MAFIA BILLIONAIRE'S SURPRISE BABY

AN ENEMIES TO LOVERS DARK MAFIA ROMANCE

VIVY SKYS

Copyright © 2024 by VIVY SKYS

All rights reserved.

No part of this book may be reproduced in any form or by any electronic or mechanical means, including information storage and retrieval systems, without written permission from the author, except for the use of brief quotations in a book review.

TABLE OF CONTENTS

Table of Contents

1

GIA

"Elio. Stop. I'm fine."

I'm grateful that the phone, and about a million miles, separates me from my brother.

Otherwise, he would probably be able to tell that I am not, in fact, fine.

Or maybe he wouldn't. I haven't been fine in a long time, and Elio doesn't seem to have noticed much.

The bitterness in that realization makes me take another long sip of the vodka that I've been slowly working through for the better part of an hour.

"Gia," Elio grumbles, my twin's voice as familiar to me as my own. "The Russians are not our friends."

"They're not your friends," I say, emphasizing the word 'your.' "But that doesn't mean they aren't mine."

They better be, after I rescued their boss' idiot daughter Stassi from the Irish in Belarus.

I drink more vodka to chase the memory.

Because with memories of Belarus, come memories of Sal.

And forgetting Sal is the whole point right now.

"The Russians have a long history with our family."

I sigh. "So do all of the crime families, Elio. That doesn't mean we can't make new alliances."

"That they will eventually betray."

"So?"

I kind of like the thrill of it all. The fact that there are alliances, favors, and obligations we all have to each other. Being part of a world that has no rules means we adhere to our own, despite what the normal boundaries of society seem to think.

It's called organized crime for a reason.

I've always loved the dance of it, even more than Elio has. That love made my mother and father absolutely crazy, but Elio isn't as locked into old prejudices as they are.

While he's out on paternity leave, I'm in charge of the Rossi family.

And I love him deeply, but I'm hopeful to make the move permanent.

Elio curses in Italian, and I smile. Usually, that means that he's annoyed with me, but he's not annoyed enough to back down.

That's perfect.

Out of the two of us, I know exactly how stubborn I need to be in order to get what I want.

"Fine. But I am sending you some backup."

"Did you finally decide who to promote to Nico's position?"

I'm genuinely curious about that. Nico betrayed Elio and me, allowing an Irish mob leader to capture Elio's wife Caterina. Well, 'allowed' is a nice term.

I'm pretty sure he sold her for a healthy payout.

"Yes," Elio says without any follow-up.

"Okay. And...?"

"He will be at your hotel within the hour."

My eyes scrunch up. I'm in Prague, which I did not tell Elio. Elio thinks that I'm in Amsterdam, where our meeting with the Russians is going to take place in one week.

Amsterdam is like Vegas in Europe. It's a lovely place to have a sit-down with a rival gang and get some delicious pastries at the same time.

A win-win, as I always say.

Amsterdam is for business. Paris is to impress someone that you want to date. Prague, however, is a city I prefer. It's a little dark, a little gloomy, but people have a great sense of humor and love to get down over a beer.

And when they drink, they tell all their secrets.

"How do you know the hotel I'm staying at?"

"I don't," Elio says flatly. "But I trust that he will."

My brother is so annoying. "Elio, you know no one has ever been able to find me if I don't want to be found."

"I know."

"So, if this is some kind of test for you new guy, you can probably call it off."

"It isn't. He already passed."

"You're annoying."

"*Ti amo*, sister mine."

The line goes dead.

I flip the phone onto the couch and glare at it. "Insufferable asshole."

My brother is many things, sadly, but an asshole is not one of them. Oh, he tries. He glowers and preens and does his whole mafia-king routine.

But deep down? Elio is as soft as a marshmallow and just as sweet.

He's always wanted to be a family man. He's cautious with his investments, he's protective of the people he loves. He adores Caterina, and their daughter Luna, and he can't wait for their twins to be born.

In another life, Elio would have been made for a suburban lifestyle.

He and Caterina could have hosted dinner parties for the whole block and made drinks for the neighbors while they watched their kids play in the streets. Sure, he's played the part of a mafia don for the majority of his life, but deep down, he's not meant for this.

Not like I am.

I fucking love it.

The politics. The intrigue. The backstabbing. All of it thrills me, and while Elio recognized quickly that I was an asset to him, I never let him see all of the things I do.

Nominally, he runs the Rossi family.

But I've been doing it for him for years.

I tell myself that I don't mind, that the thrill of it all is what I enjoy. But lately, I've noticed that I'm a little less... inclined to believe that.

I'm thirty-five years old. I'm finally starting to feel like I need to make an impact that people can see.

And I'm also kind of fed up with the bullshit that living in a world of men and machismo brings me.

I don't want to take the family from Elio. I love him deeply, and he's my brother.

However, should he decide that the stay-at-home dad life is for him...

I finish my vodka.

I'm kind of hoping he does.

I set my glass down and stroll into the living room of my suite. The hotel offers an excellent view of Old Town, and while I can't see the red-roofed buildings in the dark, the city glitters before me.

It's pretty.

There's actually a little café down on the corner that I might go to in a minute. It serves a pretty mean espresso martini, and if I want to stay awake long enough to video chat with Luna after she gets back from her first day of school, I need to mix some caffeine with my booze.

The last time I had an espresso martini was...

I shiver.

In Minsk. When I was trying to figure out who the hell sold Luna out to the Irish mob.

When Sal...

I gulp. There's no other way to remember this.

He saved me.

The memories of Belarus feel like they're crowding my mind. I sit down on the couch and sigh, closing my eyes against the images that are flashing behind my eyelids.

I'm just tipsy enough to admit that I miss him.

I don't want to miss him.

My eyes snap open.

About four weeks ago, Sal made it abundantly clear that we were friends. That despite everything we'd been through together, he didn't want to 'take advantage' of me.

I had offered him something that I'd never offered a man in my entire life.

And he said no.

So, that night, after Elio informed me that he would need me to take over some of his duties as the head of the family while he focused on Caterina, I had done the only thing I could.

I had told Sal there was nothing between us. That anything we'd had had just been because of Belarus.

Because of the way we needed each other then.

And we didn't anymore.

Two days later, he hadn't been at Luna's birthday party.

And now...

I haven't spoken to him in weeks.

The thought makes my heart ache. Despite the fact that Sal and I could never be anything other than friends, than relatives, I didn't want to stop talking to him altogether.

In the last four months, Sal became my best friend. We did everything together.

We slept in the same room because I couldn't sleep alone.

He was the only one who kept the nightmares away.

Despite the fact that he's wildly attractive, I never asked him for more. Not until I did, anyway.

And he rejected me.

The rejection still burns through me.

But alas. I need to move on. If Elio's new person is as good as he says he is, I probably don't have much time before he figures out where I am.

Or why I'm here.

The real reason that I'm lurking around Prague, aside from the fact that it's pretty convenient as far as hiding places go, is that I have a lead. And that lead is going to help me protect my family.

The family that I need to impress in order to get control of this organization.

And, be taken seriously.

Caterina, my beloved sister-in-law, is pregnant with twins. Clearly, that particular gene runs in the family, but I made a promise to her.

And I want to get it done before the babies arrive.

I promised that I would find her older brother, Marco.

At some point in the chaos of last year, Marco disappeared. I had no idea where he was, and that fact alone was annoyingly suspicious.

I am good at what I do. I am beyond good, I am *great*.

So the fact that Marco seems to have dropped off the face of the planet?

He's dead.

When Caterina finds out that he's dead, she's going to be inconsolable. If that happens while she's pregnant with two babies, she could put them at risk.

I need to find out the truth, I need to locate Marco's body. I need to control the narrative so that when we do find out, I have the ability to help Caterina through her sorrow.

So that she doesn't break down completely.

Not to mention, if I find out first, I can exact revenge on whoever killed Marco. I'm sure that Dino, their other brother, despite the absolute pack of dicks that he is, would be happy to do that.

I'm under the impression that each of the siblings had a role in their family, much like in ours. Marco, the boss. Sal, the spy. Dino, the muscle.

And Caterina.

Their heart.

Somehow, she's become our heart too.

I love her, and my niece, and my unborn niece and nephew. I'd do anything to make sure that they get the resolution that they need.

And that Marco gets the justice he deserves.

Prague is my latest lead.

I'm pretty sure that the low-level Irish gangster I tortured last week had some kind of connection here that he didn't fully grasp. He won't be talking anytime soon, and I made sure of that, but I'm here on a hunch after he spilled his guts to me.

Literally.

I smirk a little at the memory. He said something about the fact that Prague had some kind of refuge that Marco was also after.

If I can find what he was looking for, I'll likely be able to find out who killed him.

And I'll be in time to make it to Amsterdam in seven days for the meeting with the Russians.

Who, once again, better be on their knees thanking me for rescuing pretty, silly Stassi from the Irish gang's hold.

There's a noise outside of my room.

I hunch, ducking down, and slink behind the couch. The suite is large, and the living room opens to the front door. I hear a scrabbling sound again, like someone is going to pick the lock.

Quietly, I pad over to the gun I have on the coffee table. I grab it and I'm about to slink over to the side of the door when the lock clicks, and I freeze.

The door opens.

My heart kicks into my throat.

Suddenly, it's very clear why Elio was so confident that his new third-in-command would be able to find me.

Because standing in the doorway is the one man who always has.

The last man I ever want to see again.

Sal De Luca.

By the looks of it, he is absolutely livid.

I shiver.

I should not find that sexy but...

I do.

2

SAL

I FOUND HER.

I can kid myself and pretend that the thrill of the chase isn't important to me, but that would be a lie. I have been looking for Gia for two weeks, and the entire time, I've loved it.

The haze of the past few weeks is gone.

Instead, I feel sharp. Alive. Like I'm ready to hunt Gia across the world.

Like I'm ready to follow her wherever she goes.

Of course, she's not in Amsterdam. The second Elio told me that he thought she was, I shook my head.

I had been in Paris, keeping tabs on another Russian businessman.

Elio had called, telling me that Gia would need help for this meeting.

I had protested it. I had fought it in my mind.

But I would never, ever be able to walk away from helping Gia if she needed it.

My chest feels like it's heaving, like I ran all the way from Paris to Prague. I vaguely hear the door click behind me as I close it, and I warily watch Gia's thumb as it hovers near the safety on her Glock-19.

"How did you get a Glock into Prague?"

She snorts and her arm stiffens as she points it at me. "You don't think I have ways of making sure I'm well-supplied wherever I go?"

"Gia. I have no doubt. I'm just asking out of curiosity."

She gently sets it down. "The Serbians love to get chatty over a beer."

Of course they do.

I have no doubt that, were I to share a beer with those same Serbians, they'd clam up like Fort Knox.

Gia has some kind of a gift for getting people to open up to her. She's just so... *Gia.*

I know what it feels like to be on the receiving end of all of that charm.

I fell for it, after all.

The same as the rest of them.

"So, you conned them into getting you a Glock?" Russian guns would be much more popular on this side of the world. Italian guns, even.

Getting this particular model of Glock in Europe is like importing nuclear radiation. Some are made in Switzerland, but this one is 100% US-manufactured.

It's impressive that she has it. We're gangsters, true. But there are some rules to follow.

Unless you're Gia.

"I didn't con them into getting me one. I conned them into letting it get through airport security unnoticed."

My eyebrows raise. "You didn't take the jet here?"

"And risk Elio finding out? No way. I flew business class, thanks to one of my friends who happened to need a companion on his flight from Milan to Prague," she says with a smirk.

I pretend that the reference to another man doesn't make me want to throw her over my shoulder.

Show her she's mine.

Hell. I'd leave bite marks on her skin if it showed the world that she was mine.

My Gia.

She's not yours.

The thought makes my mood sour quickly. "Why are you in Prague, Gia?"

She ignores my question.

She drifts over to the couch and pulls out the handle of vodka that's on the table. She pours two glasses and offers me one.

"I suppose congratulations are in order."

If she drugged the liquor, she didn't do it recently, and I'm hopeful she won't want to kill me. All the same, I make sure she sips her drink, visibly watching the liquid slide down her throat before I drink.

It's excellent vodka.

As it would be.

Gia's taste in the finer things is somewhat legendary. Clearly, being somewhat promoted to taking over for Elio while Caterina is pregnant hasn't rid her of that tendency.

My eyes slide over her outfit. Black Chanel shirt, made of silk. Pants that could be Versace or Valentino.

They might even just be custom-tailored. Black leather.

They hug her ass and thighs, and I suppress a shiver, thinking of the muscle she's got beneath.

Gia's sexy as hell. There's no point in denying it. She knows it. I know it.

The game we play where we both pretend like we don't is maddening.

"Elio promoted you to Nico's position," she says flatly.

I nod. "He did."

"You're here to escort me to the meeting with the Russians."

Her tone isn't flat now, but laced with something that feels a little deeper than anger. "I'm here to make sure they don't shoot you or kidnap you."

"You can stop bullets now? No wonder Elio promoted you if you can do magic."

"You know what I mean, Gia," I say with a warning. "You didn't take any of the security from the house in Rome. You didn't call on anyone from Italy. You showed up here, in a completely different city. What's the plan? You're just going to waltz in there with a smile and a song, and get the Russians to ally with us against the Irish?"

She whistles. "You got me, Sal. Excellent detective work," she winks. Gia polishes off the rest of the vodka, shutting her eyes slightly against the burn.

"I know you helped out the Russian girl in Belarus," I say softly.

"What do you mean, 'helped?'"

"You saved her," I concede.

She did do that.

But at what cost?

Gia pre-Belarus was... an experience. She was smart. Sexy. She used both to her advantage, working over Elio's enemies so that they'd give her the kind of information he could build an empire on.

Gia post-Belarus?

Everything that she was before, she is now, but with an edge. She's dangerous. Hard, dysregulated in a way that she had never been before.

The Gia I pulled out of that burning warehouse in the middle of the countryside hadn't been the Gia who had gone in.

If only I had just been there ten minutes earlier. If I had known about the plot around Anastasia just a day earlier. I could have helped her then. I could have kept them from finding out, kept them from the warehouse.

I could have kept Gia from emerging from the flames as... this.

Her eyes glint. "I did save her. So, they owe me."

Technically, she's right. The Russians owe her a favor for rescuing Anastasia Novikov, the daughter of their boss.

But they also owed Elio that same favor.

And whatever the Irish had on them... it outweighed the favor of saving her life.

So that, more than anything, made them dangerous as hell.

"You need backup in case they decide they don't want you after all."

She snorts. "And Elio sent *you* as the backup."

I don't respond to her jab. "Yes. He did."

As he should have. Not only am I more lethal than anyone else in his organization right now, but he knows that with Gia, I'll do anything to save her.

Anything to protect her.

I made that clear to him when I begged him to send me to Europe to get away from her.

Unfortunately, the ocean between us hadn't' been enough. Life had a way of throwing Gia back in my face.

And I was not going to turn her away.

"I don't need you," she snorts.

She grabs the Glock off the table again, inspecting it like she's looking for a weakness. I know she won't find one.

If there's one thing Gia likes more than clothes, it's designer guns. She makes sure they're ready to go, ready to fire, and takes great pride in keeping all of her weapons clean.

"Yes, you do," I say softly.

Gia checks her weapon, the sound of the magazine clicking into place loudly in the room. "No, I don't."

"What the hell are you doing in Prague, Gia?"

"None of your fucking business, Salvatore."

The use of my full name is like a hot poker to my anger. "Don't you fucking 'Salvatore' me, Gianna."

Her nostrils flare.

I shouldn't think that is so goddamn sexy. I really shouldn't.

I'm fucked though because I think everything about Gia is sexy.

When I think about her, everything in me goes on high alert. I'm aware of her movements every time she makes them, like I have sort of stupid Gia radar.

When she breathes, my chest expands.

When she talks, I listen.

I hate how I am drawn to her. She's the sun, and I'm some kind of stupid space rock that's stuck in her orbit.

Now, I can never leave.

"You cannot walk into that meeting with the Russians alone."

"I have walked into every business deal, situation, and meeting alone!" she snaps. "Why on earth do you and my fucking soft-hearted brother think I need protection now? Why, after all this time, do I need a babysitter?"

"You don't need a babysitter!" I roar. "You need backup!"

"Like hell!"

In the time that our argument has escalated, we're inches away from each other.

This close, I can smell the expensive perfume that she has custom-made for herself. I can see the redness spotting her cheeks from where blood is flowing to her skin.

She's actually angry at me.

Gia is angry at *me*.

As though I'm the one who dismissed us. Like I'm the one who told *her* to fuck off.

I step closer until our noses almost touch.

It would take me one motion to kiss her. I wouldn't have to move more than five muscles to do so.

But kissing her...

It would change everything.

We've been here so many times. Right at the edge, somewhere between friends and...

More.

And neither one of us has leaned forward.

This is familiar territory.

But I'm not going to be the one to cross into something else.

Not unless she's there with me.

I can tell Gia is thinking the same thing. Her brown eyes search mine, begging, questioning.

Raging.

Finally, she steps back. She snaps the Glock's safety on and tucks the gun into her purse. She spins to look at me.

"Fine."

"Fine?"

"Fine," she repeats. "If you're going to follow me around like a fucking puppy, then let's go."

"Where the hell are we going, Gia?" It's almost midnight. Surely, she's not going to head out now for some kind of hare-brained thing...

"You want to know why I'm in Prague, Sal?"

"You're fucking right I do."

"I'm here to find your brother's body."

With that statement, my world shatters again.

"You don't know he's dead."

Gia glances around, but the streets around us are empty. I made sure of that before I asked the question.

Her words have been banging around in my mind, however, for the past fifteen minutes. All the way out of the hotel, into the streets of Prague, I hear them echo, like they're stuck on repeat in my brain.

To find your brother's body.

Marco isn't dead.

He can't be dead.

There's just no way that Marco De Luca, the head of the De Luca family and my oldest brother, is dead.

My whole life, my brother Marco has been something of an enigma.

He's part brother, part father, part boss. He's been in control of the De Luca family since our parents died at Caterina's engagement party six years ago.

But, even prior to that, Marco was always the one in charge of Dino and me.

He's never been just a brother.

Or maybe he's just the ultimate mob boss.

I'm inclined to think that.

He was never a kid; Marco walked out of the hospital in a full three-piece suit, cell phone glued to his ear, making deals with shipping magnates the world over. It doesn't make sense to me to picture Marco as irresponsible or childish.

Or dead.

I don't know how to live in a world without Marco in it.

"Think about it, Sal," she whispers, glancing up at me.

Gia may be significantly shorter than I am, but she makes up for it in attitude. The ten-inch height difference doesn't seem to matter at all, and sometimes, I feel like she's actually the one towering over me.

It makes me feel challenged. Like I have to be worthy of her.

Until recently, I loved that feeling.

"Yeah, I've thought about it. He can't be dead."

She tucks her head on my shoulder, clearly playing up the vision that we're just two lovers out for a late-night stroll.

Inside my chest, my heart burns.

"There's no way that he could have dropped off the face of the earth otherwise. You and I would have heard about it."

"You're assuming we would have," I say quietly.

"We would have. There is nothing that sneaks by both of us."

"You didn't know about Luna," I venture.

Her head pops up off my shoulder, fast enough that I need to dodge it in order to keep my nose from breaking. "I knew one of you had a child. I just didn't know who."

I raise an eyebrow. "Did you think it was me?"

She puts her head back on my shoulder and motions us to walk forward. "I didn't know who it was," she says, slightly defensive.

Interesting.

"Who did you think it was?"

"Dino," she says.

"Why?"

"He's shady as hell."

I don't want to laugh at that. Dino is shady as hell, always has been. It's not funny now, knowing what I know about how he sold us out, how he got Marco kidnapped, or…

I refuse to think of anything else.

"Why didn't you think it was me?"

She snorts. "You wouldn't get a girl pregnant and walk away."

"No?"

"No, Sal. You're too honorable for that. If you had a bastard, you'd marry the mom and try to make it work."

I can't tell if she approves, or if the fact repulses her.

And I don't care either way.

"Marco isn't dead," I repeat, shoving the knot of feelings down in my stomach.

"He's dead. There's no other explanation."

"What if...?"

"None," she says firmly.

We walk in silence for a minute. I let Gia tug me through the streets, pulling me this way and that until we're in an alley. There's a door in front of us, and loud music seems to pulse inside.

I turn. "A club?"

"This is the club that Marco last visited," she whispers. "An Irish guy told me about this two weeks ago."

"Under what circumstances?" I know Gia's preferred method of extorting information, and I bristle at the thought.

"I took out his organs until he saw reason."

I relax slightly. "Oh."

She raises an eyebrow. "You were worried I fucked him."

"No, Gia. You're free to fuck whoever you please."

"You're goddamn right I am," she says.

But her eyes shutter like I said something disappointing.

I'm definitely disappointed by the reaction.

And the reminder.

Gia's free to fuck whoever she likes.

And that doesn't include me.

Against the sour feeling in my stomach, I nod. "As I said. You're free to do whatever you want."

She studies me for a minute. "Marco has to be dead, Sal. There's no other explanation. The Irish man said that he saw Marco here, four weeks ago."

I do some mental calculations. Four weeks ago, Marco had dropped off the face of the earth. That was basically when we found Dino, and he had revealed that Marco was involved in something shady that he didn't want the family to know about.

Dino had ratted us out because of it.

My heart clenched. Could there be some truth to what Gia thought?

I shook my head. "No. He can't be. There's just no way."

"Sal, you have to agree…"

"I don't," I snap. "I don't agree, Gia. Marco can't be dead. There's no way that my brother is dead." My voice is hoarse by the time I'm done.

Pity, and sadness, flicker in her eyes. "Sal…"

"What else did he say," I snarl.

She sighs. "The Irishman said that Marco was here under refuge."

"What does that mean?"

She shrugs. "I don't know. But I figured that if we can find out what he was looking for, we can probably find him."

I nod. "And you want to go into the meeting with the Russians knowing what happened to Marco."

"If they did it, or if they had anything to do with it, we need to know before they do," she whispers.

It's smart.

If the Russians killed Marco and we're surprised by the news at the meeting, it's likely that our response would be pretty emotional. Emotional responses mean irrational actions, and if we act irrationally and hurt them, then they can get out of the favor they owe Gia for rescuing Anastasia.

God, she's so fucking smart I can't believe it.

Elio's great.

I like him as Caterina's husband, and while I think he's a stubborn idiot, I see how good he is for her. He's definitely intelligent—both he and Marco went to Harvard Business School.

But in this world, you don't need that type of intelligence. You don't need to know how to lead a corporation.

You need to know how to rule a kingdom.

Gia is *that* kind of smart. She's calculating, ruthless. She knows exactly what she's doing, and she's usually planned out six other moves she can make to get to her goal.

It's just another thing that I find so attractive about her.

But if she thinks Marco is dead…

I shut out the thought.

No matter what, even if he's not dead, he was here. He was at this bar in Prague, and he was searching for something.

She's right.

"Okay," I say quietly, nodding at the door. "Let's do this."

Gia smiles. It's the kind of smile that's predatory. Her pink lips part around her white teeth, and they gleam in the dim lamplight.

"Stay behind me," she warns.

I roll my eyes.

I have Gia's back. Whether she likes it or not.

I always have.

And I always will.

3

GIA

Before Sal can ask me any more questions, the door to the club opens.

A large, surly man blinks down at me. He mutters something in Czech, which is not a language that I'm fluent in.

I'm pretty sure he isn't asking for my coffee order, though.

That's really all the Czech I know. I could also tell him to fuck off, but I don't think that would be helpful either.

I'm about to give him my post pitiful *English please* look when, to my complete shock, I hear the person behind me reply.

In fluent Czech.

I whip around and try to take a peek to see if there's anyone else there, but there isn't.

Meaning that Sal speaks significantly more Czech than I do.

The bouncer gives us both what can only be described as a hairy eyeball. Sal steps forward and offers to shake his hand. I see the telltale pale edge of a banknote disappear into the bouncer's fist, and then he nods.

He lets us both in.

I fluff my hair and stand tall, strutting into the club like Sal's bribe had been my plan all along. It's only when we're firmly situated at a VIP table, which Sal also obtains by bribery and Czech promises, that I throw an arm over him like I'm bringing him close.

The music pulses around us. This club is dark as hell, as is the norm in Prague, and the flash of lights and lasers gives everything around us the impression of a stop-action film.

So I'm hopeful that it looks like I'm just another silly heiress whispering sweet nothings to her boy toy when I pull Sal's ear to my lips.

"You never told me you speak Czech."

"You never asked."

That's fair.

I never thought I had to, which is also fair. For the majority of the time I've been connected to Sal, he's readily offered plenty of information.

Now, though...

I don't really like secrets. It might not seem like that to the outside observer because I also spend a significant amount of my time gathering them like candy from a piñata, but it's less about the fact that I covet them and more about the fact that I can't stand being out of the loop.

I've been out of the loop before. Plenty of times.

My dad loved to leave me out of things because Elio was more important.

So the fact that I suddenly have no idea how many languages Sal speaks...

"Any other linguistic skills you want to share?"

"Unless you're asking what my tongue can do for you, then no, Gia."

I don't let him see that I blush at the statement.

Instead, I pull away and survey the club. The bottle girls try to do their whole song and dance with a giant magnum of champagne, but a few choice words from Sal and they're gone too.

A bottle of champagne, however, stays.

Good job, Sal.

I reach forward. He pours me a glass, and I lean back, sipping on it.

Bleh.

I prefer champagne that's a lot more expensive, but this is what I'm stuck with, I guess.

Behind me, Sal seems to glower.

I always forget how tall he is. He towers over my five-foot-two frame easily, and I know from experience that every inch of him is stacked with muscle.

He's enormous. Big, strong, much more so than his brothers in that regard, who aren't exactly weaklings either.

The whole family is pretty darn attractive.

Good genes and all that.

"What are we waiting for, Gia?"

I sigh. "For someone to look like they've seen Marco."

"Gia..."

"Hush. Let me work," I mutter.

The Irish gangster had said there was something here that Marco wanted. Something...

Oh.

Hello.

There's a guy, who is absolutely a cop, trying to dance and look chill.

Oh, bless his heart. He probably thinks he's pretty good at this too.

But I've never seen someone so clearly be a member of the FBI or Interpol in my life.

I sit down with Sal, cuddling close to him like we're just two little lovebirds. Gently, I put my hands up and tilt his face to mine, letting my fingertips linger on the curve of his jaw.

God, he smells good.

I take a breath. "See that guy who is totally not a cop on the dance floor?"

Sal's eyes dart to the crowd. I wait for him to look, then when he does, I nod.

"Yeah. The one in the obviously off-the-rack suit."

"Gia, most people wouldn't know it was off-the-rack."

"Whatever, it fits him terribly. Anyway. He's here. He's not looking for us."

He stills. "You think he's here for an arrest or to find an informant?"

"Given the fact that he's dancing like a total idiot, I'm going with informant."

Sal snorts. "Whoever it is, they're putting him through the wringer."

I grin. "Good for them."

Criminal informants sometimes make their handlers do a little song and dance in order to feel accessible. They need to take some of the power back, because ultimately, their handler has something worth having in order to get the information they need.

Whoever this guy's CI is, they're making him work for his information.

It's more than a little entertaining to watch.

When the officer takes a path to the back of the club, clearly dropping his terrible cover and making a beeline for the rooms where shady things happen, I grab Sal's hand. "Follow my lead."

He doesn't even flinch.

I have to say, that's kind of nice about Sal. It's one of the things I've always appreciated about him.

I need to be flexible in my work, and if I need someone to work with, they have to be able to change plans at the drop of a hat.

We get to the back, and I pause in a hallway. I can barely hear voices coming from a few rooms back.

I creep forward, Sal close on my heels.

We pause right outside of a dark room. There's a slight alcove next to the room, like the kind that used to hold a phone booth.

I tuck into it and Sal follows.

"...family is bound to be looking for him."

"Any reasonable person would assume he's dead," a woman's voice says.

"Well. I don't think the De Lucas are reasonable by any stretch of the imagination."

We both go stock still.

The man continues. "He's fine. When I met him here, he said he would do anything to keep the brother's kids a secret."

The woman snorts. "Yeah. Well. Anything turned out to be a whole lot for him, now didn't it?"

"True. Still. We gave him what he asked for, and he's going to give us what we need."

She groans. "I hate working with criminals. Have I said that before?"

"Sure, kid. But it's time to get you back. Babysitting duty is hard work, you know."

The door creaks. My mind is still reeling, thinking about what they said.

It's Sal who makes the decision about the door opening.

"Shit."

Faster than I thought possible, Sal moves. He rotates so that he's pinning me to the wall, his right arm braced against the flat surface so that my face is obscured by his leather bomber jacket.

He leans forward. "Act sexy," he mutters.

Then, his other hand goes around my waist, pulling our hips together.

His nose descends, brushing the line of my neck.

And his lips trace up my throat.

I don't even have to fake the gasp that explodes from me. The feeling of Sal's lips on my skin?

Holy. Shit.

There are goosebumps racing all over my skin, starting at the place where my neck meets his lips. He nibbles lightly, biting the tendon in my throat.

I don't even need to pretend to moan.

The sound is breathy and loud, and I can feel Sal's hesitation as he freezes.

There's motion next to us, and I grab the back of his neck with my hand, pressing him into me more.

I roll my hips against his, and he tilts his lips against my ear.

And he growls.

The noise makes my entire body vibrate. I want Sal to do it again.

But I want him to be much, much less clothed when he does.

The two people leave the room next to us, and I can feel them watching us for just a minute. In Italian, the man mutters, "Get a fucking room."

Sal doesn't respond, except to brush his lips over my ear.

We listen as their footsteps move back out toward the pulsing music. When I'm sure they're gone, I stand stock-still.

Sal hasn't moved.

But neither have I.

His hand is still at my waist. His nose is still inches from mine.

All it would take for us to kiss is for one of us to lean in.

Just one of us has to move approximately one half of an inch.

And we'll be kissing.

I can feel Sal breathing. I'm terrified to open my eyes and see what he's doing.

"We should go."

The words are like a bullet. They shatter the tension between us. Sal moves back, but I swear I feel his fingers linger on my waist.

"We should go," he confirms.

When he leaves, I take a deep breath before I follow.

I feel... rattled.

I never feel like this.

Salvatore De Luca, it seems, just has that kind of effect on me. I wanted to lean in to kiss him so badly.

But he didn't lean in either.

The plane ride to Amsterdam is... awkward.

There's no other way to describe it.

We're on the plane, and the plane is moving, but mentally, I'm completely preoccupied with the fact that Sal is so close to me. My mind keeps going back to the dark hallway.

To Sal's lips skating against the side of my neck.

To the feel of his heart pounding under my hand.

Sal and I have definitely recognized that we're attracted to each other. That's always been true.

However, when we last talked, I thought that maybe we had finally put a nail in that coffin. Sal made it clear he wanted more...

And I panicked.

I didn't know if I didn't want more. I didn't know that I did.

I just knew that the sight of Sal, his hands around mine, asking me for something real...

It had scared the shit out of me.

So I told him that the timing wasn't right.

That we needed space.

That I couldn't be with him because I needed to be able to work as Elio's replacement while he's on paternity leave.

I had said that.

Then, the next day, Sal had been gone. Reassigned, as he and Elio put it, to do some spying on the Russians in Europe.

I thought that it had killed the attraction.

Unfortunately, after today, I don't think the attraction between us is dead.

I think it might even be growing.

We've done a good job of dancing around this, Sal and I.

We've slept in the same bed.

We've changed, showered, done all of that in front of each other.

That was... necessity. Anxiety.

The need to be close to another human after a tragedy.

I won't say that I've never thought about Sal naked before. Because I have. A lot.

But we've never...

I shut my eyes remembering the one time we got close.

I've always thought we kind of had embers burning between us.

Now I'm worried that they're becoming flames.

After we get off the plane, Sal gently shepherds me to the location.

The bar where we're meeting the Russians is one of my favorites. It overlooks both a canal and another busy restaurant, and I like the location because it's relatively safe.

Relatively being a key word.

Sal ensures that we're there early, another perk to having him near, and when we get to the bar, he walks in first before ushering me in.

The room is empty.

I sigh. "Can't they at least have left us a bartender?"

"I think when the mob is involved, the wait staff tend to clear out," he says in a dry voice.

"Pity." This place has a great version of a French 75 that will lay you flat on your ass if you drink enough of them.

There's a knock at the door and Sal goes to clear the entry. He opens it and the Russians file in, one by one.

Three of them.

I stare at them until they sit. Nikolai and Anatoly take their seats at the table, and Damien, their muscle, hovers behind.

The air is tense.

Until Nikolai breaks out in a huge smile. "*Sestryonka*. How good to see you."

I wait for Sal's sharp intake of breath and I smirk at the implication. *Yeah. That's right. Elio isn't the only one who can build alliances.*

"Hello, Zio Nikolai."

"How have you been?"

I sigh and study my nails. "Bored, Zio. Bored to death."

"I hear you have a new niece and nephew on the way."

Ah. I see. We're firing shots. "I do. Such a blessing, you know? Well. You will know when you have grandchildren, I guess."

He laughs. "Always with the claws, *sestryonka*."

"You know it."

We make some small talk, each of us sizing the other one up. Finally, I lean back and get to it. "We need some information."

"Oh? Gia, you know that anything I know, you know."

I tap my fingers on the stone tabletop. "What did the Irish do with my brother-in-law?"

There's a flicker of unease on Nikolai's face. "I don't know, darling."

"I think you do."

He sighs. "Gia..."

"You want to tell me, Niko."

"And why's that?"

I smirk at him.

His daughter, the sweet but altogether too oblivious Anastasia, has been busy. She texted me pictures of who she was hooking up with recently in Ibiza, and Daddy Dearest is absolutely going to lose his shit once he knows.

"How's Stassie's vacation going?"

He blinks. "You knew?"

"Zio. You know I always know."

He looks over at Anatoly. "May we have the room, *sestryonka*?"

"Of course."

We rise and Sal and I exit the building. I stop outside, but Sal grabs my elbow and moves me closer to the canal.

"Something is wrong."

I frown. "What do you mean?"

"Their muscle looked twitchy."

I sigh. "He's a Russian Bratva soldier. He's not exactly…"

I don't get to finish that sentence.

Out of the corner of my eye, I see something.

Light.

Heat.

Then, before I understand what's happening, Sal throws his body on mine. He slams into me, just ahead of the billowing cloud coming out of the building, and he shoves us.

Right into the canal.

4

SAL

THE ICE COLD OF THE WATER AROUND US CLOSES over our heads, but it's so much better than the scorching heat of the blast from the restaurant.

Holding Gia, I kick off from the canal floor. When we break the surface, I immediately turn Gia's face to mine.

"Gia. Are you hurt? Are you okay? What's broken?"

She sucks in a breath.

Then, another one.

The canal is pretty slow-moving. I can hear the sound of police screaming up to the site of the explosion.

We can't be there when they pull up.

I grab Gia and kick off to the bridge that's arching over us. I pull us against the side of the cement wall, holding on while people rush overhead.

"We need to get out of here."

Gia blinks. "Where?"

My mind races.

If the bomb was meant for us, then we need to lay low. I can't tell if it was supposed to be us or the Russians, or both.

I can't discount either option, and both of them mean that we need to hide.

I shut my eyes.

"I have a place."

Gia turns to look at me. "What?"

"I have a place."

"Like, the De Lucas? There's no way that whoever it is hasn't found all of our properties, Sal..."

I shake my head. "No. I have a place. Me. Personally. That no one knows about."

I have a lot of places, actually.

The De Luca family is my family. I love every single one of my siblings and my extended family.

But watching your grandfather get slammed behind bars for RICO charges at the tender age of five does something to you.

When you know that your brother is going to inherit the family's money, the power, everything, and you're a third son who is out in the world on your own...

Well.

There are only a few options for guys like us.

One is to go all in.

Devote everything to the family. Be there when they need you, be the guy who does everything so that you make yourself invaluable.

From irrelevant to indispensable.

That pretty much went out the window for me when I saw my Uncle Andrei get put behind bars. Taking the fall, as he was supposed to.

He was a third son too.

So, when I started making real estate investments, I didn't do it for my family.

I did it for me.

And now...

Well.

It's a good thing Marco doesn't know about the properties I own. No one does.

Not even Gia.

Keeping her from finding out has been a nightmare. She's really good at what she does.

Annoyingly so, sometimes.

Now, I'm going to have to let her in on this little secret. And once I let her in, I have to tell her about all of it.

I look at her. "Gia. I have a place. It is not a family place. But we can hide. Do you trust me?"

She takes one minute to study me. Her brown eyes study mine.

And she nods. "Yes."

The whole way to the little row house that I bought about two years ago, Gia is dead silent.

If the man driving us has any questions, he doesn't ask them, which I'm grateful for.

My Dutch is barely conversational, but Gia's relatively fluent. She gives him the directions that I relay, and we manage to hunker down as he starts to drive.

The taxi brings us about a half mile away from my house.

I carry Gia the rest of the way. Curled in my arms, I can feel her shaking with the cold.

She's shivering.

Gia looks so miserable; it brings me back to the time in Belarus. I take a deep breath. I need to keep the memory where it is, at least for right now.

It belongs in the past.

Everything about that belongs in the past.

When we walk up to the row house, I set her down and I press the code that opens the garage. I have no idea if it's going to be occupied by a renter right now; there are private chambers that I keep open just in case, but most of my properties are either vacation rentals or occupied by people who just rent them from me.

It looks like there's no one here.

We walk across the cement floor of the garage, shoes squelching. When we get to the door that leads up to the living room, Gia pauses.

"Gia?"

"This... is yours?" Her brown eyes are wide, and I think she might be going into shock.

"Yes."

"How?"

I smile. "There are some secrets even you don't know, Gia Rossi."

She shakes her head.

I shut the door behind us and carry Gia upstairs to the primary suite. There are towels hanging on the rack, soap in the shower, and a bathtub built to hold an entire soccer team.

I gently set her down. "I can leave if you want."

She shakes her head. "No. I... I think I need help getting out of this."

I look down at her expensive leather Chanel suit.

"I'll bet you do."

Slowly, I help Gia undress. The cold at this point is getting to me too. Every motion that I take feels like it's taking too much time, and my limbs feel heavy.

Heavier than usual.

I turn when she's in her bra and underwear, trying to keep my eyes off of the tanned expanse of her skin. I turn and start to turn the bathtub on, testing the taps until they're warm.

"Get in," I whisper against her neck.

She shivers.

That one, tiny reaction sets off a chain reaction in my chest that's like a nuclear bomb. My skin explodes with heat, my eyes focus on Gia, and my cock starts to swell against my too-wet pants.

She liked that.

Gia Rossi. The bossiest woman that I've ever met. The woman who has haunted my dreams for nearly a year now.

She liked that I gave her an order.

And she's following it.

Still in her underwear, Gia gets into the tub. She sits there, shaking, then turns her beautiful face up to me.

"What about you?"

Fuck. *Fuck.*

I can't look at her.

Gia's nearly naked. I can see the smooth swell of her breasts under her expensive lingerie. I can see the bones in her ribs, the curve of her hip.

I want to go sit in that bathtub with her more than I've wanted to do anything in my life.

I want to tell her to sit on my cock. I want to tell her when she can come.

And when she can't.

We've been here before. Right at the edge of something between us.

The problem is that with Gia, I don't just want one night of sex. I don't want something that feels... mundane.

I'm not easy in bed. I'm very particular.

Very particular.

I don't know why, but in order for me to feel sexually satisfied, I can't just do regular, vanilla things. I know that about myself, and I generally don't look for partners who can't do that. I'm happy to get a woman off, but for me to feel any measure of satisfaction?

I have to be in control. I have to be the one in charge.

And I have no idea what Gia would do if that were the case.

I'm attracted to Gia.

I've always liked her. Always wanted to do something more with her, even when she fully rejected me the day before Luna's birthday party.

I'd be perfectly happy to live my life being the one who meets Gia's needs and forgoing my own if she decided she ever wanted to take the step that would make something sexual between us.

Well.

I had been.

Until, of course, she rejected me.

But I haven't ever known that she wants to go that far with me. And I never counted or even considered the fact that she would be interested in doing what I need to do in order to feel satisfied.

However....

Get in.

She *did* like that.

I'm not wrong.

Being that I am who I am, I'm not wrong about this stuff. Gia, though she might not know it, wants a little more control in her life. Or rather, she wants someone else to take control. Yes. That's it. Somewhere inside her, Gia wants someone else to take control. Just for a little while.

Which means that while I've always known we're compatible... if she's able to give me what I need?

The temptation of it is too much. I want to do all of that.

With Gia.

I can't just bring her into it either. If we do that, if we go that route, she's going to need to know exactly what she's getting into.

And right now? She can't consent to anything.

I give her a smile. "Let me make some calls to get some new clothes, and so that we can get the hell out of here."

The shutter of her hopeful gaze kills me. Somewhere inside, part of me crumples.

I'll never even be able to explore that with her because we can't even fucking get to that place.

"I'll be right back, Gia," I whisper.

"Okay."

I know that I'm ruining the potential for this... whatever is between us.

It's better this way, though. Gia can't be what I need her to be.

And I can't be what she needs me to be.

So, it's better just to fucking end it before it gets to be something we can never have.

I head downstairs.

The liquor cabinet, as with all of my properties, is fully stocked. I grab one of my more expensive bottles of gin, taking it out so that I can pour a ridiculous amount of it into a glass.

Gin is not fun to drink straight.

But it reminds you that you're alive.

I'm one glass in when the memories of Belarus overwhelm me.

Slowly, painfully, I remember the last time she looked this way. Since the memory is so persistent, I entertain it. You can't heal what you didn't feel, right?

So, I let myself feel it.

THE BUILDING IS ON FIRE.

As I come over the hill, that's the first thing that I think. The building is on fire.

And Gia Rossi is dead.

The thought compels me to gun the stupid Soviet-era motorcycle that I stole in Minsk, racing at a breakneck pace over the broken dirt road that leads to the warehouse.

How Gia ended up here, at a warehouse in the middle of the Belarusian countryside, is a fucking mystery.

Except, I guess it's not.

She came looking for Anastasia. Stassi, as Gia calls her.

She was convinced that this would be the way to get the Russians back on our side.

And that is going to get her killed.

I cut the bike off and run straight into the building.

"Gia!" I scream.

There's nothing.

Panicked, I look around. Everything is burning. Smoke is rolling out of the areas around me like thunderclouds, and the acrid air burns my lungs.

"Gia!"

There's something. Behind me. Somewhere.

I spin.

Flames lick at the ceiling. Any minute, that thing is going to come down. Boxes around me are catching fire.

Something crackles.

"Gia?"

Motion. Motion that doesn't look like the flames, or the ceiling breaking down. I catch a flash of a hand, grasping at the edge of a crate.

Gia.

I sprint over to her. "Gia!"

"Stassi?"

I shake my head. "She's out, Gia. She's safe. She's at the airport, just like you asked."

"'Kay."

No.

That sounded different than usual. That sounded like defeat.

I've never heard Gia be defeated before.

The boxes around us are burning, but I dive past them. I reach for her, pulling her out of the little case she made for herself.

"I'm fine..." she murmurs.

Like hell.

Roaring with a strength that I don't possess any other time, I grab her and pull her out of the pile of burning boxes. The smoke roils around us as we sprint for the edge of the warehouse.

When we get out, I gently lay Gia on the ground before falling to my knees.

We're both coughing, but the noise is sweet.

She's alive.

When Stassi told me where she was, I thought she was dead.

The motorcycle has saddlebags, and I go through them, looking for bandages or something that I can use to help her.

There's a water bottle. I pray it's water and not vodka and I open it.

Clean.

I immediately turn and kneel next to Gia. "Open your lips," I order.

They part.

Her beautiful, full lips are so cracked that I can hardly recognize them. I gently put the water bottle on them and pour.

She drinks.

When she's done, I sip some of the water before pulling Gia into my arms. My hands roam her body, checking for injuries.

There are burns. There have to be burns.

There could be cuts.

Broken bones.

She fought the fucking Irish mob by herself trying to get that stupid Russian girl out of their clutches.

There has to be...

"Sal?"

I freeze. "Gia?"

"Am I dead?"

She's delirious. I know she's delirious.

There's so much adrenaline flooding her system right now, there's no way she's going to get through this without going into shock.

"No. You're not dead."

"Prove it."

I freeze. "What?"

"Prove it. That I'm not dead."

"How?"

"Kiss me."

"Gia, I..."

I don't finish.

She leans up, pulling my head down to meet hers. Our lips crash together, and my heart squeezes because she's got to be in so much pain.

This is not how I ever envisioned our first kiss.

But holy hell.

Kissing Gia is like a shot of straight adrenaline.

Even with her cracked lips, even with her smoke-scented skin, this is the best kiss of my life.

I'm dying for her.

When the kiss ends, she slumps back. "Guess 'm not dead," she whispers.

Then, she's out.

I'm happy that she's getting rest. I need to figure out how to get us back into Minsk, then get us the hell out of this godforsaken country.

But that kiss...

I know, in that moment, that I'll never ever forget it. That kiss is everything to me. It's more than just a kiss.

It's every emotion I've felt for Gia.

Bottled. Contained.

And now, in the past.

"Sal?"

I snap my eyes open.

Gia's at the bottom of my stairs. She's wearing one of the robes that I keep in the bathroom, and the plush fabric seems to swallow her whole.

I offer her the bottle of gin. "Here."

"Do you have any vodka?"

I bring her the bottle.

Gia sits in my kitchen. She pulls up one of the chairs to the counter. She opens the bottle and takes a drink.

Looking out over the canal, she sighs.

"So, whose fucking house is this again?"

5

GIA

Each time Sal explains it to me, I still can't believe what he's saying.

We're both a few drinks in, so the shock and the alcohol might be impacting me as well, but I really can't get over it.

I stare at Sal over the rim of my glass. "So, you're like some kind of real estate magnate?"

"Basically, yes."

I narrow my eyes at him. "What's the name you have your portfolio under?"

"Are you going to tell Elio?"

I roll my eyes at him. "I'm obviously not going to tell Elio."

It's the truth. Elio doesn't need to know about this, and if Sal decided that he wanted to keep it from Elio, then I'm not going to be the one who tells him.

Sal and I keep secrets. But not from each other. We made that promise on the train back to Rome, after Belarus.

Or so I thought.

"I trade under the name Comare Holdings."

I burst out laughing. "You're the one who runs the company named after mistresses?"

"I bet you never would have thought it was me," he replies with a grin.

That's absolutely true. There is no world in which I would have thought that Sal De Luca ran a real estate company that essentially chose a name so similar to the Sopranos lore, I was sure that they were run by some white guy in New York.

"Well. I've heard of you. You made a splash when you acquired that old estate in France."

He nods. "That was my fourth one last year."

I nearly spit out my vodka. "Fourth one? Jesus Christ Sal, how many estates do you have just lying around?"

"At least four in France," he says, a smile teasing the corners of his lips.

I snort. "Smartass," I lob at him before sipping my drink. "So. Are you going to tell me where the rest of your holdings are, oh great real estate magnate?"

"No."

The word hits me harder than I expected. I resist the urge to rub my chest, my heart feeling more than a little wounded.

It shouldn't feel that way.

Sal and I aren't a couple. I told him that after he offered to be one.

So why does it bother me that he won't share the rest of his success with me?

"Okay. Keep your secrets then," I grumble. I turn in my seat, reaching for the vodka, when something in my side twinges.

Hard.

"Ah," I hiss, trying to breathe through it.

In an instant, Sal is at my side. "Gia. Where are you hurt?"

"I'm not. It's just... something down my side."

"Let me see."

"Sal, seriously. I'm fine. I don't need..."

"Let me see, damn it."

I freeze. Sal is looming over me.

From where I'm sitting on the bar stool, he seems impossibly tall. His strong arms are gripping the marble countertop behind me, and his tobacco and leather smell fills my nose.

How does he smell like that? I thought it was some kind of cologne, but since there's no way he keeps a spare bottle of that in his house that he's literally never in, I think he just smells that damn good.

That is unfair.

I make a note to search through all his bathroom cabinets for some cologne, but in that time, he's even closer to me.

I hold in a gasp as his lips are perilously close to my ear. "Let me see, Gia," he whispers.

I gulp. "It's not like you're a doctor or anything. You wouldn't be able to help."

"Gia," he growls. "Take off your robe."

Okay.

Okay.

Okay.

I'm not really sure what's going on. Because I'm not exactly the type of girl who responds well to being bossed around. In fact, I've built pretty much my whole career off of not doing that at all.

But when Sal tells me to take off my robe.

And he's two inches from my face.

And he's looking at me with those wide, brown eyes that seem to see inside my soul...

Before I know what's going on, my arms are moving. I undo the belt of the criminally soft robe, and my arms are pulling through the sleeves.

I'm still not even aware of it when Sal lifts me up onto the counter, ensuring that I sit on the robe so my butt doesn't hit the cold marble.

Thank the Baby Jesus himself that I didn't take off my panties.

Or maybe I should have.

No. Gia. No, no, no.

Aside from our admittedly very sexy situation, Sal is doing his level best to make it as unsexual as possible. He's examining my side, his eyes about a centimeter from my skin.

"Do you think you cracked a rib?"

No. "I definitely didn't crack a rib."

"Okay. I'm going to touch you and if it hurts, let me know."

I gulp.

His hands are so *big*. Like, he shouldn't ever walk into a glove store, or they'll all simply faint from witnessing hands this size.

They skate up my rib cage toward my breasts, which, while encased in a lace bra, are not exactly hidden.

It's lingerie. It's sexy. I like to wear sexy underwear.

I can't decide if that's a good or bad thing right now.

But, should Sal decide to notice, he'd see my nipples hard beneath the lace fabric, and he'd see that there are goosebumps rioting over the skin on my chest.

When his fingertips touch my naked side, I bite back a groan.

"When I put pressure here, does it hurt?"

He squeezes lightly.

No, but it makes me think of how easy it would be for you to lift me up and flip me over.

"No," I whisper.

"What about here?" his hands raise up higher, his fingertips skimming the edge of my lace bra.

"Not there," I say. God, my voice sounds hoarse. It's a miracle Sal hasn't picked up on the fact that I'm practically panting on the countertop in front of him.

I have been through hell. I was literally in a burning warehouse once. I not only survived Fyre Fest, but I made money off of people who wanted to leave on my private jet.

I can make it through Sal touching me like I'm made of porcelain.

I promise myself it won't break me. No matter how badly I want to be broken by him.

"What about on your back?"

Oh no.

He leans forward, tucking my hair over one of my shoulders so he can see down my back. Unfortunately, now he's really close to me. His chest brushes mine as he peers over my shoulder, his fingers working their way over the muscles of my back.

This is not good.

If I close my eyes, I can pretend that we're hugging. That he's holding me close, that his fingers skating over my skin are doing so out of care.

Desire.

Things that I walked away from once.

And honestly, if he offers…

I'm not sure I can do it again.

"Gia?"

"Yes?" I say. My voice is wobbly, but I managed to keep it quiet so I'm certain that he has no idea that I'm about ten seconds from ripping off his dumb soft shirt and sliding my hands up his tattooed chest…

Oh fuck.

Now I'm thinking about how his chest is full of tattoos and muscles and oh my god…

"Why are you shaking?"

"Um."

He pulls back. "Tell me where it hurts," he growls.

I shut my eyes. "Sal. It doesn't hurt."

"Then why are you shaking?"

I'm a good liar. Naturally. I'm really excellent at it.

For some reason, I've never been able to lie to Sal. He sees it almost immediately. I tried to lie to him once on the way from Minsk to Elio's house in Italy.

It didn't go well.

So instead, I tell the truth.

Kind of.

"My body is... reacting to you."

I've never seen Sal go so still.

I shut my eyes so that I can keep going.

"It's just you're so close, you know. You're warm and your hands feel really good on me and I just really like that and..."

I need to stop now. If I don't stop now I'm going to say something stupid.

Like *I really want you to fuck me on this marble countertop.*

"You're saying you're cold?"

He's just fucking with me now.

I snap one eye open and glance at him. "No. Sal. I'm not saying that."

"What are you saying then, Gia?"

His voice is barely above a growl, and it makes more goosebumps break out over my neck as I think about how that voice would feel against my skin.

I study his face. The sharp lines of his jaw are so crisp that he looks like he could cut through a two-by-four.

His eyes are dark, darker than their normal warm brown, and his fingers are curled into fists at his sides.

Like he's holding himself back.

At least one of us is.

"It doesn't matter," I say, a little more bitter than I'd intended. "It doesn't matter what I want, Sal. We can't go there. We just can't."

I hate that the second I say it, he shuts down. I swear I watch him power off, his eyes going from that dark flashing to nothing faster than the space between one heartbeat and the next.

"I'm going to shower," he says roughly.

Slowly, I gather the edges of my robe and pull it back up my shoulders. I watch him stomp up the stairs and turn the shower on.

Idly, I wonder what would happen if I walked in there with him.

You can't.

I suck in a breath and lift the glass of vodka to my lips. I need to remember that Sal is not part of my plan.

I'm going to do a good job as Elio's replacement.

I'm going to take over the Rossi family.

If I did that with a man at my side, I'd never do it.

In my world, men run everything.

They're the boss. The man of the family. They're the ones who do everything possible, and who take it upon themselves to create the world for the rest of us to live in.

Fuck.

That.

My own father loved us both, but he only ever saw Elio as the capable one. He would never say that Elio, while a great guy and a good leader, was not who my dad wanted him to become.

I was.

I'm the one who is cutthroat. I'm the one who is willing to do what it takes to get shit done. I'm the one who has no problem cutting someone's stomach open to let their intestines fall into their hands so they can really feel the outcome of crossing me.

Of crossing the family.

I'm the one who deserves to be the head of the family.

I love Elio. I'd never want to take anything away from him when it comes to the family business. If he wants to stay the head of Rossi Industries, he can do that.

But I'll strike out on my own if that's the case.

I've waited too long for this opportunity. If I had Sal at my side as... a couple, for lack of a better word, people would assume that he's the one who has the guts to do what it takes.

And they would overlook me.

Again.

I'm fine with Sal showing up as my bodyguard and backup because it's something that Elio would do as well. Elio has his own set of bodyguards, Luca and Rocco, who follow him everywhere.

But I can't let it be more than that.

The rest of the vodka burns in my throat. The pain is good, though.

It reminds me that all good things come at a price. The price of getting drunk off of good vodka? A little burn.

The price of achieving my dreams and leading the Rossi family?

Sal.

WHEN HE COMES BACK DOWNSTAIRS, I'm more than a little buzzed from the vodka. I notice first that he's wearing the same soft clothes, which look, for all the world, like linen pajamas. They give him the illusion of like... a cult leader. A tame tiger.

The fabric is so thin, however, that I can see tattoos where it stretches across his chest...

And his thighs.

"Good shower?" I ask.

Immediately I want to take it back. First of all, who asks that? Second, it makes me think about how I've been thinking about Sal in the shower.

Naked.

So very, very naked.

"We need a plan," he rumbles. "We need to figure out what happened back there, why it was that meeting, and those who were invited, who were targeted."

"I mean was it the Russians? Or was it us?"

He shrugs. "That's what we need to find out."

I nod. It makes sense.

Now, the bigger question. "What are we going to tell Elio?"

Sal frowns. "What do you mean."

"He'll hear about it. He needs to know."

"Sure," he agrees. "But aren't you acting head of the family while he's doing paternity leave?"

"Yes," I say automatically. It's the truth; I am.

"So why does he need to know all the details? Is it enough to know that we're alive and handling it?"

I freeze. "I think it is," I say slowly.

He has a point. Elio would handle this with consultation, but he'd handle it on his own.

He would send me to get intel. He'd ask Nico, which I guess is Sal now, to handle some of the muscle.

He wouldn't report back to either of us what his decision is.

"We should tell him about the meeting. We can tell him about the attack. But I'm not telling him about Marco yet."

Sal nods. "How can we explain staying in Europe after that?"

"We want to find out who did it. Get to the bottom of it," I say. "We're here to find the motherfucker who tried to kill us, Sal. That makes sense to me."

"And the business stuff?"

"It's remote for a reason. Plus, doesn't he have Dino running some of the warehouses back in Jersey?"

Sal nods. "Yeah but..."

"I know."

Dino De Luca, the third brother in the De Luca family, is somewhat of both a loose cannon and a touchy subject right now. Do I think that he's loyal, or even mentally stable? No.

Do I think he'll risk crossing us again?

Also no.

"Dino runs the business. Have him report to Luca, who will report to you," I say.

Sal smiles. "Yes, boss."

The words turn me on way, way more than they should.

I nod. "Do you want to call Elio, or do you want me to?"

"What do you want, Gia?"

Everything.

But I don't say that. Instead, I nod. "I'll call him."

It's time to be the boss bitch I have always wanted to be.

6

SAL

"So. You know how to shop now too?"

I arch an eyebrow at her over the mounds of bags that have just been delivered to the house. "What do you mean?"

Gia, adorable in her messy bun and men's silk pajamas, drifts through the living room. She trails her fingers over some of the boxes there, reading the labels.

"Versace. Gucci. Chanel. Tom Ford. Don't tell me you've developed a shopping addiction with your real estate portfolio, Sal."

I chuckle. I like to dress well when the occasion calls for it, but most of my clothes are custom-made. I find that it's the only way to make sure that I'll actually fit in the clothes that I'm given, and I don't look like a total idiot in them.

Being sized the way I am is inconvenient. Especially in European clothes.

Access to tailors, however, is significantly stronger over here, so I am able to call up my favorite one in Amsterdam and order some of the same sizes and styles that I had the last time I was in town.

You win some, you lose some.

"Gia. You know that these are for you."

"Yeah, but I want to hear you say it."

This is another game. She likes the tug of power between us.

I shut my eyes. The memory of her responses to my brief commands are...

They press at my memory.

She's interested in being commanded.

In the sexual space that I occupy, a Dom learns to read his partners well.

It's important for a variety of reasons. The least important is that it has to be clear that you're giving your partner pleasure.

The most important is that I get off from the control, sure.

But I mostly like to see them when they scream for me.

I haven't had a partner in so long I feel like my head is foggy. I can't even remember the last woman who met my needs that way, but it was definitely before I met Gia.

Because when I met her, I decided that I wanted to try to live differently. I wanted to at least put an effort into something that felt a little more normal.

Because I thought that's what Gia would want.

Then, she cut off any possibility of a future between us.

Now...

I don't even know about now.

I know that she liked it. I could see it in her body language.

But I don't know what that means for us.

"Gia," I say in a low voice that I would use if she was bound before me. "This obscene display of textiles and wealth is for you."

"Aw, thanks sweetie," she says with a smirk.

The comment floats somewhere in between us. It isn't a truth, and it isn't an untruth.

But it's an impossibility.

"Get dressed," I say, not even excited about giving the order. "We need to leave."

Gia pouts slightly. "Why?"

"Whoever it is might be in Amsterdam."

"All the more reason to stay and find them," she says with a glint in her eyes.

I tense. "Gia..."

"Elio said we had his blessing to do whatever as long as we don't fuck anything up," Gia sighs. "Come on. Let's hang around town a little. We'll put on disguises and go to the clubs and bars where the rest of the underworld meets and see what we can come up with."

"Is it going to go the same way as it did in Prague?"

She frowns. "What's wrong with that? We had a solid lead, and we found out that Marco was definitely at that bar."

"Definitely?"

Gia cocks out her hip and tilts her head. "You didn't hear that cop talking about the De Luca kid?"

"You can't think that was Marco."

"What other De Luca defends one of their siblings with a secret kid?"

I shake my head. "She didn't say kid. She said kids, plural. There are no secret De Luca kids, plural, especially from Dino or I. Only Luna."

Gia studies me. "Sal, you know by now that one lie becomes another really fast."

"I know." That's basic investigation.

"So. You don't think Dino has something to hide?"

I still. "You can't think this has to do with the reason he sold Caterina and Luna out to the Irish."

"I one hundred percent think that."

"Dino doesn't have any kids. Secret or otherwise."

"You know that for sure?"

I stare at her.

Out of the four of us, Dino is... different.

Where Caterina, Marco, and I seemed to get some kind of obedience gene when it came to our parents, he almost skipped it.

It's more than that. Dino looks different than we do. His skin is darker, eyes greener. There's been more than one person who's commented behind closed doors that Dino doesn't look like my father's son.

My father often had those people killed right after they made those comments, but that never stopped them.

It just slowed them down.

Slightly.

Gia nods. "See. I knew you weren't sure."

"That has nothing to do with the fact that Dino is... Dino," I say. "He's my brother. Marco, Dino, and I don't keep secrets from each other."

"But you keep them from Caterina?"

Gia's voice is more than a little dangerous.

"No, I don't keep them from Caterina either," I say.

Caterina is my little sister, and she's the baby of all of us.

That doesn't, however, mean that she's less capable or less intelligent. She passed all of her CPA exams about a month after graduating college, and on top of that, she's whip-smart.

She's loving, caring, and all the things that I wish I was.

We don't keep secrets from her.

Honestly, the fact that I left her out of my initial assessment... makes me feel a little weird.

Gia shrugs. "All I'm saying is that I love Elio, but he's his own person. He has his secrets. There's a lot I don't want to know about him. And there's a lot that I do know about him, even though he thinks I don't."

"What's that supposed to mean?"

Gia leans over and plays with one of the bows on a Chanel box.

"It means that I know him. I love him. But I'd never in a million years think that I can, or should, count on him to behave the way I want him to. Elio is Elio. He's my brother, and he's my twin.

"He's not the person I'm going to count on when things get hard. I'm always going to have backup so that I can ensure the outcome that I want."

It's a little chilling. "So, who would you count on, Gia?"

"Myself."

"That sounds lonely."

"It's not, Sal. It's realistic."

It still sounds lonely. Caterina, Dino, Marco, and I might have our issues, but we'll always be there for each other.

Dino's recent actions, however, pop into my mind.

He sold Caterina and Luna out.

I sigh. "Fine. I agree with you. They were talking about Marco."

"You think Dino has kids somewhere?"

"It's the only thing that makes sense," I say sadly. The fact that my older brother, who is only ten months ahead of me, would have a secret that big makes me feel more than a little hurt.

But I guess it's not like I told him anything about Gia. Or any of the other secrets I've kept for years.

My stomach twists uncomfortably.

I'm not sure what to feel.

"Fine," I mutter. "Tonight, we go see if we can scrape anything out of the low lives of this city to help us find a lead."

There's a lot to find out. The stuff with Marco is one thing. The fact that someone tried to kill Gia and me, and successfully killed the Russians?

That's also a lot.

"We're going to need a disguise," I grunt.

Gia beams. "Well. I think we did pretty good back in Prague. Speaking of, how's your Dutch?"

Excellent.

"Fine."

"Good. You'll do the talking then. I'm passable, but I sound like an American trying to speak Dutch."

I snort. "Your Russian is flawless."

"As it should be. I studied it for ten years."

My eyebrows go up. "Ten years?"

"Yep. That and ballet. I was convinced that the only way I could separate myself from Elio in my dad's eyes was to be a ballerina. And the Russian ballet? It's the best in the world." Gia smirks.

Trust Gia to think that she, an Italian girl who grew up partly in the US and partly in Italy, could join the Russian ballet.

"That's impressive."

"So is your ability to just... speak other languages," Gia says.

I can tell she's needling again. "Fine. How about this? I tell you how many languages I speak, and you leave me alone about my real estate money."

"Deal," Gia announces way too quickly.

She's definitely going to still ask me. Still, I made a bargain. "I'm fluent in Italian, French, Czech, German, and Spanish. I can get by in Russian. I can understand Japanese, but I can't say shit, and I can order food in Chinatown, or in Beijing. My Farsi is terrible, and I would do well to never speak Portuguese in my life. Oh—and Latin," I add, remembering the language that my mother painstakingly had me learn.

It was important to her, I guess.

Gia's jaw drops. "Holy shit. What are you, some kind of language prodigy?"

"I believe the term is polyglot."

"What the fuck does that mean?"

I shrug. "Languages come easily for me."

It's true. My whole life, I've been able to pick up languages exceedingly quickly.

It's more than just learning the words and phrases. I can discern the meaning of things, understand what it sounds like when people say it in their native language. I get colloquialisms. I understand nuances that others don't.

I'm just good at it.

Gia shakes her head. "Marco wasn't utilizing you well enough."

"Oh? How would you do any different?"

"I'm not sure," she sighs. "But I'd definitely have you out there with me in the world, putting that tongue to good use."

She smirks at me.

"Gia…"

"Which brings me to my next point. For cover. We did do well in the club in Prague. So. I'm thinking a couple again. You get to pick, boyfriend and girlfriend, or husband and wife."

Wife.

If there was a world where I could call Gia my wife, I'd live there in a heartbeat.

Even pretending, it's almost too painful. It's too close to something that I want. I can't pretend to be her husband.

Not when I want it so badly.

"No, Gia."

"Oh, come on," she says with a sigh. "We did good at that. We worked well together."

"We did."

"So why not?"

I can't do this.

Pretending to be Gia's husband is going to kill me.

"Gia…"

"It's the only way. Let's get dressed and think on it.

I open my mouth to protest, but before I do, the security system dings.

Flying over to the camera, I peer outside.

There's no one.

But there's something on the front step.

Unfortunately, she's running to the front door before I can say anything.

When we get to it, I open the door and snatch the package, running into the garden with it.

If there's a bomb, I'm not blowing up my fourth-favorite house.

"Stay back," I bark at Gia.

She gets behind me.

Slowly, I look at the small package. I hold it up gently, hoping that there are no tripwires hidden anywhere around it.

"What is it?"

I turn it over. "A package."

"Okay, I can see that with my own eyes, Sherlock. What's inside?"

"I'm not opening it."

I hear Gia huff from behind me. "Oh my god, Sal. Just open it."

"It could be a bomb." Or Anthrax, or any number of other powdered viruses.

"It's hot heavy enough to be a bomb."

"Gia..." I growl.

"Seriously. Just take a peek," she says from behind me.

Fine. "Take five steps back. Actually, get behind the garden wall." I jerk my head at the concrete brick wall in the garden.

"Whatever." She gives me a very annoyed look but slinks behind the cement structure.

I take a deep breath. Slowly, I unfold the edges of the package. I pull them back, holding it as far away from myself as possible—then, I turn it.

"What's in there?"

I frown. "It's...empty."

"No, it's not. Shake it."

Gently, I shake the box. A small metallic object drops out, appearing in my hand.

"It's a USB drive," I say.

Gia's out from the wall and next to me in an instant. "Okay. Let's go look at it."

"We don't have a computer," I respond dumbly.

She rolls her eyes. "Cash out one of the French castles and buy one."

I don't need to do that. I have plenty of liquid assets, so I grab the USB drive and her hand. "Let's go."

Less than an hour later, we're back, with a shiny new computer in the bag.

"It's alarming to me that you're not using the Rossi business credit card," Gia says. She narrows her eyes at me. "How much are you worth?"

"Only someone who is annoyingly rich would ask that question."

"Only someone annoyingly rich would refuse to answer it," she retorts.

I'm not going to tell her. It's enough that the computer and all of her new outfits went on a credit card with no limit, that I can pay off without blinking, in a heartbeat.

I don't answer.

Instead, I turn the computer on and plug it in. Connected to my secure Wi-Fi, I put the USB drive in.

The screen goes black.

"Fuck," Gia mutters behind me. "Did it come pre-loaded with a virus?"

"Maybe." It's a good thing this computer isn't connected to any of the usual servers, and just the Wi-Fi that's localized to the house.

The screen flickers.

It's security footage.

Gia and I both lean in.

The footage is grainy, but we can see. It looks like it's inside a bar of some kind. No, a pub. The ceiling is low, the room is dark, and it looks exactly like many of the pubs I've been in across the British Isles.

It's definitely a cell phone video. The video jostles around, and I can see that whoever is holding the camera is trying to do so without showing their hand.

Interesting.

The camera is blurry for a minute before finally focusing on something.

A person.

Two people.

A man and a woman, sitting together at a table. The man reaches forward, holding the woman's hand...

The camera finally focuses.

Next to me, Gia sucks in a breath.

I know why.

The man in the video, looking happier than I've ever seen him look in his entire life?

It's my brother.

Marco.

7

GIA

Sal and I stare at the computer screen for a solid ten seconds before either one of us speaks. The video cuts out right after Marco and the unidentified Irish woman hold hands, so when we finally do speak again, it's to the blank computer screen that's reflecting our shocked expressions.

"I told you he wasn't dead."

I throw up my hands and walk away. "Seriously Sal? That's what you're getting out of this?"

He shrugs. "I'm just saying."

"You're saying nothing! That's not the point! Where the hell is he? Why is he holding hands with that woman? And who the fuck is she?"

Questions swirl in my mind like dust from the explosion at the restaurant.

I have no idea what's going on. Marco dropped off the face of the fucking earth. He has no right to be sitting in a pub in Ireland, looking like a happy honeymooner.

He's going to fucking wish he was dead by the time I find him.

All the heartbreak Marco caused his family. All the heartbreak Marco caused me, looking for him. The way he totally fucked Elio over and left him to cover up his own disappearance.

He's so, so dead when I find him.

I walk away, pacing back and forth as I consider the options. "We have to find him. He's either gone rogue or he's been kidnapped, and either way, we need to fucking wrap up the end he's leaving loose."

Sal doesn't respond, so I continue. "I definitely think the pub is Irish. Scottish pubs feel more modern, and English pubs have soccer shit everywhere. They're definitely somewhere in Ireland, which is of course perfect because that's where our now mortal enemies live.

"Who do we know in Ireland, Sal? Who took over after we killed MacAntyre? Who..."

Instead of answering my questions, he interrupts me. "The woman looks like the one from the club in Prague."

Slowly, I turn to look at him. "What?"

"She looks like the woman from the club. Don't you think?"

"I didn't get a good look at her."

"Oh. Really?" he tilts his head.

No. OF course, I didn't get a good look at the woman in Prague when she blew past us, because I was too shocked by the feeling of Sal's body next to mine. Even *if I* had seen her, there's absolutely no way that I would remember it.

All I can remember is the feel of Sal's body next to mine in that dark corner.

All I can think about is the lust that punched through me then, and that fills my body with a simmering desire now.

"No. I didn't get a good look at her because your giant shoulders were blocking my view," I snap instead.

Sal's eyebrows go up. "Giant shoulders?"

"Yes. Giant. Like the size of a bull or something. Honestly, did you, like, crawl into a vat of HGH as a child?"

"Gia. Don't be rude."

I sigh. It was a little too far but I'm not willing to admit it yet. "I'm not being rude, but you have to admit that you're a very large person."

"And you have to admit you're being very rude for a human who I could squish under my shoes."

"Sal," I say, admonishing him.

"Gia."

"What the hell was that?"

He frowns and shakes his head, looking back at the computer. "Marco is alive."

"If he's alive, why hasn't he tried to come back?"

That's the million-dollar question.

Sure, Marco is alive. He's even doing well, it seems.

He certainly appears whole and hearty compared to how he looked when I last saw him at Caterina and Elio's.... well. The time that Marco handed Caterina over to Elio in order to try and plant her as a spy.

Laughable.

Caterina is capable and smart, but she's hardly a spy.

Still, the move brought me my favorite sister-in-law, so I'm not complaining.

Marco, however, had clearly been unhappy about the situation. Back then, he'd looked gaunt, like he hadn't slept in weeks.

This Marco looks well rested.

He's handsome, of course, like they all are. However, his whole 'older brother' thing made him too similar to Elio to ever really be attractive to me.

But this Marco?

He's glowing. I could see why the woman across the table from him is also somewhat resplendent... they both have a kind of aura around them. Two people, in love.

Maybe.

It could all just be an act.

Also, there's no guarantee that the people in the video are alive after this. It could be that whoever sent the video also kidnapped them right after and they're strung up in an Irish basement somewhere, bleeding out while Sal and I argue about how large he is.

Fuck.

"Gia?"

I glance at Sal. "Yeah?"

"What are we going to do about this?"

"What do you mean?"

"Marco's alive," he says quietly.

"Yeah. But he doesn't seem to be in any kind of immediate danger."

He shakes his head. "We don't know that."

Fuck. I should know better. Sal and I work so well as a team, it's almost like we share one brain.

I should have known that he would be thinking the same thing I am.

"I know. But presumably, whoever sent us this video wants us to know that he's well."

"Who would send it?"

I shrug. "No fucking clue."

"If it was the Russians and they wanted to make a statement because they think we killed their people…"

"Then we'd be dead. Russians don't make subtle threats like that," I sigh.

They're much more shoot and ask questions later type of people.

"Not to mention, no one knows we're here." I look at Sal meaningfully. "Unless someone knows about this place?"

"I've already told you, Gia. No one knows."

"Then how did they know to send us the video here?"

He shakes his head. "Unless we're being followed…"

My phone rings, snapping us out of the unpleasant sensation that we are likely being watched. "Elio," I say, opening the call.

"Well, it's nice to know you're alive."

Shit.

"I was just about to call you," I say breezily.

"You should have called me as soon as you did not die in an explosion, Gia. I was two seconds from sending Luca to scrape pieces of you off of the streets of Amsterdam."

"Luca's going to appreciate the fact he won't have to do that. How's Sara doing?"

"Gia. What the hell happened?"

I glance over at Sal and I put the phone on speaker. He comes behind me and leans over me. The smell of him...

I brush off the goosebumps.

"Elio."

"Sal," Elio responds. "I trust you're the reason my sister isn't painted over the pavement?"

"I'm the reason she's safe now," he responds.

Okay, that seems a little rich. Neither one of us knew about the bomb prior to it going off.

But he did pull me out of the canal.

And he did get me into the bathtub.

Shivers break out on my spine.

"I'm fine, Elio. The Russians are fucking dead though."

"So I hear. It is assumed that you two are dead as well."

Sal and I exchange a glance and I grimace. "Sorry brother. Didn't know it would come back on you like that."

"Word travels fast, especially in a small community."

The global network of hardened criminals that we belong to is hardly a small community, but I let that slide.

"Who told you?"

"Who do you think?"

I grit my teeth. "The Irish are turning out to be a fucking problem."

"That they are, Gia."

"What's the word on the street?"

"That you're dead, the Irish are proudly claiming their involvement, and they're expecting a joint retaliation from the Russians and us."

I look up at Sal. "They think we're dead?"

"Si."

Interesting. "Let them think we're dead."

"Gia?"

I look over at Sal. He's studying me, and after a while, he nods. "Yes," he whispers.

I turn back to the phone. "Let them think we're dead. It helps us out a little."

"In what way?"

"Dear brother. Please never underestimate the element of surprise."

"You are quite good at that. And with your recent public appearance, it's also significantly harder to hide. You're well known, Gia. You can't exactly sneak around Europe without someone recognizing you."

"That won't be a problem," I smile at Sal.

He frowns.

"Even if that's the case, what are you going to do? What's the purpose?"

"There's been... some other information that we found in Prague about the Irish. All of this feels too... planned for them. They're definitely the type to retaliate, but something else is going on. Sal and I are going to figure out what it is."

Elio is quiet for a second. "Gia. They're going to expect some kind of reply. If it's not written in blood, we're going to be seen as weak."

I know what he's worried about. If the world of the mafia thinks the Rossi family is weak, then they'll come for us.

Piece by piece, they'll carve parts of our empire off, until there's nothing left of us. Like a whale carcass at the bottom of the ocean, everyone with a machete will come to take a piece of us.

A big part of safety in this world is the illusion of power. As long as you're seen as powerful, the lie can be held for as long as you need to.

You can get away with a hell of a lot of people just thinking you're going to wreak havoc on them wherever you go.

If they think they're dead, though, Sal and I can do the scariest thing imaginable.

No one expects us to come back from the dead.

"They won't,' I assure him. "There's an Irish bar in Pittsburgh that has close ties to the gang. Take it out to send a message, and Sal and I will work on some stuff here."

"Stuff?"

"Trust me, Elio," I murmur.

He's silent for a minute, then sighs. "I always do."

"Love you," I say quickly.

"Love you too, sister."

The line goes dead.

I look at Sal.

He's smiling at me slightly. "Scariest thing imaginable?"

I grin. "Come on. You've never seen a zombie movie? If they think we can't be killed, that kind of takes the steam out of killing us."

"But we can be killed, Gia."

"That's the type of negative thinking that will get you demoted, De Luca."

He sighs. "Fine. What's your plan then?"

My smile grows. "Got any investment houses in Ireland?"

FIVE HOURS LATER, we have passports, bags, and clothes, and we're on the train to Copenhagen. From Copenhagen, we'll board a jet to Dublin, and go from there.

It's going into the heart of enemy territory, sure.

But it's not like we haven't done this before.

Sal is sitting across from me in the train car. He booked private, of course, cashing out some of the funds that I presume he's collected as the manager of a small real estate empire. I still can't get over the fact that Sal is as rich as God.

And he never told me about it.

He doesn't owe me that, I guess. It's not like I asked him to share his life story with me, or really for us to be something to each other at all.

Still...

Sal's closer to me than anyone. Closer than Caterina. Closer than Elio, even. He understands me in a way that I don't have to explain.

It's like having an echo.

When I move, Sal moves.

When I speak, he listens.

When I have a plan, he's already making it happen.

By the time we're at the airport, I'm so lost in my thoughts that I don't notice when he tenses.

Until his hand snakes out and grabs my wrist.

"Fuck."

"Sal?"

He wraps an arm around me, sheltering me from the bustling crowd by the ticket counters. "We need to go."

"Why?"

"Our faces are on an Interpol bulletin."

Shit. *Shit.*

"How? Why?"

I want to turn and see if I can locate our faces on the Interpol screens at the security checkpoint ahead, but Sal is already steering me out of the building.

"They're saying that we bombed the building in Amsterdam."

"Do they have our real names?"

He glances back. "No. no names. Just pictures."

"Shit."

It's not too bad. If our identification doesn't list us as Salvatore De Luca and Gianna Rossi, we can still pull this off.

"What pictures did you use for our passports?"

"Two of the ones we had on file."

"How similar do we look to the pictures Interpol has up?"

He pauses. "Very."

Fuck.

"Let's go. We need makeup and you need a wig."

"You don't?"

I sigh. "You know that I'm better at this than you are, Sal. Might as well own it."

He grabs my elbow and steers me gently out of the airport. With my sunglasses on and the Gucci scarf covering my hair, we can walk by the police without worrying too much about them.

Plus. Confidence is half the battle.

"Drugstore," I whisper.

I have no idea what drugstore is in Danish, but I'm assuming that Sal at least has some kind of working knowledge.

Sure enough, he pulls me into a sad-looking corner store. Inside, I buy makeup and some hair extensions, which Sal pays for in cash.

"When did you have time to grab Euros?"

"Why do you need to know all my tricks," he whispers.

God, I'd love to know all of his tricks.

"Follow me."

We slip into the back room when the teenage employee turns their back. I quickly take the scarf off and dig through my makeup bag.

"Did you use the pictures that you can change quickly?"

"Yes," Sal says.

"Good. We'll take new pictures after I put the disguise on and change. What did you say our names were?" I'm hopeful those can at least be salvaged as part of our new identities.

"Mr. Armando Bianchi and Mrs. Elena Bianchi."

I look up at him. "So you went for the married couple thing after all."

Sal's smile tugs at the corners of his mouth. "I figured it made sense."

Which part? The part where it was a good idea...

Or the part where it made sense for us to show up looking married?

I shake off the thought "Let's do this."

He leans down, and I start to apply makeup. This close, Sal's face is...

Goddamn it.

He's so handsome it makes my chest hurt.

His lips. His eyebrows. The way his jaw is so strong, the muscle in his cheek that twitches when he's mad. I don't want to put makeup on him for a disguise.

I want to touch the surfaces of his face, memorizing them as I lean in for a kiss.

"Gia?"

I glance at his eyes. "What?"

"Why are you staring?"

I gulp.

I look up at him.

And when I meet his eyes, my heart slams into my ribs.

8

SAL

I know Gia sees the lust in my eyes.

I can see the minute it hits her veins, flooding her system with adrenaline and hormones that make her full lips part and her eyes glaze over.

"Sal…"

I take a step forward and grab her by her elbows.

She's too close to me.

I can see the individual eyelashes against her cheeks when her gaze flutters closed, and I can see the flecks of gold in her dark brown eyes.

She's so fucking beautiful it hurts.

"What, Gia?"

"You're very close to me."

She says it as she leans closer, her eyes looking down at my lips. I can practically feel her trembling under me, and the sensation punches even more arousal through me.

I nod. "You seem to be putting us closer."

"I am?"

"Yes, Gia. You are."

"Oh."

Damn it. She leans in again, and she's up on her tiptoes, her face tilted up toward mine.

She's doing this on purpose.

I want to kiss her. I want to taste the little sigh she makes when I part her lips with my tongue, and I want to feel her as she gives in.

I want to tell her that she's mine.

But this is not the place. "Gia. We can't."

"We... can't?"

God. Her lips are brushing mine, and I can't think when her skin is so close to mine. "We're in a closet."

"I know. That means no one is watching."

"We'll ruin your makeup."

"I'm going to re-do it anyway so I look like an ugly old woman."

"You couldn't be ugly if you tried, Gia."

I hear her breath catch, and I know I shouldn't have said it.

"Sal...."

I can feel her lips brush against mine. I can feel how she sighs my name against me, and I know beyond a shadow of a doubt that in that moment, Gia would let me fuck her in this dirty Danish broom closet.

But I can't.

Not with her. Not here.

If I'm going to have Gia, I'm going to have what I've always wanted.

All of her.

And I'm going to want her to have all of me as well.

"Gia," I murmur. "We can't."

"Why?"

She's angry.

I pull her closer before she runs from me. "Gia..."

"You want me. I know you do."

One of her hands drifts over my pants and I shudder as she caresses me there.

"You're hard as a fucking rock for me, Sal. Why can't we?"

"Because..."

I suck in a breath.

I've never shared this with anyone. Not really. My brothers don't know, and it's not like I'm going to tell Caterina.

I don't really even know what to say.

"Sal?"

Gia isn't my brothers.

She's not Caterina.

She's not like anyone I've ever known.

She and I understand each other on another level. It's why after Belarus we couldn't be separated. I needed to know that she was okay at all times.

And she needed to be told she was okay.

"I... I want you," I grit out.

"I want you too," she whispers.

"But I... I can't..." I clear my throat. "I'm not interested in sex like... most people like it."

Gia freezes. "What?'

Shit. I want to stop, but I opened this door.

Now I have to walk through it.

"If I fuck you, Gia, it's going to be different than you've ever been fucked before."

"How?"

I look at her. "I need more than just... this," I pant.

My hand slowly slides around the column of her throat. She lets me, but I can see the question in her eyes.

I breathe in again. "IF you let me fuck you, Gia, then you're not going to be anyone's but mine."

"Fair. Same to you."

I smile slightly. "And I need you to do everything I tell you to."

"What?"

I tighten my hand slightly, and she breathes out. Her body relaxes under my fingers, like she's welcoming my grip.

That, more than anything, gives me the courage to go forward.

"I could take you right here," I whisper, leaning forward until I'm breathing the words in her ear. "But that wouldn't be enough for me."

"Sal..."

My hand tightens even more, and she lets out a little moan. "I need all of you, Gia."

"Okay."

"If we do this, you're doing it my way. You're mine. You won't be in control. You won't be able to boss me around."

"Oh. *Oh.*"

She lets out a breathy sigh, and my heart thumps.

She understands.

"I've wanted you from the minute I saw you, Gia. I've been fantasizing about this fucking body ever since you sauntered into that café in Turin and told me that Elio was wrong about Caterina."

"I know," she whispers.

"But once won't be enough. The way I want you, Gia... I fucking *crave* you," I snarl into her skin.

She moans.

"I want you. I want all of you. And I want to do things to you that you'd never want from anyone."

And that's the problem.

I don't want Gia unless I can dominate her. Not anymore. Once, it might have been enough to hide that part of me from her.

But now, I can't. And I know that having Gia any other way…

It won't work.

Not since I saw her bend to that one command.

It gave me a craving for more.

One that I want to fix.

As soon as possible.

"Show me," she whispers.

I drop my hand and step back.

We're staring at each other in the darkness of the broom closet.

My chest is heaving, and I feel like I'm shaking.

Here.

She wants me to show her *here*.

"Gia…"

The sound of her phone buzzing snaps us both to attention.

Gia grabs it but hesitates. She glances up at me, then back at the phone. "It's Elio."

"I figured."

"I'm going to answer it."

"Please do."

"This is not over, Sal."

I shake my head and she picks it up.

This is just beginning.

Once she puts the phone on speaker, I crowd near.

"Gia," Elio barks.

"Yes?"

"Why are you and Sal listed as wanted in the Interpol database?"

"I don't know."

"Do they not know you're dead?"

I glance at Gia, who shrugs. "Good guess?"

"You're being followed."

"By a cop?" she asks.

"There's no other explanation. You need to lay low until I figure out what's going to help. Do you have somewhere you can go?"

My mind races. We can't go to any of Gia and Elio's properties in Italy because they're going to be on Interpol's radar.

Italy, however, is safest. It's where Interpol has a tenuous hold at best, outside of Eastern Europe, and that brings us too close to the Russians for comfort. I sigh.

I didn't want to have to go here, but...

Alas.

"I have somewhere. Stay here. Five minutes, come out front."

And with that, I leave the closet.

STEALING a car is far easier than it should be.

Mere moments later, I'm back, pulling around the corner in a cheap Volvo that runs like shit.

"Your chariot awaits," I say as I open the door for Gia.

She gets in.

It will have to do for now.

"Where are we going?"

"You'll see."

The drive is long. We arc along backroads, racing south all the while. When we get to a train station in Zurich, we leave the car.

From Zurich to Lake Como, we take the train.

And when we get off, we take a taxi to a few blocks from my home.

When I use my app to open the door, everything is as I left it.

Dark, certainly, but not unclean. I hire a maid service for this house, which I bought only a year ago.

I do not rent it.

"Wow, Sal," Gia breathes.

I smirk. "Real estate pays off."

"It sure does."

I hand her the bag of her clothes. "Shower is upstairs. Pick a room. Come join me on the couch when you're done."

She nods.

I wonder if she even notices how she responds to me.

It makes me want so much more.

I can't get the closet in Copenhagen out of my mind. Part of me is hoping that she brings it up again.

Part of me hopes she doesn't.

Either way, when she comes downstairs a few minutes later, wearing one of my button-down shirts, her hair wet and sleek like a mermaid, I know something will change between us.

I hand her a glass of wine and she settles on the couch.

"Sal. This place is iconic."

With its view of Lake Como, it better be. "Yes."

"I can't believe it. It's exactly the house I want if I had one here."

I know that too. This is a more recent acquisition.

And I wouldn't be telling the truth if I denied the fact that I bought it with her in mind.

I'm standing at the opposite edge of the couch from her when she speaks.

"In Copenhagen..."

Every part of my body goes taut as I wait for her to finish that sentence.

"What about it?"

Gia tilts her head. "You're a Dom, aren't you?"

"I am." There's no point in denying it. I warned her about it back in Copenhagen, and more than that, it's part of who I am.

Part of who I want Gia to accept me as.

"How does it work? You just tie women up and tell them what to do?"

I shake my head. "It's more than that, Gia."

"Tell me."

She's sitting on my couch, wearing one of my t-shirts. With her glass of wine in hand, the scene looks so domestic, it makes my chest ache. Gia and I have been here many times before. After I rescued her from Belarus, we spent every night together, just finding comfort in each other's touch.

We've never been here, though.

"It's more nuanced than that," I say. "Sex... it's always a game of power. Right?"

"Not always."

I arch an eyebrow at her.

She shrugs. "I've heard it's about more but. I certainly don't see it that way."

Of course she wouldn't.

Gia wields sex as a weapon. It's just one in her arsenal, sure, but I know she knows exactly what I'm talking about.

"In my... situation, it's about me being in control."

"Okay. Seems selfish."

"And?"

She shrugs. "I just never pictured you as a selfish lover."

I can't help the smile that curls at my lips. "But you've pictured me as a lover."

"Sure."

It's one word that she puts out into the room, but underneath it, I can read so much more.

She doesn't want to tell me how often she's fantasized about me.

"You're correct, Gia. It isn't just about me."

I walk over to the couch and sit so that I'm facing her. We aren't close, necessarily.

But the air between us feels like it's sparking.

She sips her wine. "Okay. So, the person you're... with. They like to be submissive."

"Yes."

She tilts her head. "Why?"

I lean in slightly. "Life is full of choices, *tesoro*. Some are easy. Some aren't. But they must be made, as certain as death and taxes. When I'm with someone, I take the choice away from them."

"That sounds..."

"Freeing," I say before she can say anything else. "It's freeing."

She doesn't respond, but I can see the goosebumps on her arm.

I smile. I inch over on the couch until we're sitting side by side.

I lean in and run my fingertips over the skin of her leg. "Look at this. Your body responds to my touch. Everywhere I put my fingers," I pause, trailing the tips of them over her skin, "you feel something. Did you decide to do that?"

"No," she whispers.

"And when I go higher..." I trail my fingers just to the edge of the shirt she's wearing, stopping before they disappear beneath.

Her breath hitches.

I look up at her. "You like it."

"You don't know that."

I laugh. "Oh, Gia. I do. Your breath caught in your throat and your eyes widened. You shivered slightly when I got close, but you didn't flinch. You want me to keep going."

"What if I didn't?"

I chuckle. "You'd be making a decision based on what you think you should want, instead of what you do. That's the problem with choices," I whisper.

My hand slowly creeps toward the juncture of her thighs.

She looks down, but I use my other hand to remove her wine glass and set it on the side table. I put a finger under her chin, tilting her face to look at me.

Slowly, I move my other hand under the hem of the shirt.

"The thing about choices is you make them based on lots of factors. You calculate. You decide. You listen to a million people as you make that decision. But I only have one person to listen to."

She's breathing hard now. My fingers brush her inner thighs, and I push her legs apart slightly. "Open, Gia," I say.

Gia hesitates. That one second of hesitation makes my heart slam into my ribs.

Then, she does.

"I'm not making decisions based on what someone else thinks they should like," I whisper as I slowly trace the seam of her center.

She's wet.

I knew she would be, but the thought still makes me dizzy.

"I'm making decisions based on what I see your body react to. So when you tell me no, unless you use a special word, I'm going to keep going."

She tries to jerk her head away, but I hold it firmly. I press a finger inside of her and Gia bites her lip, trying to keep the moan inside.

"No no, *cara mia*," I whisper. "Tell me how it feels."

"I..."

I add another finger and she gasps. Her eyes close and she arches her back. She moans, loud and clear.

Exactly how I wanted her to.

"Good girl," I purr.

Then I take my hand back. I settle on the other side of the couch.

And when she finally turns to look at me, I lick the moisture from my fingers.

Her lips part in surprise.

"I want to make your choices for you, Gia," I murmur. "You wouldn't let yourself have this. But I will. Only if you want to let go."

It's an invitation.

I watch her, hoping she will answer.

Finally, she does. Her lips part and she says one word.

"Okay."

9

GIA

I have no idea what I've gotten myself into.

However, I do know that when Sal touches me, I can't think straight.

There's something in his words that makes me... not want to think straight. I understand what he's saying, and I understand the implications of it.

Sal is a Dom. I'm not super shocked by that. He's quiet, he's never pushed me into anything I didn't want to do....

But I don't know that he thinks about being a Dom the same way that I do.

I always thought that it was someone bossy. Some asshole with a superiority complex who has to be in control at all times.

I never thought it meant...

I make decisions based on what I see your body reacts to.

There's something there.

The way he describes it, I don't think he's someone who is just some asshole that needs to be in control.

I think he wants to be in control... of making me come more than I ever have in my life.

I have no idea what that means for me, but I don't hate it.

In fact... I want to see what that means.

So when I said 'okay,' I knew what I was doing.

The smile that spread across Sal's face, though?

It gives me chills.

He leans forward, shifting so that he's kneeling between my legs. "Before we start," he whispers, sliding his hands up my legs. "You need a word to tell me."

"A safe word?"

I can't believe that I'm saying that. It feels silly, and at the same time, I suddenly understand exactly why someone might need one.

If he's not going to stop...

"Cats."

Sal's hands stop an inch from where I want them.

He grins up at me from where he's kneeling between my legs. "Cats?"

"I'm not going to say it in this context," I say with my eyebrow raised for emphasis.

He laughs. "Cats it is then."

When his hands continue up my legs, I bite my lip in anticipation.

He's so close. Earlier, when he pushed his thick fingers inside of me, I almost came.

This time, I have a feeling that I'm not going to last very long.

"You liked it earlier when I put my fingers inside your pretty pussy, didn't you Gia?"

I nod.

"So honest. Such a good girl for me," he purrs.

I'm not a dog and I don't know why that's working for me…

But it is.

"Do you want me to do it again?"

"Yes," I whisper.

His eyes glint with fascination. "Okay. I'll get you close, *cara mia*, but there are rules."

I'm hyper-focused on how his hands feel on my legs. I barely notice that he's waiting for my response.

Until he lightly bites the inside of my leg.

"Don't look away, Gia," he whispers.

I nod and look down at him.

"I have three rules. Are you ready for them?"

I nod again.

"The first rule is that you can't touch me. Someday, I will tell you to touch me all you want. But not today. Okay?"

I nod. I have no other response. It's so sexy, I can't even process his words.

Sal smirks. "The second rule is you can't say anything. You can't moan. You can't tell me what you want. If you need to tell me your word you can, but other than that, no sounds. Understand?"

I nod.

He smirks again. "Good. You're already so good at following my rules, Gia."

It should bother me. It really, really should.

But, unfortunately, I'm panting and wet and all I want to do is follow his rules and find out what's going to happen next.

"The last rule, *bellissima*, is you can't come until I tell you."

I tilt my head at that. I open my mouth. "Why?"

Sal bites the inside of my thigh.

Hard.

I gasp.

He backs up. "Next time I'll mark your pretty ass with my palm, Gia. No speaking. Nod if you understand."

I freeze.

I could say the word and he would end this. I know it in my bones. I could tell him 'cats' and walk away and pretend none of this ever happened.

Or I could keep going.

I'll mark your pretty ass with my palm.

Jesus, Mary, and Joseph, that shouldn't turn me on. But at this point, I'm kind of ignoring that voice in my head that tells me what I should and should not be turned on by.

And I'm just kind of... going with the things that do.

So, I don't say anything.

I nod.

"Good girl, Gia. So good. Let's see how much you want me," he groans.

When he slides three thick fingers inside of me, I bite my lips to keep myself from screaming his name.

Hard.

"You're trying so hard not to say anything, aren't you Gia? Nod if you agree."

I nod. Vigorously.

Sal smiles.

I'm still just sitting in a long shirt on the couch, and he's kneeling in front of me. Anyone on earth who takes a boat onto the lake could see us right now. They would see me spread open, with Sal's slick fingers sliding inside of me.

With the dusk, the house is illuminated as well, meaning that we're practically a window box show. In a giant picture window.

I shouldn't like that either.

"Did you just notice that anyone can see you, Gia?"

Oh.

Oh.

He gently pulls his fingers in and out of me, pushing them in a rhythm that I know is going to drive me wild. I nod, belatedly answering his question.

"You're right," Sal growls. "They can see you. But I want them to. Because I want them to see what is mine. They can fantasize about you. They can leer at you and think about what a prize Gianna Rossi would be. But not one of them will ever fucking have you, Gia. Because you're mine," he snarls.

Oh my god.

I bend my back, arching to take more of him. His little possessive thing worked so well for me, I think I'm going to come right now. I'm just starting to feel the flutters across my stomach when he stops.

Completely.

And pulls his fingers from me.

It is all I can do not to whine with protest.

"What were my rules, Gia?"

Oh fuck.

I blink at Sal, who is looking at me with eyes so dark, they almost look black. He's still kneeling between my legs, and he looks like some kind of demonic prince, poised there to lure me into hell.

And honestly, I'd gladly go to hell for him.

"The rules, *tesoro mio*, were that you would not speak. You've done well on that one." He leans in and punctuates that with a kiss to my inner thigh.

I shiver.

"The third rule was that you can't come until I tell you to. Did I tell you that you could come, Gia?"

I bite my lip and I shake my head. *No.*

"And were you about to come?"

How the fuck did he know that? But Sal's still looking at me with that same intense gaze. I'm not going to ask him or break rule number one, that's for sure.

Slowly, I nod. *Yes.*

"Naughty, Gia," he murmurs. Slowly, he arches his fingers up my thighs again, his fingers tight. "Next time, you'll find out what happens when you're naughty."

I'll mark your pretty ass with my palm.

Shit.

"This time, I'll let it slide. But to remind you, you will not come without me saying so. Understand?"

I nod.

Slowly, Sal pushes those fingers inside of me again.

"You're going to get close, Gia. But right before you come, you have to stop."

What the hell?

"Those are the rules," he says darkly.

I nod.

His fingers twist and pump inside of me, the only sound is the noise of him moving through my wetness. I'm arching my back again, biting my lip to keep myself from crying out.

Then I feel it.

The build of sensation across my back. The shuddering of my lower belly. This time, however, I don't embrace it.

I breathe heavily and push at Sal's shoulders.

His eyes are smoldering when he pulls his hand from me.

For a minute neither one of us moves. My chest is heaving, and I'm staring down at Sal, who is looking at me with something akin to wonder.

When he smiles, though, it's an unnerving mix of lust and pure joy that sets my blood on fire.

"Oh Gia. You've done so well," he whispers. "Let's play more, shall we?"

His hands roughly tug the shirt off of me, and I let it drop onto the couch.

Sal moves so that he's kneeling close enough to lean forward and kiss me. He locks onto me with a force that I honestly can't place.

It's like he's... passionate.

The kiss is everything. There's so much in it that I feel, so much more than he's saying out loud.

When his lips move down my neck, I'm more than just gasping for air.

I'm stunned.

However, when his teeth graze against one of my nipples, my thoughts fly out of my head entirely.

That one move takes so much more concentration than before to keep quiet. I want to moan. To gasp.

I want to tell him that it feels fucking amazing.

But instead, I bite my lip. My world has been narrowed down to simple things.

The feel of Sal's teeth on my breast.

The weight of him between my legs.

And the rules.

No speaking.

Don't come.

Nothing else exists. Nothing else matters.

I'm so present in the moment, I don't think I've ever felt this way before. I've never been aware of someone like this, the way my body seems to be tuned to every single one of his movements.

When he pulls back and kisses a trail down my stomach, I feel like I might explode.

Don't come.

"Don't forget the rule, Gia," he whispers.

Then, he presses two fingers inside me again. I don't say anything, which is a goddamn triumph.

Because a second later, he adds his tongue to the mix.

And I think I'm going to crawl out of my skin.

His fingers are sliding in and out of me while his tongue works my clit. His other hand, to my joy and to my terror, climbs up my ribs to grasp one of my breasts.

Sal's fingers pinch my nipple, rolling it around, while he laps at me.

Shit

Shit.

I'm not going to make it. There's no way that I'm not going to come. There's no way that I want to stop. I mean how bad can his punishment be? He's going to what, spank me a little?

Oh no.

That thought sends a shiver down my spine that's downright dangerous. I feel it again, but this time, Sal freezes before I push at him.

He looks up.

"You're so close, aren't you darling?"

I nod. Barely. The movement is abrupt, like my neck muscles forgot how to move. But I don't know what my body is doing in the slightest, really.

His fingers are still inside me.

I feel like a violin. Like a guitar. Like a fucking bow strung so tight that any movement on his part is going to send me over the edge.

Through all of this, his rule tugs at the edges of my awareness.

Don't come.

"You've been so good, Gia. So very good. You know what happens to good girls?"

Again, a shake of my head that is absolutely terrible, like I've lost all muscle control.

He smiles again.

"They get to come."

I blink.

Is he…?

Then, he moves. His lips return to my clit, his tongue working it while his fingers move aggressively in and out of me.

I'm a mess. I feel like my nerves are going to explode. I've been here twice before, and I have no clue how I'm actually going to go through with it this time.

I bite my lips again because I need to tell him that I'm too sensitive. That I'm too wrung out. There's no way I'm going to be able to come now...

Then, he moves his fingers. In something that feels like... he's pressing something inside of me?

Oh.

Shit.

"Come for me, Gia darling," he says when he pulls up for a moment.

Oh Jesus.

I do.

I do exactly what he tells me to, and I explode.

There are stars.

Stars.

I think I might black out. Everything feels like it's rippling over me. I can't stand it. I love it. It's almost painful, it feels so good.

I don't even feel Sal take his hands off me. I definitely don't feel him tuck a blanket around me.

All I feel is the steady weight of him on the couch next to me.

His heartbeat, thundering in my ear.

A steady beat that brings my world back into alignment again.

10

SAL

IT TAKES EVERYTHING IN ME TO NOT CONTINUE.

Gia is so gorgeous. She's naked for me. She's panting. I know how she feels when she comes.

I want to push inside of her so badly and fuck her senseless. Use the cord that I have lying around somewhere to tie her into a beautiful package, for me to unwrap one piece at a time.

But I can see she's not ready for it yet.

There are levels to what I do. Ways to introduce people.

Gia's had an appetizer.

I want to know if she's ready to order a meal.

I give her a blanket and pull the curtains, settling into the couch next to her. Now that she's wrapped in my arms, I don't want anyone to see her.

We cuddle under the blanket for a while, while I listen to her heartbeat change from frantic to steady again. The feel of her around me, the way she fell apart when she came?

I'm never going to forget that. I'm going to do it again, at some point.

But not yet.

After a very long time, Gia stirs slightly. I look down at her and watch her blink up at me.

"Sal..." she whispers.

I gently press a kiss to her forehead. "Meet me in the kitchen when you're ready. The bedroom down the hall should have extra clothes, and the shower is new."

I walk away.

The house is quiet, so I can hear the sounds of Gia getting up. The floor squeaks slightly, something that I'll have to remember as I continue to improve on the house.

I'd be lying to myself if I said I hadn't pictured Gia in this house since the moment I bought it.

Hell.

I'd pictured her here when I was looking at the fucking pictures.

Having her here, and having done what we just did, puts my wishful thinking into a whole new perspective.

For so long, I've convinced myself that I can't have her. That she doesn't want me, and that even if she did, I would have to hide myself from her, never being who I truly am around her.

Now that the possibility to have both exists...

Shit.

I turn. I need something to occupy my time, so I don't end up just aimlessly pacing and thinking about things that I can't have.

I open the cabinets.

I can definitely cook something. Cooking will help me keep my mind off of Gia.

At least, I hope so.

When she joins me in the kitchen, I've got a pretty decent carbonara going. The pantry is stocked, the freezer has all the things I need, and I'm halfway through plating when I hear that floor squeak.

Gia pads into the room and settles, perching on one of the barstools at the kitchen bar.

She doesn't say anything.

I hand her a chilled vodka soda and continue plating. She sips the drink, then nods. "Carbonara?"

"Yep."

"I didn't know you could cook."

"You seem to know very little about me these days, Gia."

"I know. It's really annoying."

I smile at her.

She arches one of those perfect eyebrows. "You think it's funny?"

"I'm a little entertained."

"By me?"

Always, Gia. "That I managed to sneak some things by your incredibly extensive spy network."

"I know. I think I figured out how that happened, though," she says, sipping the vodka.

"You did?"

She nods.

I slide the pasta in front of her, coming to sit in the next seat. I hand her a fork, taking one of my own.

I wait until she takes a bite. I'm more than a little nervous to see what her reaction is.

She twirls a small amount of the spaghetti up, delicately wrapping her lips around it. When she pulls it back, I adjust myself slightly.

Gia is the most gorgeous creature I've ever seen.

I don't know how I've lived this long without her. The fact that I willingly separated from her seems not only stupid of me, but inconceivable.

She closes her eyes and moans. "Oh my god. Sal. You made this from what? Thin air?"

"Nonperishable goods in the cabinets and the freezer," I say dully.

It's the least sexy answer on the face of the planet, and I immediately regret saying it.

Gia laughs. "Wow. You tell that to all your girlfriends?"

"Are you my girlfriend?"

Her cheeks flame a bright, brilliant red. "That's not... I didn't mean..."

"Relax, Gia. I'm just joking."

The word doesn't work for us. Gia will never be just a girlfriend. She's more than that in every way.

I always suspected it.

But after what we did in the living room?

It feels more and more true every day.

"It's not a very funny joke," she mutters.

"I guess a sense of humor wasn't something you found out about me."

"No. Unfortunately, you're criminally slow. Such a shame."

I roll my eyes. "Ouch, Gia."

"Oh whatever. You like it."

I do. "So, tell me," I say, taking a bite of my own carbonara. "How do you figure you've missed so many things about me?"

She eyes me over her glass of vodka. "You hid in my shadow."

I smirk at her. "What?"

"You're so close to me. I never thought to dig into any of your stuff, because you follow me around like... a baby chick or something."

"Are you calling me a baby chick, Gia?"

"No," she muses. "I guess you're like one of those... what's the bird who takes other birds' nests?"

"A cuckoo?"

"Yeah. That. You cuckooed me into thinking you were just Caterina's older brother and the youngest of all the De Luca brothers. But you're not really just that, are you Sal?"

"I don't know what you mean."

She laughs.

I love it when Gia laughs.

"I think I got it. Since we announced the whole marriage between Elio and Caterina, you've been basically just following me around all the time, and you think that keeps you safe from my scrutiny."

Damn it.

She's pretty much correct.

I fly under the radar compared to my brothers.

Marco is… Marco. He's the heir of the De Luca family, and he's the one who ran everything until his disappearance.

Dino is… a bull in a China shop on a good day, a wrecking ball on a bad one.

Both Marco and Dino are pretty even in terms of their ability to fly off the handle at a moment's notice.

When we go out together, it's pretty much a guarantee that one of them is going to get into a fight.

Which is why no one ever seems to notice me in the background. They don't notice that I move all the things that I know will piss either one of them off out of the way.

I stay close to them too.

I wink at Gia. "Okay. You got it."

She laughs. "I knew it! And you figured out that you could do that because Marco and Dino are basically juggernauts, yes?"

"Yes, actually."

"So, if people were constantly looking at something louder and more annoying, then they'd never look at you?"

"Yes."

"And you knew I never would because I assumed pretty much the same thing?"

"I figured the fact you found me attractive helped."

Gia rolls her eyes. "You never knew I found you attractive."

I study her. "The first time I saw you, at Caterina and Elio's first engagement party, your pupils got big like saucers."

"It was night."

"Not at the incredibly well-lit party it wasn't."

"Fine," Gia huffs. "I feel like you took some kind of online course in FBI-level body language. But fine. I did always think you were the hot one."

I want to beam at her. "It wasn't an online course. Criminal justice at Rutgers."

Gia barks a laugh. "Seriously?"

"Yes."

"You. The third son of a prominent mafia family. You took criminal justice?"

"I needed to know," I say quietly. "I needed to make sure that no one would ever take members of my family away in handcuffs ever again. I needed to know how they thought.

What they looked for. So that no De Luca went to jail. Ever again."

Gia stills, her fork halfway to her mouth.

Slowly, she puts it back down. "That's really why you did it, isn't it?"

I nod.

"Sal. I'm so sorry."

I shake my head. "It was a long time ago."

But I can still see my uncles and my grandfather, the handcuffs holding them back, the shocked look on their faces.

I can still see my aunts and my grandmother after, wailing and holding onto each other.

No one died. That day.

My grandfather died in jail. Heart attack.

One of my uncles got out. Marco lets him live on one of the farms in upstate New York, some old piece of land that the family's held onto forever.

No one asks him to do anything more challenging than that.

Gia sighs. "I know. I live in mortal terror that Elio will go to jail. Or... worse."

The ghost of our past flashes between us.

"I'm going to find out, you know. Who killed our parents."

"Of that, I have no doubt."

My phone pings then, and I pull it up. It's a CNN article that Elio sent me. I open it, and nearly snort my pasta through my nose.

"What?"

"Look," I say, passing the phone to her.

Gia reads for a moment, then her eyes widen. "Holy shit. They really do think we're dead."

"According to Interpol, and now CNN, yes."

She hands the phone back to me and I look down at the article again.

Two bodies, a man and a woman, are believed to be Gianna Rossi and Salvatore De Luca. Both were caught on CCTV entering the restaurant in Amsterdam and were present for the blast.

There were no survivors, and the culprits have been named as domestic terrorists. Any information should be directed to... I look up.

Gia's staring at me in shock. "Holy shit. Did Elio put the bodies there?"

I shake my head. "No. I don't think so. That would be unusually... thorough of him."

The real word that I meant to say lingers in the air.

Not thorough.

Brutal.

Elio doesn't always have the stomach for the hard stuff. Not since he found out about Luna, anyway.

In some ways it makes sense. It's hard to show up as a family man one minute, and then turn around and order two bodies to be placed in a burning building the next.

"Whose bodies are they?"

I shake my head. "I have no idea, *cara mia*," I murmur.

We both still.

The endearment just kind of... slipped out. I didn't mean to say it, not exactly.

It's something I've thought for a very, very long time.

"I don't like how Interpol is involved," Gia murmurs.

Fine. We're not going to address the endearment. That works for me too.

"Me neither. It's just too..."

"Close?"

I nod. "Too close."

"How many people know about this place?"

"No one. I just bought it recently."

"How recently?"

Recently enough that I pictured you when I looked at the listing.

"Recently enough that it's not going to bounce to any official ledgers until about a month from now."

"So, if someone managed to find us here..."

"Impossible unless we had a tail."

Even then, there are security cameras like crazy, and they all have a feed to my phone. I had turned it on while Gia was down the hall showering.

"Odds that we have a tail?"

I look at the article. "If Interpol is involved..."

"Cops?"

"Interpol has some good ones."

"But you're a step ahead, right? Mister criminology degree?"

"No degree. Just classes."

"Do you want one?"

I glance at Gia. "What?"

"The degree."

"I..."

I'm not sure. It's never been an option for me. Marco has a business degree, but it wasn't something anyone offered to me.

"I don't know."

Gia sighs, pushing away her mostly empty plate.

"Okay. This was unfairly good. I haven't had carbonara that delicious in a long time, and now I'm stuffed. It's late. I'm tired. Let's go to bed."

"Let's?"

She studies me over the rim of her glass. "You have a problem with that?"

I want to ask her the context. We slept in a bed together after Belarus.

But I didn't make her come before then.

I shake my head. "No. I don't"

"Good."

We go through the motions quietly. Brushing teeth. Brushing hair. Gia braids her wild mane into two twin braids that arch down the back of her head, and I desperately want to run my hands over them and feel the softness of them under my fingers.

When we get into the bed, I keep my distance from Gia.

Until she sighs and grabs me, tugging me close.

I wrap myself around her. The top of her head tickles my lips, and I press them gently there, giving her a small kiss.

She doesn't say anything.

I count my heartbeats quickly. I make it the whole way to twenty, then Gia rustles.

"I needed this."

I pull her closer. "Why?"

Gia's fingernails skate over my arm. "You held me like this after Belarus."

"I did."

"I needed it then too."

"Did you?"

She sighs. "Don't make me beg, Sal."

"I have no idea what you're begging for. But if you want to beg..."

She laughs and smacks my arm lightly, cutting me off. "Don't."

"Okay."

We're quiet for another minute.

"I should have been born before Elio."

She says the words like they're rusty. Like somehow, it's the first time she's said them out loud.

"What does that mean?" I say finally.

"I want it more than he does."

I press another gentle kiss to her hair. "That is definitely true."

"I'm better at it than he is."

"You're magnificent, Gia."

"I'm smarter. I'm better informed. I do everything that he does, but I do it faster and better. And still, he's the one who gets to run the family. All because he's a boy. And he was born first."

I know exactly how she feels.

Marco is... Marco. He's my oldest brother, and he's always looked out for me. I have nothing bad to say about him, exactly.

Except that he's a terrible choice to lead our family in this world.

Marco is hot-headed. He's got a temper on him that will set fire to the world if he's not keeping it under control.

But more than that, he's so devoted to us that he can't see straight.

He'd lead the family straight into the Atlantic and sink us, if he thought it would keep all of us happy.

It makes him terrible as a leader of this family.

More than once, I've wished that I had Marco's place. I've even considered asking him for it, to tell him to step down.

Now, it's kind of a moot point.

Marco is missing.

Elio has taken over all of the dock industry, as well as all of the other stuff as well.

We've effectively been absorbed into Rossi Industries.

Ironic, I guess. Marco fought so hard to keep the De Luca family name alive and well in the world of organized crime.

Now it's basically gone.

I'm certain that it could be revived, but I don't see the point.

"I know how you feel," I whisper.

"Do you?"

I consider that. I don't know how it feels to be her, specifically.

But I know how it feels to be consistently overlooked.

"No, Gia. But I do know that you're right. You would be an excellent head of the family. You deserve it."

She tucks herself against me. "We have to find Marco. If I do, then Elio might see that I'm better than he is."

That makes me pause.

I have no doubt that Elio knows how effective Gia is. He'd be stupid not to, and he's definitely not stupid.

But I also don't think he's willing to give up on the Rossi empire either.

"We'll find him, Gia," I whisper.

She tucks herself close again, and I pull her near.

I don't think either of us sleep for a long time. But after Gia does, I listen to the beat of her heart.

I did hold her close like this after Belarus.

I don't know why Gia let me. But I knew what I needed.

I couldn't sleep without her in my arms. I couldn't sleep without knowing that she was safe. Whole. And close.

Unfortunately, I think I'm in that place again. But this time, I don't know that I can ever sleep without Gia nearby again.

Now that she's in my arms, I never want to let her go.

11

GIA

Waking up in Sal's arms has always been a treat.

I stir slightly, stretching my arms as I take in the smell of the morning. The sheets smell like Sal. The air smells like Sal.

I'm pretty sure that if I could smell the sunlight, it would also smell like Sal.

"Morning," he rumbles behind me.

I shuffle back slightly, arching my back against his front.

"Good morning," I whisper.

Sal gives a little grunt, and I scooch my butt back so it's rubbing against his cock.

Which is predictably quite hard.

I smile.

We've spent so many mornings pretending that the attraction between us doesn't exist.

It's kind of nice to admit that it does.

"Gia," Sal grunts. "You're killing me."

"It's a nice way to die though, right?"

He laughs, but his hands skate over my hips. "I'm definitely putting it on my list."

"Your list?"

"Of pleasant ways to die."

I pause. "There's more than one?"

Behind me, Sal shifts. He moves forward, one arm banding around my waist, his lips caressing my neck.

"Yes, Gia," he breathes. "I have several preferred ways to die."

"Why?"

He kisses the shell of my ear. "Because I've seen a hell of a lot of terrible ones, so I thought I might as well come up with some more pleasant ones."

In that moment, my heart aches for him.

"I know what you mean," I whisper.

"So, are you going to have a list now?"

I shake my head. "No. I'm just never going to die." *And neither are you*, I add silently.

If I have to, I'll tear the world apart to make sure that Sal never has to consult his list.

Sal laughs, and the sound rumbles through his chest. "Your confidence is simultaneously very sexy and a little terrifying."

"Sexy and terrifying is basically my brand," I whisper.

Sal's laugh feels like a balm on my soul. I can't remember the last time I felt this airy and light.

Maybe... never?

He holds me close again. "We should probably get up," he murmurs.

His impressive cock twitches against my butt, and I grin.

"Maybe," I say.

Before Sal can ask any questions, I turn in his arms. My hand glides over his chest, tracing the tattoos there, before I run my nails down his abs.

I see him gulp in a breath, the movement reflecting in the flex of his stomach.

"Gia," he murmurs.

I can't tell if it's a plea or a warning.

I blink and look up at him. "Yes?"

"What are you doing?"

Innocently, I tilt my head to the side. "Last night's rules don't apply anymore, right?"

He doesn't answer, but I see his eyes go dark with lust.

"I didn't get to touch you last night," I whisper. "It was in the rules. Which I was so good and followed just like you told me to."

I don't really care that the words sound perilously close to begging. There's something to this game between Sal and I, where we both adopt personas that are a little different than who we are normally, that's hot.

No.

That's not right either.

Because Sal is exactly the type of person who would enjoy being a pleasure Dom. Someone who notices so much. Someone who wants to be in control, even if he knows that he can't.

And I guess I'm a little bit of a manipulative princess.

I pout. "I didn't get any chances to touch you, and you were so good to me," I say.

Sal's eyes narrow, like he's fighting to keep them trained on me. "No. You didn't."

"I think I get to have my chance now, don't I?"

"That depends."

I blink. "On what?"

"On how you take me," Sal says in that voice that's so full of desire, it makes my heart slam into my chest in response.

I don't respond.

The shirt I was wearing flies over my head. My panties? Gone.

I hook my thumbs in the waistband of his soft linen pajamas, and he lifts his hips, letting me pull them down his legs.

"Jesus, Gia," he moans. "Excited much?"

I don't respond.

Instead, I smile and pull the sheets back.

I slide down the length of his body, my fingers resting on the tattoos on his thighs. They're beautiful, and this isn't the first time I've noticed them. It is, however, the first time that I've examined them up close.

One is a scorpion, twisting over his olive-skinned thigh, the details pointed and crisp.

The other is more... nebulous. It looks slightly fresher, like it was done recently. It's darkness, and there are two eyes peering out.

I gently graze that one with my fingertips. "I like these," I whisper to him.

"Thank God," he bites out. "I'd have to remove them if you didn't."

I laugh at that.

Leaning forward, I gently lick the scorpion's claws, then bite gently on its tail.

Sal rumbles in response.

I pull the covers down more, revealing his naked cock. Gently, I put my hands on it.

We both gasp.

"Shit, Sal," I murmur, my hands taking in the feel of him. "You need to come with some kind of warning label."

"Warning?"

"Impossibly huge cock. Pretty. Looks nice to lick," I say, flashing him a grin.

His eyes roll back in his head. "Gia..."

I don't let him say another word.

My lips do exactly what they've wanted to ever since I first exposed his thick length to the light of day.

I wrap them around him.

Sal arches up off the bed, hissing between his teeth. "Gia," he groans, sucking in a huge breath. "Fucking hell."

I guess that's a good thing.

One of his big hands descends on my neck, pushing me forward. "More, baby," he whispers.

Well.

He did say that I could touch him if I took him well enough.

I grin and start working him. My tongue wraps around the head of the hard column of flesh, and I use my hands to cover what my mouth can't.

"Oh, darling," he murmurs. "That's so fucking good."

I can't.

This man is a study in contrasts. He's totally in control, but willing to give it over to me. He uses language that belongs in a history book, then has the dirtiest mouth I've ever heard.

I can't fucking handle him.

I groan, shifting so I can take him deeper. I'm getting wet through this whole process, which is pretty shocking, because it's not every day that giving a blowjob turns me on as much as this.

Actually, it's never.

I don't even like blowjobs.

But for Sal?

I fucking love them.

His hand pushes me down. "Deeper, Gia," he rumbles.

I look up at him and he's watching me, his pupils blown wide. The image of him looking at me through those eyelashes, over the canvas of tattoos covering his chest, is just erotic.

Pure and simple.

I groan, and my pussy clenches with need.

Somehow, despite the fact that his fingers are nowhere near the center of my pleasure, he seems to know this. "You like this, don't you?" he purrs.

I nod.

His hand pushes me forward. "Take more, *belissima*," he whispers.

I comply.

For Sal, knowing that I like it is at least as important as liking it himself. His cock twitches in my mouth when I free one of my hands to drift down and touch myself.

Holy shit.

I *really* like this.

"You wanted to touch me so badly last night, didn't you?"

I have no response, and I suckle more of him.

"Now that you can, are you pleased?"

Glancing up at him, I make a frustrated sound. I can't exactly nod with him in my mouth.

Sal grins. "Let me go Gia. Just for a second."

I think about saying no. Keeping my lips wrapped around him.

But...

I release him.

Sal's strong arms are at my waist in seconds, and I give a little shriek as he turns me. Before I know it, my core is positioned over his face.

And his cock bobs in front of me.

"Keep going," he murmurs.

I do. His abs flex underneath me, and it's the only warning I have before his lips descend on my aching wet center.

Oh. My. God.

From there, it's kind of a mess. I can't focus on Sal when he's lapping at me, and I can barely hold him in my mouth because I keep gasping.

I try to arch down so he can get a better angle, but that makes him pop free from my lips.

Hell.

"Keep going, Gia. You're doing such a good job. I'm so close," Sal murmurs.

The encouragement is exactly what I need. I double down, sucking him down my throat as far as I can. I'm not exactly the type of person without a gag reflex, so I do my best.

And apparently, my best is exactly what Sal wants.

"Gia," he murmurs from between my legs. "I'm so close. But I need you to come first. Can you do that for me?"

In response, I shift my hips back so I'm smothering him.

He doesn't say anything, but his tongue says plenty.

Within moments, I feel the orgasm explode over my skin.

I can't focus on him anymore, not when I feel like my body is shining. Not when my vision goes dark, and when I cry out his name.

He likes that.

He grunts, and I'm moving through the air again. I'm on my back when I open my eyes, and Sal is looming over me.

"Let me show you how much I liked that," he groans.

With one of his hands palming his thick cock, I watch, mesmerized, as he leans forward. It takes two rough jerks for him to come.

And when his hot liquid sprays over my chest, I arch my back, giving him a better canvas.

"*Gia,*" Sal groans.

Oh my God. That noise, that sound. It's hotter than anything we've done so far. I totally understand the whole pleasure Dom thing in that moment.

Because knowing that I made Sal feel that much?

It's like a lightning bolt straight to my veins.

When he's done, he leans back on his heels. His chest is rising and falling like he ran a marathon, and he's staring at where he came on my breasts and stomach.

My nipples tighten in response.

"Fuck, Gia," he breathes.

I smile. "I like to touch you."

"I fucking like it too."

His weight shifts off of the bed, and he pads to the bathroom. Minutes later, he's back, and a warm towel cleans me off. "Meet me downstairs," he rumbles.

I give him a mock salute.

A few minutes later, I'm dressed in yet another set of Sal's clothes. I walk quietly down the stairs, marveling at the house in the sunlight.

When I get to the kitchen, Sal is there, coffee in hand. He hands it to me.

I breathe in and shut my eyes. "Italian coffee really is better."

"Agreed."

Opening my eyes, I sip and wander over to the living room.

The sunlight is just barely kissing the lake, making it look like some kind of metal in the morning light. There's no one out there right now, not even fishermen.

The view is stunning.

I breathe out. "This house... it really is fantastic."

"I bought it thinking of you."

The words make my heart stop.

"What?"

Sal comes to stand by me. "The house. It reminded me of you."

I know that I should think that's romantic. I do. I really do.

But it also makes my stomach squeeze.

I always knew that Sal was interested in me. Hell, I've always been interested in him. But this? It comes a little too close to something that we haven't talked about.

The reason that he left me to go to Europe.

The reason that I told him, all those days ago, that it wouldn't work between us.

I thought I might have hinted at it last night, but apparently, I'm going to have to say it out loud. I can fool around with Sal all day. I can spend many happy hours engaging in hot, sweaty stuff with him.

But at the end of the day, I need to be able to put the business, the family, first.

I thought Sal understood that. I thought that when we gave in to this thing between us, he knew that I could be his, if that meant having fun.

And I am. His. As of right now, anyway.

But will he be able to let me go?

My lips purse in a frown. "How did you…"

Sal sighs. "Don't freak out. I just… when I saw it, I saw the listing picture of this room," he gestures to the living room that's overlooking Lake Como. "And immediately, the image I had was of you, here. Having tea or coffee with me. Overlooking the lake."

It's heartbreakingly beautiful.

I can picture it too.

I'd love to wake up, have a morning like the one we just did, and then have breakfast (with coffee, since I hate tea) overlooking the lake.

Then, we could wander around the town. Go for a boat ride.

Literally do anything, as long as we were together.

I love the vision too.

But...

That kind of domestic bliss isn't the only thing that I want.

"I'm flattered, Sal," I say softly.

He tilts his head. "Are you?"

I consider this. "I am. It's really thoughtful and really nice that you pictured me here."

"You're saying that like it was neither thoughtful nor nice."

I sigh. "It is. I think it's just... I'm not only that type of girl, you know?"

He studies me. "What do you mean?"

I'm not really even sure myself what exactly I'm trying to say.

"I love the image of us waking up here together. I love the idea that you and I would just enjoy the day. But at the same time, I can't picture it without also thinking about the fact that I'm not sure how much of that I could do before it becomes..."

I stop.

Boring.

That's the word that's pounding through my mind.

Boring. Mundane.

A life where I'm completely wrapped up in someone else instead of living for myself.

Where I, like the generations of women who have come before me, don't live for what I want.

Where I live for what *he* wants.

And my dream of being the boss?

Just a dream.

"It's just a house, Gia," Sal murmurs. "Just a house. I can sell it. I can get rid of it. I can burn it down if you want."

"That would be an actual crime." I roll my eyes at him. "No. I don't want that."

But I don't want to live in that impossible dream either.

Sal studies me for a little while before he gives a sharp nod. "Well. What's next?"

I can hardly believe that he's just going to accept this and move on. I raise my eyebrows. "What do you mean?"

"Ireland?"

I sigh. He's right. It's time to focus on the task at hand. Sal and I can do... whatever this is. The fun, sexy stuff.

But when it comes down to it, business is business. While the world thinks we're dead, we need to find Marco.

And we need to find out why someone tried to kill us.

"I guess. Ireland it is."

I flash Sal a confident smile, but inside I don't feel confident at all. I feel... tangled.

In a way that definitely doesn't feel good. It doesn't feel bad.

I honestly have no idea what to feel.

So, I focus on what's here. What's now. I have Sal. We have a lead on Marco.

For now, I guess that's all that matters.

12

SAL

It doesn't take long for us to pack some things and rent another boat, heading for town. From there, we'll take the train to Marseille.

I have another boat that will take us from Marseille to Cork Harbour in Ireland.

After that...

We're behind enemy lines, to be sure.

Boat, I've decided, is the easiest way to go. It allows us for a little more cover and a little less scrutiny. Bribing people in a port is an ancient art, and one that our families have perfected over time.

I'm proud to say that I'm as good as they get when it comes to sneaking stuff in and out of a port. Much easier than a plane or train, that's for sure.

Interpol, and every police force prior, struggle to keep tabs on the ports.

It's something that I pretty much count on, in this business.

We're halfway across the lake when my eyes turn to Gia.

She's sitting on the bow of the boat, a scarf wrapped around her hair. Dark sunglasses make her look like a movie star, as does the linen outfit she's sporting.

My chest aches at how badly I want her.

However, the longing I feel for her is tempered by a darkness that has been nagging at me, ever since that first time when I asked her to be more.

And she said no.

Clearly, I'm good enough for activities that involve our bodies. The attraction between us is as palpable now as it was when I first saw her.

But I'm beginning to wonder if that's all we have.

Gia doesn't seem interested in more than sex with me. Clearly, our sexual compatibility is off the charts, even with my specific kink.

But beyond that...

She looks forward, gazing out over the lake.

My chest constricts slightly.

Beyond our physical compatibility, I have no idea. I have always assumed that Gia and I would work out as partners. We're perfectly matched in every way.

Now, though, I'm not sure that she feels the same.

We're able to dock in Como easily. From there, the train is a breeze, because in Italy when money changes hands, questions disappear.

It's so easy to travel when you know exactly who to pay to make the journey easier.

Gia, for the most part, is quiet during the trip. The countryside skims by, the landscape becoming increasingly tropical as the train huffs toward the Mediterranean Sea.

"You know, I get that America is big and has a lot of cool landscapes too," Gia murmurs. "But this? This view is something else."

I agree with her.

"You were born in Italy, right?"

She nods. "I was."

"Why does Elio have an accent and you don't?"

Gia raises her eyebrows at me over the rim of her glasses. "You, master of all languages, want to know why I learned to assimilate in America?"

I tilt my head. "I know why I learned to speak so many different languages. I'm asking you why you learned to blend in with one."

"To be fair," she stretches her legs out in the train car, her smile a flirtatious glimmer. "I know how to blend in pretty much everywhere."

That, I'll give her as well. "Fair."

She sighs. "People trust me when they think I'm like them. Being an American, and sounding like one, was more important to me than it was to Elio. He could walk around as the Italian guy and have it work. He needed people to notice him. Needed people to go 'oh, that's Elio Rossi. The boss.'"

"And you needed people to think you were their best friend."

She winks. "I knew you'd understand."

The remark is confusing. It simultaneously makes me happy and sad. I know that Gia and I are often well in alignment, and her seeing that makes me feel like she sees it too.

But then, her comments earlier make it clear that she either doesn't understand...

Or she doesn't want to.

I sigh. "So. No accent."

"No accent. I thought about doing the accent that actors used. What did they call it? Mid-Atlantic?"

I laugh at that. "The one in all the black and white movies?"

She nods. "Better that than Italian, that's for sure."

"I'd love to hear what you sound like with an Italian accent, Gia."

Gia's gaze turns wistful. You know, I don't even think I remember how anymore."

She looks out the window, and my heart aches.

I wonder if she's unhappy about that.

The train zips along until finally, we stop in Marseille. I hold Gia's hand, escorting her off, and we enter into a world of bright sun, azure seas.

And the criminal capital of Europe.

The air smells like the ocean, with a slight tinge of something burning. Not a clean scent, like the woods.

Like something that shouldn't be burned in the daylight.

It suits.

Marseille is the type of city that has never pretended to be highbrow.

This is the place where crime has reigned supreme for hundreds of years. Corsica, Sicily, Marseille.

The places where law and order is neither lawful nor orderly.

On average, tourism bureaus across the globe do not recommend travel to any of these places, outside of specifically named, heavily 'safe' destinations, aka places where the staff and the surrounding people are paid quite handsomely off of tourism dollars for their participation.

It's like protecting a cash cow, so you can milk it as often as you want. There's a vested interest in keeping tourists safe in certain areas of all three of these places, but I think Marseille may have given up on that a while ago.

The tourists stay far away from Marseille these days.

Gia sighs. "God, I love it here."

I laugh. "Come on. I have a boat this way."

"Oh. So, you have a boat now too?"

I roll my eyes at her. "Yes. And it's fully stocked, ready to go."

"How often do you use said boat?"

Snorting, I guide her past a particularly nasty pile of garbage. The trash collectors of France are famous for going on strike, and it seems like these ones are no exception.

"I haven't, really. Not since I bought it."

"Ah. I see. And is it a boat? Or a yacht?"

"I guess you'll just have to see when we get there."

"Oh, I can't wait," Gia says.

I have no doubt that she's telling the truth.

Unfortunately, my heart thumps in my chest at her response.

Impressing Gia is fast becoming my favorite hobby.

But I have to keep holding myself back. Gia might be my favorite person to impress.

And all the money in the world won't make her feel the same way about me as I do about her.

We're within sight of the marina when I feel like we're being followed.

I pause and grab Gia's hand, tucking her closer into my side. She complies easily, and I thank God again that she's so quick to pick up on my cues.

"What is it?"

"Nine o'clock. Someone's been following us for about a mile."

"Oh good. Someone's on our six as well."

Hell.

"Keep moving," I mutter. "Did you manage to pack the Glock?"

"From Prague? No, Sal. I don't have a convenient amount of Albanian thugs that I can bribe here. What about you?"

Ugh. I have a handgun jammed into my left jacket pocket, but reaching for it while Gia is on my right side will be too obvious, and I don't want to tip off the tail that we know they're following us.

However, that doesn't mean I'm completely without weapons. "There's a knife in my belt," I murmur to her.

"Since when do you know how to fight with a knife?"

"Always," I mutter.

She curses. "You have to tell me these things."

"Why?"

"Because then I can keep knives on me too. I can't use them, but you can."

"Noted," I respond.

We keep walking, and out of the corner of my eye, I watch as our tail darts along. "Do you think they're with Interpol?"

Gia snorts. "In this neighborhood? Not likely. I think it's probably…"

She freezes.

Smack in the middle of our path, a man is standing, blocking us from moving forward.

He's tall; probably a little taller than me.

He looks rangy, like he's been stretched over his frame awkwardly, but I have no doubt that he's every bit as strong as I am. His dark hair and flashing eyes remind me of Dino, as does the glower on his face.

He looks a lot like Dino, as a matter of fact, except for the scar that covers one side of his face.

He's definitely taller than Elio or I, which makes him outrageously tall. Younger, too, if the youthful grin on his face is any indication.

The contrast of his smile with the scar is a little alarming, and his eyes are so dark, they're nearly black.

He's staring at Gia.

Next to me, Gia pulls away from my embrace. I try not to grasp her as she moves forward.

She puts her hands on her hips, and she tilts her head.

"Gabriel," she calls out. "Long time no see."

She says it in flawless French.

"Look who's a polyglot now," I mutter.

"It's too similar to Italian. It was easy," she whispers back.

The man steps forward and responds in French as well. "Gia. Darling. Imagine finding you here."

"Why did that man call you darling?" I hiss.

Gia doesn't respond.

"You know, I never really thought I would find myself back in Marseille," she says breezily. "And yet, here I am, enjoying your fine city again."

"I would have been happy to host you if you would have called."

The words are light, but there's an edge to them that makes my skin prickle. I tuck closer behind her, surveying the surrounding street.

It's remarkably quiet. We're not exactly on a main thoroughfare, but we're also not in a neighborhood.

Yet, somehow, the buildings around us are dead silent.

Movement catches the corner of my eye, and the air leaves my chest in a surprised grunt.

It isn't quiet.

There are people stacked in the buildings around us. I can see their faces crowded against the glass, staring out.

Another movement and I'm definitely closing in on holding Gia.

There are people in the alleyways. People between the buildings. People everywhere, as a matter of fact.

I have no doubt that knives are definitely the tamest weapons they hold.

"Gia," I hiss. "Do you know these people?"

Gabriel, if his name is right, tilts his head. "Gia. Darling. Did you bring a boyfriend to town?"

"No," she answers swiftly. "He's my bodyguard."

I know that the lie is important. I know that it's not true.

Her easy dismissal of our relationship isn't personal, not by any means.

I am her bodyguard.

I am not her boyfriend.

But still, somewhere in my heart, my chest zings with pain.

"A bodyguard. Who walks you through the streets of Marseille. He didn't hire a car?"

At the time, I hadn't wanted to attract attention.

Gia sighs. "We know you would have crashed the car too, Gabriel."

I shoot her a surprised glance.

Had she known this would be a problem?

Gabriel takes a step closer, and some of his crew emerge from the shadows. "Ah well. You know me well enough then, Gia my love."

My love.

Who the fuck was this?

"Gia?" I hiss.

She turns back and smirks at me, and I know that right now, she's playing a part. Gia the spymaster.

"Gabriel, I'd love to introduce you to Sal De Luca. Sal, this is Gabriel."

I don't say anything.

Gabriel chuckles. "Sal De Luca? I thought you were dead. The news has all reported it, you know. Two bodies. A man and a woman in Amsterdam, and the Russians? Well. No bodies to speak of." He shakes his head sadly.

Gia shrugs. "You should know better than to count me out, Gabriel."

"Oh, I definitely should. Now, Gia. Since you are in Marseille, maybe I can show you around. You finally come to visit, I'd say it's about high time you see the city from my eyes, no?"

His eyebrows raise, and I know for sure that's not a good sign.

"We're just headed to leave," I grumble, stepping forward. I speak in English, so I can see if he understands me. "No trouble intended."

"And yet, you are here with Gia Rossi. Trouble personified," he responds.

In flawless, unaccented English.

I look at Gia. She stares at Gabriel. "Let us through, Gabriel."

"You know, Gia. When I last saw you, you said you would call. We had such fun together. But I waited," he reaches for the back of his pants, and he pulls out a gun.

I step in front of Gia, but she edges me slightly to the side.

"I waited and waited. And you know what never happened?"

Gabriel's crew is in full view now. There's no way we're getting out of this without a fight.

"What, Gabriel?" Gia says with a smirk.

"The call."

He has a predatory glint in his eye when he levels the gun at me.

The alley echoes when he clicks the safety off, and I've never heard a louder sound in my entire life. My whole body is trained on him, ready to sprint forward and knock the gun out of his hands, even if I get shot in the process.

Gia is my only priority.

Gabriel shakes his head and points the gun at her.

"Gia," he says softly. "You really should have called."

13

GIA

Gabriel Durand is a loose end that I never should have left alive.

Honestly, when Sal said Marseille, I didn't even register that we'd run into Gabriel here. When I last saw him, I was slipping out of his room in the middle of the night.

I was never going to call.

It's not because he's not handsome or anything. The man's a five-alarm French fire.

He's got dark olive skin and flashing brown eyes, which, coupled with his perpetually shaggy chestnut-colored locks, makes him just the most attractive French human I've ever seen.

Hence, why I slipped out of his bed that time. I wanted to get into it. And then I needed to leave it.

Gabriel might be handsome, and his alluring smile makes him seem like he's tame.

But he's also... dangerous.

Not in a logical way, like Elio and me. No, Gabriel is the unhinged type of dangerous that makes the hair stand up on the back of your neck and makes you check twice before stepping out into the light.

I watched him take a guy's eyes out with a grapefruit spoon.

He's *that* kind of unhinged.

It was impressive, and I'll give him that, but still.

Staring down a gun held by a man who has shown a willingness to pop eyeballs with serrated silverware isn't exactly a good place to be.

I know that I can't show him that I'm utterly terrified of his gun right now. He'll be entertained by that.

So, I step forward.

The only way to fight fire is with fire, right?

With Gabriel Durand, the only way to keep him from acting crazy is to act even crazier.

When the barrel of the gun is pressed against my chest, I give him a little smirk. "I would have called you back if I knew you were going to whip out your toys."

I can practically feel Sal radiate aggression. *Please, not now,* I plead in my mind.

He has to play along. Our lives depend on it.

More than that, this is what I was afraid of.

Sal is a good guy. Great, even.

The thing that's happening between us is something that I'm more than willing to explore.

But I have to be able to operate as myself in order to survive in this world.

And he has to accept that.

Mercifully, Sal doesn't say anything. I put out a hand and trail it over Gabriel's jaw.

"You're welcome to shoot, Gabriel. But if you're going to do it, you're going to look me in the eye when you do."

He stares at me for a minute longer, his enticing dark eyes glittering with mischief. Finally, the gun disappears, and he shifts as he tucks it back into his pants.

I want to collapse with relief, but I stay standing, smirking at him.

"Ah well. Some people were not meant to call."

"That's me, for sure. Here today, gone tomorrow. Never meant to stay."

Gabriel sighs. "Gia. At least let me show you around. Come have a drink. On me. As old friends," he says with that same half-crazy smile.

Yeah. I'm definitely not going to deny him that. "Lead the way, Durand."

"You and your..." he trails off, looking at Sal.

"Bodyguard," I supply helpfully.

"You and your bodyguard, you have somewhere else to be?"

Yes. About two thousand miles away. "No, we were just headed to the harbor to get on my yacht."

"Oh, a yacht? The Rossi, you are doing well, no?"

Gabriel turns, and I follow him, hoping Sal will continue to play along. "Well, it's not exactly Elio's yacht."

"And what in the world is Elio's sister into that she has a yacht, and he does not?"

It's not mine at all. "It was a gift."

"Gia. Surely you know better than to accept boats as gifts. They come with many strings, you know. Men who give boats are not willing to release them so easily, given the fact that both the sea and the woman have an equal stake on their hearts."

"So, who did you buy the boat for?"

Gabriel laughs. "Ah, Gia. I have never bought a boat for a woman. But I have had one take off with my heart all the same."

"Poor you."

He doesn't respond to that.

We follow Gabriel through the streets of Marseille, walking for so long that I'm certain we're going in the opposite direction from the docks when he stops.

"After you, Gia," Gabriel gestures, his hand on an ancient looking wooden door.

I press past him and duck inside.

Sal, ever behind me, follows.

Inside, there's a quaint little couch area, set up next to some windows that look pretty industrial. They might have once been a factory or something, but now light filters through them easily onto the floor, painting the furniture and the room with a golden glaze.

Gabriel settles into a chair, and we do the same. He gestures for tea, and it appears.

I take my cup. "You know I can't drink this," I say, blowing on it before I set it down.

"Gia," Gabriel puts a hand on his chest, "you wound me. You think I would poison you?"

"Yes," I answer without any other explanation.

"Ah well. You always were a smart one. Tell me, what are you doing in Europe?"

I can't tell if he's asking why we are still alive, or why we're here in general. "Oh, you know. Business."

"Business, I see," Gabriel nods. "Business like the explosion that killed the Russians?"

Fuck. "I believe we were also named as dead in that explosion."

"That you were."

"So, how will you tell people you saw ghosts?"

I'm trying to gauge his interest in this, and whether or not he'll rat us out.

Gabriel wrinkles his nose. "I find it best to leave ghosts alone. Should they come back to life, they can choose that path. Plus, it is advantageous, no? If the world thinks you are dead, they will not look for you."

"That's the idea."

"Ah. I see. Well, I am willing to keep the ghosts and leave them in their graves, if you are willing to help me."

I tilt my head. "With what?"

He gestures for something, and a dark-suited man zooms in, handing Gabriel a jar. Gabriel opens it, the metal snapping in the room. "Do you like French jellies, Gia and bodyguard?"

"Not a gelled goods person, actually," I say.

Gabriel nods. "These are delicious. They are made with the highest quality French fruits, of course. And something else."

"Like what?"

"A secret ingredient. One that I very much hope can expand, with the help of my friends the Rossi's, who also have a very good pathway for expansion."

"What's the ingredient, Gabriel?"

His smile widens. "Medicinal, of course."

"Medicinal how?"

"Well, medicinal mushrooms."

I shut my eyes, smiling despite myself. "You make jelly that gets people high."

"Ah, but it is perfect. They do not show up on a drug test. You can control your dose, and they do not taste foul, as mushrooms are known to do. I have made quite an impact with them, and they are used excessively along the coast and in Ibiza.

"I wish to expand, and I have made some effort to do that in the States, but I find myself faced with... distribution challenges. You see, I do not ever wish to leave France, and I do not know enough Americans to help my interests along."

Translation: He needs to expand his American market, and he doesn't want to move his pretty French ass to do that.

"I see," I say, studying the jelly. "And you're willing to share your profits accordingly?"

"Within the standard amounts, yes."

It could be done. In fact, I think it's a pretty darn good idea.

I smile at him. "This is a pretty neat setup you got here, Gabe."

"Only you have ever called me that, *amour*."

Amour. Oh, I can practically hear Sal's teeth grinding.

"Thank you, I'll take that as a compliment."

"No one else would have the balls to do it."

"That's definitely a compliment then," I grin at him.

Gabriel smiles back.

"Ah well. *Alors*. The very concentrated powders are placed inside my very French jellies, and they are shipped to the United States where they're unpacked and distributed, but I know this process is not reaching those I wish to reach."

"Where are they shipped?"

He sniffs. "Currently? The port of New Orleans."

"And you sell them all over?"

"*Oui*. The trucks though, they are struggling. I haven't been able to get a full shipment out to the distributors in nearly a month."

I bet they are. The Irish have been doing a hell of a job with the motorcycle gangs, paying them off to harass shipments of all kinds of goods and stuff, especially if they know they're from a rival group.

I will absolutely take this opportunity. I give Gabriel a little grin.

"I can cut your shipment costs."

Behind me Sal makes a small, surprised grunt, but Gabriel looks interested.

"Tell me more, *amour*."

"Rossi Industries recently acquired a... smaller organization. The De Luca Shipping Company trades at the dock in Long Island. I can import your jellies at a discount, and get them to you much faster, because my guys don't drive trucks."

"What do they drive?"

The smile I give is genuinely big. "Cop cars."

Gabriel bursts out laughing. "*Amour*, you pay off the police to smuggle your exports?"

"Yes, and I'd do it again. Public goods in the US are deteriorating. No one can live on a beat cop salary, and no one in another state is going to pull them over. They're perfect." I beam.

"*Alors*, Gia. You definitely have some kind of attitude to you."

"Thank you," I smirk.

Gabriel nods. "Well then. I will accept your offer. You get my jellies out in the world, and I will use you as my distributor."

"It's a deal," I stick out my hand.

We shake, and Gabriel sits back. "Well, I suppose I should be getting my new business partner and her... bodyguard out of here," he says, surveying Sal.

I don't look because I can practically feel the menace radiating off of him. "Please. We'll see you soon. I'll call you with the details about the shipments."

"And this time, you'll call?"

I laugh. "This time, Gabriel Durand, I'll actually call."

"*Bon*. It's settled then. We shall escort you to your ship and send you on your way."

"Much appreciated, Gabriel."

"Oh, it is very much my pleasure, *amour*."

That word lingers in the air. It's a tease, a meaningless thing for him to say. I don't care about it at all.

But, as I watch Gabriel walk away, I know there's one person who really, really does.

WE'RE SAFELY on the yacht and a good hour offshore when Sal finally turns to talk to me.

"What the fuck was that?"

I sip delicately at my martini. "You mean when I saved our asses?"

"How did you save them when you're the one who created the situation to begin with?"

I blink, then bristle. I set the drink down and sit up.

We're both on the leisure deck, and I was feeling pretty good about the boat ride in front of us before Sal opened his mouth.

I fix him with a glare. "Excuse me?"

"You slept with that complete sociopath, walked out on him, and left him alive? And then never wrapped him up?"

My jaw drops. "I'm sorry that I wasn't saving myself for you from the beginning, Sal. You know I'm not some kind of pure, witless virgin."

"That's not what I meant. I meant that you made a stupid decision and it came back to haunt you at the worst possible time."

"Haunt me? Um, I was able to talk us into not only getting onto this boat, but created an ally in the process."

And scored a deal in which we're going to import hallucinogenic jellies, which are going to go over like wildfire with the college crowd. People love shit that puts them in a different mindset that doesn't show up on a drug test, and jelly laced with magic mushrooms is the perfect solution.

"You almost got shot, Gia," Sal growls.

I wave my hand at him. "That? I was hardly almost shot. He was never going to pull the trigger."

"You didn't know that."

"I did."

"There was no possible fucking way to know that," Sal grits.

"Well, maybe. But I know that Gabriel would at least want me to suffer a little, so I was pretty sure he wasn't going to just pull the trigger and kill me outright. If he was going to kill me, he would have kidnapped us both and tortured us. Probably with a grapefruit spoon," I say, wincing as I remember the whole eyeball incident.

"A grapefruit... Gia, that was fucking reckless."

"It was smart."

"You had no plan. You went in blind. You had no assurances and no backup."

"You were my backup. Isn't that the whole point? Elio sent you to make sure I didn't die? Great work, you did it, woohoo," I say, twirling my finger in the air slightly.

I glance over at Sal, and despite the fact that I'm annoyed with him, I actually feel a little giddy.

His face is a remarkable color of red that feels pretty close to tomato.

Getting under his skin is just too fun. Honestly, it's so easy to get him to this state. It's so satisfying, and he gets so flustered.

I smirk at him. "Come on, you have to admit, I did a great job navigating that. I got us out of there, to the boat, and I made a new deal along the way."

"Gia..." Sal growls.

"What, did you get scared?"

The silence that descends over us is deafening. It sinks into my bones, creating tension in parts of my body that I didn't even know existed.

He really was scared.

"Come on, Sal," I say, trying to break the tension. "It was fine. It all went fine. Lighten up a little, will you?"

I don't have time to react. One minute I'm sitting on my lounge chair, and the next, Sal's hand is around my neck.

Lightly.

But firm.

It sends a shiver of arousal down my spine, and when I look into Sal's face, that shiver turns into a full-blown shake.

Sal is looking at me with fear...

And lust.

"You scared the shit out of me, Gia," he growls. "And now, you're going to pay for it."

14

SAL

When Gia's neck is in my hand, I lose my mind.

She almost died.

I keep seeing the gun pressing against her chest. The way she walked toward it. The smile on her face, which echoed the smile on that absolute sociopath.

I almost lost her.

And then, she flirted with him. Flirted. Like it was nothing. She never told me about him, and she didn't have to of course, but the fact that she flirted with him in front of my face makes me...

Jealous.

The feeling crashes over me in a tidal wave. It makes me insanely, completely jealous.

I want to brand her with my lips. Bite her hard enough to leave a mark. Spank her perfect ass until my handprint is burned into her skin.

I want to make sure that she'll never let another man call her "*amour*" again.

Part of me is practically screaming in protest. I'm doing the thing that Gia told me she couldn't do. I'm getting attached to her, in a way that means she won't be able to do whatever she needs to in order to maintain her place as the Rossi's nightmare twin.

But...

Amour.

The word sears into my mind.

Gia is not his lover. Gia isn't in love with him.

She's not in love with you either, asshole.

The thought makes my mood even darker.

She might not be in love with me.

But I have something that he doesn't.

And I'm about to make that very, very apparent to her.

I grab Gia's hips and pull, sliding her so she's further down on the chaise lounge. I adjust so that I'm standing above her, peering down at her.

My staff knows to leave me alone unless I ask them to appear, so I don't have any concerns about anyone seeing us.

Another thing I'm about to take full advantage of.

"You're not his, Gia. You're not his *amour*. You're not his anything. He doesn't own you," I growl.

Her eyes flash with challenge. "And who does own me, Sal?"

Fuck it. "I do."

It's a gamble. Gia's just as apt to hop up and slap me as she is to accept what I'm saying. She opens her mouth, and for a split second, I'm sure that she's going to protest.

Then, her eyes darken. "Prove it," she whispers.

Those two words set off a nuclear reaction in my body.

In seconds, I'm swooping down on the chaise. I growl as I grip her chin tightly, holding her face up to mine.

When I kiss her, it's with every ounce of the frustration that I'm feeling.

It's more than a kiss.

We're both lying to ourselves if we think it's not.

By the time I pull away, we're both panting. I can see the muscles in her arms shaking, and I grin.

"Do you remember your word?"

She nods.

"Good. Turn over."

She obeys, and her compliance sends a jet of lust through me that's so powerful, it feels like it's going to knock me out.

I barely recover before the next words are out of my mouth. "Put your hands up over your head."

Slowly, almost hesitantly, Gia responds. Her hands reach up and grip the top rail of the chaise lounge.

I undo my belt.

Lightly, I wrap it around her hands, then secure them to the chaise. She pulls back, startled a little, but I press between her shoulder blades, keeping her against the chaise.

"Remember, Gia. If you want me to stop, you have to use your word. Do you need to be reminded of what it is?"

"No," she whispers.

The no is shaky.

So shaky.

She's scared.

"You're doing a good job, Gia," I purr, soothing her with my voice. "Even if you were very naughty earlier, you're being such a good girl for me now."

She laughs. "You think I was bad earlier?"

"Yes. I do. And now I'm going to show you how bad."

I tug the loose pants down off of her ass, revealing her perfect pale skin. I gently caress the curve of her, noting with interest that between her legs, she's already getting wet.

She likes this.

Even if she thinks she doesn't, even if she thinks she shouldn't, she likes this.

I gently press inside of her with two fingers. "I think you like being bad even more than you like being good," I murmur as I feel her slickness clench around me.

Gia moans but doesn't answer.

I slowly plunge in and out of her. "You want to come, don't you Gia? You think that I'm going to help you, to make you come for me?"

She moans again.

I pull back. Gently, I caress her ass with one of my hands.

Then, I give it a light smack.

Gia gasps.

I give her a minute. If she's going to use the safe word, she needs a chance to process it.

My heart thunders in my chest, and I wait.

When she doesn't do anything, I take my other hand and press it inside her again.

"I think you want me to punish you, Gia. For scaring me. For acting like another man matters to you," I grunt.

With the free hand, I slap her ass again.

Harder this time.

With my fingers inside of her, I can feel her clench around me. She gasps again, and pushes back onto my fingers.

Oh yeah. She definitely likes this.

"You scared the shit out of me, Gia," I say. My voice is hoarse as I say the truth I've been feeling out loud. I slap her again, this time hard enough to make a satisfying noise.

Her flesh ripples underneath my hand, and she clenches around my fingers.

"You scared me and now you have to take your punishment like a good girl," I murmur.

I slap her again.

She moans out loud this time, thrusting herself back on my fingers.

"Gia," I grunt, repeating my pattern. Her ass is starting to turn red on both cheeks, and the impact of what I'm doing sends lust shooting through me.

She presses back again, her channel fluttering around my fingers. "Fuck, Gia," I hiss.

"Sal," she moans.

My name.

She's moaning *my* name.

"I own you, Gia," I grunt. "Not some random French fucker. Me. I own this," I smack again, hard enough that it probably hurts.

Still, she works herself up and down my fingers.

Shit.

She's going to come soon.

I reach forward and undo the belt. My hand at her waist, I lift her torso up, my other hand still deeply embedded within her.

She's pressed against me, her back to my front, and when I tug her lips over to meet mine, I slide that hand down to play with her clit.

"I own you," I whisper before I kiss her.

My fingers work her, sliding in and out while my other hand tweaks the center of her pleasure. I pull back from the kiss, gasping, and freeze. "Do you want to come, Gia?"

"Yes," she moans, breathless and needy.

I grunt. "Tell me who you belong to, Gia."

She pauses. I almost pull my fingers out, before the word falls from her lips.

"You, Sal. You do."

I growl and take her lips again, working her with my hands.

When she comes, I swallow her scream.

She's mine.

There's no world in which I'm going to let her walk away from this. Gia Rossi is mine, she's my queen, my woman.

My soulmate.

I'm never going to let her go.

AFTER SHE COMES APART in my arms, I help Gia pull her clothes back on and we head down to the cabins. We shower, change, and dress for bed.

Where we sleep.

Together.

In my arms, Gia rotates. She studies me. "You really thought that I was going to die today."

"You want to bring that up again? Now?"

She rolls her eyes. "Yeah well. We didn't really talk about it earlier."

"We processed."

"I think you processed. I... I worked through something else entirely," she grins.

I can't help it.

I smile back.

"Yes, Gia. It scared me to death when he had the barrel of the gun pressed against your chest."

"I was worried you were going to screw everything up."

I sit up on one elbow and look down at her. "What do you mean?"

"That you were going to do some macho bullshit and start fighting Gabriel."

I wrinkle my nose at her. "If you think I can't take down one Frenchman in a fight, you seriously think very poorly of me."

"He's tough! I've seen him take out a guy's eyes with a grapefruit spoon!"

Jesus Christ. "So that's why you keep bringing up the spoon thing?"

Gia giggles. "It was so fucking gross. He might be French, but don't underestimate Gabriel Durand. He's fucking nuts."

I bury my face in the pillow. "And you walked up to him and told him to shoot you?"

"You gotta fight fire with fire, baby. Fight crazy with crazy."

Mary, mother of God. This woman is going to be the death of me.

"Sal," she says, her voice serious. I look up at her, and all the laughter is gone from her face. "I'm serious. I thought you were going to get us killed."

"You thought I was going to?"

She nods. "Yeah. Gabriel might be crazy, but I can work him. I've always been able to work men to get what I want. But it requires me to... be myself. To flirt and be nimble. I need you to just roll with it when it happens, even if it pisses you off."

"And you think I didn't do that today? Gia, every time he called you amour..."

"You were back there radiating thunder like a summer storm. I could practically feel you being upset about it, Sal. And so could he."

The thought is sobering. "He didn't show it."

She shakes her head. "No. He didn't. But someone will. Someone will notice that you... react to me," she says quietly.

React.

That's one way to put it.

It's more than just a reaction. It's an overwhelming force of nature. Gia is the moon, and I'm a tide. She's a star, and I orbit her. There is never a world where I'm not going to be drawn to her.

I have to make her mine. Pretending anything else is an option is foolish.

So, if this is the only way I can have her...

"I can't not react to you," I finally say.

Gia shifts, looking at me.

She doesn't say anything, so I take a breath and continue.

"I can't pretend that I don't care about you. That I'm not drawn do you. I can't tell you that when you put yourself in danger, I won't turn around and try to get you out of it. I'll always be worried about you. I'll always want to keep you safe."

"Sal..."

I press a finger to her lips. "But I can promise that I'll try to keep my shit together. You can be whoever you want in public. As long as you're mine when you're here."

She tilts her head.

I nod. "As long as I get the real Gia, you can be whoever you want to the world. The real Gia? She's mine," I say fiercely.

Gia's eyes widen. "Sal..."

"You don't have to say anything yet. Think about it. Because Gia, if you say yes, there's no going back. There's no pretending anymore. If you agree to be mine, then you're mine."

"And what about you? Are you mine as well?"

I lean forward and press a light kiss on her lips. "Gia, I've always been yours."

I tuck her into my arms and turn out the light.

Gia's breath evens after a while.

While she sleeps, I hold her.

Hoping, praying, for things that I want so badly, it hurts.

"I CAN'T SAY that I've ever really been to Ireland," Gia says, looking out over the coastline looming in the distance. "But I feel like it's almost comically green."

I laugh, joining her on the deck. "Comically?"

"Like, we get it. They like green. You don't see Italians being so overtly… Italian about everything."

I shoot her a look. "I think we probably taught the Irish how to do it."

"Yeah. Fair, I guess. Still. The green seems like a lot."

I come behind Gia, and press against her, placing a kiss on her head. "It seems like Ireland."

We draw closer to the coast, and it is indeed, very green.

I'm not exactly happy to be here. For one, I don't know what we're going to find. Marco could be here. He could be dead.

The people who tried to kill us in Amsterdam are definitely here. I have no doubt about that.

Given the Irish vitriol toward the Rossi family and the De Luca family I have no doubt that the Irish here are going to be absolutely furious when they find out that Gia and I are here.

Well.

If they find out.

But we have to find Marco before they do. We have to get him, so they can't use him against us.

And so that we can figure out what the hell my oldest brother has been up to.

"So. You understand the cover?"

Gia rolls her eyes. "Yes. I'm Mrs. Shannon and you're Mr. Shannon and we're from Mobile, Alabama," she says, her voice shifting into a southern twang. "I always wanted to go on a trip to see Ireland 'cuz it's the land of my people, and so when I married my childhood sweetheart, he promised me that he'd take me for our second honeymoon."

"'Second honeymoon?'" I ask, my eyebrows raised.

She smirks. "The first one was to Bali."

"Ah. I see. Sexy."

"Expensive, too. My baby bought us a timeshare at the Ritz there, so we can go back over and over again," she says, patting my cheek with her hand.

"Oh, I did?"

"Yup. And after this we're going to Milan," she says, her voice softening.

"Milan?"

"To a little house on the lake," she whispers.

My heart stills. "You liked that, didn't you?"

"I did," Gia murmurs.

I gulp. "Gia..."

"Anyway. I've got the backstory down. Make sure you have your part of it, okay? Because it's almost time to rock and roll, baby. One errant elder brother, coming right up."

Gia smirks and turns, heading to grab her bag.

I watch her go.

Introducing Gia as my wife is the cover.

But she still hasn't given me her answer to my question last night. So for now, I'll pretend that she's my wife.

I can only hope that someday soon, she'll answer my question with the one thing I want.

Yes.

15

GIA

I can't keep living like this.

Waking up on a yacht with Sal is like a dream.

His smell surrounds me. His arms are some kind of cross between a full body pillow and a cloud.

I'm so comfortable, it literally takes me effort to move.

This is the absolute height of luxury. There's no amount of money in the world that I could pay to get this.

It's exquisite.

I let myself linger for just a minute.

Okay it's longer than a minute. I have no idea how much time is left on our yacht ride to Ireland, but you know what?

I don't care.

I could stay here, wrapped in Sal's arms, forever.

Which seems like it might be kind of a big freaking problem.

I can't do this. This kind of sweet, lingering morning thing, that people do when they have the time and space to be lovers...

I can't.

I'm not built for it. I'm Gia Rossi. I'm the queen of being a badass.

Queen badasses don't need to have morning cuddles.

But when Sal stretches and tugs me closer to his hard chest...

Yeah. I'll take about five more minutes of this.

I burrow my nose into his pecs. Inhaling, I shut my eyes and let him pull me closer.

I didn't need it, but damn.

It was pretty nice.

His reaction to Gabriel had been... well. I can't exactly say that it was unexpected, because I did expect that Sal would be a little miffed by me trying to be flirty to escape something.

It's the whole reason that I know we could never work long term. He's going to be jealous of the men that I give attention to. What I didn't expect, I guess, was how he would turn that around.

And that I would like it.

I'm not sure how to feel about that. I definitely did like all the orgasm that I'd gotten from the whole situation.

I just never really pictured myself as being into spanking but...

Pulling Sal closer, I throw one of my legs over his hip. I'm getting wet just thinking of the feeling of his hand on my butt.

It's a little sore.

That's kind of a nice reminder.

Sal grumbles and pulls me in, pressing a kiss to my forehead. "Well. I guess that's one way to wake up."

"It's a pretty good way, if you're asking me," I say in a tone that is more than just a little satisfied. I know that he can feel how wet I am on his leg.

Good.

Maybe he'll feel just as ready for me as I am for him.

Sal laughs and tips my chin up to meet his lips. "What did you dream about, Gia Rossi?"

"You," I answer without hesitation.

It's always you.

That thought hits me like a punch to the gut. Why would I think that?

I'm not meant for 'always' and bullshit like that. I'm the type of girl that you spend a fun week in Paris with, and then leave because I'm not the marrying kind.

I'm not 'always.'

I'm 'now.'

Still, I'm definitely in the mood, so when Sal reaches down to kiss my lips, I'm more than happy to let him.

Within a couple of seconds though, I feel like something is wrong.

On the surface, there's nothing different than the stuff we've been doing.

I'm naked. Sal is naked.

I can feel his very impressive length, getting harder and thicker by the moment. I can feel his hands on my skin, petting and caressing me as they move upward toward my breasts.

It takes me a minute to figure out what's wrong.

This feels... intimate.

This kiss is too tender.

My heart gallops as Sal gently caresses my face. His touch feels like he's worshipping me.

It's reverent.

Suddenly, his hands feel like they're tying down bindings, and not the fun kind. I twitch under his mouth, and as he moves up there, I feel less worshipped and more...

Suffocated.

I need him to stop.

What was my word...

"Cats!" I yelp.

Sal freezes. "Gia?"

"Cats. Shit. Just... give me a minute," I gasp.

Shifting back so he's sitting at my feet, Sal studies me. "Are you okay?"

"I'm fine. I am. I just... I need some space," I say honestly.

Ugh.

Usually when I tell men that I need some space, they freak out. They're all so used to taking up space, when a woman states she's not interested, they have a kind of panic.

Sal looks like he's fighting that panic.

My heart, already beating hard because of how I feel, crumples. "I just... give me a minute," I state, shutting my eyes against the sensations roiling through my stomach.

Trapped.

Trapped.

Trapped.

"Gia," Sal rumbles. "I can..."

"I just need a freaking second!" I snap.

I can't see Sal's reaction. But I can sense the emotions curling off of him like smoke.

He shuffles, and the bed dips. I hear him grab something out of a drawer.

Then, the door shutting when he leaves.

I breathe deeply, trying to contain the feelings that are running through me. I don't like this. I don't want to feel tied down, but somehow, it's only emotional. The physical restraints? I've been fine with.

Hell.

I've even liked them.

But the way Sal got too close?

I didn't like that at all.

Finally, through it all, a single thought emerges.

Sal is a great guy.

He's clearly into me.

He's clearly interested in me despite all my weird flaws.

He can keep pace with me, and if I had to be with someone, I would be stupid for it to not be him.

But this... touchy-feely stuff that we just did?

I don't like that. I should. Anyone should.

But I don't.

What the hell is wrong with me?

A SOLID HALF HOUR LATER, I get out of bed. I shower, dress in some of the clothes that Sal had the foresight to put on the boat for me, and I haul my ass up to the main deck.

Sal, of course, has already had his staff make me breakfast. He pushes it toward me without looking up from where his eyes are glued to his phone. "In case you're hungry," he rumbles.

It's a peace offering.

I should take it.

"Thanks, I'm good. Coffee?"

I hate myself for saying those words. What on earth is wrong with me? Why can't I just accept that he's a nice guy? Why can't I just enjoy the fact that a rich, insanely attractive person who knows all my needs is looking out for me?

Why don't I like this?

"Gia. What's wrong?" Sal rumbles.

"Nothing," I answer automatically. "There's nothing wrong. What's wrong with you?"

"Gia..."

"Just... I don't know. I don't want to talk about it, Sal. It's nothing you did."

His eyes study me. "But it's something I didn't do?"

"Not exactly." *I have no freaking clue. But it's something alright.* I shake my head, physically trying to shake off the sensation of guilt that's crawling up my spine. "How much longer?"

"About four hours until we get to Dublin," Sal says softly. "I've checked in with Elio. He agrees that we need to keep as low of a profile as possible."

"That goes without saying," I snort. "Why would we walk into Ireland and announce that we're there? Seems kind of stupid."

"I think he was less worried about that, and more concerned that since we met up with one of your ex-boyfriends in France, there would be some consequences related to us showing up unannounced."

I snorted. "It's not unannounced. They still think we're dead, so it's not announced at all."

"Only if Gabriel doesn't say anything," Sal reprimands me.

My temper flares. "Which he won't. Because he would be sacrificing a trade deal to sell his dumb magic mushroom jelly."

"We don't know that."

"Oh, so you're not going to trust that I know what I'm talking about?"

Sal's nostrils flare. "Gia. That isn't fair. I didn't mean..."

"I know what you did and did not mean, Salvatore," I snap at him. It's not a lie, but it's also not the truth. At this point I'm just mad, and I'm ready to pick a fight. "And it sounds like for all the talk you've done about thinking that I'm great and all that bullshit, you're just like the rest of them."

"Gia. That isn't true. You're grasping at straws now."

"Yeah well. I'd rather grasp at straws than be underestimated," I snarl.

Sal's eyes narrow. "What is this really coming from?"

"You don't think that I can argue with you without it being about something else? What, Sal. You think I'm illogical? Too emotional?"

He's definitely getting pissed off now. "Don't put words in my mouth, Gia. You're the one making assumptions."

"And I'm making them because you're showing me exactly what they all did. I'm not assuming anything if it's the truth, Sal!"

Abruptly, Sal stands. His hands grip the wood of the dining table so hard I think it might shatter.

"I am going to speak to the captain about our port of entry," he says from an impressively clenched jaw. "When you feel like talking to me like a fucking adult, I'll be ready."

"Sal..."

But he's gone.

I hiss out a breath. The adrenaline and anger are fading from me. Did I overreact to him?

Maybe.

Is it something I'm beginning to feel really, really bad about?

Also maybe.

It's all just more evidence though that something is wrong with me. Instead of coming up these stairs and sitting down and enjoying the nice breakfast this nice man set out for me, I decided to pitch a fit and blow up over what is admittedly probably not a very big deal.

Ugh.

I settle into the plush seat of the yacht, my fingers tapping the edge of the table. My phone is out in front of me, and when it rings, I startle.

It's Caterina. "Hi, favorite sister of mine," I say into the phone.

"Spoken like someone with zero other sisters, or sisters-in-law."

"Doesn't matter. You're still my favorite," I smile.

On the other end of the phone, I can hear Luna screeching in the background. "Sorry," Caterina says after telling Luna to go play in another room. "She's getting a little clingy with the babies on the way."

"Well. As she should. She's been an only child for a while. Siblings is going to be a big switch," I say. As though I have any experience with that.

"Yeah. Sibling stuff is actually why I wanted to call," Caterina says slowly.

"Oh?"

"Elio told me that you and Sal are trying to find Marco."

My fingers stop drumming on the railing. "Elio is a tattletale."

"I'm not stupid, Gia. You've been trying to find him ever since he disappeared."

Dang it. No pregnancy brain for my beloved sister-in-law. "Okay. You got me. What about it?"

She's quiet for a minute before speaking. "We don't know where he is. Or what he's done. If he's... I guess what I'm saying is that I'd rather have a brother who is loyal than one who isn't," she finally finishes. "And I don't know that Sal is going to be able to make that distinction."

Ice skates up my spine. "Cat..."

"It would kill him, Gia. If Marco did something really bad and truly betrayed us. It would kill him to see that his hero had done something like that."

"We don't know what Marco did or didn't do," I say quickly. For a long time, I've suspected that Marco might have made some kind of a deal with the Irish. He was the one who was the most set against Elio and I, convinced that we had murdered his parents.

As though we'd kill his parents and our own in the process.

Caterina sighs. "I know. But I'm just saying. For Dino and Sal, Marco was more than just a big brother. He was their world. I've always been able to kind of stay in Marco's good graces, because I've been their sister. I got the princess treatment, you know? But Dino and Sal... they got to be his brothers. And if Marco did something really, really irredeemable, then I don't know that either of them would be able to do what needs to be done."

I shut my eyes.

"I know, Caterina. And if it comes to that, I'll be the one to make the right call."

"I know you will, Gia. You're one tough cookie," Caterina laughs.

"That's the nicest way anyone has ever called me a bitch," I snort.

"Well. It's true. You're tough as nails. And Sal is a lot, but I don't know that he's on that same level. You know? At his heart, he's as much of a softie as the rest of them. Maybe even more so," Caterina sighs.

If she knew that her brother was a ruthless billionaire in his own right... Nah. Caterina deserves the image she has of her brother.

Plus, Sal's the one who hides who he is from her. It's not my place to change that.

"I know, kitty-Cat," I use a nickname that I know will drive her nuts. "Kiss Luna and my other babies for me."

"When you have babies of your own, you're going to know exactly how annoying that sentence is."

A bolt of ice hits my heart. I'm not built for having kids. I don't know how I could survive it. Having people who are constantly in my space, constantly close to me? I've seen the level of vulnerability it takes from Caterina, who is an amazing mom for Luna.

I don't know that I could do it.

"We'll see about that. Love you, sis."

"Love you too."

I hang up the phone and wonder if I should tell Sal about Caterina's thoughts. There is definitely the possibility, still, that Marco has done something truly irredeemable. That he somehow sold the family out to the Irish, and that's why he's there.

But something in my gut tells me that's not right.

I stare at the ocean, which is getting progressively darker and more choppy the closer we get to Ireland. A strange sense of dread is bubbling in my stomach.

The morning's light has long since faded.

Idly, I wonder what other horrors Ireland will have to offer. Somehow, I'm certain that once we hit the harbor, everything is going to change.

The dream of Sal and I is gone, and in its place, a cold, dreary reality sets in.

Sal and I can never be together. Not like Caterina and Elio are.

Whatever I am, I'm not meant for that.

I'm Gia Rossi.

Love was never in my cards.

16

SAL

We make it the whole way to Ireland before Gia deigns to talk to me again.

By that time, all of the anger is gone, faded from me like the setting sun on the ocean. In its place, however, is the overwhelming realization that I have to let this go.

Gia doesn't want me.

Or I guess she might want me. But she doesn't want me the same way I want her.

After seeing her interact with the French guy, it's clear to me that Gia wants people she can keep at a distance. She needs men who she can hang out with for a little while before moving on. People who don't have any sense of permanence in her life.

People she can leave.

That isn't me.

I thought that I'd accepted that between us, there really can't be a future. We can have something like this.

Sex on a boat in the middle of the ocean. Fucking each other while the sea tears at our skin.

We can do this.

But Gia will never want something more.

The thought is... heartbreaking. And surprising. I thought that maybe, we could make this work. Her reaction to my... proclivities really showed me that we could have it all.

The sex and the love.

However, her reaction earlier to me, and the more domestic moment we shared, makes it clear.

She doesn't want this.

Not one fucking bit.

The port is coming into view, and I know I need to grab Gia to get ready for entry.

We're gonna have to bribe the hell out of some customs officers, but my staff know the drill. They'll know exactly what to do.

All that's left is for me to find Marco.

Footsteps on the teak let me know that Gia's approaching. I smell her first, the expensive Gucci perfume and something uniquely Gia caressing me, singing to my very soul.

God.

I fucking want her.

It kills me to want her like this and know that I'll never be able to have her.

"I see why people wax poetic about these fucking cliffs," she says, announcing her presence.

I don't respond.

Gia trots over, leaning next to me on the rail. "Sorry," she says plainly.

My eyes slide over to her.

She doesn't look back at me. "I was a little rude earlier."

"A little?"

"Don't push it. I just...I'm not used to stuff like... that."

"Like what, Gia?"

"Like you being... when you... I don't want to get all the mushy stuff," she blurts.

I turn so I'm facing her. "The mushy stuff?"

"Yeah. Like the cuddles and sweetness and..." she trails off.

There's a note of longing in her voice that I mark.

"It's a lot," she whispers as the port comes fully into view.

I don't respond.

THE BRIBES HAPPEN EASILY. Money greases palms here in Ireland the same as it does anywhere else.

Before long, we're bundled into a car that I rented, hurtling down a road that's too small toward the best guess we have to where Marco would be.

After going over the footage for the six hundredth time, Gia and I identified a logo. For a bar, in a town outside of Dublin.

The Drunk Pony.

It's ridiculous. It sounds like a parody, like something you'd see in a movie, but sure enough, the bar is there as we pull up to it. I park the car, tossing the keys to Gia, who smoothly puts them in her Chanel bag.

Our seamless movements tug at my heart.

Why can't she see this? Why can't she see how good we are together? It kills me that Gia keeps fighting me on this when it's something that most people don't see ever in their lifetimes.

Or maybe I'm wrong.

Maybe Gia has that type of response with everyone.

And I, as always, am no one special.

"What if he's not here?" she whispers.

I shrug. "Then we'll ask around. Surely one annoyingly smug Italian American has made some kind of impression on the locals."

She smirks. "Yeah. They do tend to do that."

I pretend she's not flirting with me.

The first hour rolls by, and we each have a pint. Another one comes and goes, and nothing. Gia's flitting around the room, chatting and schmoozing with the locals.

She gets up on stage once the karaoke kit comes out and belts out a surprisingly in-tune version of "Sweet Caroline," much to the joy of the crowd.

I can't help but smile too. She really is in her element in stuff like this.

She thrives on chaos. On people. On the thrill of the chase.

I could never take that from her.

We're both on pint number four, carefully administered with food and water so we aren't drunk, when Gia sucks in a breath.

"Look," she whispers.

Marco is in the doorway.

And the woman from the video is with him.

Gia and I hunker down, making ourselves small in the corner near the door. He can't see us from where we are, because of how the tables are positioned. I look at her.

"You ready?"

She nods. We're both ready to confront him, and whoever his mystery woman is. I'm still a little enraged that, for all intents and purposes, Marco is fine.

While we've been trying to handle hell without him, he's been here.

Sitting with a pretty woman.

Drinking beer.

Just fine. Marco comes in, walking by us so close that I can feel the heat radiating from him.

The woman goes to sit, and he walks up to the bar, ordering a drink. He's about to take it to their table.

Now's as good a time as any.

I stand up, ready to follow him, when I feel a hand at my wrist.

Not Gia's.

A big, far more masculine hand.

I turn, putting myself before Gia. I look at the man, and my eyes widen.

This man is familiar.

As familiar to me as my own face.

Behind me, I hear Gia suck in a gasp.

"Dino," Gia breathes.

I square up with my brother. "What the hell are you doing here?"

Dino shakes his head. "Not here," he says. His voice is hoarse. It has been for a while now, ever since Elio beat the hell out of him for betraying Luna to the Irish.

Instinctively, I tuck up in front of Gia. If we need to make a run for it because Dino is going to pull something on us…

Dino sighs. "Not here. It will compromise him."

"Compromise who?"

He jerks his head toward the table in the corner of the pub. "Marco," he whispers.

What the hell is this?

There's a strange, sinking feeling in my stomach. "What do you know about why Marco is in Ireland."

Dino sucks in a huge breath. His nostrils flare as he exhales, and I can see the shiny scars on his neck, and the one that crosses his eyebrows, in the moonlight.

"He's here because of me," Dino whispers.

To say that I don't trust my brother right now is an understatement. The understatement of the year, actually. Because it's more than that.

I'm about ten seconds from ripping Dino to pieces.

Dino brings us back to the main town, where he points out a little shop. We go up the stairs to the left of the front door and follow him into an apartment.

Apparently, he's been sleeping here ever since he overheard Elio say that we were headed to Ireland.

I'm still pissed about this. "And how are you explaining your absence to Elio, exactly?" I say to my brother.

"He knows what I'm doing."

Gia's eyes narrow. "And he didn't feel the need to tell us?"

Dino's glare meets hers. "Well, he didn't exactly have the chance since you were floating across the ocean and all that. Cell signal sucks, especially when you're probably hitching a ride on something that has enough sea hours to count as a pirate vessel."

Ah. Of course. Neither one of them thought that we'd be on a luxury yacht that gets cell phone signal from space.

I'm happy to keep it this way. If Dino has his secrets, so do I.

I fold my arms and glare at him. "Okay. So you came the whole way from New York, abandoning whatever duties Elio assigned you to. You're here presumably so you can stop us from finding Marco. What I don't know, and what you need to start doing right now, is telling me why."

Dino sighs. He gets up and grabs a phone, then settles back at his place on the rickety dining room table. "You can't be mad."

"We're way past that," I growl. "I'm definitely mad."

"At Marco, not me," Dino clarifies.

Now that's interesting.

"I know what I've done. And I know what I asked Marco to do. And I know we didn't tell you shit about it, but we didn't tell Caterina either because you two are…" he glances at Gia. "You have more loyalties than just the family."

That hurts. "Gia and Elio are family, Dino."

"Not like you and Caterina are," he murmurs.

"So, what makes you think that you're going to spin a story that I believe now? You just told me that you don't trust Gia and Elio. You think I'm going to believe that what you have to say is the truth?"

He nods. "Yeah. Because I'm gonna tell you the truth."

"Get to going, then," I snap.

Dino sighs. "When I was graduating high school, I went on that senior trip to Pensacola. Remember?"

I barely remember. "Sure."

"When I was there, I met a girl."

Oh for the love. "You met a girl? What, Dino? You have some kind of wife that you didn't tell anyone about?"

Dino shakes his head. "No. The girl is... we aren't married. We never were. We can't be together," he says quietly. "But she..."

Instead of saying it, I watch him grab his wallet. He unfolds a picture and puts it down on the table.

Gia and I lean forward to see what it is. "Holy shit, Dino," she breathes. "What the hell is this?"

"These are my children," Dino says. His voice softens as he talks about the two babies in the picture in front of us. "They're older than Luna by about two years. Maia and Angie."

The two twin babies on the page grin up at us.

There's no doubt in my mind that they're Dino's kids. They have his same mischievous eyes and his nose.

"This is an old picture," I say slowly.

He nods. "Yeah. Like I said, they're a little older than Luna."

"And you've kept this secret for how long?"

Dino sits back. "She told me as soon as she knew."

I blink. "Dino. That was fucking *years* ago."

"I know that, Sal. But what were we going to do? I'm a De Luca. My whole life was already laid out for me, and it was laid out for me in the New York area. Hers... it's pretty much the same. She was just at Pensacola for a spring break trip. Her father..." he shakes his head.

"If her father knew that the kids were mine, we'd all be fucking dead."

Carefully, I look up at him. "Dino," I say quietly. "Who is her father."

"I'm not going to tell you. I'm sure between you and Gia, you'll figure it out eventually anyways."

I snort. "You hid twin girls from us for almost ten years, Dino. I think at this point we've earned the right to know."

Dino shook his head again, firmer this time. "I really can't tell you, man. He's too dangerous."

Gia snaps to attention. "Who in the world is so dangerous that you can't tell us? We're the Rossi family, Dino. There's no one out there more dangerous than we are."

"You don't understand, Gia. We're small potatoes compared to this guy. He's... he runs an organization so big, it would make your head spin."

I can see the wheels turning in Gia's mind. There's a pretty short list of people whose criminal activities have a greater span that Elio's so I'm curious as well.

But that's not the point. "Okay. You have secret twin girls, with someone whose father is going to burn down the world, and our family, if he knew. What makes you think he didn't find out? And he's not the one behind the deaths of our parents? Or any of this shit?"

"Because you wouldn't be dealing with an amateur bomb going off," Dino says shortly. "You'd be fucking dead. We would all be dead. Every last one of us."

I narrow my eyes. "So how does this lead us back to Marco?"

Dino sighs. "Last year, about the time that I... that I revealed Luna's location to the Irish, something happened. A guy at a bar came up to me with a picture of... her. And the girls. He said he knew where they were. He knew who they were. And if I didn't come forward to testify against the family, he would expose them, and us, to my girl's father."

I don't miss the way he says *my girl*. "So, what did you do?"

"At first? I hedged. I tried to set off a chain of events that would distract him. He was a cop, after all. Someone who had the power to put us all away."

"And it didn't work."

"No," he shakes his head. "It didn't."

Dino hadn't been behind the attack on Luna at the farm. It had been an act of violence that seemingly didn't have a root cause. A motorcycle gang war gone wrong.

But he'd told the Irish afterwards about her, and about Caterina.

That was why he did it. To start a fire to distract this cop from his family.

"So, what did you do next?"

"I went to the only person who could fix it," Dino says dully. "I went to Marco. I told him about the girls and... her," he whispers.

It's fascinating that he hasn't revealed her name yet.

"And he said that he would do it. He'd testify and make the deal. But in exchange, none of us were going to be touched. He would give them information on a different case. A different organization. And we would all stay free."

My eyes widened. "Marco offered to narc?"

This is bad.

I would rather that he would be dead.

Dino's face is angry, and I know he feels the same way.

"He did. For me. To keep my girls safe. To keep all of us from getting locked away. Marco offered to testify for one reason and one reason only, Sal. To keep all of us out of jail."

"So why is Marco in Ireland?" Gia interjects.

Dino glances at her. "Marco isn't doing anything here other than biding time until the trial."

"Trial?"

I realize what he's saying about two seconds before he says it.

"Marco's in witness protection."

17

GIA

I stare at Sal's brother in shock.

"Witness protection?" I hiss. I want to screech it louder than that, but I'm not sure who is in the little shop below. "Witness protection? Seriously?"

"Yeah." Dino glares at me. "Seriously."

Dino and I don't like each other.

It's pretty much just how it goes.

Since day one of meeting, we haven't gotten along.

And I see no reason to change that now.

There's so much to unpack with what he told us. My mind starts to go through it, and I still can't believe what he's saying.

He has kids.

Twins.

Their mom is some kind of princess, whose dad is in a gang that Dino is so afraid of, he won't even tell us who she is.

Marco offered to give testimony…

That makes me nervous.

In this situation, the cops have all the power. They can squeeze Marco if they feel like he's not giving them what they want.

"What the fuck is Marco supposed to testify on?"

Dino shrugs. "Don't know. But it has nothin' to do with us and what we've got going on, either on the De Luca or Rossi side."

"You can't know that."

Dino glares at me, ice in his stare. "You callin' me a liar?"

"I'm saying you don't know what Marco is going to say."

"I know my brother," he says fiercely.

"I thought I knew you," Sal says quietly.

That shuts Dino down pretty effectively.

I shut my eyes and hiss out a breath. "Okay. Let's say you're right, and Marco is only playing boy scout for a little while. He testifies. He pisses off every single person in our world. He can't just come back. He's going to have a target on his back. He's literally going to be the enemy number one for everyone. He can't just return to our world…"

"He's not planning on it," Dino says quietly.

I stare. "What?"

"Marco knows. He knows that he's going to be a target. He isn't coming back to the family."

Jesus H. Christ.

I look over at Sal. There's a muscle in his jaw that is twitching with emotion, and I know he's having some strong feelings about that.

Hell.

So am I.

If Elio just up and abandoned me without telling me what the fuck he was doing? If he didn't at least clue me in?

I'd be furious.

I don't know what it's like to have more than one sibling, so I can't speak to that dynamic. But I do know that with the one sibling I have, I'd lose my shit if he pulled a stunt like this.

I don't know Marco well. He was Elio's friend, and I didn't pay a ton of attention to him.

But right now?

I wish I could smack some sense into him.

"Sal," I say in a low voice. "What do we do now?"

"I don't know."

Both Dino and I stare at him. He looks calmly to both of us. "What?"

"You don't know?"

"No, Gia," Sal mutters. The frustration in his tone is evident. "I don't know."

I don't think I've ever heard Sal say that.

It's... alarming.

Instead of processing that, I round on Dino. "So what? You want us just to leave? To kindly fuck off so that Marco can continue to live in la-la land where he's protected from basically all harm?"

"Well. He's not protected from all harm..." Dino looks at Sal meaningfully.

Sal glances at me.

And I figure out what they're doing without speaking. "No. No, no. No secret brother brain communication. I'm not responsible for Marco, or anything that happens to him. Not when he chose to be a fucking narc," I hiss.

"Marco isn't at risk here. Or he wasn't until now."

"We're literally in *Ireland,* Dino! I know you're not the smart brother but surely you can put together *Ireland* and the *Irish,* the people who hate us? Like, I feel like I don't need to remind you are trying to take down everything we've built."

Dino narrows his eyes at me. "Interpol has him here for a reason."

"And the reason isn't to dangle him like a prize hog in front of the wolves?"

He snorts at me. "You showed up after being nearly assassinated by some kind of unknown..."

I throw my hands up. "Unknown? I think given the recent developments that you're telling us, it's pretty freakin' obvious who tried to assassinate us. How do we know it wasn't Interpol? That's clearly who we ran into in Prague, Sal."

"When were you in Prague?"

Sal ignores his brother. "Yeah. I agree with you, but they couldn't have known about the meeting with the Russians."

"Doesn't matter. Having Interpol's involvement is a whole different ball game," I snap.

It makes everything harder.

We're used to moving around in the shadows. We're definitely adept at doing exactly that. But having Interpol's lens on us?

That's a fucking terrible idea.

"Gia," Sal says softly.

I shake my head. "No. It doesn't matter, Sal. Marco screwed us. We have to acknowledge that. He totally, completely, and utterly screwed us over."

"No. It wasn't him. It was me," Dino says hollowly.

I point a finger at him. "Oh, you're definitely part of it. Do not mistake me, Bernadino De Luca. You're half of this fucking problem. Because you couldn't keep it in your pants..."

"I was a kid," he grunts at me.

"You have two brothers who managed to not knock anyone up!"

"And you have one who did!"

Dino and I are squared off and yelling at each other at this point. With a resigned sigh, Sal comes between us. He puts a hand gently on my shoulder, then pushes Dino back. "We don't know who could be listening," he murmurs.

"Yeah, like maybe the fucking police, or the Irish. As we are in Ireland," I snap.

I really can't resist it.

Dino bristles but Sal shoves him back. "Back off, Dino," he says in a dark voice.

"You're not the boss of me."

"I am," Sal says flatly. "As your brother, and your superior, I need you to back the fuck off."

That gets Dino's attention. Reluctantly, he takes a step back.

Sal looks at both of us. "Marco is solved, Gia. Like it or not, the reason we came here is clear."

I gape at him. "Clear? Clear as fucking mud, if that's what you mean by…"

"We know where he is. We know what happened to him. It's clear. Okay?"

No.

None of this is okay.

But I recognize the tone in Sal's voice. He's not telling me that I need to move on. He's pointing out that there's a fact here. No matter what, the purpose of our trip, the reason we came here, is over.

We know where Marco is.

We know what he's doing.

But… shit.

I can't do anything with this information.

"Caterina needs to know. Elio needs to know," I say to both of them.

Dino and Sal exchange a look. "Elio's going to like this even less than Gia did," Sal says softly.

"Yeah. I know," Dino responds.

"He's going to fire you."

"I know."

"He's going to try and make sure you never see Caterina or Luna ever again."

"He can fucking try," Dino growls. "Caterina is my sister same as yours. Luna is my niece, same as yours. He wants to be mad? Fine. I'm not going to stop Elio from being mad. But I am going to draw the line at being told that I can't see my own fucking sister, Sal."

Sal nods. "Same. Elio and Caterina are going to freak out. When's the trial?"

Dino shrugs. "Dunno. Didn't occur to me to ask, and I haven't talked to Marco since he decided to go into custody."

My eyes are going to pop out of my head. "You haven't..."

"No. Why would I? I'm not going to break his cover. He'd be a dead man if I did."

A bitter laugh escapes me. "He's a dead man no matter what so you might as well say goodbye to him! Shit!"

"We know what happened to Marco," Sal reiterates firmly. "What we don't know is who tried to kill us in Amsterdam. It could be Interpol."

"My money is on Interpol," I sigh. "Otherwise our faces would be all over the news..."

"They are, though," Dino says.

Shit.

He's right.

"You've been featured on the news ever since it happened. Two known mafia members, presumed dead after the explosion."

"Yeah, but if we're presumed dead…"

"They're trying to control the narrative," Sal says slowly. "They know that the underworld is going to more or less accept the story that they put out. We aren't going to have rivals look into this, because they're going to assume that if Interpol is putting out the report, it's real."

"Motherfuckers," I breathe.

Then, it occurs to me that we're still heavy into enemy territory here. If Marco is in witness protection here in Ireland…

"We need to leave," I whisper.

Sal nods. "We do."

Damn it. We just snuck into Ireland.

I don't want to think about sneaking out.

Ugh.

Sal looks over at me. "Why don't you shower, while Dino and I talk?"

"No. I don't need one."

"Gia," he says softly. "Please. Just give Dino and I a minute."

Well.

I guess I can't deny that either. I huff at Dino.

"Show me your bathroom. Cretin," I snap.

He does.

I shower.

Dino's been living in the tiniest living quarters possible. I have no idea how long he's been here, because the last I checked, he was running the docks for Elio.

He says Elio knows he's gone, but... how?

I'm suspicious.

And the room? Microscopic. The shower? Tiny. Neither of these guys is ever going to fully get clean scrubbing in this thing.

Especially Sal, with his broad shoulders. And his massive chest.

And his...

I shake myself. Now is not the time to be thinking about Sal's cock.

I swear, I'm getting weirdly addicted to him. If I can't make it through a full shower without fantasizing about his dick?

That's a problem.

We haven't even had like, real sex yet. I haven't felt what it's like to have him inside me. To ride him, to feel him shudder as he comes apart inside me.

Oh no. Now I'm straight up picturing him, and me.

And I'm getting wet.

I finish up, since the hot water is running out anyway, and I step out of the shower that looks like it might be made for ants. I don't really have anything new to wear, so I sit in my towel on Dino's bed.

'n not waiting long before Sal comes inside. "Hey," he murmurs.

"Hi."

"Thank you."

"For what?"

"For giving us some time."

I hug my knees to my chest, hoping the towel covers up all the stuff I need to cover.

Or maybe not.

"You don't have to thank me for that. He's your brother."

"Don't, Gia."

I glance up at him. "Don't what?"

"Don't say it like that. You know that none of us are responsible for our siblings' actions."

I hug my knees closer.

"You know, back when Elio and I were trying to figure out what was up with the whole engagement that Marco agreed to, with Elio and Caterina, I said that I knew you would never have illegitimate children. I knew one of the De Luca's did. I caught someone buying some Easter gifts."

His eyebrows raise. "You didn't think it would be me?"

"No, Sal. Like I said. You'd do the hard thing and make it work with the mom."

"Dino wants to make it work."

I shake my head again. "You wouldn't try, Sal. That's the difference. You'd move heaven and earth to make it work."

214

"I can't move heaven and earth, Gia."

Looking up, I meet his gaze. "You always do, though."

Sal moves to sit on the bed with me. Slowly, he extends an arm around me, and pulls me close. "I would like to stop finding out I'm an uncle on accident."

That gets a laugh out of me. "At least it's better than finding out you're a dad on accident?"

"Yes. That would be bad too," he whispers.

The tone of his voice pulls a question out of me. "Do you want to be a dad, Sal?"

"Yes."

"Oh," I whisper.

He presses his lips to my temple. "Do you?"

This is a complicated question.

I've never really seen myself as a mom. Cool aunt? I can do that all day. But all the women I know who are great moms seem to have some kind of... softness that I lack.

At the same time though, I want it. Like, it's an experience that I do want to have in life.

I'm just terrified that I'd be bad at it.

"I don't think I'd be a very good mom."

"I think you're pretty fucking good at whatever you put your mind to, Gia Rossi. And there's no rules on what makes a good mom."

"I would say that a lot of therapy bills say otherwise."

He laughs and his hand skims up my leg. "As long as you love your kids, it doesn't matter. You love them. You do good things for them. That's all you need."

It doesn't seem like that's it.

His hand, however, is distracting me from all of this talk about kids. It's inching toward my butt, which, since my knees are still drawn up, means that his fingers are reaching toward my center.

When his hand meets the wetness that's been gathering there, he groans. "Gia," he whispers in my hair. "Are you sitting in my brother's bed, soaking wet?"

"I wasn't thinking about him," I murmur.

"And what were you thinking about?"

Well.

I turn my face so that our lips are meeting. I smile.

"Your thick cock."

18

SAL

Gia's words send my blood from cold to raging hot in less than a second.

"Oh yeah?" I rumble. My fingers find her opening and I press inside, feeling how wet she was thinking about me. "And what were you thinking about?"

"You. Inside me. How you'd feel when you stretch me," she whispers.

Her eyes glide shut as I slowly pulse in and out of her.

"That's what you dream about when you have alone time, Gia Rossi?"

"Yes," she gasps.

My thumb brushes her clit. "Then I think we could make that dream a reality."

I withdraw my hand and stand back. "On your hands and knees, Gia."

"Sal," she whispers, her eyes wide. "Dino is probably listening."

"Dino's gone," I murmur.

I sent him away while she was in the shower. I didn't want to talk to him more than was absolutely necessary.

I am mad at him.

And Marco.

And myself, if I'm being honest. For me to just not realize that my brother had twins?

It's sloppy.

I'm not sloppy. I make it a point to know everything about everyone, so situations like this don't happen.

So no, I didn't talk to Dino long. We discussed a plan to leave Ireland, and that was it. Somehow, we need to sneak back out of here without flagging Interpol or the Irish mafia.

It wasn't a great conversation. Tired, angry, I'd been happy to find Gia partially naked as she sat on my brother's bed.

I'm angry with myself, I'm angry with Marco.

And I need her right now.

Gia's eyes narrow for one second before she complies with my request. The towel falls away and she gets on her hands and knees.

Like a good girl.

The sweet, tender lovemaking that I wanted on the yacht is over.

I need her.

She needs me.

And this is going to be fucking great.

"You liked being spanked, didn't you?" I say as I caress the globes of her ass.

"No," Gia automatically says.

I smack her lightly, and we both shudder. "Good girls don't lie, Gia," I whisper.

"I'm not lying."

I smack again, and my fingers trail through her moisture. "Oh. I think you very much are lying. Feel how wet you are, Gia."

"I'm not..." she gasps.

My fingers press inside her, and my hand smacks her ass. I can feel her clench around me, but more importantly, I can feel her soak my hand.

Jesus Christ.

I'm not going to last long.

I need to make sure that Gia comes once before I give her what she wants.

"You like it, Gia," I purr. I pull my fingers out and kneel behind her on the bed, tossing my shirt onto the floor as I go. I unbuckle my pants, pulling them down to my knees and I release myself.

With one hand, I slap her ass again.

With the other, I grip myself.

"Sal," she moans, bucking back. I release my cock and press fingers inside her again, this time leaving my thumb to press against her clit.

"Yes?"

"I..." she gasps.

I start to pump my fingers. "I know, Gia. You were hoping you'd get my cock. Is that right?"

She nods.

Smack. "You will, baby. But first, you're going to come for me."

"I... I'm not..."

Smack. "Yes, you can. You can and you will," I whisper as I rub her clit with my thumb.

Hard.

Combined with the handprint I put on her perfect flesh, it sends her over the edge. Gia gasps and shudders, her channel squeezing my fingers with so much force it makes my eyes roll back in my head.

Jesus. I need her.

I'm going to be inside her.

The thought almost makes me spill before I'm even there.

I rear back and position myself at her entrance. I press slightly inside. Just a tiny bit.

Just to see what it feels like.

We both groan.

"Sal," Gia whimpers. She bucks back, trying to take more of me. "Sal, please," she begs.

I can't wait to give her what she wants.

The sensation of Gia wrapped around me is... indescribable. She's so hot. She's so *wet*. I don't think I've been inside a woman bare...

I freeze.

I haven't ever had a woman like this before.

With the most restraint that I've ever had in my entire life, I pull out of her.

Gia looks over her shoulder. "What?"

"Goddamn it," I murmur. "I don't have protection."

"It's fine. I have the shot," Gia pants. "Just fuck me, Sal."

Well.

I can't deny her that.

And, I can't deny that the idea of being inside her bare...

It makes me shudder with happiness.

I wrap one of my hands over her shoulder, bracing myself for what I'm about to do. "You want it that bad, Gia?"

"Yes," she practically shrieks.

Well.

I can't deny her that.

I press inside her. "Jesus Christ, Gia," I grit.

"Fuck," she breathes. "You're so big."

I freeze. "Are you okay?"

"Yeah. Fine. Just... Give me a second, okay?"

I don't think I have a second.

But, I do my best. When Gia nods, I know that she's okay.

I brace my hands on her hips. Slowly, I start to move.

Oh god.

"Fuck, Gia you're so tight".

"I need your eyes *cara mia*,".

She turns and looks over her shoulder her brown eyes lock with mine.

Without taking my eyes off hers, I withdraw my cock all the way out and then I slowly slip into her, "Sal..." she whimpers.

"You can do this baby; you can have all of me".

With that I feel her get wetter and she bucks into me.

"Oh...". We both moan.

I'm never going to be able to fuck anyone else again. The way Gia holds me as I move inside her?

It's incredible.

I've never felt like this before. Gia's body is more than just perfect. It's like we fit in ways I never imagined possible.

Like she's made for me.

"Gia," I breathe, moving faster. Her ass makes a satisfying sound as it slaps against my thighs.

All she can do is give me a garbled sound in return.

I pick up the pace. I'm not going to last long. However, I'm also not going to come unless Gia comes with me.

I can feel the edges of the orgasm across my back. Quickly, I loop an arm under Gia's torso, pulling her up. Her back is pressed against my front, and her face is now next to mine.

"Fuck, Sal," she pants.

"You're going to come for me, Gia," I growl. "When I tell you, you're going to come."

"Sal, I can't…"

I use one of my hands to snake down her chest and press against her clit. "Yes, you will."

"Sal…"

My spine tingles. I capture her face in a fierce kiss as I continue to slam inside of her.

I break the kiss and press my thumb against her clit.

Hard.

"Now, Gia. Come for me, my good girl," I whisper in her mouth.

When she screams her release, my body explodes.

I capture Gia's lips with mine, swallowing her frantic shriek. It keeps me from shouting as well as the orgasm rips through me. My back bows as I pump into her, releasing jet after jet of my thick release into her body.

Fuck.

It's so insanely satisfying. I've never felt such pure joy during an orgasm as I do now.

I don't pull out.

The vision of Gia, marked by my release...

I gently try to lean both of us down without pulling away from her. We lay, panting, on the tiny twin bed.

My feet hang off the end.

"Okay. I underestimated the bed," Gia finally whispers.

"What?"

"I thought it was going to break if we fucked on it."

I laugh into her hair. "It held up."

"It held up," she repeats.

We lay there, on top of the covers, our hearts slowly moving from a race to a steady thud.

"Aren't you going to... you know," she wiggles her butt.

I'm still inside her, and the motion makes me harden again. "No, Gia."

"Oh. Okay. But why?"

I bite gently on her neck.

"Because I like marking you as mine," I growl.

She tenses, and I want to kick myself for saying it.

Too much, Sal. You're going to make her panic again.

"It's a little primal, don't you think?"

Her voice is light. Like she's trying not to panic.

That reassures me.

"You make me primal, Gia."

"Is it weird that I kind of like it?"

I laugh. Slowly, I pull out and grab the discarded towel, cleaning her up. "No, Gia, its not weird."

She turns. "It's not?"

"Of course not. Because, you want to know a secret?"

"Always."

"I like it too."

WE SLEEP, after washing off in the pathetic excuse for a shower. Gia's naked in my arms, and when I wake up, I cautiously open the little bedroom door.

Dino left clothes for us outside.

I gather them quickly, then head back to where Gia's sleeping. "Looks like Dino's a little less useless than we thought."

"Oh, I don't know about that," she murmurs as she looks at her pile of clothing.

I have to laugh.

Dino brought her the ugliest clothing imaginable. It's a shapeless dress that might be made from some kind of wool or linen, but it looks like it was made by hand by someone who had never made cloth before in their life.

"It's clean?" I say with a smirk.

Gia gets the awful sack of clothing over her head, then looks down. "Did he steal this from the eighteen hundreds?" she flops her hands down at her sides. "I look ridiculous."

"Gia. You could wear a burlap sack and it would look sexy."

"Well this is pretty darn close," she rumbles.

My clothes are a little better. Uncomfortable pants that definitely do look like he stole them from some kind of historical reenactment, or maybe a theater.

"What the hell, Dino?" I sigh, looking down at my clothes.

Gia shakes her head. "Utterly ridiculous."

She flounces to the little bathroom, and I sit on the bed. My mind is whirling with everything that's going on.

It's almost too much to process.

If what Dino said is true, then we do definitely need to leave. Interpol won't like us sniffing around their witness. More than that, it's clear to me that something else is going on with them.

Something that makes my heart clench with fear.

Plus, what I told Gia last night is still accurate. Marco's location isn't unknown anymore. He's here. He's going to be here. For the time being, Marco is safe.

At least we know that.

How Interpol is planning on keeping him safe from the underworld is... beyond me. Clearly, they have some kind of plan. Otherwise, they wouldn't have put him here...

Unless it really is in the plan to just screw him over and let him die once the testimony is done.

I put my head in my hands. I have more immediate problems to deal with than worrying about whether or not Marco is being set up as Interpol's straw man.

We need to get back. We need to figure out how to smooth things over with the Russians. We need to find a way to keep Interpol off our backs.

And why they would resort to something less than legal to kill us.

That's the only thing that bothers me about the Interpol theory. Technically, they're not allowed to assassinate people. That's not to say that they do or don't conduct questionably legal activities on a routine basis, but they're not allowed to.

If they're behind the bombing in Amsterdam… that would be new.

And definitely not a good thing.

"Ready?" I say to Gia as she comes out of the bathroom. She looks beautiful, even in the terrible dress.

She sighs. "I guess."

We leave the small bedroom. Dino is waiting at the kitchen table. He gives me a look that tells me he knows exactly what we were up to last night, and I return it.

Wisely, he nods. "Glad to see you got the clothes."

"These are terrible," Gia blurts. "Where did you steal them from?"

"A theater."

Oh. Well that explains it. "We need to leave this town."

Dino nods. "Yeah. I know."

"Any ideas?"

He gives me an infuriating bob of his head. "Some."

"Some?"

"Yeah Sal. You're not the only De Luca who has some kind of intelligence. I have some ideas about how to get us all the hell out of here."

I can practically feel Gia radiating fury, and I raise my eyebrows at him. "Okay. Well. Care to share?"

Dino settles back in the chair and narrows his eyes at me. "How did you get here? Can you take the same way out as you came in?"

I shake my head. The yacht had to leave shortly after delivering us here. Not only could I not risk it being found in the harbor, but I didn't want to risk my family finding out about my secret empire.

Secrets, apparently, are a pretty big part of our family dynamic.

"How did you get here?"

"I have my ways," Dino says airily.

Oh for the love of God. "You used to squeal if Mom so much as caught you taking a cookie before dinner."

"People change, brother."

I guess they do. "So, Dino. Do you have some kind of brilliant plan for getting Gia and I, and yourself, out of Ireland?"

"Tourists," Dino says with a smirk. "You two are going to go as tourists to Belfast. Then, you're going to get right back on whatever method of transportation you took here. Or you're going to hop a cheap flight to Scotland. There's a weird issue with customs between Ireland, Belfast, and Scotland."

"Belfast is part of the United Kingdom," I say slowly. "So we'll be able to get across without the Interpol checkpoint."

"Bingo," Dino smiles.

Gia glances between us. "How long do we have to pose as tourists for?"

Dino shrugs. "To make it really believable? About a week. If you can somehow get a passport stamp for your entry date, then it would look legit."

That it would. "I can handle the stamp."

Gia arches an eyebrow at me. "Really?"

"Yes." I'll need a printer, and there's only one of those in Ireland that I'm aware of. In Dublin.

Which means back in the crappy rental car, and back to the big city.

Where the Irish mafia run the underworld with an iron fucking fist.

Gia looks between us. "Sal?"

"I can do the stamp. But we need to get to Dublin."

Her face falls, then hardens. She looks at Dino. "You're going to get me some better clothes, you ingrate. Then, Sal and I, going to Dublin."

Dino snickers.

And I roll my eyes at the two of them.

WE AREN'T MORE than a mile down the road when Gia turns to me. "Let's go to the castle."

Gia's words jolt me out of my driving mode. "What?"

She points to a sign. "Look, that means castle, right?"

"Yeah. I guess."

"Let's go."

"Gia, we need to get to the printer in Dublin… "

"Come on. We're supposed to be tourists. Why don't we tour a little?" she grins at me.

Damn it.

I can't deny Gia anything.

The car protests as I turn when indicated, the road getting more and more bumpy as we follow it. Eventually, the castle emerges out of the gloomy sky.

When we park, Gia is all smiles. "Let's go!"

I follow her meekly.

She follows all the paths, stopping at each little sign.

"Okay. I admit. This is kind of cool," Gia says with a laugh.

"I thought you grew up in Italy?"

"Yeah but our castles are different. And I didn't live in Italy for that long."

"It still impresses me that Elio speaks with an accent and you don't."

"Admit it, De Luca," she smirks at me. "You think I'm impressive."

Looking at her, with the castle in the background, I smile.

I can't help it.

"You're goddamn right I do."

19

GIA

Playing tourist with Sal is... fun.

More than just fun. It's addicting.

And I know I'm not the only one who thinks so.

The first castle that we stay at has a name with more consonants than should exist in a sentence together, but Sal rented out the whole thing, so we have it to ourselves.

He shows me inside, and then when the staff close the doors, he winks. "Your palace, my queen."

I laugh. "Okay, laying it on a little thick?"

"I don't know. I think it fits you. You've never been a princess or a damsel in distress, Gia. You've always been my queen."

The emphasis on the word *my* feels like it lingers...

But instead of freaking out, I let it soak in.

Maybe I am Sal's queen.

That doesn't feel... terrible.

He gestures to the stairs. "This way, my lady."

I laugh. "Thank you, good sir."

"Good sir?" he teases me as we walk up the tiny winding staircase.

"Okay I don't know how people talked back in the day!"

"Good sir makes me feel like your butler."

There's a small chamber at the top of the stairs that opens up into a landing. Two massive doors, covered in wood and iron details, seal the room beyond.

I pause. "Well. That's definitely medieval looking."

Sal smiles and unlocks the doors, pushing them open.

"Sal," I whisper as we walk inside. "It's gorgeous."

The room is incredible. It might be in a castle but they've done some work to make it airy and light, and the space is filled with a blend of modern luxuries and priceless antiques. There's even what looks like a private patio beyond two more glass doors, and I skip into the room, marveling at it.

"You like it?"

I beam at Sal. "I love it. How did you know about this place?"

"Google."

I laugh as he moves our bags into the closet. When Sal turns back to me, I wrap my arms around him, my nose brushing against his.

"Hey," he whispers, smiling against my mouth.

"This is nice," I say back.

When I lean in to kiss him, it starts out slow. I'm just thanking him for the way he put all this together...

But then the kiss deepens.

Moments later, I'm clawing at him. Our clothes fly off of our bodies like leaves in a summer storm. Sal groans as his fingers run over my body, and I lick the sound from his lips.

When he puts me down on the couch, we're both desperate.

I gasp as he fills me. "Damn," I whisper.

I forget how big he is.

It's a shock, but it's one that I think I might crave.

Sal takes my mouth again as he pounds in to me. His fingers drift down my body to my core, and he tweaks at my clit.

I don't need any further guidance. I explode, clutching him to me as my orgasm rips over my body.

Sal groans, gripping my hip so hard it might bruise...

But I feel him follow me.

For a minute, we both lay there, panting. I look up at Sal.

"No games this time?" I whisper.

He blinks, then a small smile curls at the ends of his lips. "No games, Gia. I just needed you. Bad," he murmurs.

I lean in and kiss him. "Same. And you know what? There's time for games later."

Sal's eyes glint with a wicked promise.

"There is definitely time for games later, Gia."

"I THINK we should stay a little longer," Sal says later that night as we recline, sitting on our private patio. I've lost track of them at this point because they're really cool and I kind of want to see all of them.

I smile at him. "You do?"

"Yes. Everything seems stable. There's not been any new information about Interpol. No one is having a problem. Dino got back to New York earlier this week. Why not?"

I pick at my nails. "Oh, probably the threat of being dragged in by Interpol?"

"Gia. They haven't found us yet. Right?"

His eyes sparkle.

So far our cover of being a honeymooning couple has worked. Beautifully, actually. Every single Irish person who hears that we're here on our honeymoon has been absolutely overflowing with joy, and we've gotten a fair amount of perks out of it.

Not that we need them.

Sal, thinking that the best cover is being rich, has gone all out.

He's booked the nicest hotels.

Rented out entire castles.

He rents us a new car in every city, something vintage and fun that can cruise us through the Irish countryside at a painfully slow speed.

He's right.

So far, it's working.

I smile.

"Let's do it."

So, one week turns into two.

And two?

Turns into three.

Nearly a month after we arrived in Ireland, Sal and I are sitting in the last ultra-luxury palace hotel we haven't stayed in. It's just a game now. Stay in as many hotels as possible, visit all the castles.

Have sex.

Cuddle in each other's arms.

Then wake up and do it all again.

It's sort of like the best version of Groundhog Day.

Definitely not a version that I hate, for sure.

I lean back, having consumed way too many cookies with my tea. "I love it here."

"Which one was your favorite?"

I frown. There's been so many good options to choose from. "I don't know. Maybe that little one right on the coast?"

"It's yours," he whispers.

I blink. "What?"

"I bought it for you."

"Sal…"

He shrugs. "It would really fuck the Irish up to know that I own some castles, right?"

"Some?"

He smiles at me.

My heart feels like it's going to explode. Sal is... he's perfect. These past two weeks, with just the two of us, the rest of the world not existing?

It's perfect.

I don't let myself believe that this could be real. The amount of sex alone should have killed me a while ago.

But it didn't.

We haven't had anything close to the really tender moment on the boat. Sal has been introducing me, increment by increment, into more and more of the type of sex he enjoys.

I'm not even nervous to say it anymore.

I'm into some kinky stuff.

At this point, it's not even 'the sex that Sal likes."

I love it.

Maybe I just love it with him but... the fact that we've been consistently exploring more feels fantastic.

Not at all smothering like the boat.

I really don't want to get back to the real world. Pretending to be Sal's fiancé is fun.

I know it could never be real.

But it kind of makes me wonder...

No. I shut that thinking down. "How many castles are some castles, Sal?"

"You'll find out. I'm sure."

I make it a point to investigate that. But not yet.

For now, we're nearing the end of our time. Our fake visas are for a vacation, and a month is really pushing it. Technically we have ninety days before we'd be on the Garda's, and therefore Interpol's, radar, but still.

We need to get back to New York.

Getting back there, though...

I've never been this reluctant to leave a job. Ever.

Sal is a big part of that. If there was a world where I could be a boss and stay with him?

I'd do that in a heartbeat.

I can't though. Not only is it impossible because stupid mafia men would think he's in charge, it's just too risky. The only relationship that I can have with Sal that's committed in any way is a fake one.

I need to remember that. I need to break this illusion before I get too attached to it. I'm not meant for happily ever after's, families with white-picket fences, and husbands who buy me castles just for fun.

All of that is for other women. Not for women like me. Not for women with something to prove. Sal's close enough. I don't need him getting any closer to the one thing I've never given any man.

My heart.

I need to shut all of this down, however, before I lose control entirely. Sal can't have my heart if I don't give it to him, but when he pays me in great sex and castles... yeah. I really want to.

I have to stop this.

Even if doing that feels like the absolute wrong thing to do.

I sigh and reach down to where my phone is chiming lightly. I glance at it.

It's an email. From an unknown address.

I pick up my phone, my heart pounding in my chest. I click on it.

It's from... my doctor.

Normally I would pay zero attention to a reminder email from my doctor. But for some reason I click on it, signing in to the communication platform, and I open the message.

We'd like to remind you that the following routine care items need to be renewed...

I scan the list.

They're all routine things. Health tasks, an appointment reminder, a quick note about nothing in particular. It's a good, comprehensive look at my health, and a little shiver of guilt pings through me.

I haven't been to the doctor in... a long time. At least a year. I should really probably get a tetanus shot, given the nature of my work, but my eyes lock on one little line, one particular reminder, that makes panic sink into my stomach.

It's the shot I use for birth control.

The one that I told Sal I definitely had.

The one that I definitely thought was up to date but...

I haven't renewed it in over a year.

It's supposed to be renewed every three months.

No.

No, no, no.

"Gia?"

I put the phone down and do my best to smile. "I'm good. Just an email reminding me to make a doctor's appointment," I reassure him.

The best lies contain just a little bit of truth.

Inside, my mind is whirling. I'm doing mental math that seems more or less useless, as I'm not really regular with my period anyway, but it's happening all the same.

Sal squeezes my hand. "What do you want to do this afternoon?"

Find a pregnancy test. "Oh, I don't know. I'm feeling a little tired. Maybe just nap?"

"We can do that," he growls.

I sigh. "But I also really want that cake for later. You know. The one from the last town?"

God, I feel terrible for this. But I know exactly what's going to happen next.

Sal smiles.

Nods.

And gets up to go drive three hours to get me a piece of cake.

Which means that I have three hours, exactly, to find a pregnancy test.

Take it.

And then either breathe a huge sigh of relief...

Or figure out what the hell I'm going to do next.

THE THING about five-star hotels is that they really do take the whole 'service with a smile' thing seriously. The hotel concierge manages to find me a pregnancy test, the early detection kind, within about twenty minutes of me calling down.

He even believed me when I told him that I hadn't told the mister yet, so I would please appreciate his discretion.

I feel bad about that one, too.

The bellman delivers me a very discrete looking package, and I do have to say that I'm impressed. In any other situation, I'd write a nice review and let all my friends know this is the place to stay.

The situation, however, is not different.

And I need to figure this out. Tests acquired, I sit down to use one.

I always thought that people weren't serious about the whole 'waiting on two pink lines' thing. I've taken flu tests before, so I thought I kind of generally understood what all the fuss was about, but...

I didn't.

Because waiting to see if you have the flu and waiting to see if you're going to have a tiny human are two entirely different things.

There's no way that I can be pregnant.

Sure, Sal and I have had a lot of sex. Most of it unprotected.

But there hasn't been enough time.

Women aren't consistently fertile. Even for someone who has a pregnancy, it's kind of a miracle, because like... you really have to hit the timing well.

I almost laugh at my own joke because generally, Sal's timing is...

Pretty incredible.

Except not in this situation.

This would be...

My chest feels like there's a lead weight on it. If I had a baby, all my dreams of being a mafia don slip right out the window. Being a woman and leading a business is one thing.

Being a mom?

It would never happen.

When my phone chimes that the time is up, I take the test in a shaking hand. I let out a huge breath, looking down to see if it's done.

It is.

There's a result.

And when I count the lines...

There are two.

My first thought is that this can't be right. So, I whip out another test (God bless the concierge for getting multiple) and do my best to pee on it again. When I can't, I look around...

Water.

That's what I need.

I chug water. I wait a little.

And I go for it again.

In theory, I know that at some point I will have drank too much water to make the test effective, but who knows. Maybe that's when I'll finally get the result that's accurate.

Three tests later, they all say the same thing.

Positive.

Pregnant.

Yes.

Every single one of them is lined up in front of me, and Sal is going to be back at any minute, with a cake that I sent him on a fool's errand for.

I put my head in my hands.

How the fuck did this happen?

Okay, I know how it happened. The words *It's okay, I'm on the shot* and *I just want you* have been said. A lot. So often, in fact, that Sal didn't even say anything about it the last time we had sex.

Having sex without protection is apparently our thing.

I laugh, and the bitter sound echoes around the bathroom.

I've never really put thought into being a mom.

I'm definitely not the type of person who wants to be a mom in the way that I've seen other people be moms.

Like, the cutesy stuff is not for me.

My kid would probably be the one trying to hustle the other ones out of their lunch money. They'd know cuss words in nine languages.

I'd go to jail because they wouldn't ever go to school.

I'm not meant for picket fences in Jersey.

My kid would know too much about the world too soon.

"Gia?"

My head in my hands, I take one minute to collect myself. I swipe all the pregnancy tests into a drawer, then try to jam it shut by putting a towel on the metal runners on the side. Sal would look in the trash.

He won't question a broken drawer in an old castle.

"Coming," I call. I run the water, wash my hands, and smile.

I have no clue what to do.

But I know that I'm definitely, absolutely, one hundred percent not ready to tell Sal.

20

SAL

When I get back to the hotel room, Gia is acting very, very strange.

She's almost... brittle. I feel like if I hold her too tightly, she'll shatter.

I have no idea what's wrong.

"How was the drive?" she smiles.

"Good. I didn't know what type of cake you wanted, so I got you all of them," I say with a wink.

The concierge is going to send them up soon. Six boxes of cake are too much for one person to carry, and if you're staying in a five-star hotel, what's the point of doing something as trite as carrying boxes?

"Thanks, Sal," she murmurs.

Yeah. Something is wrong.

I tilt my head and look at her as she steps out of the suite's bathroom. "What's wrong with you?"

"Nothing," she says.

It's a lie.

When Gia lies, her words are too smooth. It's almost like her body lies too well.

I know the real Gia now.

So I know she's lying.

"Gia. You know you can tell me anything," I say softly.

I probably screwed something up. She's probably panicking about the endless honeymoon we've been on. It's been a lot, I know, especially for her.

But I also thought that maybe, it was okay.

Maybe the sex was... compelling enough to keep Gia from freaking out.

Mostly, I was sure that we were having a good time.

Until this moment.

"We need to talk," Gia whispers.

That makes my heart sink. "What?"

"We need to talk, Sal. I think we should go back to New York."

"As we were planning to do."

"Tomorrow."

I blink. "What's this about, Gia?"

"Nothing. We've just been away for a long time and we need to go back. It's time," she says firmly.

"What do you mean, Gia?"

She holds her shoulders back. "I mean that we've been hanging out, and it's been fun, right?"

Fun?

That word is dangerous. It's the type of word that people use to let other people down easily when they don't want to take accountability for their own shit.

I'm just having fun right now.

We're having fun, aren't we?

Let's just have fun together.

I narrow my eyes. "Having fun," I repeat dully.

"Yeah. The past month... it's been really fun. But Sal, what are we doing?"

"What do you mean, Gia?"

She sighs and plops down on the bed. "I mean, where is this going. Because the minute we get back to New York, everything is going to go back to normal."

"What is normal?" I growl at her.

"You know," she waves a hand at me. "I'm going to take over for Elio in a month when Caterina has the babies. I need to be able to pivot. I need to be able to..."

"Flirt. Fuck. Do the things you need to in order to get what you want," I say bitterly. "I'm absolutely certain, Gia, that you've told me this before."

And I'm absolutely certain that I didn't give a fuck about it then either.

"Good. We're on the same page then."

"Tell me what page you think you're on, Gia, so I can make sure it's the page that I'm on as well."

"That we need to end this."

My heart stops.

"What?"

"We should probably do it sooner, rather than later. Before we get back so that it's not weird or anything, and we can just go back to the way things were before."

"The way things were before," I repeat.

Gia raises her eyebrow at me. "For a brilliant linguist you sure do repeat what I've already said a lot."

I'm repeating it because it's surreal to hear it. It's a statement that I can't wrap my mind around.

And, more than that, it's a lie.

"Tell me when this before is that you're alluding to, Gia," I say with a tone that I normally reserve for those I'm about to destroy. "Tell me when you think this 'before' was. Because I will tell you what I know."

I step closer to her. Instinctively she moves back on the bed, her eyes widening.

She's afraid.

Good.

She should be.

"Before, when I asked you to have a relationship with me, and you told me no. You had to remain unattached in order to serve as Elio's spymaster. Before, when I held you as you cried yourself to sleep every night after Belarus. Before, when I pulled you from a fucking burning warehouse in Belarus. Before, when you and I chased each other around the globe, each one of us working to outwit the other."

She blinks. "Sal…"

"Before, when we knew before either one of our families did that our parents were not killed in a feud between the De Lucas and Rossi's. Before, when I saw you the night of Caterina's engagement and thought that I was standing in the presence of the most beautiful creature that the earth has ever seen. Before, when you opened your mouth to eviscerate Elio's foolish pride, and I knew that you were perfect in every way, not just your beauty."

Her eyes are wide. I know that I'm playing my hand here, and I'm putting down every card I have.

I've never told Gia about any of this.

About how I've watched her from afar… for years.

Even before Gia knew I existed, I knew she did. She's always been the sun, and I've always been in her orbit, waiting for her to shine the light she freely gives to others on me.

Except now I think that maybe, that will never happen for me.

Gia is never going to want me the way I want her to. Despite the fact that we're compatible in every way, she doesn't want me.

I'm not going to beg her.

I'm not going to force her.

I've never forced a woman to do anything in my life, and I'm not going to start now.

I snort. "Have it your way, Gia. I won't beg you. I won't tell you the reasons we're perfect for each other. I won't list out the reasons that I can see, perfectly, a future for us. And I know—" I hold up a hand as her mouth opens. "I know, talking about the future fucking terrifies you. I don't know where that comes from Gia because you won't. Let. Me," I roar.

"Sal..."

"I'm done, Gia. If you insist on turning me away, then turn me away. If you insist on ending this? End it. Don't fucking drag me along, and I'm happy to be done."

She opens her mouth. "I'm not..."

"If you close this door, Gia, it's going to be closed. If you are done, then we are done. There's no going back. There's nothing to return to. End it? Okay. It ends."

I wait, looking at her.

Gia's face is pale.

She looks like she's on the verge of tears, and my instinct is to ask her what's wrong. To ask if she's okay.

I don't follow it.

Gia takes a deep breath.

Tears are in her eyes.

And she says the two words that I never wanted to hear.

"It's done."

THE DRIVE IS SILENT.

The castle is about an hour away from Belfast. An hour of driving on narrow, winding roads that the Irish seem very fond of. An hour of silence, because after Gia told me that she was done, I didn't hesitate.

I packed the shit I needed.

I waited for her to do the same.

And I got us the hell out of there.

If Gia wants to end things and have a perfectly professional bodyguard, I can do that for her. If she wants to pursue her dreams of running the Rossi empire, I'll help her with that.

But she doesn't need my conversation to do that.

Finally, the road widens, and the lights of Belfast come into view.

We're flying out of the Belfast airport. Given the transparent border here, it's fairly easy to sneak our way back to England, and from there, to New York.

Interpol has a lighter presence in the UK, and as a result, we're going to be subjected to less scrutiny than if we flew out of, say, Rome.

Dino came up with this plan, and I hate to admit it... but it's a good one.

Belfast is an interesting city. Given the past and the political environment here, you'd think that they'd have tighter security but...

Bless the fact that they don't.

We're taking a back road into the city when I frown. There's a roadblock up ahead, and it feels...

Strange.

There are so few cars here, and I watch the one in front of us go through the barrier. I'm sure that there wasn't any roadwork marked here when I checked the map, which was not more than an hour ago.

I guess roadwork can come up in an hour.

I turn, following the detour. Seven minutes into the detour, I'm frowning again.

Something isn't right.

"Sal. Something feels weird," Gia murmurs.

"I know."

We turn again. I come to a stop and pull up my phone, ready to find another route, when ice skates down my spine.

I glance up...

Just in time to see the windshield shatter.

"Get down!" I bark at Gia.

She ducks.

Gunfire hails the windows, shattering it. Glass rains all over us, and I try to throw my hands over Gia to guard her.

"We need to get out of here," I shout.

Gia doesn't respond, but I hear the seatbelt click.

We need to wait for them to reload.

They're not shooting to kill. For whatever reason, they're shooting to intimidate, because if they were shooting to kill, we'd be dead.

This car isn't armored. It's not bulletproof in the slightest, as proven by the shattered glass. They know that if they shoot the side paneling, they'll kill us.

They're waiting for us to run.

So, we're going to have to do that.

Fast.

When the bullets stop, I look at Gia. "I'm going to pull you over to me," I whisper. "Then, we're going to run."

"Okay," she murmurs.

"Three, two..."

I grab her and pull her, opening the door in the same gesture. Gia and I tumble out of the car and sprint, running back the same direction we came from.

There's another shot. I throw Gia down, making sure that I cover her so that if anyone gets shot, it's me.

Gia can't get shot.

But whoever the shooter is... they still haven't shot us.

"They want us alive," I whisper to her.

There's a crunching sound. Boots. Coming closer to us.

I tense. "On my count. You run. Okay?"

"Okay."

"Three. Two... Go," I snap.

We move at the same time.

I'm on my feet and see immediately there's three people that I can count . I go for the biggest danger... then man with the rifle.

I slam my fist into his face.

I dodge when he throws a punch.

The first man is down. I know Gia's running away from here, so as long as I can keep fighting...

I move onto the next one.

It's familiar. My body knows how to do this. I've always been good at hand-to-hand. I can see the moves that they're making, and I'm willing to make sacrifices to get to what I need.

Another man drops.

Then, the third.

Three men on the ground. There's a ringing in my ears, and a cut above my eyebrow that's leaking blood, salty and hot, into my eye.

Done.

I grab the rifle. "Gia?" I call.

There's no sound.

She ran, sure. But she wouldn't have gone far…

"Gia?"

That's when I hear the noise that makes my blood turn to ice.

A scream.

I think it's coming from behind me. I turn and sprint, running down the road toward what might be a dock. The smell of the salt, the way the road is tapering down toward the harbor... it's definitely a dock.

That's not good.

My heart is in my chest. My feet feel thick and heavy, like I can't get them underneath me fast enough.

"Gia!" I scream.

I don't hear anything in response... except for the sounds of people grunting and struggling.

They have her.

I've never been so sure of anything in my life, and it utterly terrifies me.

Finally, I round a warehouse and find the dock. There are another two people, hauling someone who looks horrifyingly limp onto a boat.

"Gia!"

Gunshots echo around me. I duck behind the corner of the warehouse, grabbing the rifle I took off the body and loading it.

I want to fire back.

But I can't. because if I do...

I might hit Gia.

I need to run. I turn out, ready to sprint for the boat.

But I realize in an instant that it's too late.

I'm too late.

All of the people are on the boat. The body, that I assume is an unconscious Gia, is nowhere to be seen.

The boat roars.

And Gia disappears into the darkness.

I HAVE nothing to do except drive back to the hotel we stayed at the night before

It's a stupid idea. It feels like a stupid idea. But I have nothing else right now. My brain feels sluggish, like I took a sleeping pill, or I'm drugged or something.

Maybe I am.

Maybe that was part of the plan, to make both of us foggy with some kind of drug before taking us out.

Maybe...

The 'maybes' are going to kill me.

There's no point to them. There are only facts. The facts are that I'm here. Gia is gone, taken by someone, either the Irish or Interpol.

And I'm... here.

I need to figure out what to do.

I steal a car. It's absolutely a way to get on Interpol's radar, but fuck it.

Maybe if they arrest me too, I'll find her.

The hour back to the castle is the longest hour I've ever experienced in my life.

Longer than the one when I found Gia in a burning building.

Longer than the one when I had her in my hands in the canals of Amsterdam, swimming to get away from a bomb.

Longer than the one to the airport in New York, after she told me that there couldn't ever be a future for us.

Why didn't I believe her?

The stolen car, I abandon one town away.

I walk into a department store and use the card linked to my accounts to buy new clothes. I clean myself up in the bathroom, throwing the bloody, shredded mess into a trash can.

I hail a cab back the rest of the way to the castle.

When I walk in, the concierge from earlier smiles at me.

It's a very knowing smile.

I nod at him.

"Congratulations, sir," he says in a very bright voice.

"I appreciate it. May I ask what for?" I say, the veneer of civilization a stark contrast to the chaos that's brewing inside me.

The concierge blinks. "Oh. I apologize. I didn't realize she hadn't told you yet."

"Told me what, sir?"

He's nervous now. "I... I told her I wouldn't tell you."

"It's okay," I ease in to a smile. "I'll find out soon enough. Your discretion will not be unrewarded. In fact," I palm my wallet, digging out any of the bills hidden there. I tuck them in my palm and reach forward to shake his hand. "I'd pay you handsomely to find out what my wife kept secret from you."

"Ah. Well. I'm not sure, one way or t'other," he says in a thick accent. "But the lady had me make a little trip to the pharmacy earlier."

"The pharmacy?"

"For some tests, sir. The type of tests a woman might find... if she was in a family way."

It takes me too long to realize what he's saying.

It takes even more effort to paste an insanely fake smile on my face. "Well. No secrets were told, then. She shared the good news with me just now."

"Oh, thank the Lord," the concierge gushes.

"Indeed. I simply am having a problem adjusting to the news."

"Ah, well. Congratulations all the same," he beams.

I nod, then head to my room.

Gia asked the concierge to bring her a pregnancy test.

And I'm going to rip this fucking room apart until I find it.

I start in the bathroom. That's the most logical place. There's nothing in the trash basket. The sinks are in a large piece of furniture, riddled with drawers.

I wonder...

I start on the far left end, then work my way right.

Each drawer has something in it, but not the thing I'm looking for.

Toothbrushes.

Toothpaste.

Condoms (the irony almost makes me laugh).

Nail polish remover.

Whoever stocked this bathroom did so with care, because every fucking thing that a person could need is in here.

Except a goddamn pregnancy test.

I'm at the last drawer, ready to rip it open, when it catches.

My eyes narrow.

I pull harder. It's clear to me that something is jammed in here, keeping the drawer from pulling back smoothly. I grip the handle and pull, putting my whole body into it.

The drawer flies out. Its contents fly out too, and land on the marble bathroom floor with a slight click.

I lean down and pick one of them up.

I don't need to get the rest. This one is obviously a pregnancy test. I turn it over in my hand, my fingers shaking.

One line is not pregnant.

Two lines... pregnant.

I shut my eyes.

I take a breath.

And when I open them, all I see are two narrow, pale, but undeniably pink, lines.

My stomach roils. I turn to throw up, but I can't.

Gia's pregnant.

Kidnapped. Possibly dead.

And...

Pregnant.

21

GIA

It's the smell of fish that wakes me up.

I've never had such an aggressive reaction to it. One second, I'm out cold, the next, I feel like I'm being slapped in the face with enough fish to feed an entire aquarium.

When I get up, it's not pretty.

Because I'm throwing up everywhere immediately.

"Jaysus," I hear a distinctly Irish voice, making my stomach heave even more. "What'd you last eat, woman?"

"Fuck you," I mutter.

But it's hard to be tough and stoic, unfortunately, when you're in the middle of expelling every molecule of food that you've ever eaten.

So, instead of my usual witty retort, all that comes out is a very soft 'fuck you,' a whole lot of grumbling, and sort of a sloshing, moaning sound.

"For fuck's sake," the Irish voice hisses. "Oi! Rowan! Come bring this fuckin' bird a ginger ale, eh?"

"You sound like you're an extra in Angela's Ashes," I whisper.

The voice chuckles. "Ah well. That's the famous Gia Rossi if I've ever heard her."

"I hate you."

My eyes still haven't opened yet. I think I might be lying in a puddle of my own puke. The thought makes me gag again, and I lean to the side, right as something plastic and round appears under my face.

"This'll help," the voice says confidently.

I don't question it. I continue my incredibly disgusting evacuation, until there's literally nothing left inside my body but air.

Even that hates the fish smell.

I tense, fighting another wave of nausea as it beats through me.

"If I have nine months of this left, I'm going to turn into a stick," I mutter.

"What was that?"

Oh. Fuck.

I keep forgetting that I'm not only not alone, but I'm alone with someone who has an Irish accent. Someone with an Irish accent, who hired a group of someone's to take me down. Someone that I was fairly surprised to see, as the last I checked... he was dead.

However, I'm hardly one to speak about people being dead or alive so....

"Now. What was that about nine months?"

My heart is in my chest, and I can't believe that I said that out loud. I can't believe it because even for me, it doesn't seem true.

Nine months.

Then there will be another whole person to hang out with. Another person to worry about. Someone else that I will need to keep track of...

And I managed to get myself kidnapped.

On a fucking boat.

By the Irish.

I'm going to be sick again.

"Nothin' to say to that, then?"

I manage to screw my eyes open. Sighing, I shut them again. My heart sinks, but I know exactly what I saw.

It's him.

I lick my lips and manage to whisper, "Aren't you dead?"

The voice chuckles. "No, unfortunately. I'm not dead, even a little bit."

"Fuck."

"Aye well. That's the way of it then."

We didn't kill him. The leader of the Irish gang. Kieran MacAntyre. Because he's alive and kicking, and apparently gave me a barf bucket.

I roll over, grabbing the plastic. There's nothing left in my stomach, but I cough up everything I have anyway.

Kieran is back from the dead. And since Elio killed him the first time...

It's going to be a hell of a lot harder to make it stick now.

I'M SICK FOR HOURS. Kieran sits there the whole time, making the occasional snarky comment, barking orders either in Gaelic or heavily accented English to his crew. He's weirdly patient, which, considering that he's kind of a raving sociopath, is interesting.

And by interesting, I mean it's terrifying.

No one is this patient unless they want something. He needs me, obviously, but if Caterina's time with him is any indication, he doesn't want me for my jokes.

He wants to get revenge on Elio.

Kieran was, apparently, Caterina's original arranged husband. Prior to the deal that my dad made with her dad, she was supposed to marry Kieran. Obviously, she didn't do that, but still.

I don't want to be here. Not when I have so much at stake.

Not when I have a fucking *baby* inside of me.

"Well then. You're looking a little less green around the gills," Kieran murmurs.

"Why aren't you dead?"

"That's what you're worried about?"

"I'd say being kidnapped by a dead man is pretty high on my list of worries, yes."

He chuckles. "Jesus came back from the dead too, or so I hear."

"Surprised you can say that without it burning your mouth."

"Oh come now, Gia Rossi. I'm as God-fearing as the next Catholic."

"Again. Waiting for the smiting to begin," I say back.

He doesn't respond. I move to be in a sitting position, so that I can see him. I still can't really believe that Kieran is alive.

It's impossible.

I take a deep breath, my eyes watering against the light in the boat.

Determined, I look at him.

I blink. "I'm still not sure, exactly, why you aren't a maggot-filled bag of rotting flesh."

He smiles.

But there's a darkness there. Something bitter and vile.

My skin prickles.

"Look closer then, spitfire," he murmurs, coming near. "See what you can, while you can."

That sounds more than a little ominous.

Up close, he's Kieran.

He has to be.

He has the same flashing green eyes, the same coal-dark hair that gets into his eyes because it's just slightly too long.

The same pale skin that on a woman would look elegant, but on a man looks stark.

The hollows under his eyes are pronounced, like he's been unwell, and the tattoos on his neck...

I freeze.

The tattoos on his neck are wrong.

Kieran, or the Kieran that I remember dying of a knife wound to the gut, was covered in thick, brutal-looking tattoos. Teeth and talons and the usual animal metaphors.

This Kieran has tattoos, but they're not the same.

These ones are elegant.

They still cover his neck. His hands. I can see them on his chest too, from the little spot where his t-shirt dips down over his pecs. But his tattoos are far from brutal.

They're beautiful.

"How?" I whisper.

The man, who I'm increasingly sure is not Kieran, nods. "Think hard, spitfire. Use that famed Gia Rossi intellect."

Jesus. Pregnancy brain must really be a thing because my mind is short-circuiting. "Hand me a clue."

"I'd think someone in a similar situation would know a little faster," he smirks.

Similar....

Oh.

"Fuck," I breathe.

The man chuckles. "There it is. I'd heard you had a mouth on you, and I have to say. That, at least, does not disappoint."

"I didn't know Kieran had a twin."

"Ah, well. Our dad was the suspicious sort. There's a lot you wouldn't know then, about the MacAntyre siblings."

"Siblings... there's more than two of you?"

His eyes twinkle. "Wouldn't you love to know, Gia Rossi?"

I blink.

Kieran had a twin.

A twin brother.

Who is sitting in front of me. Wearing clothes that look like they'd be at home on an L.L. Bean model.

Fuck, he looks like a model in general.

My mouth opens. Closes. I stare at him.

"Who are you?" I blurt.

I'm ashamed of my own lack of finesse, but I really can't muster anything else.

He leans back and sighs. "What, calling me Kieran wasn't going to work?"

"No, because you're not Kieran."

He tilts his head. "At this point, does it matter?"

Fair point. "Wouldn't you rather be known as yourself?"

"Ah well, that's where you and I differ, Gia Rossi. I have a feeling you want people to know your name. Me? I'd rather not."

I narrow my eyes. "No one in our world remains anonymous."

"Wouldn't it be fun, then, if I were the first?" he winks.

Damn it. If this wasn't the worst situation on the planet, I'd be extremely entertained by this person. "Tell me your name," I demand.

"Oh, the prisoner makes demands now?"

"Hell yes. Tell me because I want to know."

He laughs. "How often does that work for you?"

"Every time."

"Even with your wee guard dog?"

I stiffen. "What did you do to Sal?"

"I, personally, did nothing."

"What the fuck happened to him," I snarl.

Kieran's brother throws up his hands in mock surrender. "Relax, spitfire. He's unharmed. You were the prize, not he."

"Why me?"

He shakes his head. "Tell me the famously arrogant Gia Rossi doesn't think she's a prize to be taken?"

"I'm pretty famous for escaping kidnappings so..."

"Not without a certain guard dog, I hear," he murmurs.

I sit back and fold my hands over my stomach. "Your name," I demand.

He sighs. He stands, then points to a door to the right. "The shower. It has a lock. Fresh clothes are under the bed."

"Name," I repeat.

He sighs, pausing in the doorway of the tiny little room. He shoots me a smile, and winks.

"Liam. I'll be in the galley when you're done," he says.

Then, he leaves.

I hug my knees to my chest. Liam MacAntyre.

Well. At least Kieran is still dead.

Small wonders, I guess.

I sigh, uncurling and stretching up. I definitely don't hate the idea of a shower, especially because if I keep smelling myself, I'm going to throw up again.

Do I believe him about the lock?

Well.

When it clicks into place...

I do.

CAUTIOUSLY SHOWERED, wearing another man's clothes, I creep upstairs. We're not exactly on a yacht; the boat smells like fish (pervasively so) and it's not going to win any awards when it comes to cleanliness.

Sal's yacht is a world away from this, that's for sure.

I hear voices coming from what I assume is somewhere important and brace myself. Liam might be not immediately murderous, but I can't guarantee that about anyone else on this fucking boat.

Plus, these assholes kidnapped me. They used chloroform or some kind of weird shit like that. I'm certainly not going to pretend that they didn't, so cautious is what I am as I creep around the boat.

"... not the one who's going to make the most impact," I hear.

Liam responds. "Ah, but she's going to have the desired impact. A fool thinks that Caterina Rossi is a better bargaining chip than Gia."

"She's his sister."

"Aye, and men burn the world down for their wives, but they'll trade it again and again for their sister, no?"

I hate men.

I make a move, stepping loudly so that I can get their attention. The talking stops, and sure enough, Liam's face pokes around the side of the doorframe. "Ah, there she is," he says with a beam.

"That whole luck of the Irish thing won't work on me," I say as I saunter in to the room.

There are two other guys sitting at a crowded little galley table in front of me. One has shockingly red hair, green eyes, and a scowl across his craggy face that would send a lesser woman running. His muscles are approximately ninety-nine percent of his body, and if I had to guess, I'd say that his neck is so thick, he probably needs custom shirts.

Should he ever wear them. Seems more like a Henley guy, if you ask me.

The other man looks... dangerous. He's slender, but clearly muscled. His hair is somewhere between brown and blonde, his skin tone somewhere between tan and pale, and his eyes glimmer a dark, murky brown.

This is Liam's spy. I know it. This man could be anyone. He could be any race, he could blend into any crowd. My instincts instantly recognize him. Some of us hide in plain sight, like me. Others, like him...

They're ghosts. You'll never see them at all.

I smile at Liam. "Thank you for the shower."

"Aye. And it looks like you've found the clothes as well."

I glance down. I'm wearing the world's baggiest sweatpants, which might have belonged to the craggy redhead, but I can't really tell. My shirt is a Metallica shirt, well loved, and I tug on it while smiling at the crew. "Who's the metalhead?"

"I'm surprised you don't already know," Liam says with an irritatingly amused smile in his voice.

"Well, you appear to have flown completely under my radar, so I think it's fair to say we're going to have to start on square one all around," I say to the crowd.

The ape scowls, and the dangerous one switches a finger.

I sigh and settle into a seat. "What's a girl got to do to eat around here?"

"Interesting question," Liam purrs. "Rowan, would you care to fetch the lady something?"

The large redhead stands, and I raise an eyebrow. "The hell kind of potatoes do you eat?"

"You don't speak," he grunts.

"You're definitely not going to keep me quiet," I inform him.

The other one leans forward while Rowan stomps to a cabinet. "You definitely gave us a run for our money, Gia."

I smirk. He's not Irish at all. Fucker's Scottish. "And what money was that exactly?"

A chilling smile creeps over his face. "I don't think you have any idea what you've gotten yourself into."

"James," Liam scolds. "You're scaring the lady."

"I think it takes far more than that to scare the lady," James responds.

I register them. James. Spy. Rowan. Muscle.

And Liam.

Whom I have never heard of before today.

Sal would have a field day with this...

The thought of his name sends an ache through me that is more than just painful. I resist the urge to gasp because it hits me like a freight train.

Shit.

I've been worried about Sal, and it's been sitting on a back burner. But now...

It's going to consume me.

I need to figure out how to keep going, or I'm going to drown in this feeling.

I take a deep breath, shoving everything that I'm feeling about Sal to the back of my mind. I can't handle it right now.

Because if I do...

I won't survive.

I smile. "So. What's the plan? Are we going to just ride this little booze cruise out until Elio pays a ransom or…"

James' smile turns dark. "That's not what this is, princess."

God, I hate it when he says that. I only like it when Sal says it. "Then inform me, Scottish James. What is the plan?"

Liam looks at the two of them. "You know how the game is played, Gia," he says softly.

I blink.

Liam's lips curl into a sad smile. "I lost a brother. I lost the chance for a sister. And unfortunately, Gia… I need to make sure both of those things happen."

I blink. *A chance for a sister…*

Oh.

Fuck.

Liam isn't going to ransom me.

He wants to marry me.

22

SAL

I'm not even sure how long I've been sitting in the bathroom. The lights have been on for so long, they're beginning to kind of sizzle, and I wouldn't be surprised if they explode.

It would be fitting ambiance.

Pregnant.

Gia is pregnant.

My family, apparently, just cannot keep from getting pregnant. Whether it's Caterina, Dino, or apparently me, every time we have unprotected sex, there's a baby that shows up.

I would laugh if it wasn't so completely terrifying.

Pregnant.

There are a thousand questions spinning through my mind. How long has she known for? What is she going to do? Was she going to tell me? I assume that if she took the test somewhat recently, then she might have just found out but...

How do I know?

I don't.

The things that I don't know are going to choke me. I breathe, steadily trying to keep panic from overwhelming me...

How do I know what's real? How do I know how to handle any of this?

I don't even know who took her. It could be Interpol. It could be any number of enemies that we've racked up over the years, or it could be the ones closest to home.

I need answers.

There are too many questions. I can't sort through them, because every time I try, my eyes drift down to the little plastic test in my hand.

Gia's *pregnant*.

There's no doubt in my mind that the baby is ours. I've been around her for the last few weeks, exclusively, and more than that, she said she had the shot.

That she was covered.

I never would have...

My heart skips a beat. Unfortunately, that's not entirely true.

I love the idea of being a parent with Gia.

The fantasy of it lingers in front of my mind like some kind of pipe dream.

Gia and I, reading books to our baby.

Having a baby shower.

Going to the doctor together.

Having insanely hot sex at night and then waking up to make the kid pancakes.

It's...

It hurts, how badly I want that.

So no, I can't think my way out of this. I can't process what I need to do. I don't even know where I should fucking start.

It's like I'm lost.

Unfortunately, I know exactly what I need in order to be found.

I need the one person who can help me.

My eyes squeeze shut.

I need my big brother.

I GET my chance nearly four days later.

It's an excruciating wait.

I keep sending Elio's phone calls to voicemail, even though they're hardly coming in fast and thick. It seems that whatever Dino told him about what Gia and I are doing is still holding up as far as cover, because if Elio knew Gia had been kidnapped...

Yeah.

He'd be doing a little more.

Luckily, it's giving me time. Time that I need in order to track down Marco and figure out how I can get him alone, without the blonde woman he's living with.

The woman who, I can only assume, is his witness protection handler.

They do everything together. For all intents and purposes, it looks to me like they're a happy couple. However, there are some places where the illusion seems to fall apart.

Every now and then, he looks at her with longing. Naked, unabashed, clear longing.

And every now and then, she looks at him with so much pain, it makes my heart clench in response.

She does, however, go for a run. Every other day. For exactly one hour and thirty minutes.

Like clockwork.

When she leaves the little cottage that he's hiding in, I don't hesitate. I saunter up to the door, ready to pick the lock.

It opens.

I freeze, waiting for the click of a gun. Instead, I just see Marco.

My heart skips in my chest.

Seeing him like this, whole and hearty and definitely not dead, makes me feel a rollercoaster of emotions. I'm happy he's alive. Thrilled, because the brother that raised me is in front of me.

Angry, because he did something to get himself here. Something that I don't necessarily want to know about.

Furious, because he's going to sell us out.

And sad, because while I'm going through all of this, he's just... watching me.

Marco, as always, doesn't have emotions. His face shows nothing as he stares at me before he shrugs.

"Might as well come in," he grumbles. "She'll be back soon."

"An hour and," I check my watch. "Thirteen minutes."

"Twelve, if she decides to sprint up the hill. Seventeen if she stops for a coffee around the corner. Either way, we're burning it up, so get in here."

Cautiously, I follow my brother into the little cottage.

Inside, it's exactly what I thought it would look like. Clean, neat as a pin. Simple. It could easily be a romantic honeymoon cottage for two lovebirds, exactly like the scene that Marco and whoever she is are playing at.

The fact that it's so flawless makes my teeth hurt, and I grind them together in my skull.

Marco sits down at the kitchen table, and gestures for me to follow.

I do, eying him suspiciously.

"I would get you tea, but I don't think you like tea," he rumbles.

His voice. It makes me want to... throw a punch at him, right now.

"I thought you were dead," I snarl.

Marco shrugs. "That was kind of the idea."

"You wanted us to think you were dead? Elio thinks you're dead. Caterina thinks you're dead. *Luna* thinks you're dead, for fuck's sake," I snarl.

Luna's name makes him wince. "I am sorry about that. But it's for the best, Sal."

"It's for the best that you're just here? Playing house with someone, waiting to give testimony against us?"

"I guess you heard from Dino then," he says coolly.

I roll my eyes. "For fuck's sake, Marco. You're not going to do anything to explain what the hell is going on?"

"No."

"Why?"

He rolls his eyes. "Because you've clearly got it already figured out, so why would I bother."

"Jesus Christ Marco!" I'm almost shouting. "It would be great to hear what the fuck is going on with you without thinking that you're just a piece of shit who abandoned your family and is just shacking up with some blonde woman, pretending that you're what? In love with her? Her husband? What the fuck kind of game is going on here?"

He doesn't respond. Marco at least has the decency to look away, but I can tell that I made him angry. Something about my comments about the girl are hitting a nerve with him, and I need to figure out what it is.

Finally, he takes a breath. "She's not who you think she is."

"Oh? Who is she? Interpol? Irish mafia? Can't be both so which is it?"

Marco's eyes gleam. "Did you think that I'd just let myself be arrested?"

"No," I answer honestly. "But Dino told us that you were doing it to protect him."

"Sure. I'm glad Dino thinks that."

I narrow my eyes. "You weren't trying to protect Dino's secret kids?"

"I protect all my nieces and nephews. And my family," he adds meaningfully. "I wish you'd remember that, Sal, before you go through whatever bullshit you have for me today."

I splutter. "Bullshit?"

"I know that's why you're here. You want to beg me to come back, to help you with something. To re-join the family and do... something," he sighs.

I snort. "That's not at all why I'm here."

"Then why are you?"

The question feels like it should be easy to answer. But when I open my mouth to tell him...

I don't know where to begin.

Gia's been taken by someone isn't enough. Because technically, the sentence is correct. However, there's so much more behind it.

Gia's been taken.

But it's more like the mother of my child has been taken.

The only woman I've ever wanted to be part of my life has been taken.

Gia, who is the sun to me, the only star in my life that I orbit around...

She's been taken.

It doesn't feel like the words *Gia's been kidnapped* work to describe how terrifying this is for me.

My mouth opens. Closes. Marco leans back in his chair and crosses his arms. "Well fuckin' say it," he barks.

"Gia's been kidnapped," I finally manage.

It's woefully short of the terror that I feel when I think of that, but it's factual. There is something to it, and it's the best I can do without getting too deeply into how I feel for her.

"Okay," Marco says.

I blink. His casual reaction is making me feel like I'm losing my mind. "Okay?"

"Yeah. Okay. Did Elio send you to get her or something?"

"No..."

I see understanding flash across Marco's eyes. "Oh. I see. Elio didn't send you. which means that you're here of your own volition. Which means that, in a truly stupid move, you've gone and fallen for Gia Rossi."

"I can't look out for my sister-in-law?"

He snorts. "Gia Rossi will never be anyone's kin like that. She's fucking feral, Sal. That's never going to change."

"You don't know her."

He sits back in his chair, his eyebrows pinching together in surprise. "Jesus, Mary and Joseph, Sal. It's bad, is it?"

"I don't know what you mean," I say quietly.

He sighs. "Look. Gia's a fun girl. I've always known that. She's a hell of a soldier, and makes an even more effective capo. But she's not... she's Gia," he says by way of explanation.

Everything that he's saying is making my skin prickle. "So?"

"So, she's kidnapped. She's going to fuck or fight her way out of it and turn up in a couple of weeks with a great story and a new set of Jimmy Choo's. She's Gia. She doesn't get stuck. She doesn't need rescuing. She doesn't need anyone, actually, and she's pretty clear about that."

I growl. "This time, she needs me."

The emphasis on the word *me* makes Marco pay attention to me in an alarming way. He puts his elbows on the table, leaning over them as she studies me. "She needs you, huh?"

"Yes."

"Did she lose her tongue or something?"

"Marco..."

He throws his hands up and leans back again. "Fine. Whatever. No Gia trash talk. But what I still don't get is how you play into this."

"She needs me," I say again.

He shakes his head. "Gia Rossi needs nothing and no one."

"She does."

He tilts his head. "Does she need you, Sal? Or does she want you?"

I don't answer that.

Marco's eyes narrow. "How do you know that she wants you."

"The fuck?"

"How. Do you know. That. Gia Rossi. The queen of flirtations. The one woman that I think would rather die than be tied down. How do you know that she's interested in you as well?"

I don't.

That's the long and short answer. I know that Gia and I care about each other, and I know that she cares about me. She wouldn't... seek me out for comfort if she didn't.

"Gia needs me," I say from between my teeth. "And that's all you need to know."

"Does she?"

I tilt my head. "Marco..." I growl.

He throws his hands up. "All I'm saying is that Gia Rossi isn't just a spy. She's not just in charge of all Elio's intelligence for shits and giggles. She's dangerous, Sal. And I don't know that it's because she's smart or brutal, because both of those things are true. Gia's dangerous because you can never really know her."

That's not true. "I know her," I insist.

"You know who she wants you to know. But even Elio doesn't know her," Marco says softly. "He's said multiple times that he wouldn't be surprised if Gia betrayed him one day and tried to take over the Rossi empire."

"She wouldn't take it over. He would give it to her."

Marco barks out a laugh. "You're smarter than that, man. Come on. I know you're smarter than that."

I ignore him. "Are you going to help me or not?"

For a long, terrifying moment, I think his answer might be no. That he's not going to help me with her.

That he's going to turn me down and decide to send me away.

Finally, Marco sighs. "We won't have enough time while Maeve is out. Meet me later, here," he says, scribbling down an address.

I take the paper from him and pocket it. "Marco…"

"Just meet me there. But after this, Sal? No more." He shakes his head. "You're just as bad as Gia. Always have been. You're nosy and have to know everything, but I'm here to tell you now that even you can't control this," he says.

The finality in his voice makes me feel like a kid, and I hate it.

"Marco…"

"Don't, Sal," he says quietly. "Just don't. I've chosen this path. I know why. You don't have to."

But I do.

I very much do want to know.

If I don't fully know why Marco is doing this, then I'm always going to wonder why.

Why he didn't choose me.

Why he's abandoning his family.

Why he doesn't want to be part of us anymore.

There's something inside my chest that aches, and it's not until I get back in the car and look at the address Marco gave me that I realize what it is.

I am always overlooked.

I'm never the brother people fear. I'm never the one that stands out. Everything about me, and who I am, is designed to hide.

To stay hidden.

I haven't even told my family about my successful real estate business, and Marco's exasperation is a stark reminder of why.

They've never seen me as capable. As someone worth noticing.

So why would I want to prove them wrong, if they never believed in me in the first place?

That, at least, feels familiar in terms of my baggage with my family.

Layered in, however, is an entirely new hurt.

Gia.

As I drive away, the biggest, and most pressing, bubbles up through me like heartburn.

Why the hell am I not enough for her?

And, more importantly... Marco's words are getting to me. They're making me realize that, under everything, there's one more question that's demanding my attention.

Loudly.

Given what Marco's already said, and what Gia's told me, I keep wondering one very pivotal, crucial thing.

Will Gia ever choose me?

23

GIA

It takes three days on the damn boat to get anywhere.

Which means, disconcertingly, I have absolutely no idea where we are. I'm not an old-timey sailor. I can't read the stars or the currents or whatever else they used to do in order to not be totally lost at sea.

Because that's what I am right now.

Lost.

One hundred percent, completely and totally, lost.

The fact that I'm harboring a little stowaway makes everything a little worse.

The fact that Liam MacAntyre, the long-lost twin brother of Kieran (and honestly I'm assuming there is either a third triplet or sibling to deal with at this point) has quietly insisted, over and over again, that we get married, makes it even worse.

Every time I think about Liam, or him asking me to marry him, or any number of things associated with that whole situation, there's a Gordian knot of emotion in my chest that makes me pretty sure I'm going to have a panic attack.

I can't think about Sal.

If I think about Sal...

The panic attack is something I can't have. Not here. Not when I'm trying to survive.

Not when someone very small, and very much inside my body, is also counting on me to survive.

When we finally get off of the stupid boat, it's not anywhere crazy like Florida or the Bahamas. The coastline is rocky and cold. Like, really cold. There's ice and mountains and the tiniest, barest scrap of green.

"Where the hell are we?" I say to Liam as he helps me onto the dock.

"You know full well I can't tell you that, love."

"Don't call me love," I snap immediately.

The words send that pit of terror swirling inside me.

Liam shrugs. "Well. Suffice to say that we're not anywhere your devoted bodyguard will find you, nor will any of his brothers, or your own. We have time and space here to discuss, so that you and I can arrive at a solution that's palatable to all."

I shoot him a glance. "Palatable?"

"Acceptable?"

Something about that makes me cringe. I can say many things about my relationship with Sal, but none of them are that our relationship is palatable.

Electric.

Thrilling.

Shocking.

Comforting.

Magical...

I shut the thoughts down. It doesn't matter what Sal and I had.

Whatever I am doing here, with Liam? That's reality.

The reality is, I might need to marry this guy to survive.

My stomach clenches.

"You alright then?" Liam's voice weaves around my ears.

"Fine," I grumble.

"Lookin' a mite green around the gills again."

"Yeah well. I'm on yet another fishy coastline."

"What's with you and fish, hmm?"

My unborn child has an extreme aversion. "Are we going to go somewhere or just sit here and freeze?"

Liam offers his arm to me, and I take it.

The coastline is... well, it's not pretty. Not like the rolling green hills of Ireland.

The rocks are dark, and everything smells like bird shit and fish.

There are areas of moss gathered on the rocks around the pier, and a small road winds away to the north of us, leading to a disturbingly small town.

The buildings hug the ground like a stiff wind would take them away.

Or like they've weathered much, much worse, and they are afraid to let go.

As we walk down the road, it's clear that we aren't alone. A small crowd of people is gathered on the road in front of the town.

Rowan, surprisingly, waves at the small crowd of people gathered in front of us. A language that I've never heard before in my life pours out of his mouth.

Slack-jawed, I stand back.

"Oh, that's a new one for you?" James sneers at me.

That guy is about to catch the first knife I can toss in his stomach. "You know what, James the Giant Shithead? I'm humble enough to admit that I don't know every language in the world."

Sal might, though.

Deep breath.

Shut that down, Gia.

If I can figure out what language they're speaking, then I can get a clue about where we are. I listen in, trying to hear anything that I recognize…

I've got nothing.

It's not even remotely close to any language that I've ever heard.

Shit.

Okay, Gia. Where have you not been?

Ugh. It could be any number of indigenous central American languages. Any number of non-European languages. Fuck, now that I think about it, I really only know two language groups.

Let's hope you get your dad's gift for language, little one.

Ohhhh no.

My eyes are getting hot. I rub my hands against them as tears press, rather insistently, against the edges of my focus.

No. No Gia, keep your shit together.

I don't even recognize myself right now. I couldn't talk my way out of a wet paper bag, let alone get back to Elio and my people.

What the fuck is wrong with me?

"Gia. This way," Liam says, gesturing with his shoulder.

Meekly, I follow.

Meekly.

I am never fucking *meek*. When I get to wherever we're going, I'm going to absolutely lay into him. Liam thinks that I've been subdued, but I haven't.

I'm Gia fucking Rossi.

I don't do *meek*.

Liam leads me to a little shack that's situated, mercifully, above all the fish smells. The air is marginally clearer, but I still can't see shit. There's nothing but snow and ice and rock and that sad, spongy looking moss grass.

Iceland, maybe?

I would guess northern Scotland but I think there's more people in Scotland than this weird, scrappy little village. Could be Canada, but I don't think we were on the boat long enough to get to Canada.

Where the hell are we?

Liam opens the door to the little shack and I duck inside. At some point, Rowan and James have disappeared, and I'm alone with Liam.

I look around. There's a pretty nice couch, what I assume is a bedroom, and a small kitchen. The furnishings look kind of vaguely Nordic, like something that Ikea might have sold, but they're clean.

Nothing smells like fish.

Blissfully.

I zoom over to the couch and sit. "So, now that we're here, do you want to have your wicked way with me?"

"Ah, well. I thought we could talk about the offer I made you on the boat."

"That didn't seem so much like an offer as it was a demand, but I'm interested to hear what you've got."

Liam smirks. "You really are something, Gia Rossi."

"Don't forget it," I say with a wink.

"I won't anytime soon."

Liam settles on to the couch across from me. "So. Like I said. I aim to make you my wife."

"Wow. And you're not even going to buy me a drink first?"

He chuckles. "I've a feeling that many men have bought you drinks, and yet none have made you theirs."

Sal.

I shake that off. Sal wasn't mine. I'm not his.

Except...

A strange montage of our time pretending to be husband and wife flashes before my eyes. Sure, I wasn't Sal's wife.

But I pretended to be.

And I didn't hate it.

"No," I say cautiously. "But have you considered that fact has a lot less to do with the fact that no one gave me an offer, and more with the fact that I just don't want to be married?"

"I'm afraid, Gia, that I'm about to make you an offer that you can't refuse."

My instincts hear his voice drop into something more sinister, and ice skates down my spine. "Do tell," I murmur.

Liam leans back. "What do you know of my brother?"

"He makes a better dead man than a living one?"

I'm curious how that will land.

Liam breathes slowly, but he doesn't look mad. I'm under the impression that very little ruffles him, which is a pretty stark difference from his admittedly very volatile twin.

"I'll let you have that one, Gia. But I won't suffer much disrespect for the dead."

"Oh? I'm sorry that you two were close."

"We weren't," he says sharply.

That gets my attention. "Why the sense of fraternal duty, then?"

"Family's family," Liam says from between clenched teeth. "You, of all people, should know and understand that."

I nod. "Fair."

"And, it's not right to talk poorly of the dead," he adds.

Fascinating. It appears that Liam is just a tad superstitious.

I wonder if I can work with that.

"Well. I see what you're saying, but he kidnapped my very favorite sister-in-law and scared the shit out of her, tried to rape her, and kept ranting about some kind of deal that his... well, *your* father made. Does that about sum up what I know?"

"Aye," Liam's eyes darken. "It appears, though, that dear old dad's legacy runs a little more deep than either Kieran or I had imagined."

"Explain," I say crisply.

"Dad ran Ireland," Liam says softly. "But he was a family man at heart. Or, he was, until our mum passed."

"I'm sorry to hear that," I say automatically. I know how terrible it is to lose a parent.

Liam nods. "After her death, we were sent to separate homes. I was raised by my uncle Sean. Kieran, by Da, since he was older and Da wanted him to take over the business anyway."

"And your other sibling..." I prompt.

Liam shakes his head. "No, darlin.' I can't give you that unless you're my wife."

Interesting. He also wants to protect his sibling, whoever that is.

I guess I can understand that as well.

"Okay. So. Kieran and dear old dad," I prompt.

Liam nods. "Aye. Losing mum changed him. A lot. I'd say that dad became right cracked, and he decided somewhere along the line that in order for one of us to inherit the empire, we needed to be married. To a good girl, in a good family."

"Ah," I nod, understanding dawning. "Hence, Caterina."

Liam nods. "Good girl. Good family. Someone whose family was in a position to be controlled. They made that marriage contract before the De Luca's had any children, so they didn't know how long they'd wait before a girl came 'round."

"Was it the De Luca father? Or the grandfather?"

Liam tilts his head. "Does it matter, love?"

Love.

I hate how casually he throws that around.

I guess it is kind of a relief, though. I know that he doesn't mean it. It's like seeing his cards on the table. Liam doesn't love me, but he's willing to flatter me.

That's something.

"It does," I say quietly. In the back of my mind, I still have so many questions about who planted the attack on our parents that day.

I'm beginning to suspect that I know exactly who.

Liam shrugs. "It doesn't. We are, however, in a position where I need to inherit this empire. I'm no' going anywhere. Kieran royally fucked this up for us, and I'm here to undo it. But I can't do that, Gia, unless I have a wife."

Everything clicks into place. "That's why Kieran kidnapped Caterina."

"And it got him killed."

My eyebrows skyrocket. "You don't think this is going to get you killed?"

"I think that I'm in the presence of a much better negotiator than Caterina De Luca."

He doesn't know her at all, but that's not the point.

Liam's words bite at me like mosquitos.

He leans forward. One of his hands slips into mine, and I stare at it.

Everything in me wants to pull back, but I can read the room.

I know that would be a bad idea.

Liam's hand isn't terrible to hold. It's rough, and strong.

"What were you doing before this?" I blurt.

I'm curious about why his hand has calluses on it.

Liam gives me a little quirk of a smile. "I'm a farrier."

"No shit," I laugh.

"Aye. Have my own business in the countryside near Cork. Been doin' it since Uncle Sean taught me how."

"A farrier. Well, it explains the hands, I guess."

"Were you worried they'd be too rough for you, princess?"

I hate the teasing lilt to his voice.

"No," I say idly. "Just curious."

"Well. Ask anything you want. If I can answer it for you, I will."

He hasn't moved his hand. "I'm more interested in you finishing up our discussion with the point," I say softly.

Liam nods. His thumb rubs over my hand. "I'll no' mistreat you, Gia," he says softly. "I'm a decent man. I've done what I need to in order to get to where I am, and redeem my brother in the eyes of the business, but I'll not harm you. I'll not make you suffer. I know well the worth of the woman in my house, and I'd treat you like my equal. Being married to me wouldn't be so bad, and we'd both get something we want out of it."

"What, exactly, do I get out of it?"

His eyes gleam. "Power. The ability to help me run the organization. More than you'll get in your brother's shadow, that's for sure," he murmurs. "You'd be my partner, Gia Rossi. My equal. My counterpart. So. What do you say?"

I shut my eyes. Sal never treated me like an equal.

He treated me like a fucking queen.

I nod, aware that I'm swimming with sharks in blood-soaked water. I gently slip my hand from his. "I need some time to think about it," I whisper.

Liam gives me a half-formed smile. "I'd expect you'd say that."

He stands. "The cottage is yours. I'll give you a radio, but be aware, you've no idea where in the world you are. You've no resources, no way to talk to the people to sweet talk your way into an escape. Rowan, James, and I are the only ones who know this place, and we're the only ones who know how to get off of it. You can't hide. You can't leave. Plotting to do so will be fatal," he says in a low voice.

"Romantic," I say dryly as I blink up at him.

He shrugs. "Romance is not for people like you and I, unfortunately. Besides, I can offer you much more than romance. I can offer you power. Money. Stability. All things that I think you, being a very practical woman, know and care about more than romance, yeah?"

I don't answer that.

Liam nods. "Time it is then. I'll send a woman up from the village with a radio. Let me know when you're ready to talk, then."

With a squeak, the door to the cabin shuts. Liam's gone.

Then, and only then, do I let myself do the thing that I've been dying to do since the word *wife* escaped Liam's lips.

I put my head on my hands.

I take a deep breath.

And I let the tears that I've been holding back come roaring out.

24

SAL

I've been pouring over nautical charts and shipping records for an hour.

Marco's idea was to connect me to someone who could trace the boat, which wasn't a half bad idea. Marco's instructions brought me to the Belfast port authority, who was more than happy to loan me the office in exchange for an amount of money that would have been exorbitant in any other situation.

In this one though, it's not.

Gia is on the line.

It makes everything more urgent. And it makes me feel like I have no clue what I'm doing.

I've never been this helpless. Not in a very, very long time.

Not since I saw my family, one by one, be cuffed and put behind bars, and I couldn't do anything about it. I wanted to save them, that time.

But I didn't know enough. I had no control over the situation.

Now, though?

I should have control.

The problem is that I don't.

My mind also lingers on what Marco said to me earlier, in the pub when he gave me the tip about the shipping and port records.

I can't leave her for long.

I can't for the life of me tell if that means that he's being trapped by her...

Or if he doesn't want to leave.

There's no doubt in my mind that the woman Marco's living with is an Interpol agent. However, what's unclear to me is if there's anything else going on with her.

For some reason, I get the feeling that there's more to her and Marco's relationship than meets the eye.

I force myself to look back at the charts.

It's far too shortly, however, before my phone rings, jarring me out of my concentration.

I look down at my cell. I pick it up, my hands clumsy as I try to calm myself down.

It's Elio.

I don't want to take this call. I thought that Elio might give us just a little bit more time before he summoned me.

I had thought that, perhaps, he would think that Gia and I were still under cover.

But clearly... that isn't happening.

I gulp around the lead pit in my stomach and answer.

"Elio," I say into the phone. "How are you."

"Would you like to explain why a marriage contract came across my email this morning?"

I blink. "What?"

"There's an Irish man offering to marry my sister. Care to explain who the fuck this is?"

Elio's voice is absolutely vibrating with rage.

"I have no idea," I say honestly.

"You've been gone for months. You told me that you were going to bring Gia back in one piece. That you would look out for her. That you'd bring her back to me," he emphasizes that last part in a snarl. "And now not only are you not here, but you expect me to believe that you have no fucking clue why an Irishman named Liam MacAntyre is offering to marry my sister?"

I frown. MacAntyre?

The name is too familiar, because MacAntyre is the name of the man who kidnapped Caterina.

"Liam MacAntyre?" I say slowly.

"Si," Elio hisses and swears in Italian. "And I too wondered why the name sounded so familiar. Kieran was the one we killed. And we did kill him, did we not?"

"Stone cold dead," I mutter. I handled the body of the fucker myself.

Putting the man who kidnapped and assaulted my sister into the ground was pure joy.

"Then why the hell," Elio's voice is thick, his Italian accent pronounced as it often is when he's upset, "is someone named *Liam MacAntyre* saying he is going to marry Gia?"

I take a deep breath. There isn't an explanation for this, but more than that, I don't want to think about what's implied here.

That whoever kidnapped Gia is going to marry her.

When she's pregnant.

With my. Fucking. Baby.

"I don't know," I finally manage to get out.

The line is silent. So silent that I'm about to ask Elio if he's still there when he makes a noise that's somewhere in between a scream and a roar.

"Find her, Sal. Find her or I'm going to unleash hell on the world."

"Not before I rip it apart," I growl back.

Elio's clearly upset still, but I can hear him as he simmers down slightly. "You'd do that, wouldn't you?"

I can't tell him. Elio would be devastated if I told him about the baby and Gia didn't.

Hell, I'm still destroyed over the fact that she didn't tell me herself.

"Tear it to shreds, Sal. She's my sister," he says in a threatening voice.

And she's the love of my life, I want to add.

Instead, I open my mouth and bark out a quick "Copy," then shut the phone down.

There are so many feelings buzzing around in my mind, I can't keep them all straight. Terror. Anger. Confusion.

Then, back to that deep, soul-sucking terror the information Elio gave me brought on.

Gia can't be getting married.

There has to be some kind of threat embedded here. I'm missing something and I can't quite place what it is.

I dig for my laptop, opening it up and connecting it to the VPN for the port authority within moments.

Liam MacAntyre. Who the fuck is he?

Why does he have my Gia with him?

Why did he intentionally kidnap her? Why target specifically her?

Why the fuck did he leave me alive.

I'm staring at the blank screen. My mind is moving faster than the technology in front of me, and it's making my skin crawl. Finally, the computer boots up. It's still painfully slow, but at least it's functional.

Immediately, I start to search.

Liam MacAntyre.

I'm not sure if it's the fact that I'm in Ireland, and therefore on the correct VPN, or just stupid luck, but the search almost immediately brings something up.

My jaw drops.

This man is a fucking ghost. He's a corpse.

He shouldn't be alive. I watched him die.

I lean in closer, frowning.

No, he's not Kieran.

For one, his name is different, which sounds like a stupid difference until I realize that there are other subtle differences. Different tattoos.

Kieran's face had a cruel look to it, while Liam's has a stoic one.

He doesn't, however, look unhinged like Kieran did.

That's a relief, I think.

The tattoos are also totally different. Both of them are (or had been) covered in tattoos, with only their faces exposed, but Liam's tattoos are artful. They look more like they're done intentionally, whereas Kieran's tattoos had looked like they'd been done by a drunk pirate somewhere around the end of his career.

Or maybe by someone who had been given a tattoo gun for the first time.

Either way, I can appreciate the elegance in Liam's ink. It doesn't mean I like the guy, but it does mean that he doesn't appear on the surface to be a total fuckwit.

That also means he's going to be a pain in the ass to deal with.

He wants to marry Gia.

My email pings, and I open it. Elio's forwarded me the email from MacAntyre.

I scan through it.

Every sentence burns through me like a branding iron.

It's well-worded. The man is perfectly logical. Perfectly sane. He's absolutely thought every aspect of this, and I fucking hate him for it.

It's a good bargain. He's proposing that he and Gia get married in order to satisfy the terms of an old debt that his father had. In return, Elio would receive a fighting force nearly triple our current numbers. He would have unfettered access to the Irish supply of weapons that flowed from Eastern Europe, and he would have exclusive trading rights with the diamond mines that the Irish somehow had a hand in.

I didn't know what else they have a hand in across the world, but I knew what was being offered in the letter was good.

There is one line, however, that lingers in my mind. The words waver in front of my face.

I would give her a position as my equal. The organization would benefit from having Gianna Rossi at my side, and I would never be unaware of that.

He sounds like he knows her.

Like he's talked to her.

And, like he understands her.

My hackles are up. No one understands Gia except me.

Or at least... that's what I thought.

My heart thumps.

I shut my eyes and I take deep breaths. Gia isn't mine. She made that very clear. Even though I thought we were on the same page...

We aren't.

I can't let our personal situation interfere here. I need to find Gia.

Even if when I find her, it breaks me.

AN HOUR LATER, I find it in the harbor's video recordings. An unmarked ship left and headed north.

North.

There isn't much north when it comes to Ireland. Scotland. Maybe Iceland. Canada?

God, it would be fucking terrible if she was back on North American soil and I didn't have a clue.

Elio's words ring in my mind, but more than that, I can't stop thinking about the fact that Gia is with some guy who wants to marry her.

Who didn't exactly give us an "or else" when he sent his message, but the implication was clear all the same.

North.

I pour over a map, doing everything I can to figure out what 'north' might be. Russia?

God I hope it's not fucking Russia.

It's not exactly like I can reach out to any of the Russians, either. Even if she didn't get taken to Russia, they have pretty much a monopoly on shipping anything above the latitude of New York City. Their network of ships and containers and the movement of goods is vast, and if anyone knows where Gia's been taken in the general direction of 'north,' it's them. If they know directly, they'd tell Elio, since Elio and the Russians are fairly tight, but even if they don't know...

They definitely have an idea of where the Irish would hide her, especially in the north.

However.

They also think that Gia and I are dead. If I show up and announce that not only are we very much alive, but we managed to survive the blast that took out two of their top guys, they're immediately going to suspect one person.

Me.

No matter how strong we've been as allies in the past, when it comes to stuff like this, people are pretty predictable. The Russians are absolutely going to think that we had something to do with all of this.

Unless...

An idea pops into my head. It's stupid, potentially to the point of being reckless, but it's the only lead that I have.

I shuffle through my pockets until I find Gia's phone. I tap in her password, then scroll through her contacts.

There's one Russian who owes Gia more than the other ones. Do I think she will be particularly helpful, considering that she got herself kidnapped in Belarus and Gia had to be the one to save her.

And I had to be the one to save Gia.

But she won't squeal. She can't. It would mean violating one of the more sacred rules of this life, which is that people who save your life basically own it until you repay them.

Usually, by saving theirs.

A life for a life. That's how the world goes.

So when the phone rings and a bubbly, valley girl voice answers, I know that no matter what, I have no regrets. The Russians will know that I called their precious princess, but they'll also know why.

And that I had no choice.

"Gia!" Anastasia Novikov, also known as Stassi, chirps into the phone. "Oh my god, it's been like, forever. What are you doing? What are you up to?"

I take a deep breath. "Anastasia. It's Sal De Luca."

She's quiet for a second. "Where's Gia?" Stassi says in a small voice.

"That's why I called. Gia's been taken, and I need your help to find her."

There's a shuffling sound. I think Stassi has put the phone against her chest and she's walking somewhere.

I'm hopeful that it's somewhere private.

"I'm back," she whispers. The ditzy, bottle-blonde voice is gone.

In its place, there's a throaty, even-toned sound.

"Tell me everything," she demands.

I steady myself. There's a moment of regret before I launch into the story.

Gia needs us.

Stassi is the key to finding out where she is.

Even though I don't like it, and even though it's a risk, it's the only way.

With that in mind, my mouth opens.

"Let me start at the beginning."

25

GIA

It's been five days and Liam still hasn't come back, and I'm beginning to think that he's actually kind of devious.

Like, I think this might be a form of torture.

Because I am so fucking bored I'm going to pull my hair out.

There is nothing to do. Literally nothing.

There's wind.

Cold rain that I'm pretty sure is just snow, but in disguise.

Lots of birds and bird noises.

I heard a ruckus and Rowan told me that it was a polar bear in town, but I didn't actually get to see it.

You know that you're bored when you want a polar bear to show up.

Inside the cabin, there is no TV. No computer. There's a bunch of books but I think they might be all in Danish, and so I'm literally just alone with my thoughts.

Well.

And my body, which is doing everything that it can to kill me.

I can't keep anything down. I don't know if it's the fishy smell of bird poop that occasionally wafts up from the beach, or the fact that I'm more anxious than I've ever been in my life, or the fact that I'm stuck in a cabin somewhere so far away from the rest of the world I might as well be on the fucking moon.

But it's getting really bad.

I can see that I'm losing weight. Normally, I'm not necessarily skinny, and I'm curved. I'm short and so all of those curves look quite pronounced on my body, a fact that I'm very proud of, but as I look at myself in the mirror, I can see things I haven't seen on my body in a long time.

There are a lot more bones in my shoulders than I've ever seen before, for example.

It's been somewhere around a week since I had a solid meal. There are lots of weird Danish crackers and things that I'd never eat, and I do my best to keep them down, but it's really difficult.

I do not feel well. At all.

Beyond my body, there's my mind. I'm still completely unsure of what to do about the proposal from Liam.

Do I want to marry him?

My gut, which I'm assuming at this point is 99% baby, says hell no. This, of course, makes sense to me.

The baby would like its father to be married to me. I think there's some kind of biological imperative there, like the baby is in my body telling me what to do with its little baby-mind control stuff.

I huff.

Okay.

Even I know that's illogical. If babies could control people's brains, the world would probably be a much more interesting place. Nicer for babies. Everyone would have paid parental leave...

Huh. Baby mind control.

I'm never going to achieve my dreams of being the first female mafia don with a baby.

Our world is so male-dominated, I have to be as tough as the boys if I stand a chance of getting there. It's like in old Hollywood, where women could never have kids and be considered for a role.

If I'm going to do it, I have to be... different. Curated, sort of, so that the men around me are equally terrified and attracted to me.

That's the only way I know how to function as a woman in this world. It's how I've had success for years.

There's just simply no possible way that I can do any of that with a baby.

I think about the fact that I told Sal I couldn't even date him. Be with him. Fuck, I don't know what exactly I turned down, but I know that the idea of Sal and I together is one that scared the shit out of me, and I didn't want to lose myself in him.

But that happened anyway.

Now I'm lost without him, and I'm pregnant with his baby and...

A familiar feeling creeps up my stomach and I dash to the toilet.

A solid ten minutes later and I'm lying next to the (again, oddly Danish-looking) toilet. My stomach hurts. My body hurts.

If I'm being honest with myself... my heart kind of hurts.

This is the worst. Literally, I would do anything to not be pregnant right now...

As I think that, however, another round of bile rises in my throat.

It's not exactly true.

If I really look into my heart of hearts, I'm not upset about being pregnant with his baby, exactly.

A little squirt who looks like Sal? It's kind of... it's sweet. And if I think about it I get all weepy and soft and I want to curl up into a ball and just hug myself.

I wish Caterina were here.

Honestly, at this point I'm missing my mom.

She and I didn't exactly get along. Well, that's not true.

She was my mom and I loved her more than anything in the world, but we were oil and water.

When I said that I wanted to be a boss like Dad, she had nearly exploded with frustration.

She wanted me to be like Caterina. Sweet. Kind.

A perfect wife and mother.

Those are not bad things by any means, and as an adult I'm now re-thinking what it takes to be a mother (I refuse to think of myself as anyone's wife) but I am not, nor have I ever been, sweet.

Or biddable, which is what my mother had said a good wife should be.

Instead, I turned into a goddamn nightmare. My mother knew it, and she did her best to tame me, but as per usual...

I refuse to be tamed.

However, in this situation, when you're pregnant and so sick you feel like crumpling into a tiny ball, and you have no idea how to get through the next few minutes, let alone the next few days or hours...

You just kind of want your mom.

I'm still lounging in front of the toilet (which is clean, bless the woman who came to clean it earlier) when I hear the front door open.

I shut my eyes but I don't move. If someone wants me dead then... part of the job is already done.

"Gia?"

I recognize that voice. It's one that I haven't heard in a while, but I'd know anywhere all the same.

He's back.

For a heartbreaking second I think that the person walking through the door is Sal, but I know better. Their voices aren't the same. They don't look alike, not really.

But it's the fact that I'm so hopeful for Sal to walk in that makes me kind of hallucinate for a second.

At least, that's what I think.

When a face peeks around the side of the bathroom, my heart does a little sinking thing.

Which, in turn, makes me nauseous, and I turn to use the toilet again.

The man behind me patiently waits. "Well. That was the type of greeting that any gent would be happy to receive."

Yeah, definitely not Sal. The man behind me is definitely the one I've been hoping would never come back.

Because now, I owe him an answer.

I sigh. Through my haze, I smell him. He's got some kind of fresh scent— I'd simply overflow with joy if it was Irish Spring – and I inhale it, noting how it smells before realizing there's another scent as well.

Just Liam.

"Are you well, Gia?" he asks.

I'm pretty sure that there's genuine concern in his voice, which is not helping. A major part of my debate is the fact that Liam is...

Not terrible.

He's attractive. He's actually kind of nice. He's funny in a different sort of way, like he's got an accountant's sense of humor, and he does his best to incorporate feedback from his men.

That, more than anything, has been surprising to me.

What he's done in the last five days? Who knows. I assume that he has access to a helicopter of some kind, because he can't have gone anywhere interesting for a couple of days then come back via boat.

I think.

Again, having no clue where I am is somewhat disorienting.

"I'm fine," I mutter.

Liam arches an eyebrow and looks at me. "You don't look fine."

"Harsh, Irish."

He chuckles. "So that's what you're doing now? Calling me Irish?"

"It's the nicest thing that I can think of," I snort.

Liam sighs and slides down along the wall until he's facing me. He puts his hands on his knees, leaning forward. "Am I so bad then?"

"I don't think I know what you mean," I whisper back.

I know exactly what he means, but I'm not sure that I can answer the question.

He's not bad. Not really.

And I think it's probably about time to give him an answer.

I sit up, my head swirling as I lean against the bathroom wall. "You want me to marry you."

"Yes," Liam says somewhat confidently.

"I don't want to get married, Liam."

He turns, and I realize that I've never said his name before.

His reaction makes everything worse.

Liam's face softens, and his green eyes look down on me with something that seems less like a business partner, and more like fondness.

And I hate that.

He doesn't need to be pleasant to me. We shouldn't be fond with each other.

He's essentially kidnapping me and forcing this marriage, after all.

Whatever path we go down, it can't be one that includes fondness.

My heart feels bruised and sore as I think about what that word means to me.

He nods. "I understand. But there isn't another option, Gia. I can't just let you go."

"You could," I counter.

Theoretically, it's possible.

"You could. We could build another contract. You and..." my voice trails off.

I was going to say that we could tell him to marry Elio's daughter Luna. But she's seven.

He'd have to wait eleven years. And he'd easily be almost thirty years older than his child bride.

And I'd be selling out my niece to save myself.

Liam's eyes harden. "I'll no' be '

"Men in your position marry children all the time," I hiss.

"Maybe. But I won't," Liam confirms.

Damn it.

Why does he have to be so fucking *good*? It's so annoying. Of all the people in the world, the last one that I was expecting to be such a goddamn likeable person is the twin of the person who really was kind of an evil gremlin.

And now he's... offering to be my husband.

There are worse fates. There really are.

But right now, I can't think of one.

"I sent the offer to your brother," he murmurs.

That makes me sit straight up. "What?"

"I emailed Elio a copy of the contract. I want him to be involved because something tells me that Elio is as important to you as my... he's an important sibling."

"Nice dodge there, Ace."

He chuckles. "Would it be so bad?"

"The bad part is that I don't have an option. I'm not in a position to negotiate. It's either marry you or die, I assume," I whisper.

"I'm not a killer, Gia..."

"But you won't let me go, either. So even if I don't agree to marry you, I'm not going to be going home, am I?"

"A prolonged captivity is something that I was expecting, yes," he says slowly.

I snort. "Prolonged captivity. That's what we're calling it?"

"It's kinder than another term."

I shut my eyes. "Maybe we don't need to work with kindness here, Liam."

"Wouldn't you prefer it, though?"

I open my eyes.

Liam shuffles and pulls his legs up closer to his chest. I can tell from the way he's flexing that the muscles in his legs are thick.

Again, normally I'd be attracted to him.

But I just... I can't.

There's nothing when I look at him. Nothing that makes my blood beat or my heart thump or anything even remotely close to attraction.

It's like looking at him through a wall. On one side, there's this knowledge that he's an attractive man, and I can see that. I can see what he offers, and anecdotally, I know that he's a nice human being.

Or at least, one of the nicer ones in the world that I occupy.

But I don't feel him. I don't experience him in any way. All I can feel for Liam is a kind of halfway appreciation of him as a human being.

I definitely don't... care for him like Sal.

My heart skips. I had a very different word in mind, but my brain deleted it right away.

"I'd make you my consort, love," Liam adds.

"Don't say that," I say quickly.

He tilts his head. "What?"

"The L word."

"Lo..."

"That one," I cut him off.

Liam shrugs. "If it's that important to you, I'll do it," he says.

I nod.

"I wouldn't keep you away from the world that we live in, Gia. I know what an asset you are. I know what I have with you."

He might.

But that's not what I want to be seen as. Sal never saw me as an asset.

Sal saw me as... I'm not sure.

But around him, I feel worshipped.

Not tolerated.

A future with Sal though? It's impossible. More so now than ever before. Liam isn't going to give me up, especially if his vision for this is long term.

If I escape, I'm going to start an incident.

If I get rescued, Sal, my brother, Caterina, Luna, the twins... they're all at risk.

The only way out...

Is in.

I sigh. I shut my eyes.

"I'll marry you," I whisper.

The faster we get married, the faster we'll have sex.

And the faster we have sex...

The easier it will be to pass my baby off as his.

Liam sighs. "I wish it was under better circumstances, lo... Gia."

"Yeah," I sigh. "Me too."

Or no circumstances at all.

LIAM OFFERS to write the letter to Elio, and then I can sign it. The terms will be accepted.

I'm going to marry him.

He offers to stay with me for the night, but I decline. I don't want to be around anyone right now.

I just want to be alone.

I still haven't eaten. I haven't had hardly any water. I can't keep anything down, so there's really no point.

Instead of just sitting in the house, I get every blanket I can find and I bring one of the dining room chairs outside. I put it on the porch.

And I look up at the stars.

It's super dark here. I know I'm probably somewhere north of the Arctic Circle too, or nearby, because there's the strangest display of dancing lights that whisper across he horizon.

"Pretty," a familiar voice says.

I give James a hefty side eye. "I'll fucking stab you if I have to, creep."

James slinks onto the porch and settles in. He leans back against the wall and puts a leg up like a cardboard cutout of a cowboy.

"You look ridiculous," I say without looking over at him.

"Says the woman wrapped up like a damn penguin."

"The fact that you think penguins have blankets leads me to believe you're stupid," I retort.

James sighs. He's quiet for a minute. He's genuinely unsettling. The way he can be completely dead silent and quiet at the same time makes me feel nervous. Plus, he just looks shifty.

Red flag if I've ever seen one.

"He has to marry," James finally says.

"You know, I did figure that. When he told me he had to marry to run your stupid empire."

"No," he shakes his head. "I don't think you understand. He has to marry. All of the children did."

I look to the side. "What do you know about that?"

James' gaze darkens as he looks down "More than I should," he grumbles.

Interesting.

"He's no' a bad man."

"I know that," I say from between gritted teeth.

"He deserves a wife who doesn't have... attachments to another man," James rumbles.

I shoot him a quick glance.

Does he know about the baby?

"You and Sal De Luca. You've been making waves," James clarifies.

"Most of the world thought we were dead."

"Clearly," James lets himself have a satisfied little smirk. "I'm no' the rest of the world."

"Oh my god, that's annoying."

He laughs and pushes off of the wall. "Annoying I may be, Gia Rossi. But Liam deserves someone who can see who he is. Someone who recognizes the sacrifice he's made. And someone who cares for both of those things."

I narrow my eyes, but James is already slinking away.

Life with Liam will be fine.

He's level-headed. He makes good decisions.

He's going to let me have power.

I can't marry Sal. Doing so would ruin our relationship. But I have to marry Liam to save Sal.

My hand goes to my stomach.

I'm sorry, little one.

26

SAL

Anastasia Novikov happens to be in London.

For Fashion Week.

Not for the first time, I regret calling her as I wait for her at the Belfast airport. She flew on a regular plane, which is shocking in and of itself, but at least it's a somewhat smart move.

Somewhat.

I'm here to pick her up, and I definitely don't need anything to figure out who she is. Stassi is as recognizable as a famous statue. People turn their heads to look at her as she glides by, and I can't help but be a little impressed.

She's a beautiful, striking woman.

She has skin that's so tan, it looks almost out of place on her thin frame.

She's willowy, tall with long limbs like a model, and even though she's wearing a black sweater dress that covers everything up, she moves in a way that seems more than a little bit sexual.

Her eyes are the ice blue of her father, and her hair is so blonde it's almost white.

Stassi is the exact opposite of Gia. In every way.

Most people do think that she's beautiful, and that's pretty easy to see.

But all I can do is just appreciate that she's pretty. Like one would find a monument beautiful, or a work of art.

Stassi does nothing for me.

She smiles, and I swear the group of high-school aged boys beside me fall apart. "Stassi," I say by way of greeting, taking her bags.

"Oh thank god. I would have been so pissed if you called me Anastasia."

I gesture her out of the airport. I'm aware that she's drawing attention, and that's the type of thing that we don't need right now.

Stassi gets in the car and I shut the door. "Gia told me that you preferred to not be called Anastasia."

"She's the freaking best," Stassi trills.

Her Valley-girl accent is so out of place it's a little jarring. I start the car and we move toward the port. "She is," I rumble.

Stassi grabs some lip gloss and puts it on. "So. She got herself kidnapped, huh?"

"Yes," I grunt again.

"Guess it's a little easier to get kidnapped than even the great Gia Rossi thought, isn't it?"

I shoot her a look, but there's no malice in her face. Stassi's a little concerned, but her lips are curled into a catlike smile.

"Was I right to call you?" I say flatly.

She sighs. "Yeah, duh. I'm like, totally the right person for this."

"And your family?"

She smirks. "Daddy thinks that I'm at Fashion Week, and he has no idea that I left."

I arch an eyebrow. "I find that hard to believe, considering that you've slipped your leash a few times in the past few years."

Stassi's hand flies to her chest in mock indignation. "Slipped my leash! Oh my god, that is so mean!"

"You know what I'm saying, Stassi."

She huffs. "Fine. Daddy doesn't know that I'm here, for sure."

"How?"

"Well, he sometimes gives me bodyguards that are like, really easy to distract."

"Meaning..."

She looks at her nails. "You know that I have a ton of model friends, right? From when I was signed as a model in New York?"

I had no idea. "Yes."

"They're good distractions. And since my bodyguards are usually pretty hot, they like the challenge."

I shake my head. "What happens when they find out you're gone?"

"Um, do you think that any one of them is going to freely admit to my dad that they lost me?"

She has an excellent point.

"That's pretty clever," I say slowly.

Stassi shrugs. "I'm just so over it. Daddy doesn't need to put me under lock and key, you know?"

"You do know that Gia rescued you from the Irish in a warehouse in Belarus?"

"Duh," she rolls her eyes. "How do you think I met her? Or why I'm here? I owe her. A life for a life. That's the code, right?"

"Right," I observe slowly.

Stassi Novikov might be a little more competent than I gave her credit for.

She nods. "So. You think they took Gia north."

"According to the harbor log, yes."

"Did they give coordinates?"

"What?"

She gives me another look. "So there's like, a couple of ways to look for this. They might have registered the RFID under a false name, that's tagging the cargo. They also need to have some kind of declaration of goods for customs, and if they were carrying anything good, someone should have had a UIID card," Stassi says in a very matter-of-fact tone.

All I can do is gape at her.

"I think that if they were trying to like, be under the radar, that they would totally fake the RFID that they registered. But also like people aren't super smart when they do that, so there might be a pattern we can look for in the name..." she trails off after looking at me. "What?"

"How do you know all of that?"

"Do you think I just like, don't pay attention when Daddy and all of my uncles talk?"

I open my mouth. Shut it. Open it again. "Yeah but... I didn't think you'd pay attention."

"Why. Because I'm blonde?"

Because until right now I thought you were shallower than a kiddie pool. "No. Your hair color has nothing to do with it."

"Well. Like I said. My money's on the RFID being false, and maybe even the UIID."

"Can you figure those things out?"

Stassi rolls her eyes at me again. "Duh. Why did you think I agreed to this?"

"To make your debt with Gia even."

"But like, you didn't think that I could figure out how to do that? I need to save her for it to be even. Right?"

She's not wrong. "Right."

Stassi proceeds to unwrap a piece of gum, then smacks it in her mouth. Loudly. "'Kay. So to even the score, I need to save her."

"Yes..."

"Cool. So, I'm going to save her," Stassi says.

"Just like that?"

She grins. Snaps her fingers.

"Like, totally."

It's the RFID tag.

Stassi figures out by looking through the log that it's not only registered under a false name, but it's one that the Irish absolutely were doing their imports and exports with. The ID tag is labeled as 'leprechauns.'

That's rich.

Stassi is chatting with the harbormaster, slowly caressing his face with her fingers. It reminds me so much of Gia that I almost choke.

Instead, I'm running the records looking for a port destination that has logged the same RFID tag.

The computer beeps, and the upload completes. I grab the hard drive that I downloaded the log onto, then get up to leave. Once I do, I sent Stassi a text.

She meets me outside in the car moments later.

"He smelled like, so gross," she says, wiping her hands on her dress. "Seriously, has he even heard of a shower?"

"Here," I ignore her. "Let's check the port destination."

I pull it up on the computer, the flash drive slow to load. Stassi grabs it, scanning through the document.

"There." She points.

I lean in. "Do you know the code for the port...?"

"Yup. That's an easy one. Greenland."

Greenland.

Gia is in fucking *Greenland*.

"Let's go," I say with a snarl.

Stassi's eyebrows raise. "With you and what army?"

"Um. Just me?"

"You think that's going to get Gia back, out of the hands of these Irish dudes who totally have her on the most remote island in the world?"

I frown. "It's not the most..."

"Whatever." Stassi holds up a hand. "It's fucking *Greenland*, dude."

"Okay. So what?"

"You think that he doesn't have like, a whole army holed up there in case someone finds them?"

"I..."

She flips her hair. "I have a better idea."

"What's the idea?"

She smiles. "How good are you at acting? And do you know anything about science?"

"Stassi..."

"Oh, shut up. This is going to be so much fun!"

I shut my eyes.

God save me from smart women.

I think they're going to be the death of me.

OF ALL THE languages that I speak, Nordic languages like Danish are some of the ones that I've never touched. For one thing, those types of languages aren't really involved in my work all that often.

For another, I have no interest in learning them.

So Stassi has to do all the talking for us.

She, apparently, not only speaks Russian, but Danish, Polish, Norwegian, and Swedish.

When I ask her about Finnish, she snorts. "I'm not like, trash, you know."

I have no idea what that comment is supposed to mean.

But Stassi speaks Danish. And apparently, so do some of the people in Greenland.

We manage to use my yacht, which does not look anything like a scientific vessel, into port. Stassi, apparently, can fake an RFID tag with the best of them, and our clearance passes inspection with flying colors.

I also don't know how she sold that we're a science team.

"Why did they believe you," I ask quickly.

She smiles. "I told them that we were on our honeymoon and I'm like so excited to see the type of moss that I've been studying for my whole life."

"And they believed that?"

She smirks at me. "Why wouldn't they? I told them I had a PhD in arctic ecosystems, especially in grasses and moss. And I couldn't wait to see Salix Arctica in its like... natural habitat."

I gape at her. "Salix Arctica?"

"It's the grasses you see out there," she waves at the dingy countryside.

"And you knew this..."

"Oh. I do like, definitely have a PhD in biochemistry. Not in grasslands though."

My eyes are going to pop out of my head. "What?"

"Yeah. It's what I was doing when I got kidnapped."

"You were doing a PhD?"

She shakes her head at me. "Nope! I was doing field research for some post-doctoral stuff."

I have no words.

"Stassi..."

"Yeah, I know," she sighs. "Daddy tells me that people get really weirded out when they hear about the PhD. I don't care though. I love it and I know it's weird."

"It's not weird. It's really damn impressive." My mind goes back over some of the things she said. "Wait. And you model?"

"Yeah. That started out as like a fun thing, but then I got the cover of Vogue France and it kind of blew up from there."

I'll bet it did.

"Okay. Well. Thank you," I say lamely.

Stassi shrugs. "Totally."

"So now, we..."

"I have to wait to see if they have an idea where she is."

"Oh," I nod. "That's logical."

"Like, if the Irish have her here, she's probably hidden. But that guy," she points to someone who looks like a cross between an orc and a giant that's lumbering across the dock, "likes blondes."

"Oh, does he?"

"Yes." She smirks. "And I'm about to like, totally blow his mind."

I watch her saunter away.

She's an incredible woman. I had quite honestly severely underestimated Stassi Novikov. I imagine that lots of people do.

Idly, in another world I realize that I would have been very interested in her. She's insanely attractive and she's ridiculously competent.

Even with her strange Valley girl accent (I didn't know, but maybe she grew up in California?) I feel like she's just running circles around me.

I like that. I like smart women.

But even though Stassi is an amazing woman, I don't think I'm attracted to her. I don't think she does anything for me, actually, other than make me realize that she's pretty awesome.

There's no room in my heart for anyone except Gia.

It's fucking terrifying.

So I watch Stassi shamelessly flirt, in Danish, with the harbor master. I sit back and let my mind drift to the next thing, which includes one of the most terrifying things that I've ever thought of.

I'm in love with Gia. I have been for months. Maybe even years.

If she doesn't love me back...

I don't know what I'm going to do with myself.

Stassi returns, her tennis shoes squeaking on the dock. "I know where she is."

I gape. "What?"

"Gia. I know where she is."

"How...?"

"I promised him that I'd come to his house later. Which I will not be doing," she says in a low voice. "But he told me that there's a guy in town whose father was Irish, and whose mother was on the island. He brought some friends to his town, which is a ways away from here, about a week ago. The friends are two men and a woman," she says with a smile. "So that's totally where Gia is."

"How...?"

"And, if we go now, there's no one up there. The one guy, the one with the Irish father, he's gone to look for supplies. The other two might be there but according to his auntie, who is the person who cleans the cabin, they go out during the day and come back in the evening," she examines her nails.

I heave out a breath. "Stassi. That's incredible."

"Thanks, Sal. So come on. Let's go get your girl," she smiles.

"She's not... I'm doing this for Elio."

Stassi snorts. "Sure. Same as you like, pulled her out of a smoking warehouse in Belarus for Elio? And you totally made sure that she never had to sleep alone until she was okay? And how you like, really seem to be into her?"

"How often do you talk to Gia?"

"Often enough that I know a lot about you," she winks.

She *winks* at me.

"I mean if you weren't so obviously head over heels for Gia, I'd totally do you," she says with a flip of her platinum blonde hair.

"I'm not quite sure how to respond to that."

"So don't," she smiles. "But let's get the hell out of here, okay?"

"Okay," I murmur.

We get back onto the yacht. Stassi has the crew put in the correct village, and we're hauling ass within moments.

As the forlorn coastline whips by, my heart is in my throat. I truly have no idea what I'm going to say to Gia. How we're going to get her out of here. If Stassi doesn't have another trick up her sleeve, and the Irish come for us...

It's going to be an all-out war.

Elio's going to wage war on them anyway if we don't get Gia.

We can't do that.

There's too much at stake.

Caterina is about two seconds from giving birth to twins. Luna's just a kid. Dino has kids who are going to be caught in the crosshairs if anyone ever finds out about them, and God forbid anyone does, because it sounds like his children's grandfather is also going to be hell if he finds us.

Marco is in police custody. To testify against us in a case.

We're so fucked.

In my head, there's a logical path. But I refuse to acknowledge it. If Gia did get married to Liam, then everything would change.

There would be no war.

And we'd have a massive number of allies.

Allies that can protect us from the threat of whoever is the grandparent of Dino's twins. Allies that can help us to secure our new shipping lanes, courtesy of the Irish, who do have some pretty decent networks for smuggling across Europe.

It's the logical choice.

But I will be absolutely fucking damned if it's the choice that I make.

27

GIA

When I wake up, there's a note from Liam on the kitchen table.

Went to grab some bubbly to celebrate. Back soon. X

Next time I see him, I'm going to ask him if he knows how to sign his name or if he just leaves the "X" like a pirate.

The thought should bring me more joy but... it doesn't.

I agreed to marry him.

It was the only way.

I'm just sitting at the kitchen table. My hands are flat in front of me. It's so quiet around me that I'm pretty sure I can hear my hair growing.

I'm pretty sure that I can feel my body feeding the baby inside me. Which is definitely a weird sensation.

"Well," I murmur to it. "At least you'll have some kind of a dad."

Kids don't care who their parents are. They're kind of programmed to love them no matter what. I just never really saw myself as a mom. I mean in theory I wanted to have children, but that was a *very* big theory.

I always knew that I couldn't.

Sighing, I sit back and massage my temples. The nausea is okay this morning, just a light simmer instead of an outright boil. That's a nice respite from the torture that's been plaguing my body.

Liam better not come back with champagne.

I have no idea how to tell him that I can't drink it.

I wish I could look up if having just like a sip is okay in your first trimester. Caterina's been pregnant... I search my memories, trying to think if I've ever seen her drink anything while she's been pregnant with the twins.

I haven't.

But I also don't remember. I mean women find out they're pregnant late and then have drinks while pregnant all the time.

Right?

Fuck. I'm not willing to risk it. I have to make good decisions now, ones that protect this little person.

That's a lot of pressure.

It makes me ache for my own parents. They weren't perfect by any means, and God knows I had plenty of altercations with the both of them over the years.

At the end of the day, though, they loved me. They supported me. They wanted the best for me.

And sometimes you just really want to hug the people who raised you.

Instead, I hug my belly. "I guess that I can hug you, huh kid?"

Predictably, it doesn't say anything back.

"Well," I murmur. "At least I was right about the fact that I needed to be able to pivot and make alliances, and that I couldn't be with Sal to do that."

Ugh.

Maybe I manifested this for myself. Some dark god somewhere is having a hell of a laugh at my expense. Literally, this is the reason that I told Sal he and I couldn't be in a relationship.

I had to be able to preserve my relationship status for strategy.

To get what I wanted from this world that we live in.

"But I didn't get that either, did I?" I murmur to the chillingly quiet cabin.

The lack of noise echoes around me, pressing against my eardrums.

The silence on this godforsaken stretch of land is so pervasive that I can literally hear people in the village a half mile away. I can't make out their words, of course, but the tone and the cadence are familiar.

So when there's an unfamiliar voice in the mix, it's really, really clear.

Mostly because everyone is making excited noises. Or nervous ones. Either way, the tone of the little village has changed.

Nervously, I wander outside.

From the porch, I can see the road that comes from the village. There's a couple of people walking up it. I see a flash of platinum-blonde hair that seems familiar.

And a shape that makes my heart clench.

No.

I sit down on the kitchen chair that I left on the porch last night.

I blink.

That man has to be Sal.

There's no way it's not. I can practically sense the way he walks. He prowls like a jungle cat, and he's got his eyes locked on one thing.

Me.

The blonde comes to me now. There's only one person I know who has a shock of hair like that and is that tall.

Stassi.

My heart sinks. If Sal brought Stassi in to find me, then this is about to be really, really bad.

The Russians don't know that Sal and I are alive. In order to bring Stassi in to find me, Sal would have had to get permission from her father.

And if her father knows...

My eyes widen. Of course her father knows. Liam told me that he reached out to Elio. Which means that Elio knows.

Which means that Sal had to bring in anything he could, because Elio is about to freak the fuck out.

And if Elio freaks out...

My heart feels like it's going to explode. If Elio freaks out, this is going to hell in a handbasket so fast, because he's going to start a war.

Which means that everyone is at risk.

Elio. Caterina. Luna. Dino. Marco.

Sal.

Elio would take care of them, I know. But even though he's good at what he does, that doesn't guarantee anyone's safety.

If he goes to war, it's going to be a fucking blood bath.

I have to tell them to go back. Before Liam comes back. I gather myself and I start marching down the road.

I make it about ten feet before the gunshots ring out.

Sal and Stassi drop down, and I can't help but cry out. I'm reasonably sure that whoever's shooting won't be shooting at me.

Reasonably.

So, I sprint down the road, waving my arms.

"Hey!" I shout. "Leave them alone!"

I don't even know where the shooter is. He could be a sniper positioned somewhere behind me, on the rocky cliffs that appear to be holding back an entire world of ice. He could be in the town.

The gunshots ring out again, and this time I drop. I swear that I heard one whizz by my head.

Why the fuck are they shooting at me?

"Gia!" I hear Stassi yell. She's still probably a quarter mile away so the words are faint. "Are you okay?"

I don't respond. Instead, I look up. I kind of half crawl, half scramble, keeping low.

There's another shot. The dirt road in front of me explodes. Then, there's a shout, and the gunshots stop.

Thank God.

Tumbling forward, I'm half walking, half rolling to where Stassi and Sal are lying in the road. I'm covered in dirt and I'm praying with everything I have that I don't find just the bodies there.

That they're alive as well.

It's the longest quarter mile that I've ever moved. It takes me forever.

When I get there, I kneel down. "Stassi," I say, breathing heavily. "Are you okay?"

She smiles. "Oh my God. Gia. That was crazy."

Stassi. God, I love her. "Stay down," I murmur.

I can't look at Sal yet.

Stassi nods. Then, she frowns. "Have you lost weight? I mean this in the nicest way, but you look like, really terrible."

"I know," I say. "I..."

I don't finish that sentence because two things happen.

First, Sal turns over and stares at me. I feel like he's looking into my soul, and it freezes me.

I've missed him so much that I think I might throw up if I keep looking at him.

Second, I hear the sound of a small-caliber pistol being chambered.

"Get up," Liam's voice says.

Slowly, we rise.

I turn to look at him, my hands on my head.

Any trace of the somewhat passive, gentle man who talked to me yesterday is gone. In its place, there's someone else entirely.

Now, I understand completely why Liam wants to run the Irish mob.

He's a fucking killer.

Every edge of his body seems to have sharpened. His tattooed forearms are cut like marble, and he's holding the Glock like he could shoot us full of holes in his sleep.

Holy shit.

This is worse than Kieran. Kieran at least was crazy out front.

I think that I've completely underestimated Liam.

And, given that Sal and Stassi are sitting right in front of me, that's a very, very bad thing. An hour ago, I would have said that Liam could be reasoned with, and that my chances of talking Sal and Stassi off of this... wherever we are were good.

I do not think that anymore.

"So. Which one of you fuckin' found out where I was hiding her," Liam snarls.

"Um. I did," Stassi says in a soft voice.

My eyes snap to her.

Anastasia Novikov, princess of the Russian Bratva, has a mom who is a big-time entertainment lawyer. She grew up in Beverly Hills, and thus, everything about her screams 'California Girl.' The accent, the hair, the boobs, the legs... she's basically a Beach Boy's wet dream.

But she's fucking smart as hell.

And she doesn't let a lot of people know that.

So if she let Sal in and showed him how smart she really is...

That's kind of a big deal.

For a second, a little wave of insecurity passes over me. Stassi literally is a model. She's hot and she's smart and if she and Sal had to be together to get here...

Then, Sal looks at me, and all of my doubts fly from my mind.

I have no doubt that he's still mine.

He was never yours.

"How?" Liam snarls, pulling my attention back to the moment.

Stassi smirks. "Whoever is in charge of coding the RFID for your cargo smuggling sucks," she says with a little smack of her lips.

Good. She's trying to disarm him by being sexy.

I taught her that.

Slowly, I try to look around, determining the angle of where everyone is standing. If I can just move so that I'm in between Liam and Stassi and Sal...

"You freeze too, Gia," I hear Rowan's voice.

Damn.

"You're expectin' me to believe that you found my boat. You decoded the tag on the RFID for the cargo. And you figured out it was going to Greenland?"

That's where I am? Fucking Greenland? I turn to Liam. "Greenland? Seriously?"

He shrugs. "Rowan has a connection."

Of course he does.

Stassi makes a little noise. "What, like it's hard?"

Liam blinks at her. "Aye. I'd say it is, as no one else has ever found it before."

"Well obviously that's because I didn't try," she says. "Duh."

If I wasn't so nervous, I'd laugh.

"So, you had nothin' to do with this?" Liam growls, pointing the gun at me.

Oh shit.

If Sal thinks that I'm being threatened...

"She didn't know," Sal barks.

His voice is rough. Gravely. Like he's been holding it in for a long, long time.

Or like he's been upset.

Shit.

"She didn't know. Elio sent us because you told him that you wanted to marry his sister."

"And how do you know she wasn't willing to marry me too?"

Sal snorts. "Everyone knows Gia doesn't want to get married."

Ouch.

"Plus, I was there when you took her, you fucking asshole."

Ah. Okay. There's the anger I've been looking for.

Liam swings the Glock at him. "Call me an asshole again and I'll pump you so full of lead you'll make the water toxic when I dispose of your body."

"That's like, a very specific threat, but I kind of appreciate it."

Everyone looks at Stassi, who is staring at Liam with genuine amusement.

Fuck.

I forgot that she's kind of weird too.

"Maybe Gia didn't want to marry someone else because she hadn't met me yet," Liam snarls.

Sal shakes his head. "She would never marry you voluntarily."

Liam looks at me.

Sal looks at me.

Stassi looks at me.

I can't see Rowan, but I'm sure he's looking at me too.

I have to say it. Everything depends on me saying it. I have to look Sal in the eye and I have to absolutely fucking sell this.

His eyes flick down to my stomach.

Ice skates up my spine. *Does he know?*

No. That's just paranoia.

I have to sell this. I drop my hands from my head and saunter over to Liam's side. I wrap my arms around him, and his scent overwhelms me.

He smells nice.

But I prefer cedar to leather.

"Liam makes a very persuasive argument," I say in my lowest, huskiest voice.

I can't look at Sal.

If I look at him, I'm going to fucking lose it, and everything is going to hell.

Underneath my hands, Liam tenses. I can tell that he's surprised by my actions.

Good.

I gently lower his weapon, then slide my hand into his free one. "I guess that you didn't send Elio the good news yet, babe," I smirk.

Liam shakes his head. "No, love. I haven't shared a thing."

I can practically feel Sal's anger. I can't pay attention to that.

Instead, I focus on Liam.

"You know, with news like this, I think it's probably better to deliver a message in person, right? More convincing than an email. More authentic. And I think that Elio did us a nice favor. He gave us the perfect two people to send back to him."

I can't look at Sal. I can't.

"What are you thinking, Gia darling?" Liam rumbles.

I smile. I lean in and plant a kiss on his cheek. Stassi sucks in a huge breath, and I know that if I glance at Sal, I'm going to collapse.

"I'm thinking that we send them back, hale and hearty to share the good news."

"And what good news is that?"

I shut my eyes.

I smile.

"Liam and I are getting married," I say.

Inside of me, something breaks.

I'm never going to be the same.

Nothing is ever going to be the same.

All because of one stupid sentence.

28

SAL

LIAM AND I ARE GETTING MARRIED.

Gia's words rattle around in my mind. I think everyone around us has gone kind of quiet, and they're just staring at me.

Or I'm just hearing the echoes of what she said and everything else is quiet.

Liam and I are getting married.

If she's faking it, she's making a good fucking show out of it.

Because she does not, in any capacity, look like she's faking it.

Gia's fingers glide over Liam's arm. He steps closer to her, like he's protecting her.

From me.

My fingers clench into fists, and I gulp against the pain that's gripping my chest.

Liam and I are getting married.

"Well, first of all, totally want to just say congratulations," Stassi leans in and blows them both a kiss. "I most def want an invite to the wedding." she beams.

"Salvatore," Liam says with a tilt of his eyebrow. "Care to share your congratulations?"

If I open my mouth, I'm going to rip his throat out with my teeth.

I give him a curt nod.

"Oh, come on now. That's the type of felicitations you'd give to your sister-in-law?"

Gia rolls her eyes. "That's so silly, and definitely not how you describe that. Come on, pumpkin," she coos. "Let's go."

"But how will I know that they give Elio the message?" Liam growls.

My eyes go warily to the gun still hanging from his fingers.

The types of messages that we like to leave are not exactly legal.

And if it were me?

I would not leave someone to walk away from me with a message.

I would send a fucking statement.

Liam's eyes glitter, and I see the calculation in them. He's thinking the exact same thing that I've been thinking.

Fuck.

I need to get Stassi out of here.

Leaving Gia behind is going to kill me, but…

Liam and I are getting married.

"We'll go," I manage to grunt.

Stassi's fingers find mine. They're delicate, petite. Elegant.

I'd give anything to feel Gia's fingertips on my skin.

Hell, I'd throw Stassi to Liam if I thought that he had any interest.

I can't see that he does, not any more than I do. We can both appreciate Stassi is a beautiful woman, but…

Gia's the prize, and we both know it.

"Cool. Totally cool. I think Sal and I need to bounce, but again. You're going to just be the cutest couple," Stassi says with a little wrinkle of her nose.

"Come on, Sal," she smiles.

"Follow them," Liam barks at his red headed henchman.

The last thing I want to do is turn my back on them. On Gia. On the baby I know she's carrying.

Fuck.

Fuck.

My heart slams against my ribs. How is this fucking real? My skin feels hot. My muscles refuse to move, and my knees are locked.

I open my mouth.

Shut it.

I stare at Gia.

She stares back. Her hand snakes into Liam's, and she squeezes it.

Her eyebrow arches at me. Like she's daring me to prove her wrong.

Like she's daring me to do something.

That, more than anything, makes my heart feel like it's being shredded.

Gia is fucking with me. She's playing some kind of fucking game. I have no doubt that she doesn't really love Liam, and she's just making him play whatever tune she has in her head. She's going to walk out of this someday, head held high, bullets raining down around her like hail, but she's going to be fine.

Gia has a plan.

Which means that ultimately, my deepest fear is true.

Gia doesn't care about me. She's never cared about me the way that I care about her.

She doesn't love me.

It's that final thought that decimates me.

My chest feels like it's been broken in half, shredded more effectively than any bullet ever could. I'm barely breathing, and when Stassi tugs me toward the dock and the boat, I just follow her.

The red-haired mother fucker follows us the whole way. He has a pump-action shotgun, with two rounds chambered.

I wonder if I'd be able to swing on him before he can unload one of them...

Stop.

There's no point in going over this again in my mind. Gia made her choice. Even if she doesn't feel anything for the Irish fuck, she's not choosing me.

She's choosing the life she always wanted.

I'm the idiot who thought she would change for him.

It's my fault. She told me exactly who she was. Exactly what she wanted.

I'm the one who fucking believed her.

Stassi gives all kinds of orders in Danish that I'm barely tracking on. Somehow, the boat is pulling away from the dock. I'm still halfway impressed that we haven't been shot.

Maybe I'm hoping that I will be.

It would hurt less, I think. I know, actually. Having been shot before, the physical pain is manageable.

What I'm feeling now is agony.

Pure, simple agony.

When the shore of Greenland is finally curving away over the horizon, Stassi comes to sit by me in the dining area. She pulls up two chairs, putting her long legs out over one of them.

"So, like... what's the vibe?"

I stare at her. "What?"

"You look like you've been really through something," she says.

She's braided her platinum blonde bob into two braids that arch over her head. She looks like something out of a sci-fi film with the long cashmere wrap she has on.

How the hell did she get a cashmere wrap?

"I'm fine," I say.

My voice sounds hollow, and Stassi's eyebrows raise. "That sounds like someone who is totally not fine."

"I'm fine."

Stassi sighs. She leans back in the chair and shuts her eyes. "You know, that's who kidnapped me."

I turn to look at her.

"The like... tattooed guy. Except I think the guy who captured me in Belarus was like, totally meaner. This one looks like he could be his twin."

"He is," I say slowly. "Kieran was the one who died."

"Well, he sucked," Stassi says, like she's an Emperor sending a Gladiator to death.

I laugh, a humorless sound that's lost in the roar of the engines. "He kidnapped my sister too."

"Oh my god. No way," Stassi turns, her eyes wide. "Like, what's his deal?"

"I think there's probably some type of inheritance clause. Neither one of them can be the full leader of the gang until they're married."

"Ew. That's like, a thing?"

"Yeah. It's definitely a thing." God, am I going to come out of this talking like Stassi? That's a fucking nightmare.

"Why kidnap Gia, though?"

I shake my head. "I don't know," I say hollowly.

"Like, aren't you guys and the Irish kind of really mad at each other?"

I tilt my head. "Yeah. Why?"

"So, is he trying to be your enemy, or your bestie?"

Bestie... I frown.

I hadn't actually considered that.

There are plenty of women to marry in the world. Plenty of women in the mafia. Hell, there's plenty of women in Ireland.

Why the hell *did* he go for Gia?

"Anyways. Just seems weird, you know? Like I was probably an easier target."

"You sell yourself short, Stassi," I say curtly. "You're pretty fucking formidable."

Stassi makes a little gasping sound. "Oh my god. That is so nice. Thank you so much."

"You're welcome," I respond, a little bemused.

Stassi settles back in her chair. "I bet Gia's planning something."

"She is," I confirm.

"Well, that's like good then, right? Because if she's just planning something, then she'll escape, and you guys can be together forever!"

"She doesn't want me," I say roughly.

Stassi sighs. "Oh my god. Totally not true. I can tell from the way she talked about you..."

"She doesn't want me, Stassi. She wants what she wants more than she wants me."

"You don't think..."

"Don't fucking talk about Gia again," I snarl.

Stassi blinks.

Oh god.

It's like yelling at a puppy.

I feel like a fucking monster. "Stassi, I'm sorry..."

"It's fine," she sniffles. "I know when I'm not wanted."

Jesus fucking... "I'm just a little tired right now."

"Okay," she sniffles again.

Fuck.

Now I made her cry.

I stand and turn. "Where do you want to go?" I ask her abruptly.

Stassi blinks up at me. "What do you mean?"

"Now. Where do you want to go? Where should I return you to?"

"Um... I don't know. Where are you going?"

I narrow my eyes. "Why?"

"Well like, this isn't over yet, right? So don't we need to follow Gia?"

"No," I say curtly. "I'm not following her anywhere."

"Okaaaaay," Stassi draws it out. "So where are you going then?"

I stare out over the ocean.

There's only one place I want to go.

"Italy," I grunt.

I DROP Stassi off in Marseille. I refuse to find out if that asshole French gangster is still there, so I personally see her to the airport.

She gets back on the plane to London without any issue.

And I go to the house that I bought for us.

I don't know how long I'm going to be there. I don't know how long I should be. I assume that eventually, life will resume its flow around me.

Eventually, I'll move on.

Elio will know by now that Gia chose to marry Liam.

Everyone will know soon enough that I failed.

But no one will know how devastated I am. No one is going to see it.

Because I'm not going back.

There's nothing for me there, in that life. I'm not Elio's spy. I'm not anyone's protector. I'm a failure.

A failure who couldn't get the person he loved to love him back.

Days kind of blur together. I eat food if it's delivered. I drink myself under the table, more than once. Wine is free flowing in Italy, and I have a pretty good cellar here.

One that I built for *her*.

Eventually, I decide that I need to change. I'm not sure how long I've been sitting in these clothes, but it's long enough that I'm aware of how I must smell.

When I strip off the jeans I've had on for longer than I remember, something falls out and clatters on the tile floor of my bedroom.

It's my phone.

I haven't looked at my phone in...

A while.

I plug it in to the charger. When the phone is finally charged enough to turn on, I open it and tap my password in.

A barrage of messages flood the screen. They're from everyone. Dino. Elio. Lots from Elio. Caterina.

My eyes tear up at the next ones. *Luna.*

She wants to know where her uncle Sal is.

That one almost kills me, but the next set of messages...

They're from Caterina.

I'm having my babies now, you butthead! Where the heck are you!

Please come home. I need you.

Sal, I'm scared.

Please come back.

Fuck.

I slam my head back against the wall.

I missed the birth of my new niece and nephew. And my sister needed me.

But I missed it.

I'm sulking, pissed at myself, when I hear a knock.

There's someone at the door.

I grab my gun and march toward the door, pointing it down and out of the way.

No one knows about this place, I reassure myself.

The knocking, however, is loud.

Firm.

Like someone knows I'm here.

I get next to the door. I'm still trying to bank on the fact that no one knows I'm here, when a very, very familiar voice floats through the door.

"Sal! I gave birth a week ago and I had to drag my butt all the way out here and if you don't open up I'm going to lose my mind!"

Caterina.

I take my finger off the trigger and toss the gun down. I open the door.

Caterina is standing in front of me. She looks like hell. Her hair is up in a messy bun, her skin is really pale. Her eyes are kind of watery, and she's holding herself against the doorframe like it hurts to stand.

I've never been happier to see my sister in my whole entire life.

For just a minute, I don't care how she got here. I don't care why.

I'm just so happy to see her that I want to collapse.

"Cat..." I start.

She pushes in and wraps her arms around me.

And starts sobbing.

Cautiously, I put my arms up and hold her. "Um. Hi?"

"You're so mean, Salvatore De Luca!"

Uh-oh. It's never good when Caterina uses my full name. I cringe, ready for the lecture that's definitely about to follow.

Caterina pulls back, her eyes streaming tears. "You are the worst out of all my brothers! I hate you! Why the heck did you do that?"

"Do what?"

"No one has seen or heard from you in three weeks!"

Three...

"Oh," I say softly.

"Yeah. Oh," she snarls at me. "I literally had the babies a week ago. One. Freaking. Week. And no one has heard from you. Stassi Novikov, of all people, was the last person to see you alive. I swear to God, Sal...My body hurts so much right now and if I don't sit down in the next ten seconds I'm going to pee on you so let me in!" she cries.

Meekly, I move out of the way. My sister hobbles into my house.

And collapses on the couch.

Gingerly, I move over to her. "Um. Are you okay?"

"No!' she shrieks. "I thought you were dead!"

"How did you find me? No one knows where..."

"Oh, your secret real estate empire? The fact that you're secretly a billionaire and you just never wanted to tell us?"

I blink. "How..." my voice trails off.

Then, I shut my eyes. "Stassi."

"Yeah, Stassi. Did you know she has a master's degree in like computer hacking or something like that?"

"And a PhD in biology," I mutter.

"Didn't know about that, but yeah. Stassi Novikov. She found your little real estate side hustle," Caterina waves her hands at me. "And she found you here. And she helped me get on a plane while her uncle distracts Elio at like a Russian spa, so you better get the hell back on this plane and come back with me!"

"No," I whisper.

Caterina sits up. "Huh?"

I shut my eyes. "No, Cat. I can't go back."

"Why not?"

I don't know if it's the fact that she's, my sister. Or that she flew on a jet one-week postpartum. Or that she's here in front of me.

But I take one breath.

And then I tell Caterina...

Everything.

29

GIA

"So. Will you tell me the reason that you refuse to have some bubbles, then?"

I look up from the bed in the little cottage.

Sal and Stassi left... a while ago. I'm not really sure. Days, maybe.

A couple of them at least.

Maybe more.

I can't really tell time, as it is. All I have is just the sickness. It's nearly constant. I haven't eaten anything in days. Weeks. No clue. My body feels terrible, and my skin looks like I'm actually turning into a ghost.

I should be worried about myself.

But I'm... not.

There's kind of a strange distance around me. It's like I'm watching myself sink further and further into a kind of weird, corpse-like state, but I can't really do anything about it.

I'm watching myself from a distance, while also being inside myself...

Yeah.

I don't know how to explain it, but it's all that I have.

I look up at Liam. "I don't do alcohol," I say weakly.

He shakes his head. "You know, I'm not a fool, Gia," he whispers. "I think there's something a little more wrong with you than a need to take care of your liver."

Fuck.

I turn back, facing the wall and hiding from him. "I said I'd marry you," I say dully. "It's too late for you to back out of it now."

"We aren't married yet, Gia."

"Might as well be," I mutter.

The bed dips as Liam sits next to me. He's quiet for a minute.

"I'll say the baby is mine, if that's what you're worried about."

I laugh.

It's a bitter, harsh sound, even to me. I laugh and laugh until I want to cry, because any more motion is going to bring my stomach up again.

"Gia?"

"I wasn't worried," I mumble.

That strange, distant feeling is back. Except this time, I also feel like I'm not even in my own body.

I kind of feel like I'm... floating.

Interesting.

"Gia..."

"I wasn't worried, Liam. Even though you're a piece of shit and I can't stand you, you aren't a bad man."

"No?"

" 'S why I offered to marry you," I slur.

Now I feel kind of drunk. My body doesn't respond to my commands anymore. Also, there's a long black hole at the edge of my vision.

It's getting narrow....

"Gia?"

Liam's voice is so distant. How did he end up so far away from me? He was just on the bed next to me.

"Gia," he says.

God, he sounds kind of frantic. Idly, I feel motion, like someone is gripping my arms.

If I knew how, I'd giggle, because it feel so silly that someone would be holding my arms and I don't even know what they're doing.

"Gia. Stay with me," Liam's voice sounds high-pitched. I should probably reassure him. That's what a wife does, right?

Fuck, I wish it was Sal with me.

Sal...

As Liam's voice fades into the darkness, I let myself think of Sal.

I miss him so fucking much, it feels like it's part of my body. Like I'm growing my pain, just as quickly as I'm growing the baby inside me.

The darkness takes me.

And Sal's face is the only thing I see.

THE DREAMS of Sal fade away. In their place, an annoying beeping sound, and bright, blinding lights, appear.

Groggily, I try to figure out what the hell shifted. I cling to the memories of Sal like they're some kind of lifeline.

There are more voices around me.

Ones I don't recognize.

"Where am I?"

The question is on my lips as I blink, opening my eyes and looking around.

"Ireland, darlin'," an older man's voice says.

I shuffle up before groaning and flopping back down. "Why am I in Ireland?"

"Because you passed out and Liam MacAntyre is not the type of man who lets a woman pass out on him."

I blink again.

The world around me swims into focus. There's an older man, presumably a doctor if his white coat is anything to go by, in front of me.

He's staring at me.

So, I stare at him.

"How are you feeling?"

I look down, frowning.

I'm in a hospital bed. In a hospital gown. There's an IV in my arm that's steadily dripping fluids into my body.

But I feel a little better. "Um. Well, if I felt like I was at a zero beforehand, I feel like I'm probably a three now?"

"That's good. Strong improvement. I'd take a three over a zero any day," the older man says.

"Who are you, again?"

He smiles. "I'm Dr. O'Malley."

"No. Like the cat in Aristocats?"

Dr. O'Malley laughs again. "Sure. Not Thomas, though. My first name is Joshua."

"Missed opportunity on your parents' part," I grumble.

"Aye. Well. They still got a doctor for a son out of the bargain, so I suppose that's alright then, now isn't it?"

I lean back on the hospital bed. "Okay, Dr. O'Malley. Catch me up. What happened?"

He rolls a chair over and sits on it. I like this guy. Something about him reminds me of like, the grandfather I always wanted.

My actual grandfather, the one that's still alive, is wanted in Sicily for crimes against the state.

Dr. O'Malley leans his head on his arms. "You're pregnant."

"Yeah. And?"

"Would you like to know more about the status of your wee one?"

My heart stops. "Oh my god. Is the baby okay? Please..." my voice trails off.

Dr. O'Malley nods. "Aye. The baby is fine. Growing like a weed, and you're about nine weeks in."

Nine weeks.

It's been nine weeks since Sal and I...

That's a long time. It's a long time for me to be in Greenland, too. My mind strays to what's going on at home. Elio will be losing his mind, of course. After Liam sent Sal and Stassi packing, they would have informed Elio about me.

I bet Marco has given his testimony. I wonder if he's been let back into custody.

And Caterina...

Shit. Caterina will have her twins any day now.

And I'm going to miss them.

I squeeze my eyes shut. "Okay. Baby is fine."

"Do you want to know the gender?"

I shake my head. "No."

That's something that I would have wanted to do with Sal. If I'm on my own... I'm happy to just have a healthy baby.

"Well that's settled then. A fine choice, to be surprised like in the old days. Baby's fine. But you, mom," the word feels very weird to me, but I also realize that it's the first time I've been called that, "you are not fine."

I blink. "I'm not?"

He shakes his head. "No, sad to say it. You've got something called hyperemesis gravidarium."

"Hyper..."

"-emesis gravidarium," he finishes.

"What's that?"

"Means that you've got extreme morning sickness."

I laugh. "Okay well. I didn't need to go to the doctor to know that."

"You did, though, because you were on a fast path to organ failure if you didn't."

"Oh," I say softly.

"Yes. Oh."

"How can I fix it?"

He shrugs. "Might go away on its own soon. Past nine weeks, it diminishes somewhat. I've given you fluids and some anti-nausea drugs. You'll be up to eating soon enough."

I grimace. "Will I?"

"That's the idea, darlin'."

I lean back in the bed again and sigh. "So did I already screw this whole parenting thing up?"

"Oh, sweetheart," Dr. O'Malley says. I peek at him, and he's looking at me with genuine kindness. "You've been doin' the best you can, or so I hear."

"Yeah. And now I have hyperemesis gravidarium."

"Something you never would have known or been able to control for. No one knows why some women get it and some don't. Just part of the process."

I shut my eyes. "I'm not prepared for this," I whisper.

"Being a mother? Or being married to my Liam?"

I peek at him. "Your Liam?"

"Aye. He didn't tell you about me, then?"

My eyes widen. "You're the uncle."

His chest puffs up. "One and the same, love."

"You're the reason he's not a total sociopath."

O'Malley's eyes go soft. "Well, I tried."

"You did a good job. Really," I say.

He gives me a little half grin. "As will you. The two of you, I presume?"

"Who do you mean?"

"You and my Liam."

"Oh." I nod. "Yeah. He's... he's going to be the dad."

"He's a good boy," the doctor says. "Now, let's get you something to eat..." he turns, ready to grab a tray that's behind him on the counter.

But, in that time, something happens.

I hear gunshots.

O'Malley and I recognize the noise at the same time. He dashes over to me and starts to pull the IV out of my arm.

"I'm sorry," he whispers. "This might hurt."

It does. It very much does.

I clench my teeth against the pain. The tubes are out, and O'Malley is handing me some clothes.

"Here," he says, "Take these."

He pulls at a drawer and grabs a pistol. The sound of yelling, and the echo of gunshots, is much louder now.

"Where are we?" I ask in a hissed whisper.

"Dublin. If you can get..."

He doesn't finish the sentence.

The door explodes open in a haze of smoke and dust. I scream and duck, trying to hide underneath the gurney. There are two shots. A yell. A grunting noise that sounds suspiciously like someone being choked.

Then, silence.

Hiding under the hospital gurney, I'm shaking. My breath feels like it's too loud. I know that they can hear me.

There's no way they can't.

There are three sets of feet in the room. Three men.

I'm going to have to shove the bed on them. Then I'll have a chance to run.

I shut my eyes.

One.

Two.

Three...

I shove.

There's a bunch of male grunts, and then I'm running. I sprint down the hallway, wearing my hospital gown, my boobs wiggling underneath them. I'm so thankful for the pants, I think that I could kiss Liam's uncle.

I can see the end of the hall. I book toward it, my feet slapping on the hospital tile.

I'm almost there. I can touch the door. I reach my fingers forward…

There are arms around my middle.

I grunt, aware that they're pushing down on my lower belly. I curl back, lessening the pressure there.

No one is going to hurt my fucking baby.

I kick and scream, scratching at the person with everything I have. Based on the scratchy outfit, though, he's wearing some kind of tactical gear…

"*Puta*," the man hisses.

I'll fucking show you a bitch.

I twist, ready to scratch at his ears, when there's a sharp pain in my neck.

Like a needle, plunging into my flesh.

I start to feel groggy. My arms grow heavy. I have one last, lucid thought before the darkness consumes me.

Please don't be a sedative that will hurt my baby. Please.

THIS TIME when I wake up, it's not gentle. It's like coming out of a nightmare.

God damn it.

"Where the fuck am I now?" I gasp.

"Well. At least they were right about something. You have a mouth on you."

I do not know that voice.

Also, it's so fucking hot that I don't know what to do with myself.

With a groan, I struggle to open my eyes. I blink, looking around the room.

I'm in another fucking hospital. That's good, at least.

Now my hyperemesis won't kill me.

Or the baby.

"Tell me where I am," I demand.

From the shadows in front of me, a shape emerges.

I study him.

Another old man. Severe eyes. Gray hair that's carefully coiffed. He's wearing a suit, wool, despite the absolute swamp like heat.

He smirks. "Good morning, Gia Rossi."

"Where. The hell. Am I?" I grit.

The man sighs. "Do you know who I am?"

"No," I say flatly.

I don't have time to fuck around with this person. I need to get out of here. I need to get back to…

Shit.

The only person I can think of is Sal.

He's the only person that I want. I've been passed out in too many places. I'm weak. I'm vulnerable.

I want someone to protect me.

And the only person I trust in the entire fucking world is Sal De Luca.

"Hmm," the man says, pacing closer. "Well. You should."

"I should what?"

"Know who I am."

"Why's that?" I bark.

He smirks. "Because I think you know the father of my daughter's children."

Oh.

Fuck.

He nods. "Let us start again. You, Gia Rossi, are in Brazil."

I blink. "Brazil."

"Yes. Brasilia, the capital, to be precise."

"And why am I in the capital of Brazil?"

His grin spreads. "Because you're a problem."

"How?"

He tilts his head. "That question is odd."

"Not really. I'm just a problem for a lot of people. You're going to have to be more specific."

The man chuckles. "Ah, the rumors about you appear to be true to the very letter."

"Can't say I know the same about you," I challenge.

The man sighs. He stands. He surveys me, looking down his nose.

"Let me introduce myself then. I am Benicio Souza."

Oh.

I'm super fucked now.

My eyes must give something away because his smirk widens. "I see you've heard of me."

I need to play it cool. "I heard you didn't do so good in that last election. Frog farm failure, was it?"

This man is a fucking nuclear bomb.

He's not just a mob boss. He's a politician.

A bully.

A warlord.

He's the king of the castle down here in his little corner of the world, and he rules his kingdom with an iron fucking fist and absolutely zero morals.

I'm so fucking dead, it's not even funny.

I have to leave.

"And why am I a problem to you, again?"

"Two reasons." Benicio settles into a chair across from me. The pulse meter on the screen next to me twitches, and I curse it.

I don't want him to know how nervous I am.

Benicio extends one finger. "First, you are going to marry someone who needs a wife to rule his kingdom, and I cannot have him inherit that throne."

That's Liam. I stay silent, staring at Benicio.

"Second—" He adds another finger. "You are the sister of my most bitter rival. By marriage, you are the sister-in-law to the father of my grandchildren, and when they come for you..." His smile is wicked.

It sends chills down my spine.

"When they come for you, Gia Rossi, they're going to wish they had never once heard my name."

30

SAL

After I finish, Caterina stares at me for a second.

Then, she nods. "Okay. So. You love Gia."

"Yes," I whisper.

"And you're just going to give her up?"

I blink. "It's not that simple."

"Yeah, I think it's pretty flippin' simple, brother of mine."

"Gia doesn't want me," I say bitterly.

"And you think that would stop her?"

Glancing up at her, I can see that Caterina is serious. "What does that mean?"

She huffs. "I mean, if I know one thing about Gia Rossi, it's that she's more than just a dog with a bone. She's a wolf with a kill. She practically invented the whole concept of being persistent. She wouldn't stop if she loved you."

"Caterina," I sigh. "I know. That's why I know she doesn't love me back. Because if Gia loved me back, she'd do everything in her power to show me."

"Except... she wouldn't, would she?"

"What do you mean?"

"She's Gia. So, she'd do everything in her power to keep you safe. If she thought that the only way to keep you safe was to tell this Liam guy that she was going to marry him..."

I shut my eyes. "She doesn't want me, Caterina. Just leave it alone."

"That's not true!" Caterina says.

Her voice is shrill. I realize, looking at her, that she's more exhausted than I thought.

"Caterina," I say gently. "How did you get here?"

She waves a hand. "Helicopter from Milan. Jet from New York."

"I think we should probably go back..."

"No. Not until you admit you can't give up on her."

"Then she shouldn't have given up on me!" I yell.

Caterina blinks.

My chest is heaving, and I feel like I'm panting. I look at my sister, and the full force of my pain cracks through me.

"She should have chosen me. She shouldn't have given up on me. She should have showed me that she's just as into me as I am into her," I croak. "She should have loved me back."

"Oh, Sal," Caterina says.

I put my head down. I don't want to cry.

That's not what I'm going to do right now.

Caterina rushes forward and pats my back. "It's okay," she soothes. "It's okay."

"I…"

Caterina kind of stumbles, and I catch her. I look down and realize that the bags under her eyes are dark, and her lips look a weird shade of bluish purple.

I remember that my baby sister just gave birth, not even a week ago, to twins.

"Come on," I say, lifting her up in my arms. "Let's get you back to New York."

"Ugh. Fine," she mumbles sadly. "But only if you come back with me. I can't lose you, Sal," Caterina says sadly.

"I'm sorry, Cat," I say sincerely.

I am sorry.

I missed my niece and nephew being born.

I missed Luna's end-of-year celebration.

I missed a lot of things.

As we head back to the helicopter pad, where Elio's helicopter is waiting, shiny and sleek in the night, I have a glimmer of hope.

Maybe I can't be loved by Gia.

But Caterina loves me. My nieces and nephew will.

Maybe I don't need to be loved by Gia to survive.

The lie sounds so good that as I put Caterina onto the helicopter, I almost believe it.

Almost.

THE TWINS ARE... loud.

Elio and Caterina's house has gone from being a place of relative peace, with Luna as the only source of chaos, to being complete and utter mayhem.

Two are a lot of babies to have at once.

Caterina and Elio need all the help that they can get.

And I guess in this situation, that comes in the form of... me.

Dino's kind of around. He's actually been helping more in the warehouse and with the shipping stuff. He and I take turns running the business and running the organization, while Elio and Caterina do their best to keep up with Luna and the babies.

It's insane.

We have to call in multiple Zia's and Nonna's for backup, and still, these babies run us like we're a military regiment.

No one talks about Gia.

However, I know that I'm not the only one who feels her absence everywhere.

Everyone does.

Luna, true to form, is the most direct about it. She asks for Zia Gia all the time. She's taken to sitting in Gia's room in the house, writing her letters and notes and sprinkling them around like some kind of summoning spell.

It doesn't work, of course.

None of us have the heart to tell her that it won't bring Gia back to us.

I don't know if she's married by now. It's been two weeks since I came back with Caterina from Italy, and none of us have heard anything.

She probably is married.

She's probably somehow managed to convince Liam that the baby...

My eyes shut.

I can't think about our baby. It's an area of me that hurts so badly, I can't even reach for it.

Caterina knows.

But she promised not to tell anyone.

I know she'll keep my secret. There's no point, not really.

Gia made her choice. She chose to make the alliance for the organization, for the family.

She chose Liam.

And she chose Liam for both of them.

One day, I'm just coming off of baby duty, heading to the garden of the house. I need a minute to catch my breath, to breathe in the dusk, and to just be outside. Elio and Caterina have kept a nice garden, which is unusual for the somewhat suburban home that he's purchased for them in upstate New York. I'm just coming around the hedge of roses that Caterina is so proud of, heading toward the cement benches that border a fountain, when I run into Elio in the garden.

He shoots me a guilty look, leaning back against the concrete bench. "Apologies. I needed a moment to breathe and enjoy the silence."

I laugh. "Yeah. I get that. I thought that Luna had a set of lungs as a baby, but she's got nothing on your two."

He wrinkles his nose. "I think that they try to out-compete each other in terms of the decibel levels of their cries."

"Possibly," I nod. "Either way, it's damn impressive that two people who are so small and so helpless can be so powerful."

Elio quirks a small smile at that. "They are fierce," he says in an approving voice. "Just like their mother."

Only time will tell if they're fierce like their Zia Gia as well.

I don't respond. After a while, Elio nods at me. "Caterina has the babies then?"

"Yeah, but they're sleeping," I say. "Put them down just now."

"Good. And Dino's coming to take over?"

"On his way now."

Elio sighs. "I am glad Dino has this chance to redeem himself."

I think about what Marco told us. I haven't revealed that to Elio yet either. There will be time for that.

There will be time for everything, I guess, once life settles in around the babies again.

"How are you doing, brother?" I ask Elio.

He shoots me a look. "I am... I don't know," he says honestly.

I tilt my head.

Elio sits back and shuts his eyes. "I am happy to have the babies here. I am happy to see my family. Being around Caterina makes every one of my days brighter," he says, knocking his head lightly against the cement retaining wall that the bench is positioned against.

I nod, settling into the bench across from him. "Yeah. That's kind of nice."

"It is a dream, Sal. One that I did not think I could ever hope for," Elio says softly.

I still.

My brother-in-law is a stoic man. He rarely shares anything about himself, and I'm pretty sure that Caterina is the only person who really knows him inside and out.

Well.

Caterina and Gia, of course.

"I did not think that, in this life, I could ever have such a treasure as a wife and children. Let alone a wife that I liked. Let alone one that I love as much as I love your sister."

"You're good for each other," I say.

Elio nods. "The only thing missing today, is my sister."

I freeze.

Continuing, Elio nods his head at me. "I know that you two had something. That was made clear to me after you took her back from Belarus. The fact that Gia consented to this marriage with the Irishman... I did not think it was real, Sal. I truly thought it was some kind of plot, made up by the fucking Irish to get back at us once again."

"I did too," I add.

"But then Stassi told us that Gia agreed to it. That she saw with her own eyes. But I have not yet heard from my sister. So I still do not believe that this is true," Elio adds.

"So why haven't you gone after her?"

"Gia is smarter than I am," Elio says. "She is more ruthless. More competent. She is built for this in a way that I'm not. I trust that if Gia decided to do this, then she has her reasons, and she will someday tell them to me."

I snort. "Yeah. Someday."

"The biggest surprise, however, is that she decided to marry someone who wasn't you."

I freeze.

I don't want to look at him, because if I do, I'm going to... I don't know. I've kept my feelings about Gia on a pretty tight leash and bottled up deep inside my soul.

I can't let them out, or I'm going to probably explode into a thousand pieces.

"Gia has never wanted to love someone. Not anyone other than myself, or Luna. She has always kept everyone at arm's reach, because I think it would have been too big of a betrayal if they didn't see her for who she was. For what she wanted. I didn't think such a man could exist. And then you came along," Elio looks at me. "You pulled her out of a burning building. You treat her like a queen. You recognize all that Gia is, and for the first time ever, her excuses were futile."

"Futile?"

"She had no choice but to love you, Sal. I think for someone as in control of herself as Gia is, the inevitability of falling for you was probably more terrifying than anything. She could not control for the variable that was you, and it probably scared her."

"And that's why she married him?"

Shaking his head, Elio looks at me. "We do not know that they are married yet."

"We can assume…"

"We should not assume," he says firmly. "If your sister has taught me anything, it is that we should never assume."

"Oh yeah? Anything else Caterina's taught you?"

Elio's lips curl. "To hope, Sal. She has taught me to hope."

He pulls himself off the bench and stretches. "One of the guards is out tonight. I'm going to patrol the outer perimeter, and then I will head inside to relive Dino."

"Rodger," I nod.

Elio walks away, leaving me in the garden.

I let the stillness of the night consume me.

Everyone but Gia, it appears, knew that we were meant for each other.

It's validating, but it doesn't mean anything.

In the end, Gia chose him. She didn't choose me.

And I need someone to choose me.

I'm out in the garden for a lot longer before a noise registers in my mind. It's weird, like shouting…

Elio.

I sprint for the front gate. By the time I arrive, I can see two shapes in the area in front of the driveway, on the outside of the gated entrance to Elio's home.

I move closer, my eyes searching in the dim light to figure out what's going on.

Elio has someone out front, somewhere in front of the iron gate to his home.

At gunpoint.

As I get closer, I recognize the tattoos, and the lean, almost whip-like stature. The mop of dark hair.

The irritatingly green eyes.

Yeah, I'd know this man anywhere. The very sight of him is burned into my brain, and I'll never be able to get it out again.

Liam.

Rage pours through me, and it takes every scrap of my self-control to not haul off and punch this asshole in the face.

"Here to gloat, you Irish fuck?" I spit at him.

Liam looks up at me, and rage simmers in his gaze too.

Good.

Beating the shit out of him might cause an inter-organization war, but I don't fucking care anymore.

All of the peace that I thought I'd made in this situation is gone. In its place, all I have, all I am, is anger.

He is the one that Gia chose. For better or worse, this man is the one who has access to her body right now.

To her heart.

And I don't give a shit anymore about him.

"It is altogether unclear to me what this man is doing at my house," Elio grunts.

His accent is thick. He's tired, he hasn't slept well in weeks, and he's more than a little protective right now.

I nod, looking at him. "Looks like he doesn't know when he's fucking invited," I snarl.

"No. No indeed. Which begs the question, Irish," Elio says coolly. "Why the fuck are you at my home?"

Liam looks at Elio. He clenches his jaw. I can see it working in the lamplight from Elio's front gate.

When he turns back to look at me, his words fall like boulders, sinking into the ground around me.

Anchoring me to something that I'm terrified to hear.

"Gia's been taken."

Elio and I both explode.

"What the fuck?"

"What do you mean? Didn't you take her from us?"

"Why the fuck weren't you watching her?"

"Why the fuck did you not...?"

Liam holds up a hand, and we both pause. He looks back at me, his eyes locking with mine.

"She's been taken. She's in Brazil."

My eyes widen.

Next to me, I hear Elio suck in a breath. "No," he murmurs. "There is no way."

Liam nods. "She's been taken by Benicio Souza.

The name hits me square in the chest.

"What the fuck?" I murmur.

Benicio is bad fucking news.

He's a despot. A politician who functions somewhere between a cartel leader and a warlord.

Getting something small from Benicio? Impossible.

Stealing back a person?

It's a fucking death sentence.

Liam shakes his head. "I'll have time to explain later. But Benicio took her because she belongs to me."

I growl at that.

Liam shakes his head again. "But I can't get her back alone. I need your help," he says.

Elio and I look at each other.

I look back at Liam.

I know that Elio's waiting on me to respond, but the answer is the easiest fucking thing I've done in a long time.

I nod. My mouth opens.

And without hesitation, I decide.

"Let's go get her."

31

GIA

In all the places that I've been kidnapped lately, this one is definitely my least favorite.

It's so fucking hot that I think I'm going to explode.

True to form, though, as Dr. O'Malley predicted, the severe morning sickness is diminishing. I can actually function, get around, and after about a day, Benicio's doctor who has been taking care of me takes me off of the IV fluids.

It's great.

What's not so great, however, is the fact that I'm a prisoner in this giant, hot house with no air conditioning.

Benicio hasn't been here since my arrival. I've seen the doctor twice, then after the IV ended, I haven't seen him either.

Since then, for the last few days, I've been completely alone.

Someday, I'm going to get kidnapped in New York City, or Los Angeles, or somewhere cool.

Bora Bora.

Tahiti.

Somewhere that I'm not so miserably bored the entire time.

The house is clearly set up for captivity.

There's food that shows up every day. The house gets cleaned, except for the room that the doctor showed me to after he released me from the hospital bed that's in yet another room.

It's on the third day, during a shower, that something catches my eye.

There's a hair in the shower that's not mine.

I lean closer, picking it up off the bottom of the wall next to the floor. I hold it up like it's some kind of evidence and I'm at a crime scene, and I look at it in the light.

Despite the fact that it's super weird, and that I normally would be completely grossed out at the fact that someone else's hair is in the shower with me, this time, I'm a little excited about it.

Because it means something really important.

I'm not alone. Well, I'm less alone than I was before. Because while I knew about the guards, and I knew about the doctor and Benicio himself, there's an element that I didn't know about in the beginning.

There's another woman here.

Someone who might be sympathetic to my cause.

Someone who might be able to help me get the hell out of here.

I shut the shower off and grab a towel. I wrap the towel around myself, getting out of the shower.

This is definitely someone else's hair. It's way longer than mine and stick straight, but dark brown, maybe even black.

I've never been so happy to see someone else's hair in the shower.

I dress quickly in some of the clothes provided for me, wondering if these also belong to the other woman.

It's highly possible. If that's true, she's somewhere around my height, with curves similar to mine.

I try to not pay attention, though, to the way that the pants stretch across my stomach.

There's definitely a baby in there. And it's about to get harder and harder to hide that.

I have got to get the fuck out of here.

But how can I find this other person? Is she a prisoner like I am?

Or is she in on it? She's voluntarily here?

Ugh.

I can't count on any of those things.

I've been in Brazil for about a week when the pattern of the people around me becomes clear.

The guards switch at three-hour intervals. They watch a bunch of telenovelas in Brazilian Portuguese, for several hours.

They are truly terrible guards.

Which makes me think that we're probably in some kind of remote area.

If they're not worried about someone coming up to the house and have the time to lay around and not do anything but watch telenovelas, then there's some other security involved.

I don't think there's an army posted around us. I think we're probably on some kind of estate in Brasilia.

That would explain the security lapse.

Meals all come in on a truck, delivered from what I assume is a catering company. That's probably my best bet for escape.

The meal truck is my ticket out of here.

Other than the guards, I don't see another soul. Haven't all week.

But there's another woman here.

Step one, find her.

Step two, convince her that I'm just a run of the mill pregnant lady, and I need some goddamn help to get out of here.

Step three...

Escape.

Today, after I've dressed and I'm ready to go on my usual wander, I wander around the house, eying it for weaknesses or places that I've missed in terms of assessing the structure for possible ways to escape. I have renewed interest in this now because I feel like I can finally see a light at the end of the tunnel.

Except, in order to achieve step three of my plan, I need to find a way out. Poking around the house, that's what I'm looking for.

To my knowledge… yeah. There's nothing. No hidden escape routes

Except, there's a hint of perfume in the hallway.

Hmm.

After lunch, I go back to the room that I've been sleeping in. I grab a piece of toilet paper and an eyeliner, which appears unused (I will not be putting it on my eyes though… gross) and I scribble down as much as I can. I write my name. I write that I'm a prisoner.

I write that I want someone to help me leave.

I write it in English and Spanish because I figure somewhere between those two languages, I'll hit something that looks accurate to someone.

Then, I leave it on the sink.

To my knowledge, no one has cleaned this bathroom except me.

To my knowledge.

I take another walk around the house. After about an hour, when the guards are switching their shifts, I head back to the room.

The scrap of toilet paper on the sink is gone.

THE NEXT DAY AT BREAKFAST, I smell that perfume again. It lingers in the dining room, something deep and floral. Rouses and oud, maybe. Just something that smells halfway between something my grandmother would wear, and some kind of classic floral smell.

I have to say, being pregnant and having a super nose is partly really cool, and partly God awful. Identifying scents on the first try? Cool.

Realizing that an entire country smells like fish and you never want to go there again?

Let's just say, Greenland has been well and truly ruined for me, forevermore.

Take that one off of the tourism list.

But the perfume encourages me. She's here.

Somewhere.

I just have to find her.

The day progresses as normal. I move through the house. The guards watch their telenovelas. I eat food. I pretend I'm not pregnant.

I pretend that I'm fine being here, trapped in Benicio's house.

Right before dinner, I go to take another shower. At this point, the showers are the only thing that are keeping me from going nuts because they're just something to do with my day.

I open the closet, ready to grab the stupid sweatpants and shirt that just keep appearing for me in there when I freeze.

There's a woman looking at me. From the closet.

If it wasn't something that I've been hoping for, this would be literally the stuff of nightmares.

I do everything I can to hold my shit together. I stare at her.

She stares at me.

She's definitely my height. She's curvy, like me, but with the sheet of dark, straight hair that hangs down her back in a glossy wave. Her eyes are brown, her skin is dark brown, and she has full lips and high cheekbones.

She's very pretty.

I narrow my eyes at her. "You?"

She nods. "My name is Marisol. You're a captive of my father, no?"

"I am," I say quietly. "I'm Gia." Her accent is barely there, but I can still tell that she's probably from somewhere local. Her English is good though, so I'm sure she's spent some time in the States as well.

Marisol gives me a quick up and down before she continues. "And you're pregnant."

How the fuck... do I just broadcast this information on a freaking billboard every time I walk into a room?

"How did you know?"

"Hard to hide it now," she gives me a meaningful glance. "Those sweatpants were the only ones that fit me back when I was pregnant with my twins."

Pregnant with...

My eyes widen. "Holy shit," I murmur. "You're Dino's girl?"

The name makes her whole body transform. First, an unmistakable longing crosses her face. I know in a split second that Dino is definitely the father of the twins she referenced a minute ago.

Then, her face hardens, and her eyes flash.

I know then that while Dino has something of a special place in her heart, she's also not going to be begging him back anytime soon.

"How did you know about Dino?" she says with a hiss.

I raise my eyebrows. This is a calculated risk that I'm about to take.

"You're not going to believe this," I say with a small grin. "But I'm kind of his sister-in-law."

Marisol's eyes get big. Her fingers clench.

This is going to go one of two ways. Either she's going to hate Dino so much that she's going to completely betray me and tell the guards that I've been trying to get loose.

Or she's going to help me get out of here so that she can find Dino herself, and rip into him.

I have a feeling that she isn't going to betray me.

Marisol looks at me for another minute. She narrows her eyes. "You really know Dino?"

There's a touch of longing in her voice, that makes my own heart echo in response.

"I do."

"If we get out of here, can you take me and my kids to him?"

The kids? Shit.

"I'll do my best. Where are they now?"

"With my mother."

"And is she on good terms with your father?"

"She shot him in the chest. She's the reason he has to use a machine to help him sleep at night, to inflate his lungs while he's resting."

I tilt my head. "I appreciate how your mother solves problems."

"As do I." Marisol grins.

"'Kay. So. Kids are secured. You want to talk to Dino?"

Marisol nods. "I have some things to say to him."

I love a woman hell bent on vengeance.

"Cool. So. We getting out of here or what?"

She deflates slightly. "I've been trying for months," Marisol admits. "I am also being held here."

"By your own father?"

She nods.

"Why?"

"I... have disobeyed his wishes," she manages to grit out.

I wrinkle my nose. "Well. I suppose that's a problem that does come with having a father."

"Sorry."

I wave my hand. "It's fine. Old news. More to the point, we need a way to get the hell out of here."

Marisol shrugs. "Like what?"

I feel positively feral when I look at her.

"Can you drive one of those food trucks?"

We make our move the next day.

The guards watch their stupid telenovela. They don't think we can do anything important. Clearly, someone's taught them that women are not to be concerned with.

They're clearly fucking stupid.

One of the things that Marisol and I do is put something special in their afternoon coffee. Marisol showed me the little greenhouse that's attached to the house, and there's something in there, taking advantage of the sweltering heat.

Aloe Vera plants.

Which make a great laxative.

We put enough in the afternoon coffee of the guards and the food delivery workers, to make them more than a bit uncomfortable. Marisol delivers the coffees, as she is always supposed to do, apparently, and she makes sure that every single one of the six men around us drinks their coffee to the fullest.

It's not a sedative.

But...

It's enough of a distraction.

When the last guard leaves, clutching his stomach, that's when we make our move.

"Come on." I grab Marisol's hand.

She's more than happy to comply.

We sprint for the little pickup truck connected to the kitchen via a doorway. The door is still open, and we book it straight through.

Climbing in the truck, Marisol starts it.

It roars to life, and she throws it in gear.

We rumble away.

"Does this thing go any faster?" I look back out the back window. We probably have about ten minutes before they notice we're gone.

Maybe more. It's not like they did a great job of checking on either of us during the day.

"No," Marisol says. "The estate is on seven hundred acres of land…"

"Seven hundred! I thought we were in a city?"

"Brasilia is kind of like Washington DC. It's a district and a city and also contains a lot of wildlife parks, because, you know. We protect our forests," she adds.

I raise my eyebrows. "Is that true?"

"I'm not about to get into the politics of Brazil with you, white girl."

"I'm Italian, if that helps."

"Doesn't help me," she says with a snort.

I smile. "I like you, Marisol."

"You just need to trust me, Gia. We're going to get out of here. You don't have to like me one bit."

"Guess it's a bit of a bonus then," I say, slamming into the side of the truck as she whips around a curve.

The next curve, she takes slower.

But unfortunately, there's gunshots that ring out over us as we trundle around.

"Shit," I say looking back. "They found us. Put this into high gear," I look at the truck.

"It is in high gear," Marisol grits.

We both duck as more bullets rain down on the truck's roof.

"Shit, Marisol. Maybe we could take like a side…"

There's someone coming up the road at us.

Three ATVs. Three men in helmets.

Three men with giant, semiautomatic rifles strapped to their chests.

"Fuck!" I snap.

Marisol turns the wheel, and the truck screams, turning slowly. For a second, I think we're going to tip over, and I brace myself to roll.

But the truck, heavy, tips back. Instead, we come screeching to a halt.

My heart is in my throat. We're dead. We're caught.

One of the men with a helmet lifts his rifle. He points it toward us.

"Get down!" I yell at Marisol, shoving her forward.

I wait for the round to puncture the truck.

I hear the gun go off. I wait for it to shatter my world.

Nothing happens.

Cautiously, I lift my head.

The guys on the ATVs aren't shooting at us.

They're shooting at the guards, racing down the trail at us.

Who the hell…?

One of the riders pulls his helmet off. He looks straight at us.

My ears ring.

My eyes feel like they can't focus on anything. There's something surreal about this.

Because the man in front of me, beautiful and bloody, his eyes staring into mine.

That man is Sal De Luca.

He came for me.

32

SAL

THE GUARDS WERE NEVER EXPECTING US.

That much is absolutely clear.

We wipe them out in about ten seconds. I hate to admit it, but Liam's plan isn't a terrible one.

And it fucking worked.

What none of us expected, however, is to see two women hop out of an extremely beat up Ford F-150.

One of whom is the woman that I love more than anything in the world.

Gia.

She looks terrifyingly thin.

God. Has she been eating? What the fuck has the Irish fuck been trying to feed her? I'm about to round on him to yell at him, but I can't tear my gaze away from her.

I hear Liam dismount his ATV, and Elio follows.

"Gia," Elio calls. "Are you hurt?"

She snaps back in Italian. She says she's okay. She's not hurt. She's fine and she would appreciate not being treated like a child.

All I can do is watch her perfect lips wrap around each word.

I want to run to her so badly. I want to gather her in my arms. I want to kiss her and make sure that she never, ever has to worry about anything ever again.

The whole world feels frozen around us.

Until gunshots once again break out, and we hear shouting coming up the road.

"Fuck," Elio says, ducking down. "We need to split up. Irish, you come with me. Grab the girl and let's go. Sal, take Gia and get the fuck out of here," he shouts. "We'll meet back at the airstrip."

The airstrip is about ten miles back down the road.

I don't question him. I just obey.

I grab Gia by the waist, hauling her up on the ATV. I seat her in front of me. I put the helmet on her head, not bothering to be delicate about it.

The ATV roars to life, and I hit the throttle.

We scream away. While the trail flies by us, my mind is swirling through all of the dozens of things that I want to say.

There aren't enough words in my mind to describe how I feel right now.

Seeing Gia alive? Whole? Fine? It's a huge relief. When I first saw her pop out of that truck, I had never been more relieved in my entire life.

I've also never been angrier.

She looks like hell. She got kidnapped. Twice. By two different, very dangerous, people.

I want to tell her how I feel about her. I want to tell her everything…

The ATV jerks, tossing us both sideways. I hold Gia, trying to keep us both on the stupid thing.

"Fuck," I mutter.

It's blown a tire.

I hit the brake before it can throw both of us off, and I grab Gia. She pulls off the helmet. "Stop manhandling me, asshole!"

"Come with me," I say, grabbing her hand.

"Sal…"

But she doesn't take her hand away from mine.

Vaguely, I remember that we passed some horse stalls down the road. I pray that we're close enough to get there…

I smell them before I see them. "Bingo," I mutter.

Gia tenses. "You can't be serious."

"Why?"

"I'm not supposed to ride a horse when I'm…"

She pauses.

She looks up at me.

I know what she's about to say, but she doesn't say it.

Fine.

"You can ride a horse while pregnant, Gia," I murmur to her. "You were a champion equestrian in high school. Remember?"

Her eyes widen, but I don't take the bait, instead, I grab her and pull her forward. "It's the only way out."

Gia looks at me for a minute longer, then nods.

Twenty minutes later and we're riding a horse down the trail toward the airstrip, where Elio and the jet are waiting. The threat of retaliation from Benicio Souza is very real. He's luckily out of town right now, so the challenge is not the man itself, but the three hundred or so men in his private militia that he's left behind.

And the fact that he appears to have some kind of burning grudge against Liam and the Irish that surpasses even my dislike of the Irish.

The urgency is there. But as long as there's no one actively pursuing us, we can afford to be slow and steady and careful.

This all factors into the horse I chose, the pace we set, and how firmly I have my hand wrapped around Gia's waist.

I went for a chestnut horse. I'm not sure why, exactly, but it seemed the calmest one of the bunch, which is pretty fucking important at the moment. I'm well aware that a fall for Gia could risk both of them, so I try not to push the horse past anything faster than a trot.

We also don't have a saddle. And the sketchiest halter that I've ever seen.

But the horse can take a trail that the ATV couldn't. The horse, also, is apparently a very intelligent creature, and seems to know the way east.

The way back to the airstrip.

"So how do you know how to ride a horse," Gia asks.

"It's the one thing Caterina and I wanted to learn how to do. That was different than Marco and Dino," I clarify.

"The girl I was with is Dino's baby mamma," Gia murmurs.

"No shit?"

"No," she whispers.

We lapse into silence. I can't hear anything behind us, other than the jungle creaking and moving through its' day. I assume that Liam and Elio can take care of the people coming from wherever they were keeping her.

But Gia is with me.

And even though this is very, very wrong, it's hard for me to not feel like it's very, very right.

"I know about the baby, Gia," I finally say.

In front of me, she twitches. My arm tightens around her waist.

"Why didn't you tell me?"

"Don't ask me that," she whispers. "Please Sal. Don't ask me…"

"Are you going to go back to him?"

"Who?"

"Liam."

"I don't... I don't know," Gia says.

I've never once in my life heard Gia sound so unsure.

"Do you care about him?"

"No," she answers quickly.

"So then why did you do it?"

"Because, Sal, I had to," Gia says.

The horse flicks its ears back, like it's listening to our conversation.

"Explain to me how you had to," I grit out.

"He fucking kidnapped me. I wasn't going to escape Greenland on my own. And, if Elio came for me, he was going to start a war. Against the Irish, who have the most foot soldiers out of any of the gangs we know," she barks at me. "I wasn't going to have you die just because I was stupid enough to get kidnapped!"

"You weren't worried about me..."

"Yes I fucking was, Sal!"

The genuine fear in her voice echoes, falling off of the leaves of the forest around us like rain.

"I was terrified. If there was a war, do you think that everyone I love would have made it out okay? Do you think that you and your brothers, and your sister, and my brother, and our nieces and nephews, all would have fucking survived? I've lost my parents. I've lost aunts and uncles and cousins. I can't and I won't fucking lose you, Sal. Not like that. Not in some kind of a war that's being fought over me, and absolutely not when it's well within my power to prevent it. So you can just fuck right off with all your dramatic bullshit, okay?"

I snort. "Dramatic bullshit?"

"Yes, Sal. That's what it's called when you're not being practical or logical or..."

"How the fuck is it practical to say that the woman I... that you are going to marry another man!"

"You don't get any say in that..."

"Gia. You are carrying my goddamn baby!"

"And if I didn't want to have the baby then I wouldn't!"

"Of course, but you are! And if you have the baby and you let another man raise him, don't you think that it's not fair to me? To rob me of the chance to be a father? A hus..." I stop at that.

We won't get to that.

Gia doesn't respond.

The horse continues to clop down the trail.

Neither one of talks as the trail eventually widens back into the road. There's no one on it.

"Are the other two Elio and Dino?"

I shake my head. "Elio and Liam." She must not have heard Elio yelling orders earlier.

Gia tenses.

"Liam was the one who came to get Elio and me. You were taken from his custody, and he didn't have the resources to come get you. He showed up at Elio's house..."

"And you were there?"

"Yes," I confirm, aware that if she's in front of me she can't see me nod. "Caterina brought me back."

"Did she have the twins?"

"Yes."

"And everyone's okay?"

"The twins have a set of lungs on them like you would not believe."

Gia gives the tiniest chuckle at that. "That was me. Our mom joked that I screamed loud enough for the two of us and Elio was the silence I lacked."

"They're fine, Gia. Luna misses you."

She tenses again. "Fuck me, Sal. Why did you have to say that?"

"Because it's true."

"But when you stay stuff like that..."

"What, Gia? It reminds you that people love you? That they care about you and miss you? That you're more than just someone who's useful?"

"No," Gia mutters. "It just makes me feel like shit."

I stop.

We manage to get to the air strip without incident. The horse, luckily, seems to know the way home, and after Gia and I slide down off of its back, it gives us a little shake of its head and plods back the way it came.

Gia still isn't speaking to me.

The plane is open, and we hop on. Minutes later, Elio, Liam, and the woman get on. Gia immediately whisks the woman into the airplane's back room, locking all of us out.

We stare at the door while the pilot boots the plane up.

Elio turns to Liam. "What can we expect now that we've taken her back."

"I think the bigger issue is probably the other woman, who looks suspiciously like Marisol, Benicio's daughter."

"Fuck me," I say, looking at the door.

Liam shrugs. "An eye for an eye. Isn't that how it works?"

The plane's engines roar, and we start to taxi down the runway.

Elio sighs. "But since we're all in this together now, it seems appropriate to make a truce, no?"

Liam nods. "The enemy of my enemy," he sticks his hand out. Elio shakes it.

I don't bother.

The plane climbs in the sky, and I settle back in my seat.

We have Gia.

I can figure the rest out.

BACK AT ELIO'S HOUSE, both women shower. Caterina cries. Luna is thrilled to have her Zia back.

Finally, Gia retires to the room we used to share together. When I go in to bring her some food, I find that she's dead asleep in the bed.

I would love to watch her, but that would be too fucking weird, even for me.

So, instead, I leave.

There's a shape huddled next to the door. I turn to address it as I step forward.

"She's sleeping," I say, coming out of the room.

Liam's lurking outside. He leans against the wall like some kind of parody of a Marlboro man.

I shut the door, clearly closing him out of the room that holds the mother of my child.

And my unborn child.

"She loves you, you know," Liam whispers.

I look over at him.

"When I saw you two looking at each other in the forest, I knew. I think I knew long before that, if I'm bein' honest with you," Liam says slowly.

"And are we honest with each other?"

He looks me up and down. "You love her too, don't you?"

Honesty. "Yes," I say clearly. "More than anything in the world."

He nods.

"She wouldn't tell me about the baby. She just... kept throwing up her guts. Over and over. Every day. When I took her to my doctor in Dublin, he said something was... a condition she had. He knew it right away though," Liam adds. "Something to do with extra bad morning sickness."

My eyes shut. "You don't have to make me feel terrible for not being there for her. I already feel like shit," I snap.

"I'm no' tryin' to do that, Sal."

It's the first time he's said my name.

Liam sighs and peels himself off of the wall. "I need to marry to solidify my title as the leader of the gang. It's in the rules of the organization. Signed, sealed, delivered."

I glance up at him.

He makes it sound like he hasn't married Gia...

Yet.

"I need to marry. But I'll no' have a wife who hates me. Call me an idiot if ye must, but like fuck am I going to marry another man's bride," Liam says with a little shrug of his shoulders.

"Irish..."

"And I'll be havin' you use my name," he says, glaring at me.

I shake my head. "Liam."

"I'm no' a bad man, Sal. And I'm certainly no' going to stand in the way of what is between you two."

"Why?"

The question has multiple layers. *Why not stand between us? Why not take what you want in order to run your organization? Why back off now?*

"Part of it? Whatever's going on between you is white hot, and if I'm in the middle of it, I'm gonna just end up burned," he says with a wry grin.

Liam claps a hand on my back. "When she wakes, make it right," he murmurs.

"If you think I can make Gia do anything, then you're fucking crazier than I am."

He laughs. "Gia won't be forced. But I've a feeling that you can offer her something no man can. And that, my friend, is going to lure her more than anything I could ever offer."

With that, Liam MacAntyre walks out of the hall. I hear him say goodbye to Elio.

Beyond that, I don't fucking care.

I turn to the door.

My hand shakes when it's on the handle. I turn it, the door squeaking lightly on its hinges.

I take one deep breath. I push the door open.

Gia is everything.

She's my queen.

She's my future.

She's the love of my life.

If I have to spend every day for the rest of my life making that future happen for us, I will.

And that future starts now.

As long as I can convince her.

33

GIA

For the first time in what feels like forever, I wake up in a familiar bed.

With familiar surroundings. Familiar smells.

And a familiar shape lurking in the chair in the corner.

"Watching me sleep is pretty creepy, you know," I grunt at him.

Sal shifts. "How are you feeling?"

"Fine. Wasn't feeling bad," I mutter.

Except for the fact that I crashed, slept for around sixteen hours, woke for approximately five seconds to pee, then fell back asleep again.

It's been nearly a full day since we got back to New York.

So no, I'm not feeling well. Not by a long shot.

But I'm not quite ready to let Sal know that either.

I'm still recovering from the mad dash out of Brazil.

There was, of course, the whole situation with Marisol. Marisol, once we landed in New York, asked to be put on a plane to Florida.

Her kids were there.

Her dad wouldn't find her, she assured us, if she was with her mom in Fort Lauderdale.

I hadn't been a fan of the idea, but I also didn't want to say anything against her. I gave Marisol my number, then watched her head right back onto the plane.

"She doesn't want to see Dino," Elio had murmured.

I was inclined to agree.

From there, we went back to the house. Then, of course, the sleep.

Now, I'm here, in my room.

And Sal is just lurking.

"You sure you weren't feeling bad?"

"Can it," I mutter. "I'm fine now."

I curl around my stomach, ever so slightly, and Sal's eyes drift down to my abdomen.

"We haven't talked about this," he says softly.

I shut my eyes.

I don't have any other way to stem the tears that are pressing at the edges of my eyes.

We haven't talked about it because we didn't have a chance.

Because we didn't have any time alone yet.

Because I haven't told Elio, and I assume Sal hasn't either, and neither one of us is willing to tell him without talking about it first.

But we don't want to do that either.

"Sal…"

"Gia…"

I laugh softly. This is what it's like with us.

Always on the same page.

Never at the right time.

"I want the baby," I say.

The words echo in the room. I haven't said them out loud. It's a little late now, certainly, but I realize that I definitely want to keep this little kiddo.

Sal nods. "Okay."

"And I don't know what else I want," I say.

"Okay."

"Because I still want to have the whole thing. The organization. I want to be the boss. I want to live here. I want to live in Italy. I want to take a plane all over the world. I want to stay home. I want…" My voice trails off.

Sal's silence is looming.

"I don't know what I want," I say honestly.

The truth is, I want everything. But what I want more than anything in the world is to be…

Myself.

Whoever that is.

Maybe it changes. Maybe I am never just one thing.

But right now, the thing that I want is to be Gia Rossi, and I don't know how to do that anymore.

"Will you marry him?"

I look over. "Liam?"

Sal doesn't answer. His eyes, however, are drilling into mine with an intensity that's so powerful, I almost can't look back at him.

"I..."

I don't have an answer.

I can't.

I have to.

I can't.

I must.

My stomach tightens, and I put a hand on my abdomen.

Fuck.

Sal rises. He looks down at me.

There's something simmering in his gaze that looks a lot like a word somewhere close to wrath.

Rage.

Pain.

Torture.

I ache to have him look at me with the love that he once had.

But from the way he's looking at me now…

I think I might have ruined that entirely.

"You need to decide," Sal says roughly. "And Gia, I don't want to be left out of my kid's life. Even if you marry him. I want to be the father that… I want to be something to my child," he grunts.

God, the pain in his voice is absolutely killing me.

For the first time, I realize something.

Sal has been unwaveringly on my side.

He's been my biggest fan. My most devoted follower.

He's lifted me up every step of the way and I've never, ever, not once, doubted the fact that Sal cares about me.

But the way he's looking at me now…

Abruptly, Sal turns. He marches out the door, which slams shut behind him.

I shut my eyes.

I think I might have broken Sal De Luca. For good.

And I've never been really good at fixing anything.

Especially not when it comes to saying things like "I'm sorry' and 'I was wrong.'

And, even most especially, 'Please forgive me.'

When the door opens again, I'm not even facing it.

I'm turned to face the wall.

I couldn't bear it if Sal came back in. But I also wanted it to be him.

Either way, I am one hundred percent too scared to look over at the door.

"Gia?"

I know this voice too.

Reluctantly, I rolled over. "Liam," I murmur.

Liam sits in the chair that Sal had occupied... an hour ago? I couldn't keep track of time anymore.

Liam studies me. "How are you then?"

"Shitty," I answer honestly.

"Aye. You look it too."

"Thanks. Really nice words to say to your future wife."

Liam leans back. "Somehow, Gia darling, I feel that's no' going to happen."

I sit up. "Are you rejecting me?"

He shakes his head. "No. But I'm no' stupid. I can practically feel the tension between you and Sal. I'm not about to step into that. Not in a million years," he growls at me.

"Why does it matter?"

"What do you mean, why does it matter?"

I snort. "The type of relationship that we're going to have. Why does it matter if I am... hung up on someone else?"

Liam casts a meaningful glance down at my stomach.

"Okay well that aside, why does it matter?" I retort.

"It will always matter," he says softly. "And I…" he stops.

My eyes widen. "You were hoping that we… that you and I would…Oh. Liam," I say. I'm genuinely sad for him.

Liam really wanted us to be a thing. An actual thing. He wanted us to be in love. Someday.

His lips tilt slightly. "Well, a guy can dream, can't he?"

"Liam MacAntyre. Dreaming of falling in love. I think that's really sweet," I say.

"Aye well. I'd appreciate you keepin' that little observation to yourself," he says softly.

"If you keep my secret, I'll keep yours."

"That, I can do."

We're quiet for a moment. Then, I look over.

"What will happen to the truce between our organizations?"

"I think we're in for a penny, in for a pound at this moment."

"Meaning?"

"Meanin', I'll be around. And you'll have a hard time stopping me. I think that makin' a mutual enemy of Benicio Souza is gonna be a little more than hell for all of us, so I'd say that we need to stick together, yeah?"

I grimace. "That's not exactly a good thing, is it?"

"Enemy of my enemy."

"Okay then."

He stands, ready to leave. Suddenly, something occurs to me.

"You still need to marry someone in order to inherit, right?"

"Aye."

"What about… Stassi Novikov?"

He shakes his head. "I think my brother already tried that, remember?"

"Sure. But Kieran was an unhinged sociopath. You… Stassi might be interested," I say.

Liam studies me for a moment. "Anastasia… comes with more than just a starter pack of problems."

"Yeah but—" I shrug. "Don't we all?"

Liam gives me a little, tight smile at that. "I would have liked to have been your husband, Gia Rossi."

"I would have made a terrible wife, if it's any consolation."

He nods. "I think that wife is not the role for you."

My doubts come back, swarming me like bees. "Um. Okay."

"Because Gia, there is no role that fits you. You are your own thing. A force of nature, an enigma. You are no one's wife. But I think that maybe someone will be worthy of being your consort. The moon has the sun. Darkness has light. Even forces of nature have a balance, Gia. I hope you find yours. I truly, truly do."

My mouth hangs open.

With those admittedly amazing words, Liam walks out.

Leaving me alone. Shocked. Processing his words. Trying to figure out what the hell is going on.

Again.

THE THIRD TIME the door opens, it's Elio.

"Hello Gia," he says in Italian.

Oh boy. If Elio's speaking Italian, it means that he's too emotional to use English.

"Hi brother," I respond in Italian. I gesture to the bed, and he comes to sit next to me.

We're quiet for a minute.

"How are the babies?"

"Doing well," he murmurs. "Caterina is such a fantastic mother. Every day I am in awe of her."

Of course she is. The stark contrast between us pulses. Caterina is the perfect mother.

I'm not.

"That's good. Congratulations."

"You sound less than thrilled."

I look up at him. "Not at all, Elio. Really. I'm so happy for you. You have everything you wanted. You have Caterina. You have three beautiful children. Good for you, making all your dreams come true."

I shut my eyes, because even I can tell that comment was a little bitter.

My brother's arms wrap around me. I relax, sagging into his hug.

Elio is my best friend. He's the only person in the world, aside from Sal, that I trust.

I love him like he's a piece of my own heart.

So, when he hugs me, I can't hold the tears back anymore.

I start sobbing.

It takes forever, but when I'm done, Elio leans back. "Do you want me to have Sal killed?"

I blink. "What? No."

"Is he the source of your pain? I can have him killed. In an instant."

"First of all, that would make Caterina very upset," I say with my eyebrow raised.

Elio shrugs. "She would understand."

"Second, you lunatic, no. Even if Sal is the source of my pain... he's also the source of all my joy."

Elio tilts his head.

I let my hand drift to my stomach. "Don't freak out. And don't kill anyone."

"No promises."

"Okay, then no truths."

"Gia," he sighs.

"Fine. But seriously, no murders. Pinky swear." I hold up my hand, hoping the childish gesture pulls him out of his funk.

Elio groans but shakes my pinky. "Fine. Pinky swear, no murders."

"I'm pregnant."

A flood of curses in Italian and English pours out of Elio's mouth. He leaps up off the bed, roaming back and forth in the room.

He spins. "I'll fucking kill that Irish shit."

"You said no murders."

"I'll…"

"Elio!" I shout.

He pauses.

"It wasn't Liam," I say softly.

It takes Elio a solid ten seconds to understand. His eyes go wide, then narrow.

"Are you fucking kidding me? Sal?"

I nod.

The Italian curses are back. This time, they're mostly directed at the people in the Rossi and De Luca families, and our inability to use reliable birth control.

Finally, he seems to remember that I'm there, and that I told him I'm pregnant.

Elio comes over to me. "Are you well?"

"I'm fine. For real."

"And Sal…"

"He knows. He's fine with whatever I choose."

Elio snorts. "He better be."

"I'm having the baby."

His eyes go soft. "Gia…"

"But Elio, I don't want to be limited to one thing. I want to have the baby. I want to run the Rossi gang with you. I want to be able to fight and flirt and fuck—"

He cringes at that, which I do find hilarious, "And do whatever I need in order to make myself happy."

"You want to run the organization."

I freeze.

I've never actually told him that before.

"Yes?"

"Why didn't you tell me?"

There's genuine relief in his voice.

My mouth opens. It shuts. It opens again. "That's it, just why?"

"Yes. Why didn't you tell me sooner?"

I blink. "Um. Because I thought you'd laugh at me like Dad did?"

"Jesus, Mary, and Joseph. No, Gia," he sits, with relief crossing his face. "I want you to be my equal. We can divide it. We can each take a section. We can do whatever it takes. I'm so fucking tired of doing this alone. I want to spend time with Caterina and the children. I want to be able to fucking relax sometimes."

"Oh," I whisper. "I thought you only wanted to do that when the babies were born."

He shakes his head. "No. If you are offering help, I want it. Two siblings. Together. That sounds remarkably wonderful, don't you think?"

"Well. Yeah..."

Elio swoops in and hugs me. "Done, sister dearest."

Well.

That was easier than I thought.

When the hug is done, Elio looks at me. "So. Are you marrying the Irish?"

"I don't think he'll have me," I sigh.

"Good. I'd rather not have him for a brother-in-law anyway."

I roll my eyes. "As if you get a say."

"Of course I don't, Gia. And I know better than to tell you what to do. But whatever you choose, I love you. And I will love my niece or nephew as much as I love you," he grins.

I shrug. "Thanks, brother."

With that, Elio leaves.

Sitting on the bed, I smile.

I guess that some things were a little easier than I thought.

34

SAL

Elio has a shooting range in his backyard.

Today, I am taking full advantage of that fact.

I have earmuffs over my ears. My eyes have protection on them.

And I'm absolutely pulverizing the target in front of me.

In my mind, it's just a stand-in for all the things that I can't control, and all the issues that I have with the world at large. It's just me, shooting the hell out of everything that bothers me.

It's no wonder that I don't hear Elio come in.

He waits until I need to reload, then hits the button on the target that drags it closer to me. I turn, not realizing it's Elio until I see him behind me.

I don't say anything.

He steps forward and looks at the target. "Well. That's one way to do it then."

"What do you want?"

He looks at me square in the eye. "You're going to be a father."

Ah. "Gia told you?"

"She did. which begs the question as to why my own brother-in-law, and my second in command, did not?"

"That's complicated."

He sighs. "You know, you and Gia are two fucking peas in a fucking pod."

"Is that a good thing?"

"No," he grunts.

I turn back to the target, hitting the button that will pull it back out into the space. I aim my pistol at the target, emptying another magazine into it.

"So, what are you shooting?"

"Nothing specific."

"A certain Irish bastard?"

I lower the weapon and look back at Elio. "Why do you ask?"

"He left; you know."

I blink.

"Liam MacAntyre. Left a phone number and walked right on out. Asked for Stassi Novikov's number too."

"Did you give it to him?"

Elio shrugs. "*Sì*, I did."

"Why?"

"If he marries the Russian girl, he'll stay away from the women in my family, no?"

It's a little brutal, maybe even ruthless.

But it is practical as hell.

"Stassi isn't what you think," I say.

Elio shrugs. "Are any of the women in our world?"

I don't answer that.

He sighs again and sits on the metal bench next to me. "Marry Gia."

"No."

He looks up at me. "You're going to knock up my sister and not marry her?"

"I would if she would let me," I sigh.

Elio nods. He puts his hands on his knees.

"You know, Gia sometimes gets in her own way."

"You don't say?"

"You can't tell her what to do. You can't change her mind. But the thing about Gia is that, pretty reliably, she can be convinced."

"Convinced?"

He nods. "For my dad, it was money. He could buy her anything and she'd be happy to do what he asked. My mom would bring her to the spa to get her nails done. For me, I'm her twin, so I just have to annoy her into it."

"And this has what to do with me?"

He stands. "I'm sure you have your way of convincing her," he grunts.

With that, Elio leaves.

I'm more than a little stunned. Because if I'm not mistaken, I think Elio just told me to seduce his sister.

And I think, unfortunately, he might be right.

Of all the things that Gia and I have, the way we connect best?

It's with no talking whatsoever.

I DON'T REALLY KNOW how to go about this.

While I know that I need to step in there and show Gia exactly who we are and why we work, I'm also... hesitant.

There are doubts, each one circling my mind, preying on my own concerns like sharks in the water.

For all that Gia and I have been through... maybe it's for the best if we don't fight for this.

I know that I want her. Badly. She's the most important person in the world to me.

I also know that I can't take another rejection from her. I have shown up at Gia's side through everything, and she has consistently pushed me away.

At what point do I accept that she just doesn't like me all that much?

She does.

There's a war inside of me. The certainty of knowing that Gia and I are meant for each other battles against the fear deep in my stomach that she's just not that interested.

Both feel equally present in my mind.

And, both cause me equal amounts of anguish.

Which means that both, effectively, prevent me from walking in to see her.

I'm standing outside of Gia's room, practically twiddling my thumbs with anxiety. I know that Gia's in there. No doubts about that whatsoever. According to Caterina, she hasn't moved in days, and that seems like a big problem.

It kills me that she's trapped herself in her room.

One way or another, if I go in there, at least she'll have some kind of motivation to move.

Caterina walks up to me. She looks at the door, then looks at me. "Elio filled me in on what you're doing right now," she says with a smirk.

"Going to pretend you didn't say that because it's pretty weird," I say as I screw my eyes shut. No one wants their little sister to know that they're planning on having sex with anyone, let alone said little sister's sister-in-law.

Caterina laughs. "Listen, in our family, I think it's probably time we talk about sex more, since all of us have fucked it up somehow."

"Luna is hardly a fuck up," I give her a glance.

"Yeah well. Neither is your baby," she smiles. "Honestly? I'm excited to be an auntie for once."

I make a mental note to force Dino to tell her about his twins and nod. "Yeah. Well. I'm pretty scared to be a dad."

"You're going to do great." She smiles. "But you need to get in there and do a little magic first."

"Gross, please don't say it like that ever again."

"What, you want to call it something else? Like making..."

"Okay, thanks, sis." I visibly shudder. "I'm going to crawl into a hole."

"I think Gia can help you with that," Caterina snorts.

"Oh God. Please stop."

She sighs. "Remember how Dad used to talk about his grandpa being in World War Two, and how nervous he was before he got off the boat in France?"

"Yeah," I mutter.

"I hate to say it Sal, but this is it. The boat is done. The shore is in front of you. Get off of it and just get it over with. D-Day can only happen once, so might as well get in there." She nods.

"I'm also going to pretend you didn't refer to my... to Gia and I as D-Day."

"Whatever floats your boat, brother," she laughs before she turns, Luna's voice summoning her from another floor.

I watch her go. My baby sister is hardly a baby anymore, but the way she knows how to annoy me?

That will never get old. And probably never go away.

She's right though.

I'm wasting time just sitting here in the hallway. The place I need to be is inside that room, with the woman that I love.

Gia and I have always been doing this kind of dance.

But, when we were in Ireland, I realized that the thing that has always worked between us isn't begging or pleading.

It isn't a bargain or negotiation or trying to change Gia in the slightest. Gia doesn't want me to be weak for her. She doesn't need me to be the one who is asking her what to do.

Most of the time, Gia knows exactly what to do.

But now, like all the other times when it's been just us?

She doesn't.

So, the thing that works between us isn't up for debate or negotiation.

It's me.

Telling Gia what to do.

Telling her to take her pleasure.

And in that...

I always take mine.

My body settles into a strange kind of stillness as I reach for the handle. I turn it and propel myself into the room, shutting and locking the door behind me.

The sound echoes in a very weird way as I survey the room.

Inside, it's very still. The door closing is definitely the loudest sound that happened, and for a minute, I wonder if Gia is even breathing.

The bed rustles slightly, though, which lets me know that she's in there. The room is just so quiet...

And dark.

Gia has all the lights off and the curtains drawn. She's laying on the bed facing away from me, and I can just make out the curl of her hair in the dim light.

"Gia," I say softly. "Are you awake?"

"No," she mutters.

Okay. I guess we're starting then.

Purposefully, I stride over to the bed. I sit so that my hips bump against the curve of her ass.

I'm not going to scare her.

But I am going to get her the hell out of the darkness.

"I think you're awake, and we need to talk."

"We've done a lot of talking. I'm tired, Sal. Just..."

I gently run my hands up her neck and fist them in her hair. I tug slightly until Gia's turned over, laying beneath me.

Her eyes are wide, and her lips part slightly in surprise.

"You're right," I say roughly. "I think we're done talking."

Then, I kiss her.

For a heartbreaking second, I'm terrified that Gia won't kiss me back. Then, she moans and melts into my mouth.

And from there, everything sets itself right.

I tighten my grip on her hair as she sits up to put her nails on my scalp, running her fingers up and down as she devours my lips. My other hand drifts down to the curve of her hip, where her soft silk nightgown has risen up over the tops of her thighs as she writhes closer to me in the bed.

"Fuck, Gia," I pant, breaking the kiss for a second to lick the skin of her neck. "You fucking wore this for me, didn't you?"

"No," she says aggressively.

I growl. "When you put this—" I roughly tug the dress up, exposing the naked curve of her hip, "on, you put it on for me. Because no one else is going to do this to you," I grunt.

I punctuate my grunt by sliding two fingers inside of her.

We both moan at that.

"This is mine," I say against the skin of her neck as I pant against the wetness I feel. "All of this is fucking mine, do you understand?"

"Yes," Gia breathes.

"Say it, Gia," I groan.

I'm like a fucking animal right now.

Her smell, the sounds she's making, the fact she's pregnant with my baby... it's lighting something up in my brain that runs deeper than anything I've ever felt before.

I feel like I'm beating my chest and screaming at the world.

This woman is *mine.*

And if you want her, you have to fucking go through me first.

She moans, but I bite the tendon where her neck meets her shoulder. I do it a little hard and she gasps.

Good.

"Say whose you are," I snarl.

"Yours," Gia whispers. "I'm yours, Sal. I've always been yours. It's always been you," she whispers.

The words send that same primal hormone spiraling through me. My muscles flex and my cock is harder than steel against my pants.

I need to fuck her. Right fucking now.

"Good girl, Gia," I croon as I gently push her back on the bed. In one motion, I tug all of the covers off, revealing her on her clean white sheets.

With the other, I take off my belt. Gia watches, eyes round as I unhook it and slide it from my pants.

My grin feels wicked. "Not today, *amore mio*," I say, letting the words come from me. "Today, the only thing holding you is me."

Gia's lips part, but I'm already shrugging out of my shirt. Her eyes rove the tattoos on my chest, and I smirk.

"You're mine, Gia," I growl.

I fall down onto the bed, parting her legs as the soft silk of the nightgown reveals her to me. I notch myself at her entrance, watching her eyes roll back in her head as I push inside.

"Tell me again," I groan as I'm part of the way there.

"Fucking... You're so fucking big, Sal," she whispers.

A flush of satisfaction has me pushing in more. "You take me so well, Gia," I purr. "You're meant to take me, all the way, understand?"

She bites her lip and nods. "I..."

I push in all the way, and Gia shrieks.

I need to make sure that she's not in pain.

The thought is alarmingly dim against the reptilian roaring in my brain. Part of me is pleased that she knows, that she remembers how I feel inside her.

Part of me wants her to feel it so she never forgets how I fuck her.

But I also want her to love this as much as I do, so I free one of her beautiful breasts and roughly palm it, pinching her nipple between my fingers.

"Oh fuck." She arches back. "Careful, they're so sensitive," she groans.

Oh.

Oh.

I forgot that the pregnancy hormones might make these a little more tender. Instead of pinching, I let the calluses on my hand rasp against one nipple, and then the other, abrading them into perfect peaks that beg to be licked.

Gia, meanwhile, is writhing on my cock, and from the way she slides on me, I would say that I've done my work.

"Good, Gia," I whisper as I slowly start to pump in and out of her. "You're doing so well, *amore mio*. See, I told you that you could take me so well."

"Fucking hell, Sal," she moans. She's arching off the bed, offering her perfect breasts up to me. "Just keep fucking going."

"Only if you come for me, my love," I say.

I can tell that the l-word gets to her, but I don't stop. Instead, I push my hips to a punishing pace, slamming into her so that I steal the breath from her.

"I love you, Gia," I grunt. "And unless I'm wrong, you fucking love me too."

"You're..."

I lean forward, scooping one hand under her hips and pulling her up higher. She wraps her legs around my back, and I pound into her.

The new angle is going to drive her absolutely crazy.

"Here's the thing, love," I say, my breath harsh and hissing between each word. "I am. Not. Wrong."

I press down on her clit at the same time as I lean down, pressing a kiss on her lips. She gasps as the orgasm swamps her, and I can feel her tight walls tugging on my cock, draining me as I steal the scream from her mouth.

When I come, it feels like the stars themselves have realigned for us. It rips over me, taking my own sanity as I pour everything I have, everything I am, into Gia.

I'm not sure how much time passes as we stay connected, my hips flat against hers, our bodies one. I'm staring down into her eyes, daring her to say I'm wrong.

That she doesn't love me too.

Gia's staring back. Her cheeks are flushed. I can see tracks where tears have come down her cheeks. With one of my hands, I gently wipe one of them away.

She sighs. "Okay. Fine. I love you too."

The smile that blooms across my face is so filled with joy, I want to shout. "Was that so hard to admit?"

"Yes, you giant oaf." She wiggles a little, but the movement makes us both moan.

"Unless you want to go again, I'd advise you to stop." I smile.

Gia snorts. "And I'd advise you... yeah. Maybe we need a minute," she whispers.

Gently, I extract myself from her. I get a towel to clean her up, but Gia waves a hand. "Make me a bath. And get in it with me."

I smile. "Done."

NOT TWENTY MINUTES LATER, I'm holding her in the bathtub. There are so many bubbles that I can't see her beautiful curves, but I feel them against me, and I'm not going to hide it.

The fact that she's cuddled into my chest makes me very, very hard.

Gia plays with the bubbles in front of us. "I do love you, Sal," she says finally.

"I know."

"You didn't know."

"I knew the minute you were in my arms after Belarus."

I can't see her face, but I'm sure she's making that cute little frown that she makes when she doesn't think I know what I'm talking about.

"I knew every time you asked to spend the night in my room. I knew from when I kissed you in Prague. I've always known, Gia Rossi, that you're the one for me. Mostly because I know that you love me."

"I literally tried to dump you. Multiple times."

"And if you ever try it again, I'll take you up on it," I warn her.

Gia sighs and melts into my arms. "What else do you know about me that I don't know?"

"Nothing. That was it. You're an amazing woman, Gia. You're my queen and I'll do anything for you. But all I ask..." I shuffle, shifting her so my lips are next to her cheek. "All I ask is that you love me."

"Fine. I can do that," she grumbles.

But I can hear the smile under it.

"Good. Now. Are we ready to talk baby names?"

She shudders. "No. This little jerk already tried to kill me."

"No way."

"Seriously. That's how I got kidnapped by Benicio. Liam had to take me to Ireland for treatment."

"Well. Maybe he was just allergic to Irish fuckers," I say thoughtfully.

"Liam isn't that bad..." She doesn't finish that sentence because I pinch one of her nipples.

Hard.

"I thought we were waiting," she pants as she wiggles against me.

"That's overrated." I smile, pulling her in for a kiss. "Never say his name again, okay?"

"But what if...?"

I seal my lips over hers.

Gia Rossi is mine.

My queen.

My heart.

My whole world.

I'm never letting her go.

EPILOGUE: GIA

"No. I am not having a meeting today, Gia," Elio barks at me.

I roll my eyes and adjust the baby on my hip. "Come on. We just need to go over those contracts with the Russians..."

"I said no. No business today. It's the twins' birthday. We can't have business on such a day," Elio thunders.

Francesca giggles, and Elio's face softens. "Gia, why must you insist on bringing my niece to business meetings? She's going to be two years old, swearing and swindling Russians for all they're worth."

"And I will be so proud of her," I say, snuggling my daughter into my arms.

He sighs. "I suppose it would be too much to ask you to move her to another room?"

"Yep."

There's been quite a few conflicts like this recently. The newborn stage was pretty challenging, but now that

EPILOGUE: GIA

Francesca's almost a year old, I'm enjoying her.

Sal and I both dote on this little girl, as does everyone else in the house. Her cousin Luna often refers to Francesca as 'her' baby, which all of us find hilarious except for Caterina.

Elio puts out a hand and Francesca latches onto his finger. She giggles and he smiles.

"Fine," he says softly. "You do the video call with the Russians, and I will make sure the bounce castle is installed correctly."

"Deal." I smirk.

Elio leaves the office and I hop into the desk, opening the computer. Elio and I use the same laptop. Same computer. Same accounts. Same everything.

This is a tag team situation. Elio and I both run the Rossi enterprise. Equally.

It's the only way that we can make this work, honestly, with all the kids and whatnot.

The call opens, and Stassi's father, Boris Novikov, beams at me. "How is the little one today?"

Francesca's face is halfway in the frame. "She's ready to get this deal done."

He laughs. "Already so fierce, like her mother. I agree. Let's get to the brass tacks, as you would say."

The trade deal is a good one, and when we're done, Boris nods. "Say hello to my Stassi for me today."

"Will do." I smile.

With that taken care of, I sigh and look at my baby. "You ready to go party, nugget?"

EPILOGUE: GIA

She coos back at me.

Leaving the relative calm of the office, the house is a whirlwind of activity. There's catering. Flowers, vendors, toys, everything is just flowing through the mansion.

I'm so glad that Sal and I have our own place, but it's kind of fun to be here. It's always chaos.

"There are my girls," Sal says.

I turn and Francesca giggles, putting her hands out for her dad. He takes her and peppers kisses all over her before tucking her under his arm.

I sniff. "I see where I rank."

"Ah, but I just needed a little longer for your kiss." Sal smiles.

He leans in and makes good on that, leaving my heart pounding and my blood pumping after a very, very good kiss.

"How did the call with Boris go?"

"Good. Signed, sealed, delivered."

"Excellent. Now, ready to celebrate?"

My nose wrinkles.

"You know, a birthday party for one year old babies is really a lot," I say for what is probably the millionth time.

I mean, when I look at Francesca, she's just happy to be here. She giggles her little baby giggle and smiles her little baby smile, and she's good to go.

For her one-year-old birthday, Sal and I are going to invite family over. We're going to have a picnic and take a few pictures of Francesca eating some cake.

EPILOGUE: GIA

Then we're going to send everyone home.

"Let's go, *amore mio*." Sal offers his other arm.

I take it, and we head outside.

The twins are also just a year old, and they're halfway toddling around outside, carefully supervised by Caterina as they take in the chaos around them.

The only one who's really having a hell of a time today is Luna, and she's practically shrieking with delight as she bounces off the exorbitant bounce castle that Elio rented.

Dino's sulking in the corner.

Marisol didn't come back from Brazil with us. She chose to go to Florida instead, where, by all accounts, she's living in peace away from her father, with her mother and her children.

But not with Dino.

While Elio and Caterina know something of Dino's story now, they don't know everything.

That's Dino's business to tell.

Luna's face lights up as she looks past us to the patio. "Auntie Stassi!" she shrieks.

Like a tornado, she barrels over and knocks into Stassi, who is holding the single largest mass of balloons that I've ever seen in my life.

"Oh my god, babe." Stassi looks at Luna. "I totally love your hair. Did you do it?"

Luna requested an elaborate mass of braids, including some that look like bows, from the hairdresser Caterina hired. "No. But my mommy let me." She beams.

EPILOGUE: GIA

"Totes adorbs. Hey girl, and Sal," Stassi says, smiling at us.

I like having Stassi around more. She keeps everyone on their toes, and since she's been in the running for the Nobel prize with her work on sea moss lately, she's been in New York more frequently.

I smile. "Hey, Stassi."

"How's the world's tiniest tyrant?"

Francesca burbles as Stassi takes her. "Yeah, I know," she says in a high-pitched voice. "Auntie Stassi is here, so the fun can begin."

"Sure." Sal rolls his eyes. "What am I, chopped liver?"

"Ha. Very funny, Sal," she winks.

The party begins to heat up, which means that there are just more children screaming. And food.

Okay, it is kind of fun.

Or at least, it is fun until my brother sidles up to me and whispers something in my ear that makes my skin feel cold.

"Gia," Elio rumbles. "There's a woman and two children at the front gate."

Sal and I shoot each other a look. I hand Francesca to Caterina, and together, Sal and I head for the front gate.

By the time we get there, the guards have basically swarmed out front. They're standing in front of someone, weapons drawn.

The second I realize who it is, I yell. "Stand down!"

Sal and I push toward the front and open the gate. "Who is it?" a voice rasps.

EPILOGUE: GIA

I look over and Dino is at my elbow.

I don't know what to tell him, so instead I just wave him forward.

The guards, bemused, look over at us.

The woman, and two children, in front of us look battered. They look like they've been through hell. Their clothes are torn, and they're covered in mud, and the woman is bleeding from a cut on her forehead.

It takes me a second to realize who this is.

But, when I do, my heart feels like it's going to collapse.

It's Marisol.

She looks at me. "Help," she whispers.

She pushes the two children toward Dino.

Then, she collapses.

Thank you for reading Sal and Gia's story. I hope you enjoyed reading it as much as I enjoyed creating it.

Please leave me a review, it helps me grow as a new independent author.

If you haven't read the first two books in The Ruthless Mafia Kings, you're in for a spectacular treat.

Book 1 Mafia Heir's Secret Baby: An arranged Marriage Enemies To Lovers Romance. Xander and Mel's story.

You will loose your mind over Xander's alpha male protective and possessive nature. "Nothing is enough when you're my

EPILOGUE: GIA

woman Mel...".

Book II Mafia King's Secret Baby: An Enemies To Lovers Billionaire Romance. Elio and Caterina's Story. They will leave you breathless and aching.

Coming soon is Dino and Marisol's story so don't miss out, follow me on Amazon to be the first to know when it's on pre-order.

If you have completed the mafia series, I have a dangerously hot alpha and a Secret Baby he just about faints when he discovers.

Your next book starts now in Sera and Alan's story, Broken Billionaires Secret Baby: An enemies To Lovers Boss Romance.

Blurb

He broke my heart eight years ago when he left me pregnant and disappeared without a word.

Mr. Grumpy billionaire took over my family's resort, which made him my boss.

After all these years he's back, pretending like nothing happened.

And yeah...he's still my type.

One look is all it takes and I'm against the wall begging for release in a public bathroom.

We have a deal. Agree to pretend to be his girlfriend for one week, and he will leave me and the resort alone.

EPILOGUE: GIA

Against my better judgment I'm falling for him again.

And I have a secret, one that is eight years old. She has his eyes and his stubborn personality.

I have to protect her from him.

Trouble is now I am expecting his second child, and he has a bigger secret of his own, the reason he left us.

Read Broken Billionaire's Secret Baby: An Enemies To Lovers Dark Romance.

Here is a little sneak peek into Sera and Alan's story...

Prologue

SERA

His hands traveled over every inch of my body, igniting skin, and his soft lips planted kisses on my hair, on my eyelids, on my nose, on my mouth, underneath my jaw, behind my ears, and down and down he went, his lips creating a moist trail across my body.

There's a hunger to his touch, a ferocity to his kisses like he's desperate to claim me.

Every touch, every kiss, every bite is an act in the private symphony that he's directing. His hands maneuver me expertly, deftly, prompting me to follow.

Every stroke of skin, every light brush of his lips is a deliberate attempt to unravel me.

And it's working.

In one fluid motion, he tugs his shirt over his head, revealing rock-hard abs, a ripped chest, and perfectly sculpted, yet surprisingly tender, arms. His muscles ripple as he moves, like waves undulating under his perfect skin.

I let my hands travel across his neck, his chest, his stomach, his arms, and his back. I dig my fingers into his back, feeling more turned on by how hard the muscles plating his back are.

I push my fingers into his hair, enjoying how soft it feels under the pressure of my finger pads. *How can one man be so beautiful?* I wonder to myself, but I know the answer to the question. *It's because he's Alan Dirkman.*

I lean into him, reducing the inches between our naked skin, savoring the feel of his sweat-slicked body against mine, his scent, and his warm breath on my neck.

In the dark, his eyes blaze like pinpricks of blue light, and I feel myself falling into them, eyes that seem deeper than any well, any pool, any ocean.

He plants kisses under my chin, on my throat, and slowly, torturously, begins to make his way down between my breasts, my navel, the hair between my legs ... *Ooooh.*

He flicks his tongue over my lips and a shudder ripples through me. His expert tongue explores me, kissing, licking, biting, nibbling, each motion a glorious slice of heaven.

I arch my back, raising my hips to meet his tongue, his fucking glorious tongue. I feel his grin against my vulva, and it's the thing that undoes me. I feel myself unraveling, seismic waves of pleasure rippling through me all at once, a sensation I never want to end.

It's his name that escapes my lips as I cum around his mouth, a silent prayer, a dark secret. Goosebumps erupt all over my skin, and a brief nothingness blossoms in my mind as my entire essence seems to stretch in every direction.

EPILOGUE: GIA

After an eternity, I come back into my body. And in the dark, I see that he's grinning. I must look like a mess for him to find this funny. Soundlessly, he pulls himself over me, and he kisses me, forcing me to taste my delicious wetness.

Quick as an eel, he flips me over, and I'm lying face flat on my stomach. I feel the heat of his skin as his weight presses down on me, his hardness pressing against my ass. His hands travel across my back, massaging my shoulders and rubbing my arms.

Despite the non-sexualness of the act, the very fact that he's doing it only serves to turn me on the more. His hands on me ignites me, and I know without a doubt that I've never felt as alive as I feel at this moment.

The sharp sound of ripping foil pierces through the air, and I turn to look at him. A lone shaft of moonlight spills into the room, illuminating his face. Silver strands of moonlight ripple across his hair, and in the low light, the condom glistens.

Then he moves out of the light, and once again, he's obscured by the darkness, his silhouette one of lust and sin.

He presses against me, and he kisses my earlobes, occasionally pausing to give each of them a delicious bite. He splays his fingers under my stomach, a low moan escaping the back of his throat.

"How can you be so soft all over, Sera?" he whispers against the back of my ear, his words punctuated by kisses. "What are you doing to me?"

I want to ask him what *he's* doing to *me,* but I don't get the chance. He raises me up gently and slips a pillow under my stomach, guiding me with the back of his palm.

He angles me until my back is arched and my ass is literally high-fiving the ceiling. He spanks me, the sharp pain only

EPILOGUE: GIA

compensated by the pleasure that tears through me. He rubs my ass cheek gently as if apologizing for being unable to resist spanking me.

"You're so soft," he says, and he leans and plants identical kisses on both of my cheeks. He saves one for the lips of my vulva, and I have to bite down hard on the pillow to keep myself from howling in pleasure.

He kneels behind me, his legs pushing my thighs apart. He leans in and trails kisses from the back of my neck down my spine until he gets to my waist.

Then he traces his way back.

"Don't scream," he whispers against my ears, a threat, a warning.

Then he slams into me.

And I scream.

His hardness stretches me, filling me—a sweet sensation. I bite into the pillow to keep myself from howling out in pleasure, but it's no use.

There's absolutely no way I haven't woken up the entire neighborhood.

He pushes himself in and out of me, filling me, claiming me, each practiced thrust a deliberate attempt at unraveling me. "Yes, yes, yes!" I moan into the pillow because I want it too. I want this.

His thrusts are merciless. The bed jerks underneath us, and in some part of my mind that isn't addled by the feel of this man inside me, I register that it would be really embarrassing if the bed broke down under us.

EPILOGUE: GIA

"Give it to me," he groans against my ear like he's angry I'm not coming apart yet. "I can sense that you're holding back. Don't. Or you'll regret it."

I want to tell him that I'm not holding back, not intentionally anyway and that I just don't want this to end. That this is what I want to be doing for the rest of my life until I die.

But the words don't come. His dick must have hit the part of my brain that oversees my motor controls, and my tongue feels clumsy in my mouth, like a bloated thing.

"Fuck this," he growls, and he pulls out of me, ruining the magic. But I don't have time to complain because he lies down back on the bed and pulls me on top of him. "Climb," he orders, and I hasten to obey.

There's a cruel smile on his handsome face, and I know that this is his way of punishing me for holding back.

Grabbing each of my hips, he guides me onto his waiting member. I shut my eyes, savoring the feeling of Alan pushing into me because that's what he does. His hips meet mine in the air, and a moan escapes from the back of my throat.

Then he's moving, really moving, his pace and speed torturous. I hang my head back and let out a cry as he pushes in and out of me, each of his thrusts perfectly aimed and merciless.

It's like our lower bodies have merged. I don't know where the opening of my vagina begins and where the shaft of his dick ends. It's the way he fills me and seems to fit me perfectly like we were made for each other, like there's no way I could feel this same way if I was doing this with another person.

EPILOGUE: GIA

At this moment, there's no one but Alan Dirkman, no sound but the moans that escape his lips, no sensation but the feel of his skin against mine.

"Sera," he says, his tongue rolling across each syllable in my name like it's a prayer, a plea. His eyes snap open, and his fierce blue eyes pierce into my green ones, and time seems to slow around us.

There's a rising feeling in my chest, and it's like I'm floating through the clouds. But that dark look in his eyes forces me back down. "Sera," he says again, no trace of warmth in his voice, no trace of anything but hot, dark lust.

"Come for me, Sera," he whispers breathlessly, and I unravel at his words, exploding around him as I climax and splinter into a million pieces on top of him. And as he comes, he calls out my name, thrusting hard, then stilling as he empties himself into me.

We lay that way for a while, my head resting on his chest as I try to time my heartbeat to coincide with his. We don't say anything to each other, and the comfortable silence is only broken by our ragged breathing.

I feel worn out like I have just run a marathon, although sex with Alan might have been just that.

"Sera," he whispers against my ear, but there's a wrongness in his voice. I whip my head around, hoping to see those same blue eyes I want to stare into for the rest of my life, but the eyes of the man underneath me are the wrong color.

"Sera," he whispers again, but it's like he's far away.

He raises his hands and grabs my throat and begins to squeeze. My vision is tinged with a sick red, and when I'm about to pass out, the pressure of his grip loosens. My eyes snap open, and

EPILOGUE: GIA

I'm staring at a formless void that had once been the man I loved.

"Sera," he whispers again, but his voice is unnatural, and he seems to be falling apart, dissipating like clouds of black smoke.

"Sera," he whispers again, and I feel the bedsheets tugging at me, like snakes, wounding themselves around my arms and legs as they pull me into the bed.

"Sera," he whispers again, only he's no longer here. He never was. And this time, he never will be.

"Sera," he whispers again, and I wake up ...

... In a pool of my own sweat. My heart hammers against my chest like it wants out, and it takes me a moment to realize that I was dreaming, that Alan wasn't really here.

My fingers find the area between my legs, and they come away sticky. I flush with embarrassment at the erotic dream I had of Alan.

My bedside clock glows an emerald 2:30am, and I know without a doubt that I won't be able to go back to sleep again. I climb out of bed and make my way downstairs.

"Mo?" I call when I see the only other person that lives in this house with me.

Her hair hangs around her face in wild tufts, and she rubs her eye with her fist. "I can't sleep," she says as a manner of explanation.

I sigh. "I can't sleep, too."

"Bad dream?" she asks. And I'm grateful for the shadows that hide the faint blush that appears on my cheeks.

EPILOGUE: GIA

"Something like that," I reply, biting my lower lip.

"Me too," she says. And we just stand there, mother and daughter, staring at each other. The silence hangs between us for a while before I decide to break it.

Then finally, I say, "Come on. I'll read you a story, then we'll see about you getting some sleep."

"I'm eight, Mom," she says, but her eyes light up. And when I extend my hand to her, she places hers in it.

Chapter 1

SERA

The sky above Seattle is as clear as a calm sea, with only thin wisps of cloud drifting across its dark surface. It's 6 am in the morning, and only the purple tinge of the horizon is any indication that the sun plans on rising today.

Despite the hour, traffic rages on the main roads, a beast with a thousand glowing eyes. There's a light downpour, and people shuffle around with umbrellas and discarded newspapers held over their heads as they make for their respective destinations.

I sit on the floor with my legs crossed. Across from me sits an eight-year-old child, and she's jutting her chin out stubbornly. A sketch pad sits between us, like a barricade, and it is covered in a swirl of so many colors that it would have rivaled any rainbow. I sigh, fingering the dark shadows under my eyes and patting my ragged hair into place.

"You were supposed to paint a fire extinguisher, Mo," I say, shaking my head.

EPILOGUE: GIA

"I know," Mo says. And we sit like that for the next two minutes, me staring at Mo, Mo staring at her sketchpad.

"Right," I say, finally breaking the silence. "You know you're going to have to redo it, right?"

She snaps her head and faces me, and her bright green eyes flash with obvious malice. I face her scrutiny head-on, giving her a look that I hope says, *"I'm your mom, young lady; your glares won't burn holes through me like heat vision."*

When she finally looks away, I let out a breath I don't know I've been holding in. *They're the wrong color,* I think to myself, *They're the color of leaves in summer, but they're the wrong color.* She has *his* eyes.

I shudder at the thought, trying to hide the heat that flushes my cheeks as I remember the erotic dream I had with Alan in it.

Mo is content with glaring at the sketchpad in front of her as if reprimanding it for tricking her into painting something else. For a moment, I'm sure she looks surprised that the sketchpad isn't apologizing.

"Fine," she says, wrinkling her nose like she has smelled something particularly disgusting. I raise my arms and smell both pits to be sure. "Okay," I say when I'm convinced I'm not the one.

With my help, we get to work immediately. There's no way to salvage the ruined page, so I tear it out. Out of the corners of my eyes, I see Mo's nostrils flare, but luckily she doesn't say anything. With that page out of the way, I directed her on how to paint a fire extinguisher.

It's more like we argue over what to do and what to put where, with Mo stubbornly insisting that we do it her way, despite my

EPILOGUE: GIA

arguments that the only reason we're doing it again is because we did it her way in the first place.

Being a mom is hard work—don't let anyone tell you differently. Being Mo's mom is even harder.

"You should be helping me," she says, exasperated, so I apologize and get to work immediately.

With my hands busy, my mind is free to wander. I think about a lot of things in the space of precious seconds, but it's hard to keep my mind trained on any of them. My mind, like water passing through holes in a basket, always finds its way back to the one thing that's truly been bothering me: Alan.

His name stirs up a wave of emotions inside of me, and it's hard to make sense of any of them. It's been eight years since I last saw him, eight years since Mo and everything her coming along meant for me, eight years since my world broke cleanly along its center, eight years since the best thing that could ever have happened to me did.

Those eight years haven't been the easiest, and being a single mom who just got her heart broken and still had to try her best to save the resort that Alan left to its devices in his haste didn't make any of it easier.

But I pulled through. The days were dark and darker, and on some of them, I didn't feel like waking up. But I did. Partly because I had a little girl to be a superhero for now, because anyone who knows anything about anything knows that little girls need superheroes like Fredrik Backman would say. And partly because I wanted to prove a point.

There's no doubt that when Alan left, he was expecting that my walls would come crumbling down ... And they did, but I didn't want that to be the end of my story. So I pieced back

455

EPILOGUE: GIA

those walls as best as I could, and I went on functioning, losing myself in my efforts to be a not-crappy mom and a not-crappy CEO.

And it worked. At some point, everything got a whole lot easier, and the nightmares and the panic attacks lessened somewhat, and I could finally look forward to the next day like a slightly normal person.

But now, I'm surprised that I'm thinking of Alan again, eight years after I promised to bury him under a mountain of new memories. I shudder at how my dream-self responded to his touch, how she craved his lips on her throat, wanted ... no, *needed* him inside of her. I want to drown myself in a bathtub of too-hot water and scrub till my skin is red and raw.

Till I forget what it felt like to be kissed by a man as impossibly and annoyingly perfect as Alan Dirkman. Till I forget what it felt like to be loved by such a man, even if it was for a moment too brief for words. But above all, I want to forget the gnawing hole he created in my heart when he left. Because, despite my best efforts, that hole has stubbornly refused to be filled up.

It's 8:12 am, and one look at the sky is all the promise I need that it's going to be a beautiful morning. The clouds look like some god had left their creation to an eight-year-old. They're all in odd shapes; if I squint my eyes, I'll see that one of them is shaped like a boot.

I'm driving Mo to school, partly because I feel guilty that we're not spending enough time together—with work and all the drama in between, I feel like we're drifting apart, and my daughter is growing too fast. But the other reason I'm driving her to school is because I don't trust her to get to school by herself.

EPILOGUE: GIA

As if on cue, Mo snorts. "You don't have to drive me to school every day. I CAN GET THERE BY MYSELF!"

"Stop yelling," I say, perhaps less authoritatively than I intend to. With Mo, it's hard to know who the parent is.

"I'M NOT SHOUTING!" Mo shouts. Then she falls back into her chair and, thankfully, in a much quieter tone, adds, "You don't trust me."

I bite my lip. "You don't make it very easy," I say, looking ahead, so Mo has to glare at the side of my face. I can tell from her petulant snort that it's not as gratifying.

I sigh. The last time I let someone else take you to school, you convinced her that you had permission from me and the principal to go to the zoo. By the time I got there to get you, the poor woman was in tears.

Mrs. Tamara was just trying to help, but you made doing even that such a hell for her." I frown. The incident happened some weeks ago, and I'm surprised that I'm still mad about it.

Mo is special in that she doesn't have the grace to seem chastened. "It's not my fault she wasn't so smart," she says, pouting.

I sigh. "Mrs. Tamara is not dumb, Mo."

"I DIDN'T SAY THAT!" Mo roars, exasperated, and I'm sure if someone was looking in through the car windows, they would think that one of the two of us needs hearing aids. "'Dumb' is a bad word," she says as if that explains everything. "I just meant she wasn't so smart."

"And that's why you intimidated her into helping you skip school?" I ask.

EPILOGUE: GIA

Mo glares at me, and this time I see it. The unmistakable way her lips press against each other like they're trying to hide away from something. The way her nostrils flare like a bull's when it's setting up for a fight. When Mo glares at you, she does with her whole being, and there's only one other person that glares as she does.

"I didn't intimidate her," Mo says after a while, turning so she's facing the road. "I asked her to take me to the zoo instead. It's not my fault people always do as they're told when I'm the one giving the orders.

"Okay," I reply after a moment's hesitation because I know that's Mo's equivalent of an apology. Being a mom is hard work; I'm sure I mentioned that earlier.

I drop Mo off, and in hindsight, I realize that our goodbye had been too hasty. And that's only because it's hard not to look at her and see the man who turned my happiest memories into ash in my mouth.

And I'm happy Mo is too angry to look at me because that way, she won't see that her mom doesn't want to look at her because she's afraid that she'll see the man who hurt her in those emerald green eyes.

"You're just stressed," Piper says the moment I'm done narrating the events of the morning, which, to my eternal shame, includes my erotic dream with Alan in it. "Not to mention horny," she adds, and I can swear that she's grinning on the other line of the phone.

I'm sitting in my office. Golden sunlight pools in through the window, falling over the polished black tiles. I tap my fingers on the mahogany table, mainly to have something to do with my hands.

EPILOGUE: GIA

"It's hard to argue with that analysis," I say rather glumly. It's just the thing I've been expecting to hear her say, but I'm surprised by how much it stings.

Because I *am* stressed. We're weeks away from the holidays, and things at the resort have been hectic. I rub my eyes with the ball of my palm, knowing, without having to look at the mirror, that I have crescent-shaped dark circles underneath them.

"You should get laid," Piper says, as she has been saying for quite a long time as if getting laid will magically fix all of my problems. "How have you avoided meeting anyone? Beats me. You're smart, you're beautiful, and you're the fucking CEO of one of the most popular and successful holiday resorts in Seattle. You should have hot studs coming out of your ears."

I grin, surprised that it's genuine. It's hard not to feel a swell of pride at Piper's words, even if it lasts only a moment. "I can't," I say, uttering my line in this play we've both been participating in for as long as I can remember. "Things are not at their best right now, and I don't know how Mo will feel about me seeing someone."

"My goddaughter is eight, Sera," Piper says. "Five years ago, what you're saying would have been a valid excuse, but it isn't anymore. You're stalling, and now that you've told me that you're having dreams about *him*"—there's so much vehemence in her tone when she talks about Alan—"I think I know why."

"This is not about Alan," I say, rolling my eyes even if she can't see me.

"Then what is it about?" Piper asks, exasperated. "You're refusing to see anyone. You keep finding new ways to dodge out of taking a vacation—"

EPILOGUE: GIA

"That sounds like a good idea at the moment," I say, even if I don't really think it's the right time for a vacation. But at least it'll keep Piper distracted, and hopefully, she won't keep pestering me about seeing someone, and I won't have to confess that I've tried, but none of them seem to work out, and I think that Alan broke something inside of me when he left, and there's no way to fix it.

Piper is quiet for some time, and I wonder if she even heard me. "You're agreeing to a vacation?" Piper asks like she can't believe her ears.

"Yeah," I lie through my teeth. "Mo can stay with my mom. She and Bob seem to get along quite well. At least, she doesn't think he's incompetent at being an adult, and he doesn't think she's a complete idiot, which is about the highest compliment anyone can get from either of them. So she'll be fine."

"THIS IS BRILLIANT!" Piper roars through the phone, and she's so loud that I have to take the phone away from my ear to keep myself from going deaf.

"God, this is brilliant!" Piper exclaims like I didn't hear it the first time. "I should start making plans. So much to do ... So much to do. It's a terror." She pauses, then in a slightly more menacing tone, she says, "You could have made up your mind sooner, you know? Ugh."

I want to point out that until this very moment, I wasn't planning on going on a vacation, but it's no use because Piper interrupts me. "It's no use dwelling on such issues now," Piper says. "Where are we going?"

"Paris," I blurt out immediately. Alan promised to take me once but ... but ... *Don't think about Alan!* I tell myself firmly.

Piper snorts in the way only people that have been around the world and consider Paris a poor venue for a vacation do. "I'll get back to you with tickets and an estimate of our expenses," she says. And after that, there's not much to talk about, so we say our goodbyes and end the call.

And I spend the rest of my day trying to be excited about going to Paris. It doesn't work out very well however.

Chapter 2

ALAN

There's an incredible wrongness about waking up feeling like a bag of shit in the most expensive suite in a five-star hotel in one of the most visited places in human history. I'm talking about Paris, of course.

My head pounds like I have a little person caged in there that is tired of being locked behind my skull and wants out. It's a very unpleasant feeling, and I know without a doubt that it's going to be a crappy day.

Still, I pull my body out of the soft bed, fighting the saner part of me that keeps insisting I sleep in. I have a meeting with a business partner in a few hours, and while it's not uncharacteristic for Alan Dirkman to skip his meetings, I don't think it's a good idea for me to stay indoors today.

Grudgingly, I make my way to the bathroom, intent on getting to the end of today as soon as possible.

The man sitting across from me has eyes the color of dark chocolate, and his wild bush of a mustache twitches nervously with each word he forces out of his mouth. We've been talking

EPILOGUE: GIA

for over an hour, and during that time, he's avoided eye contact with me entirely.

It's all very boring, and it's obvious it's not going to get better, so I look out through the window and take in Paris.

I'm not one for needless dramatics, and I like to say things as they are, but damn, it's like I just stepped into a fairyland. Paris stretches around me in every direction like an unrolled map, and despite myself, I take in a deep breath, savoring the site.

Then, predictably, almost like I'm in a play with a preordained script, my mind drifts back to her, and I can't help the way my heart begins to hammer in my chest. It's like Paris has suddenly lost its grandeur, impossible as that is, and every sight that had once seemed marvelous now looks empty and dejected, just like me.

The craziest thing about time is that it doesn't really exist. Not the way space and matter do. We define time to make our lives less complicated than it already is, a sorry quest if there ever was one.

Time is before and after, a reference point, that tiny footnote at the bottom of a page that explains something that's hard to understand. And as I sit here and philosophize about time, or try to, I realize that my world stopped moving when I left Sera.

I shake my head, trying to dispel the thoughts. But it's too late, and my morning is already ruined. A ball of rage swells inside of me, and I can't be sure if it's directed at myself or at the man in front of me trying to convince me to invest in his start-up.

I reach inside of myself and try to force it back down, but now I realize that it's no longer the harmless cur it had been eight years ago. During that time, it has grown, feeding on negativity and my restlessness, and now I realize that I can't dismiss it as I could at its early stages. This only serves to aggravate me further.

I raise my hand to stop the man mid-sentence. He looks like he's relieved, but in a fraction of a second, his look changes to that of worry.

"Where do you see ... er ... What's the name of your company again?" I ask, snapping my fingers and trying my best not to sound irritated. It's not working.

He looks affronted, like my not remembering the name of his start-up is a personal insult, which it probably is, and I realize that it's the only reaction I've managed to get out of him since the time we started talking.

"Fluffy Ears," he says, and he seems to be sitting up straighter.

"A fashion brand?" I ask, incredulous. I want to ask if he's soft in the head, but I keep my mouth shut.

"No!" he says indignantly, and seems to realize who he's talking to and adds, maybe a bit too hastily, "Sorry." He's quiet for some time, then he says, "Fluffy Ears is not a fashion brand, but we're going to make clothes.

However, it won't be from leather and skin and all those other things that encourage poaching. It'll be synthetic and biodegradable, which will help the environment a great deal. The major hurdle we're facing now is cost, but in five years, we're hoping we'll be able to make them at a much cheaper rate.

Then in a decade after that, we want to give out the clothes for free, so it acts as an incentive for people to ditch their environment-harming tendencies and reduce the pollution.

EPILOGUE: GIA

When he's done, he draws in a deep breath and blinks rapidly, like he has something in his eyes. He looks stunned like he's surprised he's been able to utter so many words, and I know that the look on my face must probably mirror his.

"It's brilliant," I say, surprised that I mean it. "We should talk about this another time." I push back my chair, stand up and straighten my suit. Then I give him a warm smile and hope that I don't look like the scary Alan Dirkman people are used to. "My assistant will be in touch. I look forward to investing in your start-up. Fluffy Ears is the future."

The man—who I now remember as Mr. Kevin Edmund—doesn't say anything for a while, but his eyes are glistening as if with unshed tears. Finally, in a voice that is trying really hard not to sob, he says, "Thank you."

"It's nothing," I say, extending my hand for him to shake it. When he does, I say, "Your start-up will change the world, Kevin. I'm just glad I'll be able to help. Whatever you need, don't hesitate to call."

He nods, probably because he's too overwhelmed to force out words. I nod in understanding. I don't have to be a soothsayer to know what it's like to be told that your dream is actually feasible and that someone believes in it, too.

There's some small talk, but it isn't forced, and we pass the time pleasantly. After a while, we say goodbyes, and I'm surprised that I feel bad when he stands up to leave.

For months, this is the only conversation I've had without another person that didn't make me feel like clawing out my eyes with my fingers. I have to admit that I like the feeling.

On a whim, I offer to see him out. There's a whole city out there below me, and I've spent my time sequestered in this

EPILOGUE: GIA

bubble of my making.

By the time we get to the door, Austin and Jake, my bodyguards, take their place beside me, and we continue the rest of the way in pleasant silence.

It's an hour later and I've spent a good part inhaling lungfuls of the Parisian air. I briefly consider buying a house here; moving to Paris can't be such a bad idea now, can it? After Seattle, I've been finding it hard to settle down. I've been living in hotel suites for as long as I can remember, and it's probably time I move into a new place.

There's a restaurant in front of my hotel, and that's where I head to, Austin and Jake tailing me like overprotective mother hens. I have another meeting in two hours, but I've decided that it can wait, at least until I'm well-rested and fed.

My French is not that good, so I can't read the signs. I don't need to anyway; when Austin pushes open the door, I can tell from the scents that rise to meet my nostrils that I'm in the right place.

Austin goes to find a table for me in a secluded section of the restaurant—while publicity is like a second shadow to me, I'm not in the mood for it at the moment.

The waiter, a rather tall man with pale green eyes and a wry frizz of a mustache, comes to take my order, and feeling famished, I ask for a little bit of everything, duly asking Jake and Austin to join me. And that's when I hear it.

Laughter. Full and lovely, and the sound of it stirs memories in me. I turn around in my seat, my eyes searching for the source of the sound. Out of the corners of my eyes, I can see that Austin and Jake have identical worried looks on their faces, but I pay them no mind.

465

EPILOGUE: GIA

As I walk through the restaurant, trying to find the source of that sound, the faces of people blur in front of me. The only thing I can focus on is the sound of that laughter.

She is sitting at a table beside one of the windows that look to the streets outside. Her dark hair falls behind her head, a stream of onyx. Everything about her is familiar like I've just stepped into a dream. *Funny*, I think to myself, amused at the chances. *She looks just like ...*

Then, as if sensing my gaze, she turns to face me, and suddenly, there's not enough air in the room to breathe. Those green eyes flicker from surprise to shock to anger in the space of a few seconds, and I'm too stunned to move.

It's like my legs are made of clay, and I'm rooted to the spot. Time seems to have frozen or is otherwise moving far too slowly.

She's wearing a black sleeveless dress that hugs her frame like a glove, accentuating her curves. Her lips are scarlet, and they're curved into a smile when she turns to face me, and then those lips curve downward, and her eyes register shock, then outright anger.

"Sera," I say, and it's halfway between a sigh and a whisper. And in the thin bubble of silence that surrounds the two of us, I know that she's heard me.

"Alan," she says after an eternity, and with so much vehemence that I cringe inwardly.

Sera Pierce is in Paris. And she still hates me.

Continue reading Broken Billionaire's Secret Baby Free With Kindle Unlimited Audible and available on Paperback.

ABOUT THE AUTHOR

VIVY SKYS the author of Steamy Contemporary Romance novels, featuring smart, strong, sassy and witty female characters that command the attention of strong protective alpha males, from Off limits, Age Gap, Bossy Billionaires, Single dads next door, Royalty, Dark Mafia and beyond Vivy's pen will deliver.

Follow Vivy Skys on Amazon to be the first to know when her next book becomes available.

Printed in Dunstable, United Kingdom